THE CLASSIC WORKS OF J. SHERIDAN LE FANU

18 SHORT STORIES FROM ONE OF THE FIRST AND GREATEST WRITERS OF GHOST STORIES

British Library Cataloguing-in-Publication Data
A catalogue record for this book is available from
the British Library

Contents

THE FORTUNES OF SIR ROBERT ARDAGH

In the south of Ireland, and on the borders of the county of Limerick, there lies a district of two or three miles in length, which is rendered interesting by the fact that it is one of the very few spots throughout this country, in which some fragments of aboriginal wood have found refuge. It has little or none of the lordly character of the American forests; for the axe has felled its oldest and its grandest trees; but in the close wood which survives, live all the wild and pleasing peculiarities of nature—its complete irregularity—its vistas, in whose perspective the quiet cattle are peacefully browsing—its refreshing glades, where the grey rocks arise from amid the nodding fern—the silvery shafts of the old birch trees—the knotted trunks of the hoary oak—the grotesque but graceful branches, which never shed their honours under the tyrant pruning hook—the soft green sward—the chequered light and shade—the wild luxuriant weeds— its lichen and its moss—all, all are beautiful alike in the green freshness of spring, or in the sadness and sear of autumn—their beauty is of that kind which makes the heart full with joy—appealing to the affections with a power which belongs to nature only. This wood runs up, from below the base, to the ridge of a long line of irregular hills, having perhaps in primitive times, formed but the skirting of some mighty forest which occupied the level below.

But now, alas, whither have we drifted?—whither has the tide of civilization borne us?—it has passed over a land unprepared for it—it has left nakedness behind it—we have lost our forests, but our marauders remain—we have destroyed all that is picturesque, while we have retained everything that is revolting in barbarism. Through the midst of this woodland, there runs a deep gully or glen ; where the stillness of the scene is broken in upon by the brawling of a mountain stream, which, however, in the winter season, swells into a rapid and formidable torrent.

There is one point at which the glen becomes extremely deep and narrow, the sides descend to the depth of some hundred

:eet, and are so steep as to be nearly perpendicular. The wild trees which have taken root in the crannies and chasms of the rock, have so intersected and entangled, that one can with difficulty catch a glimpse of the stream, which wheels, flashes, and foams below, as if exulting in the surrounding silence and solitude.

This spot was not unwisely chosen, as a point of no ordinary strength, for the erection of a massive square tower or keep, one side of which rises as if in continuation of the precipitous cliff on which it is based. Originally, the only mode of ingress was by a narrow portal, in the very wall which overtopped the precipice ; opening upon a ledge of rock which afforded a precarious pathway, cautiously intersected, however, by a deep trench cut with great labour in the living rock ; so that, in its original state, and before the introduction of artillery into the art of war, this tower might have been pronounced, and that not presumptously, almost impregnable.

The progress of improvement, and the increasing security of the times had, however, tempted its successive proprietors, if not to adorn, at least to enlarge their premises, and at about the middle of the last century, when the castle was last inhabited, the original square tower formed but a small part of the edifice.

The castle, and a wide tract of the surrounding country had from time immemorial, belonged to a family, which, for distinctness, we shall call by the name of Ardagh ; and, owing to the associations which, in Ireland, almost always attach to scenes which have long witnessed alike, the exercise of stern feudal authority, and of that savage hospitality which distinguished the good old times, this building has become the subject and the scene of many wild and extraordinary traditions. One of them I have been enabled, by a personal acquaintance with an eye-witness of the events, to trace to its origin ; and yet it is hard to say, whether the events which I am about to record, appear more strange or improbable, as seen through the distorting medium of tradition, or in the appalling dimness of uncertainty, which surrounds the reality.

Tradition says that, sometime in the last century, Sir Robert Ardagh, a young man, and the last heir of that family, went abroad and served in foreign armies, and that having acquired considerable honour and emolument, he settled at Castle Ardagh, the building we have just now attempted to describe. He was what the country people call a *dark* man ; that is, he was supposed from the utter solitude of his life, was upon no terms of cordiality with the other members of his family.

The only occasion upon which he broke through the solitary monotony of his life, was during the continuance of the racing season, and immediately subsequent to it; at which time he was to be seen among the busiest upon the course, betting deeply and unhesitatingly, and invariably with success. Sir Robert was, however, too well-known as a man of honour, and of too high a family to be suspected of any unfair dealing. He was, moreover, a soldier, and a man of an intrepid as well as of a haughty character, and no one cared to hazard a surmise, the consequences of which would be felt most probably by its originator only. Gossip, however, was not silent—it was remarked that Sir Robert never appeared at the race ground, which was the only place of public resort which he frequented, except in company with a certain strange looking person, who was never seen elsewhere, or under other circumstances. It was remarked, too, that this man, whose relation to Sir Robert was never distinctly ascertained, was the only person to whom he seemed to speak unnecessarily; it was observed, that while with the country gentry he exchanged no further communication than what was unavoidable in arranging his sporting transactions, with this person he would converse earnestly and frequently. Tradition asserts, that to enhance the curiosity which this unaccountable and exclusive preference excited, the stranger possessed some striking and unpleasant peculiarities of person and of garb—she does not say, however, what these were— but they, in conjunction with Sir Robert's secluded habits, and extraordinary run of luck—a success which was supposed to result from the suggestions and immediate advice of the unknown—were sufficient to warrant report in pronouncing that there was something *queer* in the wind, and in surmising that Sir Robert was playing a fearful and a hazardous game, and that in short, his strange companion was little better than the devil himself.

Years, however, rolled quietly away, and nothing novel occurred in the arrangements of Castle Ardagh, excepting that Sir Robert parted with his odd companion, but as nobody could tell whence he came, so nobody could say whither he had gone. Sir Robert's habits, however, underwent no consequent change; he continued regularly to frequent race meetings, without mixing at all in the convivialities of the gentry, and immediately afterwards to relapse into the secluded monotony of his ordinary life.

It was said that he had accumulated vast sums of money—and, as his bets were always successful, and always large, such must have been the case. He did not suffer the acquisition of wealth, however, to influence his hospitality or his housekeeping—he neither purchased land, nor extended his establishment; and his mode of enjoying his money must have been altogether that of the miser— consisting, merely, in the pleasure of touching and telling his gold, and in the consciousness of wealth. Sir Robert's temper, so far from improving, became more than ever gloomy and morose. He sometimes carried the indulgence of his evil dispositions to such a height, that it bordered upon insanity. During these paroxysms, he would neither eat, drink, nor sleep. On such occasions he insisted on perfect privacy, even from the intrusion of his most trusted servants;—his voice was frequently heard, sometimes in earnest supplication, sometimes raised as if in loud and angry altercation, with some unknown visitant—sometimes he would, for hours together, walk to and fro, throughout the long oak wainscotted apartment, which he generally occupied, with wild gesticulations and agitated pace, in the manner of one who has been roused to a state of unnatural excitement, by some sudden and appalling intimation.

These paroxysms of apparent lunacy were so frightful, that during their continuance, even his oldest and most faithful domestics dared not approach him; consequently, his hours of agony were never intruded upon, and the mysterious causes of his sufferings appeared likely to remain hidden for ever. On one occasion, a fit of this kind continued for an unusual time—the ordinary term of their duration, about two days, had been long past—and the old servant, who generally waited upon Sir Robert, after these visitations, having in vain listened for the well-known tinkle of his master's hand-bell began to feel extremely anxious; he feared that his master might have died from sheer exhaustion, or perhaps put an end to his own existence, during his miserable depression. These fears at length became so strong, that having in vain urged some of his brother-servants to accompany him, he determined to go up alone, and himself see whether any accident had befallen Sir Robert. He traversed the several passages which conducted from the new to the more ancient parts of the mansion; and having arrived in the old hall of the castle, the utter silence of the hour, for it was very late in the night, the idea of the nature of the enterprise in which he was engaging himself, a sensation of remoteness from anything like human companionship, but more than all the vivid but undefined anticipation of something horrible, came upon him with such oppressive weight, that he hesitated as to whether he should proceed. Real uneasiness, however, respecting the fate of his master, for whom he felt that kind of attachment, which the force of habitual intercourse, not unfrequently engenders respecting objects not in themselves amiable—and also a latent unwillingness to expose his weakness to the ridicule of his fellow-servants, combined to overcome his reluctance ; and he had just placed his foot upon the first step of the staircase, which conducted to his master's chamber, when his attention was arrested by a low but distinct knocking at the hall-door. Not, perhaps very sorry at finding thus an excuse even for deferring his intended expedition, he placed the candle upon a stone block which lay in the hall, and approached the door, uncertain whether his ears had not deceived him. This doubt was justified by the circumstance, that the hall entrance had been for nearly fifty years disused as a mode of ingress to the castle. The situation of this gate also, which we have endeavoured to describe, opening upon a narrow ledge of rock which overhangs a perilous cliff, rendered it at all times, but particularly at night, a dangerous entrance ; this shelving platform of rock, which formed the only avenue to the door, was divided, as I have already stated, by a broad chasm, the planks across which had long disappeared by decay or otherwise, so that it seemed at least highly improbable that any man could have found his way across the passage in safety to the door—more particularly, on a night like that, of singular darkness. The old man, therefore, listened attentively, to ascertain whether the first application should be followed by another ; he had not long to wait ; the same low but singularly distinct knocking was repeated ; so low that it seemed as if the applicant had employed no harder or heavier instrument than his hand, and yet despite the immense thickness of the door, so very distinct, that he could not mistake the sound. It was repeated a third time, without any increase of loudness ; and the old man obeying an impulse for which to his dying hour, he could never account, proceeded to remove, one by one, the three great oaken bars which secured the door. Time and damp had effectually corroded the iron chambers of the lock, so that it afforded little resistance. With some effort, as he believed, assisted from without, the old servant succeeded in opening the door ; and a low, square-built figure, apparently that of a man wrapped in a large black cloak, entered the hall. The servant could not see much of this visitant with any distinctness ; his dress appeared foreign, the skirt of his ample cloak was thrown over one shoulder; he wore a large felt hat, with a very heavy leaf, from under which escaped what appeared to be a mass of long sooty-black hair ;—his feet were cased in heavy ridingboots. Such were the few particulars which the servant had time and light to observe. The stranger desired him to let his master know instantly that a friend had come, by appointment, to settle some business with him. The servant hesitated, but a slight motion on the part of his visitor, as if to possess himself of the candle, determined him; so taking it in his hand, he ascended the castle stairs, leaving his guest in the hall.

On reaching the apartment which opened upon the oak-chamber, he was surprised to observe the door of that room partly open, and the room itself lit up. He paused, but there was no sound—he looked in, and saw Sir Robert—his head, and the upper part of his body, reclining on a table, upon which burned a lamp ; his arms were stretched forward on either side, and perfectly motionless ; it appeared that having been sitting at the table, he had thus sunk forward, either dead or in a swoon. There was no sound of breathing ; all was silent, except the sharp ticking of a watch, which lay beside the lamp. The servant coughed twice or thrice, but with no effect—his fears now almost amounted to certainty, and he was approaching the table on which his master partly lay—to satisfy himself of his death—when Sir Robert slowly raised his head, and throwing himself back in his chair, fixed his eyes in a ghastly and uncertain gaze upon his attendant. At length he said, slowly and painfully, as if he dreaded the answer—

"In God's name, what are you?"

"Sir," said the servant, "a strange gentleman wants to see you below."

At this intimation, Sir Robert, starting on his legs, and tossing his arms wildly upwards, uttered a shriek of such appalling and despairing terror, that it was almost too fearful for human endurance ; and long after the sound had ceased, it seemed to the terrified imagination of the old servant, to roll through the deserted passages in bursts of unnatural laughter. After a few moments, Sir Robert said—

"Can't you send him away? Why does he come so soon? Oh God! oh God! let him leave me for an hour—a little time. I can't see him now—try to get him away. You see I can't go down now—I have not strength. Oh God! oh God! let him come back in an hour—it is not long to wait. He cannot lose anything by it—nothing, nothing, nothing. Tell him that—say anything to him."

The servant went down. In his own words, he did not feel the stairs under him, till he got to the hall. The figure stood exactly as he had left it. He delivered his master's message as coherently as he could. The stranger replied in a careless tone—

"If Sir Robert will not come down to me, I must go up to him."

The man returned, and to his surprise he found his master much more composed in manner. He listened to the message; and though the cold perspiration stood in drops upon his forehead, faster than he could wipe it away, his manner had lost the dreadful agitation which had marked it before. He rose feebly, and casting a last look of agony behind him, passed from the room to the lobby, where he signed to his attendant not to follow him. The man moved as far as the head of the staircase, from whence he had a tolerably distinct view of the hall, which was imperfectly lighted by the candle he had left there.

He saw his master reel, rather than walk down the stairs, clinging all the way to the banisters. He walked on as if about to sink every moment from weakness. The figure advanced as if to meet him, and in passing struck down the light. The servant could see no more; but there was a sound of struggling, renewed at intervals with silent but fearful energy. It was evident, however, that the parties were approaching the door, for he heard the solid oak sound twice or thrice, as the feet of the combatants, in shuffling hither and thither over the floor, struck upon it. After a slight pause he heard the door thrown open, with such violence that the leaf struck the sidewall of the hall, and it was so dark without that this was made known in no other way than by the sound. The struggle was renewed with an agony and intenseness of energy, that betrayed itself in deep-drawn gasps. One desperate effort, which terminated in the breaking of some part of the door, producing a sound as if the door-post was wrenched from its position, was followed by another wrestle, evidently upon the narrow ledge which ran outside the door, overtopping the precipice. This seemed as fruitless as the rest, for it was followed by a crash-ing sound as if some heavy body had fallen over, and was rushing down the precipice, through the light boughs that crossed near the top. All then became still as the grave, except the moan of the night wind that sighed up the wooded glen.

The old servant had not nerve to return through the hall, and to him that night seemed all but endless ; but morning at length came, and with it the disclosure of the events of the night. Near the door, upon the ground, lay Sir Robert's sword-belt, which had given way in the scuffle. A huge splinter from the massive door-post had been wrenched off, by an almost superhuman effort—one which nothing but the gripe of a des-pairing man could have severed—and on the rock outside were left the marks of the slipping and sliding of feet.

At the foot of the precipice, not immediately under the castle, but dragged some way up the glen, were found the re-mains of Sir Robert, with hardly a vestige of a limb or feature left distinguishable. The right hand, however was uninjured, and in its fingers was clutched, with the fixedness of death, a long lock of coarse sooty hair—the only direct circumstantial evidence of the presence of a second person. So says tradition.

This story, as I have mentioned, was current among the dealers in such lore ; but the original facts are so dissimilar in all but the name of the principal person mentioned, Sir Robert Ardagh, and the fact that his death was accompanied with circumstances of extraordinary mystery, that the two narratives are totally irreconcileable, (even allowing the utmost for the exaggerating influence of tradition,) except by supposing report to have combined and blended together the fabulous histories of several distinct heroes of the family of Ardagh. However this may be, I shall lay before the reader a distinct recital of the events from which the foregoing tradition arose. With respect to these there can be no mistake ; they are authenticated as fully as any thing can be by human testimony ; and I state them principally upon the evidence of a lady who herself bore a prominent part in the strange events which she related, and which I now record as being among the few well-attested tales of the marvellous, which it has been my fate to hear. I shall, as far as I am able, arrange in one combined narrative, the evidence of several distinct persons, who were eye-witnesses of what they related, and with the truth of whose testimony I am solemnly and deeply impressed.

Sir Robert Ardagh was the heir and representative of the

his father, the estates descended to him in a very impaired condition. Urged by the restless spirit of youth, or more probably by a feeling of pride, which could not submit to witness, in the paternal mansion, what he considered a humiliating alteration in the style and hospitality which up to that time had distinguished his family, Sir Robert left Ireland and went abroad. How he occupied himself, or what countries he visited during his absence, was never known, nor did he afterwards make any allusion, or encourage any inquiries touching his foreign sojourn. He left Ireland in the year 1742, being then just of age, and was not heard of until the year 1760—about eighteen years afterwards—at which time he returned. His personal appearance was, as might have been expected, very greatly altered, more altered, indeed, than the time of his absence might have warranted one in supposing likely. But to counterbalance the unfavourable change which time had wrought in his form and features, he had acquired all the advantages of polish of manner, and refinement of taste, which foreign travel is supposed to bestow. But what was truly surprising was, that it soon became evident that Sir Robert was very wealthy—wealthy to an extraordinary and unaccountable degree ; and this fact was made manifest, not only by his expensive style of living, but by his proceeding to disembarrass his property, and to purchase extensive estates in addition. Moreover, there could be nothing deceptive in these appearances, for he paid ready money for everything, from the most important purchase to the most trifling.

Sir Robert was a remarkably agreeable man, and possessing the combined advantages of birth and property, he was, as a matter of course, gladly received into the highest society which the metropolis then commanded. It was thus that he became acquainted with the two beautiful Miss F——ds, then among the brightest ornaments of the highest circles of Dublin fashion. Their family was in more than one direction allied to nobility ; and Lady D——, their elder sister by many years, and some time married to a once well-known nobleman, was now their protectress. These considerations, besides the fact that the young ladies were what is usually termed heiresses, though not a very great amount, secured to them a high position in the best society which Ireland then produced. The two young ladies differed strongly, alike in appearance and in character. The elder of the two, Emily, was generally considered the handsomer—for her beauty was of that impressive kind which never failed to strike even at the first glance, possessing all the advantages of a fine person, and of a commanding carriage. The beauty of her features strikingly assorted in character with that of her figure and deportment. Her hair was raven black and richly luxuriant, beautifully contrasting with the even, perfect whiteness of her forehead—her finely pencilled brows were black as the ringlets that clustered near them—and her eyes, full, lustrous, and animated, possessed all the power and brilliancy of the black, with more than their softness and variety of expression. She was not, however, merely the tragedy queen. When she smiled, and that was not unfrequently, the dimpling of cheek and chin, the laughing display of the small and beautiful teeth—but more than all, the roguish archness of her deep, bright eye, shewed that nature had not neglected in her the lighter and the softer characteristics of woman.

Her younger sister Mary was, as I believe not unfrequently occurs in the case of sisters, quite in the opposite style of beauty. She was light-haired, had more colour, had nearly equal grace, with much more liveliness of manner. Her eyes were of that dark grey which poets so much admire—full of expression and vivacity. She was altogether a very beautiful and animated girl—though as unlike her sister as the presence of those two qualities would permit her to be. Their dissimilarity did not stop here—it was deeper than mere appearance —the character of their minds differed almost as strikingly as did their complexion. The fair-haired beauty had a large proportion of that softness and pliability of temper which physiognomists assign as the characteristics of such complexions. She was much more the creature of impulse than of feeling, and consequently more the victim of extrinsic circumstances than was her sister. Emily, on the contrary, possessed considerable firmness and decision. She was less excitable, but when excited, her feelings were more intense and enduring. she wanted much of the gaiety, but with it the volatility of her younger sister. Her opinions were adopted, and her friendships formed more reflectively, and her affections seemed to move, as it were, more slowly, but more determinedly. This firmness of character did not amount to any thing masculine, and did not at all impair the feminine grace of her manners.

Sir Robert Ardagh was for a long time apparently equally attentive to the two sisters, and many were the conjectures and the surmises as to which would be the lady of the choice. At length, however, these doubts were determined; he proposed for and was accepted by the dark beauty, Emily F——d.

The bridals were celebrated in a manner becoming the wealth and connections of the parties; and Sir Robert and Lady Ardagh left Dublin to pass the honeymoon at the family mansion, Castle Ardagh, which had lately been fitted up in a style bordering upon magnificent. Whether in compliance with the wishes of his lady, or owing to some whim of his own, his habits were henceforward strikingly altered, and from having moved among the gayest if not the most profligate of the votaries of fashion, he suddenly settled down into a quiet, domestic, country gentleman, and seldom, if ever, visited the capital, and then his sojourns were brief as the nature of his business would permit.

Lady Ardagh, however, did not suffer from this change further than in being secluded from general society; for Sir Robert's wealth, and the hospitality which he had established in the family mansion, commanded that of such of his lady's friends and relatives as had leisure or inclination to visit the castle; and as the style of living was very handsome, and its internal resources of amusement considerable, few invitations from Sir Robert or his lady were neglected.

Many years passed quietly away, during which Sir Robert's and Lady Ardagh's hopes of issue were several times disappointed. In the lapse of all this time there occurred but one event worth recording. Sir Robert had brought with him from abroad a valet, who sometimes professed himself to be a Frenchman; at others an Italian; and at others again a German. He spoke all these languages with equal fluency, and seemed to take a kind of pleasure in puzzling the sagacity and balking the curiosity of such of the visitors at the castle as at any time happened to enter into conversation with him, or who, struck by his singularities, became inquisitive respecting his country and origin. Sir Robert called him by the French name, JACQUE; and among the lower orders he was familiarly known by the title of "Jack the devil," an appellation which originated in a supposed malignity of disposition, and a real reluctance to mix in the society of those who were believed to be his equals. This morose reserve, coupled with the mystery which enveloped all about him, rendered him an object of suspicion and inquiry to his fellow-servants, amongst whom it was whispered that his man in secret governed the actions demnify himself for his public and apparent servitude and self-denial, he in private exacted a degree of respectful homage from his so-called master, totally inconsistent with the relation generally supposed to exist between them.

This man's personal appearance was, to say the least of it, extremely odd; he was low in stature; and this defect was enhanced by a distortion of the spine, so considerable as almost to amount to a hunch; his features, too, had all that sharpness and sickliness of hue which generally accompany deformity; he wore his hair, which was black as soot, in heavy neglected ringlets about his shoulders, and always without powder—a peculiarity in those days. There was something unpleasant, too, in the circumstance that he never raised his eyes so as to meet those of another; this fact was often cited as a proof of his being SOMETHING NOT QUITE RIGHT, and said to result not from the timidity which is supposed in most cases to induce this habit, but from a consciousness that his eye possessed a power, which, if exhibited, would betray a supernatural origin. Once, and once only, had he violated this sinister observance: it was on the occasion of Sir Robert's hopes having been most bitterly disappointed; his lady, after a severe and dangerous confinement, gave birth to a dead child. Immediately after the intelligence had been made known, a servant, having upon some business, passed outside the gate of the castle yard, was met by Jacque, who, contrary to his wont, accosted him, observing, "so, after all the pother, the son and heir is still-born." This remark was accompanied by a chuckling laugh, only, the only approach to merriment which he was ever known to exhibit. The servant, who was really disappointed, having hoped for holy-day times, feasting and debauchery with impunity during the rejoicings which would have accompanied a christening, turned tartly upon the little valet, telling him that he should let Sir Robert know how he had received the tidings which should have filled any faithful servant with sorrow; and having once broken the ice, he was proceeding with increasing fluency, when his harangue was cut short and his temerity punished, by the little man's raising his head and treating him to a scowl so fearful, half demoniac, half insane, that it haunted his imagination in nightmares and nervous tremours for months after.

To this man Lady Ardagh had, at first sight, conceived an antipathy amounting to horror, a mixture of loathing and dread so very powerful that she had made it a particular and urgent request to Sir Robert, that he would dismiss him, offering herself, from that property which Sir Robert had, by the marriage settlements, left at her own disposal, to provide handsomely for him, provided only she might be relieved from the continual anxiety and discomfort which the fear of encountering him induced.

Sir Robert, however, would not hear of it; the request seemed at first to agitate and distress him; but when still urged in defiance of his peremptory refusal, he burst into a violent fit of fury; he spoke darkly of great sacrifices which he had made, and threatened that if the request were at any time renewed he would leave both her and the country for ever. This was, however, a solitary instance of violence; his general conduct towards Lady Ardagh, though at no time bordering upon the uxorious, was certainly kind and respectful, and he was more than repaid in the fervent attachment which she bore him in return.

Some short time after this strange interview between Sir Robert and Lady Ardagh, one night after the family had retired to bed, and when everything had been quiet for some time, the bell of Sir Robert's dressing-room rang suddenly and violently; the ringing was repeated again and again at still shorter intervals, and with increasing violence, as if the person who pulled the bell was agitated by the presence of some terrifying and imminent danger. A servant named Donovan was the first to answer it; he threw on his clothes, and hurried to the room with haste proportioned to the urgency of the call.

Sir Robert had selected for his private room an apartment, remote from the bed-chambers of the castle, most of which lay in the more modern parts of the mansion, and secured at its entrance by a double door; as the servant opened the first of these, Sir Robert's bell again sounded with a longer and louder peal; the inner door resisted his efforts to open it; but after a few violent struggles, not having been perfectly secured or owing to the inadequacy of the bolt itself, it gave way, and the servant rushed into the apartment, advancing several paces before he could recover himself. As he entered, he heard Sir Robert's voice exclaiming loudly "wait without, do not come in yet;" but the prohibition came too late. Near a low trucklebed, upon which Sir Robert sometimes slept, for he was a whimsical man, in a large arm chair, sate, or rather lounged, the form of the valet, Jacque; his arms folded, and his heels shapen legs, his head thrown back, and his eyes fixed upon his master with a look of indescribable defiance and derision, while, as if to add to the strange insolence of his attitude and expression, he had placed upon his head the black cloth cap which it was his habit to wear.

Sir Robert was standing before him at the distance of several yards in a posture expressive of despair, terror, and what might be called an agony of humility. He waved his hand twice or thrice, as if to dismiss the servant, who, however, remained fixed on the spot where he had first stood; and then, as if forgetting every thing but the agony within him, he pressed his clenched hands on his cold damp brow, and dashed away the heavy drops that gathered chill and thickly there. Jacque broke the silence.

"Donovan," said he, "shake up that drone and drunkard, Carlton; tell him that his master directs that the travelling carriage shall be at the door within half an hour."

The servant paused as if in doubt as to what he should do; but his scruples were resolved by Sir Robert's saying hurriedly, "Go, go, do whatever he directs; his commands are mine, tell Carlton the same."

The servant hurried to obey, and in about half an hour the carriage was at the door, and Jacque having directed the coachman to drive to B——n, a small town at about the distance of twelve miles, the nearest point, however, at which post horses could be obtained, stept into the vehicle which accordingly quitted the castle immediately.

Although it was a fine moonlight night, the carriage made its way but slowly, and after the lapse of two hours, the travellers had arrived at a point about eight miles from the castle, at which the road strikes through a desolate and heathy flat, sloping up distantly at either side into bleak undulatory hills, in whose monotonous sweep the imagination beholds the heaving of some dark sluggish sea, arrested in its first commotion by some preternatural power; it is a gloomy and divested spot; there is neither tree nor habitation near it; its monotony is unbroken, except by here and there the grey front of a rock peering above the heath, and the effect is rendered yet more dreary and spectral by the exaggerated and misty shadows which the moon casts along the sloping sides of the hills. When they had gained about the centre of this tract, Carlton, the coachman, was surprised to see a figure standing, at some distance in advance, immediately beside the road, and still more so when, on coming up, he observed that it was no other than the person whom he believed to be at that moment quietly seated in the carriage; the coachman drew up, and nodding to him, the little valet exclaimed, "Carlton, I have got the start of you, the roads are heavy, so I shall even take care of myself the rest of the way; do you make your way back as best you can; and I shall follow my own nose;" so saying he chucked a purse into the lap of the coachman, and turning off at a right angle with the road he began to move rapidly away in the direction of the dark ridge, that lowered in the distance. The servant watched him until he was lost in the shadowy haze of night; and neither he nor any of the inmates of the castle saw Jacque again. His disappearance, as might have been expected, did not cause any regret among the servants and dependants at the castle; and Lady Ardagh did not attempt to conceal her delight; but with Sir Robert matters were different; for two or three days subsequent to this event, he confined himself to his room; and when he did return to his ordinary occupations, it was with a gloomy indifference which showed that he did so more from habit than from any interest he felt in them; he appeared from that moment unaccountably and strikingly changed, and thenceforward walked through life as a thing from which he could derive neither profit nor pleasure. His temper, however, so far from growing wayward or morose, became, though gloomy, very, almost unnaturally, placid and cold; but his spirits totally failed, and he became silent and abstracted.

These sombre habits of mind, as might have been anticipated, very materially affected the gay housekeeping of the castle; and the dark and melancholy spirit of its master, seemed to have communicated itself to the very domestics, almost to the very walls of the mansion. Several years rolled on this way, and the sounds of mirth and wassail had long been strangers to the castle, when Sir Robert requested his lady, to her great astonishment, to invite some twenty or thirty of their friends to spend the Christmas, which was fast approaching, at the castle. Lady Ardagh gladly complied, and her sister Mary, who still continued unmarried, and Lady D—— were of course included in the invitations. Lady Ardagh had requested her sisters to set forward as early as possible, in order that she might enjoy a little of their society before the arrival of the other guests; and in compliance with this request

- - -

15

they left Dublin almost immediately upon receiving the invitation, a little more than a week before the arrival of the festival which was to be the period at which the whole party were to muster.

For expedition's sake it was arranged that they should post, while Lady D—'s groom was to follow with her horses ; she taking with herself her own maid and one male servant. They left the city when the day was considerably spent, and consequently made but three stages in the first day ; upon the second, at about eight in the evening, they had reached the town of K——k, distant about fifteen miles from Castle Ardagh, Here owing to Miss F——d's great fatigue, she having been for a considerable time in a very delicate state of health, it was determined to put up for the night. They, accordingly, took possession of the best sitting room which the inn commanded, and Lady D—— remained in it to direct and urge the preparations for some refreshment, which the fatigues of the day had rendered necessary, while her younger sister retired to her bed-chamber to rest there for a little time, as the parlour commanded no such luxury as a sofa.

Miss F——d was, as I have already stated, at this time, in very delicate health ; and upon this occasion the exhaustion of fatigue, and the dreary badness of the weather, combined to depress her spirits. Lady D—— had not been left long to herself, when the door communicating with the passage was abruptly opened, and her sister Mary entered in a state of great agitation; she sate down pale and trembling upon one of the chairs, and it was not until a copious flood of tears had relieved her, that she became sufficiently calm to relate the cause of her excitement and distress. It was simply this. Almost immediately upon lying down upon the bed she sank into a feverish and unrefreshing slumber ; images of all grotesque shapes and startling colours flitted before her sleeping fancy with all the rapidity and variety of the changes in a kaleidoscope. At length, as she described it, a mist seemed to interpose itself between her sight and the ever-shifting scenery which sported before her imagination, and out of this cloudy shadow, gradually emerged a figure whose back seemed turned towards the sleeper ; it was that of a lady, who, in perfect silence, was expressing as far as pantomimic gesture could, by wringing her hands, and throwing her head from side to side, in the manner of one who is exhausted by the over indulgence, by the very sickness and impatience of grief, the extremity of misery. For a long time she sought in vain to catch a glimpse of the face of the apparition, who thus seemed to stir and live before her. But at length the figure seemed to move with an air of authority, as if about to give directions to some inferior, and in doing so, it turned its head so as to display, with a ghastly distinctness, the features of Lady Ardagh, pale as death, with her dark hair all dishevelled, and her eyes dim and sunken with weeping. The revulsion of feeling which Miss F——d experienced at this disclosure—for up to that point she had contemplated the appearance rather with a sense of curiosity and of interest, than of any thing deeper—was so horrible, that the shock awoke her perfectly. She sat up in the bed, and looked fearfully around the room, which was imperfectly lighted by a single candle burning dimly, as if she almost expected to see the reality of her dreadful vision lurking in some corner of the chamber. Her fears were, however, verified, though not in the way she expected; yet in a manner sufficiently horrible—for she had hardly time to breathe and to collect her thoughts, when she heard, or thought she heard, the voice of her sister, Lady Ardagh, sometimes sobbing violently, and sometimes almost shrieking as if in terror, and calling upon her and Lady D——, with the most imploring earnestness of despair, for God's sake to lose no time in coming to her. All this was so horribly distinct, that it seemed as if the mourner was standing within a few yards of the spot where Miss F——d lay. She sprang from the bed, and leaving the candle in the room behind her, she made her way in the dark through the passage, the voice still following her, until as she arrived at the door of the sitting-room it seemed to die away in low sobbing.

As soon as Miss F——d was tolerably recovered, she declared her determination to proceed directly, and without further loss of time to Castle Ardagh. It was not without much difficulty that Lady D—— at length prevailed upon her to consent to remain where they then were, until morning should arrive, when it was to be expected that the young lady would be much refreshed by at least remaining quiet for the night, even though sleep were out of the question. Lady D—— was convinced, from the nervous and feverish symptoms which her sister exhibited, that she had already done too much, and was more than ever satisfied of the necessity of prosecuting the journey no further upon that day. After some time she persuaded her sister to return to her room, where she remained with her until she had gone to bed, and appeared comparatively composed. Lady D—— then returned to the parlour, and not finding herself sleepy, she remained sitting by the fire. Her solitude was a second time broken in upon, by the entrance of her sister, who now appeared, if possible, more agitated than before. She said that Lady D—— had not long left the room, when she was roused by a repetition of the same wailing and lamentations, accompanied by the wildest and most agonized supplications that no time should be lost in coming to Castle Ardagh, and all in her sister's voice, and uttered at the same proximity as before. This time the voice had followed her to the very door of the sitting room, and until she closed it, seemed to pour forth its cries and sobs at the very threshold.

Miss F——d now most positively declared that nothing should prevent her proceeding instantly to the castle, adding that if Lady D—— would not accompany her, she would go on by herself. Superstitious feelings are at all times more or less contagious, and the last century afforded a soil much more congenial to their growth than the present. Lady D—— was so far affected by her sister's terrors, that she became, at least, uneasy ; and seeing that her sister was immoveably determined upon setting forward immediately, she consented to accompany her forthwith. After a slight delay, fresh horses were procured, and the two ladies and their attendants renewed their journey, with strong injunctions to the driver to quicken their rate of travelling as much as possible, and promises of reward in case of his doing so.

Roads were then in a much worse condition throughout the south, even than they now are; and the fifteen miles which modern posting would have passed in little more than an hour and a half, were not completed even with every possible exertion in twice the time. Miss F——d had been nervously restless during the journey. Her head had been out at the carriage window every minute ; and as they approached the entrance to the castle demesne, which lay about a mile from the building, her anxiety began to communicate itself to her sister. The postillion had just dismounted, and was endeavouring to open the gate—at that time a necessary trouble ; for in the middle of the last century, porter's lodges were not common in the south of Ireland, and locks and keys almost unknown. He had just succeeded in rolling back the heavy oaken gate, so as to admit the vehicle, when a mounted servant rode rapidly down the avenue, and drawing up at the carriage, asked of the postillion who the party were; and on hearing, he rode round to the carriage window, and handed in a note which Lady D—— received. By the assistance of one of the coach-lamps they succeeded in deciphering it. It was scrawled in great agitation, and ran thus—

My Dear Sister—my dear Sisters both,— In God's name lose no time, I am frightened and miserable; I cannot explain all till you come. I am too much terrified to write coherently; but understand me—hasten—do not waste a minute. I am afraid you will come too late.   E. A.

The servant could tell nothing more than that the castle was in great confusion, and that Lady Ardagh had been crying bitterly all the night. Sir Robert was perfectly well. Altogether at a loss as to the cause of Lady Ardagh's great distress, they urged their way up the steep and broken avenue which wound through the crowding trees, whose wild and grotesque branches, now stript and naked by the blasts of winter, stretched drearily across the road. As the carriage drew up in the area before the door, the anxiety of the ladies almost amounted to sickness; and scarcely waiting for the assistance of their attendant, they sprang to the ground, and in an instant stood at the castle door. From within were distinctly audible the sounds of lamentation and weeping, and the suppressed hum of voices as if of those endeavouring to soothe the mourner. The door was speedily opened, and when the ladies entered, the first object which met their view was their sister, Lady Ardagh, sitting on a form in the hall, weeping and wringing her hands in deep agony. Beside her stood two old, withered crones, who were each endeavouring in their own way to administer consolation, without even knowing or caring what the subject of her grief might be.

Immediately on Lady Ardagh's seeing her sisters, she started up, fell on their necks, and kissed them again and again without speaking, and then taking them each by a hand, still weeping bitterly, she led them into a small room adjoining the hall, in which burned a light, and having closed the door, she sat down between them. After thanking them for the haste they had made, she proceeded to tell them, in words incoherent from agitation, that Sir Robert had in private, and in the most solemn manner, told her that he should die upon that night, and that he had occupied himself during the evening in giving minute directions respecting the arrangements of his funeral.

Lady D—— here suggested the possibility of his labouring under the hallucinations of a fever; but to this Lady Ardagh quickly replied,

"Oh! no, no! would to God I could think it. Oh! no, no! wait till you have seen him. There is a frightful calmness about all he says and does; and his directions are all so clear, and his mind so perfectly collected, it is impossible, quite impossible;" and she wept yet more bitterly.

At that moment Sir Robert's voice was heard in issuing some directions, as he came down stairs; and Lady Ardagh exclaimed, hurriedly—

"Go now and see him yourself; he is in the hall."

Lady D——accordingly went out into the hall, where Sir Robert met her; and saluting her with kind politeness, he said, after a pause—

"You are come upon a melancholy mission—the house is in great confusion, and some of its inmates in considerable grief." He took her hand, and looking fixedly in her face, continued— "I shall not live to see tomorrow's sun shine."

"You are ill, sir, I have no doubt," replied she; "but I am very certain we shall see you much better to-morrow, and still better the day following."

"I am *not* ill, sister," replied he: "Feel my temples, they are cool; lay your finger to my pulse, its throb is slow and temperate. I never was more perfectly in health, and yet do I know that ere three hours be past, I shall be no more."

"Sir, sir," said she, a good deal startled, but wishing to conceal the impression which the calm solemnity of his manner had, in her own despite, made upon her, "Sir, you should not jest; you should not even speak lightly upon such subjects. You trifle with what is sacred—you are sporting with the best affections of you wife——"

"Stay, my good lady," said he; "if when this clock shall strike the hour of three, I shall be anything but a helpless clod, then upbraid me. Pray return now to your sister. Lady Ardagh is, indeed, much to be pitied; but what is past cannot now be helped. I have now a few papers to arrange, and some to destroy. I shall see you and Lady Ardagh before my death; try to compose her—her sufferings distress me much; but what is past cannot now be mended."

Thus saying he went up stairs, and Lady D—— returned to the room where her sisters were sitting.

"Well," exclaimed Lady Ardagh, as she re-entered, "is it not so?—do you still doubt?—do you think there is any hope?"

Lady D—— was silent.

"Oh! none, none, none," continued she; "I see, I see you are convinced," and she wrung her hands in bitter agony.

"My dear sister," said Lady D——, "there is, no doubt, something strange in all that has appeared in this matter; but still I cannot but hope that there may be something deceptive in all the apparent calmness of Sir Robert. I still must believe that some latent fever has affected his mind, as that owing to the state of nervous depression into which he has been sinking, some trivial occurrence has been converted, in his disordered imagination, into an augury foreboding his immediate dissolution."

In such suggestions, unsatisfactory even to those who originated them, and doubly so to her whom they were intended to comfort, more than two hours passed; and Lady D—— was beginning to hope that the fated term might elapse without the occurrence of any tragical event, when Sir Robert entered the room. On coming in, he placed his finger with a warning gesture upon his lips, as if to enjoin silence; and then having successively pressed the hands of his two sisters-in-law, he stooped over the almost lifeless form of his lady, and twice pressed her cold, pale forehead with his lips, and then passed motionlessly out of the room.

Lady D—— followed to the door, saw him take a candle in the hall, and walk deliberately up the stairs. Stimulated by a feeling of horrible curiosity, she continued to follow him at a distance. She saw him enter his own private room, and heard him close and lock the door after him. Continuing to follow him as far as she could, she placed herself at the door of the chamber, as noiselessly as possible; where after a little time, she was joined by her two sisters, Lady Ardagh and Miss F——d. In breathless silence they listened to what should pass within. They distinctly heard Sir Robert pacing up and down the room for some time; and then, after a pause, a sound as if some one had thrown himself heavily upon the bed. At this moment Lady D——, forgetting that the door had been secured within, turned the handle for the purpose of entering; some one from the inside, close to the door, said, "Hush! hush!" The same lady, now much alarmed, knocked violently at the door—there was no answer. She knocked again more violently, with no further success. Lady Ardagh, now uttering a piercing shriek, sank in a swoon upon the floor. Three or four servants, alarmed by the noise, now hurried up stairs, and Lady Ardagh was carried apparently lifeless to her own chamber. They then, after having knocked long and loudly in vain, applied themselves to forcing an entrance into Sir Robert's room. After resisting some violent efforts, the door at length gave way, and all entered the room nearly together. There was a single candle burning upon a table at the far end of the partment; and stretched upon the bed lay Sir Robert Ardagh. He was a corpse—the eyes were open—no convulsion had passed over the features, or distorted the limbs—it seemed as if the soul had sped from the body without a struggle to remain there. On touching the body it was found to be cold as clay—all lingering of the vital heat had left it. They closed the ghastly eyes of the corpse, and leaving it to the care of those who seem to consider it a privilege of their age and sex to gloat over the revolting spectacle of death in all its stages, they returned to Lady Ardagh, now a widow. The party assembled at the castle, but the atmosphere was tainted with death. Grief there was not much, but awe and panic were expressed in every face. The guests talked in whispers, and the servants walked on tiptoe, as if afraid of the very noise of their own footwteps.

The funeral was conducted almost with splendour. The body having been conveyed, in compliance with Sir Robert's last directions, to Dublin, was there laid within the ancient walls of Saint Audoen's Church—where I have read the epitaph, telling the age and titles of the departed dust. Neither painted escutcheon, nor marble slab, have served to rescue from oblivion the story of the dead, whose very name will ere long moulder from their tracery—

Et sunt sua fata sepulchris.

The events which I have recorded are not imaginary. They are FACTS; and there lives one whose authority none would venture to question, who could vindicate the accuracy of every statement which I have set down, and that, too, with all the circumstantiality of an eye witness.

SCHALKEN THE PAINTER

You will no doubt be surprised, my dear friend, at the
subject of the following narrative. What had I to do with
Schalken, or Schalken with me? He had returned to his
native land, and was probably dead and buried before I
was born; I never visited Holland nor spoke with a native
of that country. So much I believe you already know. I
must, then, give you my authority, and state to you frankly
the ground upon which rests the credibility of the strange
story which I am about to lay before you. I was acquainted,
in my early days, with a Captain Vandael, whose father
had served King William in the Low Countries, and also in
my own unhappy land during the Irish campaigns. I know
not how it happened that I liked this man's society in spite
of his, politics and religion : but so it was; and it was by
means of the free intercourse to which our intimacy gave
rise that I became possessed of the curious tale which you
are about to hear. I had often been struck, while visiting
Vandael, by a remarkable picture, in which, though no
connoisseur myself, I could not fail to discern some very
strong peculiarities, particularly in the distribution of light
and shade, as also a certain oddity in the design itself, which
interested my curiosity. It represented the interior of what
might be a chamber in some antique religious building – the
foreground was occupied by a female figure, arrayed in a

species of white robe, part of which is arranged so as to form a veil. The dress, however, is not strictly that of any religious order. In its hand the figure bears a lamp, by whose light alone the form and face are illuminated; the features are marked by an arch smile, such as pretty women wear when engaged in successfully practising some roguish trick; in the background, and, excepting where the dim red light of an expiring fire serves to define the form, totally in the shade, stands the figure of a man equipped in the old fashion, with doublet and so forth, in an attitude of alarm, his hand being placed upon the hilt of his sword, which he appears to be in the act of drawing.

"There are some pictures," said I to my friend, "which impress one, I know not how, with a conviction that they represent not the mere ideal shapes and combinations which have floated through the imagination of the artist, but scenes, faces, and situations which have actually existed. When I look upon that picture, something assures me that I behold the representation of a reality."

Vandael smiled, and fixing his eyes upon the painting musingly, he said :

"Your fancy has not deceived you, my good friend, for that picture is the record, and I believe a faithful one, of a remarkable and mysterious occurrence. It was painted by Schalken, and contains, in the face of the female figure, which occupies the most prominent place in the design, an accurate portrait of Rose Velderkaust, the niece of Gerard Douw, the first, and, I believe, the only love of Godfrey Schalken. My father knew the painter well and from Schalken himself he learned the story of the mysterious drama, one scene of which the picture has embodied. This painting, which is accounted a fine specimen of Schalken's style, was bequeathed to my father by the artist's will, and, as you have observed, is a very striking and interesting production."

I had only to request Vandael to tell the story of the

painting to be gratified; and thus it is that I am enabled to submit to you a faithful recital of what I heard myself, leaving you to reject or allow the evidence upon which the truth of the tradition depends, with this one assurance, that Schalken was an honest, blunt Dutchman, and, I believe, wholly incapable of committing a flight of imagination; and further, that Vandael, from whom I heard the story, appeared firmly convinced of its truth.

There are few forms upon which the mantle of mystery and romance could seem to hang more ungracefully than upon that of the uncouth and clownish Schalken – the Dutch boor – the rude and dogged, but most cunning worker of oils, whose pieces delight the initiated of the present day almost as much as his manners disgusted the refined of his own; and yet this man, so rude, so dogged, so slovenly, I had almost said so savage, in mien and manner, during his after successes, had been selected by the capricious goddess, in his early life, to figure as the hero of a romance by no means devoid of interest or of mystery. Who can tell how meet he may have been in his young days to play the part of the lover or of the hero – who can say that in early life he had been the same harsh, *unlicked*, and rugged boor which, in his maturer age, he proved – or how far the neglected rudeness which afterwards marked his air and garb, and manners, may not have been the growth of that reckless apathy not unfrequently produced by bitter misfortunes and disappointments in early life? These questions can never now be answered. We must content ourselves, then, with a plain statement of facts, or what have been received and transmitted as such, leaving matters of speculation to those who like them.

When Schalken studied under the immortal Gerard Douw, he was a young man; and in spite of the phlegmatic constitution and unexcitable manner which he shared (we believe) with his countrymen, he was not incapable of deep and vivid impressions, for it is an established fact that the young painter looked with considerable interest upon the beautiful niece of his wealthy master. Rose Velderkaust was very young, having, at the period of which we speak, not yet attained her seventeenth year, and, if tradition speaks truth, possessed all the soft dimpling charms of the fair, light-haired Flemish maidens. Schalken had not studied long in the school of Gerard Douw, when he felt this interest deepening into something of a keener and intenser feeling that was quite consistent with the tranquillity of his honest Dutch heart; and at the same time he perceived, or thought he perceived, flattering symptoms of a reciprocity of liking, and this was quite sufficient to determine whatever indecision he might have heretofore experienced, and to lead him to devote exclusively to her every hope and feeling of his heart. In short, he was as much in love as a Dutchman could be. He was not long in making his passion known to the pretty maiden herself, and his declaration was followed by a corresponding confession upon her part. Schalken, however, was a poor man, and he possessed no counterbalancing advantages of birth or otherwise to induce the old man to consent to a union which must involve his niece and ward in the struggles and difficulties of a young and nearly friendless artist. He was, therefore, to wait until time had furnished him with opportunity and accident with success; and then, if his labours were found sufficiently lucrative, it was to be hoped that his proposals might at least be listened to by her jealous guardian. Months passed away, and, cheered by the smiles of the little Rose, Schalken's labours were redoubled, and with such effect and improvement as reasonably to promise the realization of his hopes, and no contemptible eminence in his art, before many years should have elapsed.

The even course of this cheering prosperity was, however, destined to experience a sudden and formidable interruption, and that, too, in a manner so strange and mysterious as to baffle all investigation, and throw upon the events them-selves a shadow of almost supernatural horror.

Schalken had one evening remained in the master's studio considerably longer than his more volatile companions, who had gladly availed themselves of the excuse which the dusk of evening afforded, to withdraw from their several tasks, in order to finish a day of labour in the jollity and con-viviality of the tavern. But Schalken worked for improve-ment, or rather for love. Besides, he was now engaged merely in sketching a design, an operation which, unlike that of colouring, might be continued as long as there was light sufficient to distinguish between canvas and charcoal. He had not then, nor, indeed, until long after, discovered the peculiar powers of his pencil, and he was engaged in com-posing a group of extremely roguish-looking and grotesque imps and demons, who were inflicting various ingenious torments upon a perspiring and pot-bellied St. Anthony, who reclined in the midst of them, apparently in the last stage of drunkenness. The young artist, however, though incapable of executing, or even of appreciating, anything of true sublimity, had, nevertheless, discernment enough to prevent his being by any means satisfied with his work; and many were the patient erasures and corrections which the limbs and features of saint and devil underwent, yet all without producing in their new arrangement anything of improvement or increased effect. The large, old-fashioned room was silent, and, with the exception of himself, quite deserted by its usual inmates. An hour had passed – nearly two – without any improved result. Daylight had already declined, and twilight was fast giving way to the darkness of night. The patience of the young man was exhausted, and he stood before his unfinished production, absorbed in no very pleasing ruminations, one hand buried in the folds of his long dark hair, and the other holding the piece of charcoal which had so ill executed its office, and which he now rubbed, without much regard to the sable streaks which it produced, with irritable pressure upon his ample Flemish inexpressibles.

"Pshaw!" said the young man aloud, "would that picture, devils, saint, and all, were where they should be – in hell!" A short, sudden laugh, uttered startlingly close to his ear, instantly responded to the ejaculation. The artist turned sharply round, and now for the first time became aware that his labours had been overlooked by a stranger. Within about a yard and a half, and rather behind him, there stood what was, or appeared to be, the figure of an elderly man : he wore a short cloak, and broad-brimmed hat, with a conical crown, and in his hand, which was protected with a heavy, gauntlet-shaped glove, he carried a long ebony walking-stick, surmounted with what appeared, as it glittered dimly in the twilight, to be a massive head of gold, and upon the breast, through the folds of the cloak, there shone what appeared to be the links of a rich chain of the same metal. The room was so obscure that nothing further of the appearance of the figure could be ascertained, and the face was altogether overshadowed by the heavy flap of the beaver which overhung it, so that not a feature could be discerned. A quantity of dark hair escaped from beneath this sombre hat, a circumstance which, connected with the firm, upright carriage of the intruder, proved that his years could not yet exceed threescore or thereabouts. There was an air of gravity and importance about the garb of this person, and something indescribably odd, I might say awful, in the perfect stone-like movelessness of the figure, that effectually checked the testy comment which had at once risen to the lips of the irritated artist. He, therefore, as soon as he had sufficiently recovered the surprise, asked the stranger, civilly, to be seated, and desired to know if he had any message to leave for his master.

"Tell Gerard Douw," said the unknown, without altering his attitude in the smallest degree, "that Minheer Vanderhausen, of Rotterdam, desires to speak with him on tomorrow evening at this hour, and, if he please, in this room, upon matters of weight – that is all – goodnight."

The stranger, having finished this message, turned abruptly, and with a quick but silent step quitted the room, before Schalken had time to say a word in reply. The young man felt a curiosity to see in what direction the burgher of Rotterdam would turn on quitting the studio, and for that purpose he went directly to the window which commanded the door. A lobby of considerable extent intervened between the inner door of the painter's room and the street entrance, so that Schalken occupied the post of observation before the old man could possibly have reached the street. He watched in vain, however. There was no other mode of exit. Had the old man vanished, or was he lurking about the recesses of the lobby for some bad purpose? This last suggestion filled the mind of Schalken with a vague horror, which was so unaccountably intense as to make him alike afraid to remain in the room alone and reluctant to pass through the lobby. However, with an effort which appeared very disproportioned to the occasion, he summoned resolution to leave the room, and, having double-locked the door and thrust the key in his pocket, without looking to the right or left, he traversed the passage which had so recently, perhaps still, contained the person of his mysterious visitant, scarcely venturing to breathe till he had arrived in the open street.

"Minheer Vanderhausen," said Gerard Douw within himself, as the appointed hour approached, "Minheer Vanderhausen of Rotterdam! I never heard of the man till yesterday. What can he want of me? A portrait, perhaps, to be painted; or a younger son or a poor relation to be apprenticed; or a collection to be valued; or – pshaw, there's no one in Rotterdam to leave me a legacy. Well, whatever the business may be, we shall soon know it all."

It was now the close of day, and every easel, except that of Schalken, was deserted. Gerald Douw was pacing the apartment with the restless step of impatient expectation, every now and then humming a passage from a piece of music which he was himself composing; for, though no great proficient, he admired the art : sometimes pausing to glance over the work of one of his absent pupils, but more frequently placing himself at the window, from whence he might observe the passengers who threaded the obscure by-street, in which his studio was placed.

"Said you not, Godfrey," exclaimed Douw, after a long and fruitless gaze from his post of observation, and turning to Schalken – "said you not the hour of appointment was at about seven by the clock of the Stadhouse?"

"It had just tolled seven when I first saw him, sir," answered the student.

"The hour is close at hand, then," said the master, consulting a horologe as large and as round as a full-grown orange. "Minheer Vanderhausen from Rotterdam – is it not so?"

"Such was the name."

"And an elderly man, richly clad?" continued Douw.

"As well as I might see," replied his pupil; "he could not be young, nor yet very old neither, and his dress was rich and grave, as might become a citizen of wealth and consideration."

At this moment the sonorous boom of the Stadhouse clock tolled, stroke after stroke, the hour of seven; the eyes of both master and student were directed to the door; and it was not until the last peal of the old bell had ceased to vibrate, that Douw exclaimed :

"So, so; we shall have his worship presently – that is, if he means to keep his hour; if not, thou may'st wait for him, Godfrey, if you court the acquaintance of a capricious burgomaster; as for me, I think our old Leyden contains a sufficiency of such commodities, without an importation from Rotterdam."

Schalken laughed, as in duty bound; and after a pause of some minutes, Douw suddenly exclaimed :

"What if it should all prove a jest, a piece of mummery got up by Vankarp, or some such worthy? I wish you had run all risks, and cudgelled the old burgomaster, stadholder, or whatever else he may be, soundly. I would wager a dozen of Rhenish, his worship would have pleaded old acquaintance before the third application."

"Here he comes, sir," said Schalken, in a low admonitory tone; and instantly upon turning towards the door, Gerard Douw observed the same figure which had, on the day before, so unexpectedly greeted the vision of his pupil Schalken.

There was something in the air and mein of the figure which at once satisfied the painter that there was no *mummery* in the case, and that he really stood in the presence of a man of worship; and so, without hesitation, he doffed his cap, and, courteously saluting the stranger, requested him to be seated. The visitor waved his hand slightly, as if in acknowledgement of the courtesy, but remained standing.

"I have the honour to see Minheer Vanderhausen of Rotterdam?" said Gerard Douw.

"The same," was the laconic reply of his visitant.

"I understand your worship desires to speak with me," continued Douw, "and I am here by appointment to wait your commands."

"Is that a man of trust?" said Vanderhausen, turning towards Schalken, who stood at a little distance behind his master.

"Certainly," replied Gerard.

"Then let him take this box and get the nearest jeweller or goldsmith to value its contents, and let him return hither with a certificate of the valuation."

At the same time, he placed a small case about nine inches square in the hands of Gerard Douw, who was as much amazed at its weight as at the strange abruptness with which it was handed to him. In accordance with the wishes of the stranger, he delivered it into the hands of Schalken, and repeating *his* directions, despatched him upon the mission.

Schalken disposed his precious charge securely beneath the folds of his cloak, and rapidly traversing two or three narrow streets, he stopped at a corner house, the lower part of which was then occupied by the shop of a Jewish gold-smith. Schalken entered the shop, and calling the little Hebrew into the obscurity of its back recesses, he proceeded to lay before him Vanderhausen's packet. On being ex-amined by the light of a lamp, it appeared entirely cased with lead, the outer surface of which was much scraped and soiled, and nearly white with age. This was with difficulty partially removed and disclosed beneath a box of some dark and singularly hard wood; this too was forced, and after the removal of two or three folds of linen, its contents proved to be a mass of golden ingots, closely packed, and, as the Jew declared, of the most perfect quality. Every ingot under-went the scrutiny of the little Jew, who seemed to feel an epicurean delight in touching and testing these morsels of the glorious metal; and each one of them was replaced in its berth with the exclamation: "Mein Gott, how very perfect! Not one grain of alloy – beautiful, beautiful." The task was at length finished, and the Jew certified under his hand the value of the ingots submitted to his examination, to amount to many thousand rix-dollars. With the desired document in his bosom, and the rich box of gold carefully pressed under his arm, and concealed by his cloak, he retraced his way, and entering the studio, found his master and the stranger in close conference.

Schalken had no sooner left the room, in order to execute the commission he had taken in charge, than Vanderhausen addressed Gerard Douw in the following terms:

"I may not tarry with you tonight more than a few minutes, and so I shall briefly tell you the matter upon which I come. You visited the town of Rotterdam some four months ago, and then I saw in the church of St. Lawrence your niece, Rose Velderkaust. I desire to marry her, and if I satisfy you as to the fact that I am very wealthy, more wealthy than any husband you could dream of for her, I expect that you will forward my views to the utmost of your authority. If you approve my proposals, you must close with it at once, for I cannot command time enough to wait for calculations and delays."

Gerard Douw was, perhaps, as much astonished as any one could be, by the very unexpected nature of Minheer Vanderhausen's communication, but he did not give vent to any unseemly expression of surprise, for besides the motives supplied by prudence and politeness, the painter experienced a kind of chill and oppressive sensation, something like that which is supposed to affect a man who is placed unconsciously in immediate contact with something to which he has a natural antipathy – an undefined horror and dread while standing in the presence of the eccentric stranger, which made him very unwilling to say anything which might reasonably prove offensive.

"I have no doubt," said Gerard, after two or three prefatory hems, "that the connexion which you propose would prove alike advantageous and honourable to my niece; but you must be aware that she has a will of her own, and may not acquiesce in what *we* may desire for her advantage."

"Do not seek to deceive me, sir painter," said Vanderhausen; "you are her guardian – she is your ward – she is mine if *you* like to make her so."

The man of Rotterdam moved forward a little as he spoke, and Gerard Douw, he scarce knew why, inwardly prayed for the speedy return of Schalken.

"I desire," said the mysterious gentleman, "to place in your hands at once an evidence of my wealth, and a security for my liberal dealing with your niece. The lad will return in a minute or two with a sum in value five times the fortune which she has a right to expect from a husband. This shall lie in your hands, together with her dowry, and you may apply the united sum as suits her interest best; it shall be all exclusively hers while she lives – is that liberal?"

Douw assented, and inwardly thought that fortune had been extraordinarily kind to his niece; the stranger, he thought, must be both wealthy and generous, and such an offer was not to be despised, though made by a humorist, and one of no very prepossessing presence. Rose had no very high pretensions, for she was almost without dowry; indeed, altogether so, excepting so far as the deficiency had been supplied by the generosity of her uncle; neither had she any right to raise any scruples against the match on the score of birth, for her own origin was by no means elevated, and as to other objections, Gerard resolved, and, indeed, by the usages of the time, was warranted in resolving not to listen to them for a moment.

"Sir," said he, addressing the stranger, "your offer is most liberal, and whatever hesitation I may feel in closing with it immediately, arises solely from my not having the honour of knowing anything of your family or station. Upon these points you can, of course, satisfy me without difficulty?"

"As to my respectability," said the stranger, drily, "you must take that for granted at present; pester me with no inquiries; you can discover nothing more about me than I choose to make known. You shall have sufficient security for my respectability – my word, if you are honourable : if you are sordid, my gold."

"A testy old gentleman," thought Douw, "he must have his own way; but, all things considered, I am justified in giving my niece to him; were she my own daughter, I would do the like by her. I will not pledge myself unnecessarily however."

"You will not pledge yourself unnecessarily," said Vanderhausen, strangely uttering the very words which had just floated through the mind of his companion; "but you will do so if it *is* necessary, I presume; and I will show you that I consider it indispensable. If the gold I mean to leave in your hands satisfies you, and if you desire that my proposal shall not be at once withdrawn, you must, before I leave this room, write your name to this engagement."

Having thus spoken, he placed a paper in the hands of Gerard, the contents of which expressed an engagement entered into by Gerard Douw, to give to Wilken Vanderhausen of Rotterdam, in marriage, Rose Velderkaust, and so forth, within one week of the date thereof. While the painter was employed in reading this covenant, Schalken, as we have stated, entered the studio, and having delivered the box and the valuation of the Jew, into the hands of the stranger, he was about to retire, when Vanderhausen called to him to wait; and, presenting the case and the certificate to Gerard Douw, he waited in silence until he had satisfied himself by an inspection of both as to the value of the pledge left in his hands. At length he said :

"Are you content?"

The painter said he would fain have another day to consider.

"Not an hour," said the suitor coolly.

"Well then," said Douw, "I am content – it is a bargain."

"Then sign at once," said Vanderhausen, "I am weary."

At the same time he produced a small case of writing materials, and Gerard signed the important document.

"Let this youth sign the covenant," said the old man; and Godfrey Schalken unconsciously signed the instrument which bestowed upon another that hand which he had so long regarded as the object and reward of all his labours. The compact being thus completed, the strange visitor folded up the paper, and stowed it safely in an inner pocket.

"I will visit you tomorrow night at nine of the clock, at your house, Gerard Douw, and will see the subject of our contract – farewell"; and so saying, Wilken Vanderhausen moved stiffly but rapidly out of the room.

Schalken, eager to resolve his doubts, had placed himself by the window, in order to watch the street entrance; but the experiment served only to support his suspicions, for the old man did not issue from the door. This was very strange, very odd, very fearful; he and his master returned together, and talked but little on the way, for each had his own subjects for reflection, of anxiety, and of hope. Schalken, however, did not know the ruin which threatened his cherished schemes.

Gerard Douw knew nothing of the attachment which had sprung up between his pupil and his niece; and even if he had, it is doubtful whether he would have regarded its existence as any serious obstruction to the wishes of Minheer Vanderhausen. Marriages were then and there matters of traffic and calculation; and it would have appeared as absurd in the eyes of the guardian to make a mutual attachment an essential element in a contract of marriage, as it would have been to draw up his bonds and receipts in the language of chivalrous romance. The painter, however, did not communicate to his niece the important step which he had taken in her behalf, and his resolution arose not from any anticipation of opposition on her part, but solely from a ludicrous consciousness that if his ward were, as she very naturally might do, to ask him to describe the appearance of the bridegroom whom he destined for her, he would be forced to confess that he had not seen his face, and if called upon, would find it impossible to identify him. Upon the next day, Gerard Douw, having dined, called his niece to him and having scanned her person with an air of satisfaction, he took her hand, and looking upon her pretty, innocent face with a smile of kindness, he said :

"Rose, my girl, that face of yours will make your fortune." Rose blushed and smiled. "Such faces and such tempers seldom go together, and, when they do, the compound is a love potion, which few heads or hearts can resist; trust me, thou wilt soon be a bride, girl; but this is trifling, and I am pressed for time, so make ready the large room by eight o'clock tonight, and give directions for supper at nine. I expect a friend tonight; and observe me, child, do thou trick thyself out handsomely. I would not have him think us poor or sluttish."

With these words he left the chamber, and took his way to the room to which we have already had occasion to introduce our readers – that in which his pupils worked.

When the evening closed in, Gerard called Schalken, who was about to take his departure to his obscure and comfortless lodgings, and asked him to come home and sup with Rose and Vanderhausen. The invitation was, of course, accepted, and Gerard Douw and his pupil soon found themselves in the handsome and somewhat antique-looking room which had been prepared for the reception of the stranger. A cheerful wood fire blazed in the capacious health; a little at one side an old-fashioned table, with richly carved legs, was placed – destined, no doubt, to receive the supper, for which preparations were going forward; and ranged with exact regularity, stood the tall-backed chairs, whose ungracefulness was more than counterbalanced by their comfort. The little party, consisting of Rose, her uncle, and the artist, awaited the arrival of the expected visitor with considerable impatience. Nine o'clock at length came, and with it a summons at the street door, which being speedily answered, was followed by a slow and emphatic tread upon the staircase; the steps moved heavily across the lobby, the door of the room in which the party which we have described were assembled slowly opened, and there entered a figure which startled, almost appalled, the phlegmatic Dutchman, and nearly made Rose scream with affright; it was the form, and arrayed in the garb of Minheer Vanderhausen; the air, the gait, the height were the same, but the features had never been seen by any of the party before. The stranger stopped at the door of the room, and displayed his form and face completely. He wore a dark-coloured cloth cloak, which was short and full, not falling quite to the knees; his legs were cased in dark purple silk stockings, and his shoes were adorned with roses of the same colour. The opening of the cloak in front showed the under-suit to consist of some very dark, perhaps sable material, and his hands were enclosed in a pair of heavy leather gloves, which ran up considerably above the wrist, in the manner of a gauntlet. In one hand he carried his walking-stick and his hat, which he had removed, and the other hung heavily by his side. A quantity of grizzled hair descended in long tresses from his head, and its folds rested upon the plaits of a stiff ruff, which effectually concealed his neck. So far all was well; but the face! – all the flesh of the face was coloured with the bluish leaden hue which is sometimes produced by the operation of metallic medicines, administered in excessive quantities; the eyes were enormous, and the white appeared both above and below the iris, which gave to them an expression of insanity, which was heightened by their glassy fixedness; the nose was well enough, but the mouth was writhed considerably to one side, where it opened in order to give egress to two long, discoloured fangs, which projected from the upper jaw, far below the lower lip – the hue of the lips themselves bore the usual relation to that of the face, and was, consequently, nearly black; the character of the face was malignant, even satanic, to the last degree; and, indeed, such a combination of horror could hardly be accounted for, except by supposing the corpse of some atrocious malefactor which had long hung blackening upon the gibbet to have at length become the habitation of a demon – the frightful sport of satanic possession. It was remarkable that the worshipful stranger suffered as little as possible of his flesh to appear, and that during his visit he did not once remove his gloves. Having stood for some moments at the door, Gerard Douw at length found breath and collectedness to bid him welcome, and with a mute inclination of the head, the stranger stepped forward into the room. There was something indescribably odd, even horrible, about all his motions, something indefinable, that was unnatural, un-human – it was as if the limbs were guided and directed by a spirit unused to the management of bodily machinery. The stranger said hardly anything during his visit, which did not exceed half an hour; and the host himself could scarcely muster courage enough to utter the few necessary salutations and courtesies; and, indeed, such was the nervous terror which the presence of Vanderhausen inspired, that very little would have made all his entertainers fly bellowing from the room. They had not so far lost all self-possession, however, as to fail to observe two strange peculiarities of their visitor. During his stay he did not once suffer his eye-lids to close, nor even to move in the slightest degree; and farther, there was a death-like stillness in his whole person, owing to the total absence of the heaving motion of the chest, caused by the process of respiration. These two peculiarities, though when told they may appear trifling, produced a very striking and unpleasant effect when seen and observed. Vanderhausen at length relieved the painter of Leyden of his inauspicious presence; and with no small gratification the little party heard the street door close after him.

"Dear uncle," said Rose, "what a frightful man! I would not see him again for the wealth of the States."

"Tush, foolish girl," said Douw, whose sensations were anything but comfortable. "A man may be as ugly as the devil, and yet if his heart and actions are good, he is worth all the pretty-faced, perfumed puppies that walk the Mall. Rose, my girl, it is very true he has not thy pretty face, but I know him to be wealthy and liberal; and were he ten times more ugly" – ("which is inconceivable," observed Rose) – "these two virtues would be sufficient," continued her uncle, "to counter-balance all his deformity, and if not of power sufficient actually to alter the shape of the features, at least of efficacy enough to prevent one thinking them amiss."

"Do you know, uncle," said Rose, "when I saw him standing at the door, I could not get it out of my head that I saw the old, painted, wooden figure that used to frighten me so much in the church of St. Lawrence of Rotterdam."

Gerard laughed, though he could not help inwardly acknowledging the justness of the comparison. He was resolved, however, as far as he could, to check his niece's inclination to ridicule the ugliness of her intended bridegroom, although he was not a little pleased to observe that she appeared totally exempt from that mysterious dread of the stranger which, he could not disguise it from himself, considerably affected him, as also his pupil Godfrey Schalken.

Early on the next day there arrived from various quarters of the town, rich presents of silks, velvets, jewellery, and so forth, for Rose; and also a packet directed to Gerard Douw, which on being opened, was found to contain a contract of marriage, formally drawn up, between Wilken Vanderhausen of the Boom-quay, in Rotterdam, and Rose Velderkaust, of Leyden, niece to Gerard Douw, master in the art of painting, also of the same city; and containing engagements on the part of Vanderhausen to make settlements upon his bride, far more splendid than he had before led her guardian to believe likely, and which were to be secured to her use in the most unexceptionable manner possible – the money being placed in the hands of Gerard Douw himself.

I have no sentimental scenes to describe, no cruelty of guardians, or magnanimity of wards, or agonies of lovers. The record I have to make is one of sordidness, levity, and interest. In less than a week after the first interview which we have just described, the contract of marriage was fulfilled, and Schalken saw the prize which he would have risked anything to secure, carried off triumphantly by his unattractive rival. For two or three days he absented himself from the school; he then returned and worked, if with less cheerfulness, with far more dogged resolution than before – the stimulus of love had given place to that of ambition. Months passed away, and, contrary to his expectation, and, indeed, to the direct promise of the parties, Gerard Douw heard nothing of his niece or her worshipful spouse. The interest of the money which was to have been demanded in quarterly sums, lay unclaimed in his hands. He began to grow extremely uneasy. Minheer Vanderhausen's direction in Rotterdam he was fully possessed of; after some irresolution he finally determined to journey thither – a trifling undertaking, and easily accomplished – and thus to satisfy himself of the safety and comfort of his ward, for whom he entertained an honest and strong affection. His search was in vain, however; no one in Rotterdam had ever heard of Minheer Vanderhausen. Gerard Douw left not a house in the Boom-quay untried; but all in vain – no one could give him any information whatever touching the object of his inquiry; and he was obliged to return to Leyden nothing wiser than when he had left it. On his arrival he hastened to the establishment from which Vanderhausen had hired the lumbering, though, considering the times, most luxurious vehicle, which the bridal party had employed to convey them to Rotterdam. From the driver of this machine he learned, that having proceeded by slow stages, they had late in the evening approached Rotterdam; but that before they entered the city, and while yet nearly a mile from it, a small party of men, soberly clad, and after the old fashion, with peaked beards and moustaches, standing in the centre of the road, obstructed the further progress of the carriage. The driver reined in his horses, much fearing, from the obscurity of the hour, and the loneliness of the road, that some mischief was intended. His fears were, however, somewhat allayed by his observing that these strange men carried a large litter, of an antique shape, and which they immediately set down upon the pavement, whereupon the bridegroom, having opened the coach-door from within, descended, and having assisted his bride to do likewise, led her, weeping bitterly and wringing her hands, to the litter, which they both entered. It was then raised by the men who surrounded it, and speedily carried towards the city, and before it had proceeded many yards, the darkness concealed it from the view of the Dutch charioteer. In the inside of the vehicle he found a purse, whose contents more than thrice paid the hire of the carriage and man. He saw and could tell nothing more of Minheer Vandehausen and his beautiful lady. This mystery was a source of deep anxiety and almost of grief to Gerard Douw. There was evidently fraud in the dealing of Vanderhausen with him, though for what purpose committed he could not imagine. He greatly doubted how far it was possible for a man possessing in his countenance so strong an evidence of the presence of the most demoniac feelings, to be in reality anything but a villain, and every day that passed without his hearing from or of his niece, instead of inducing him to forget his fears, on the contrary tended more and more to exasperate them. The loss of his niece's cheerful society tended also to depress his spirits; and in order to dispel this despondency, which often crept upon his mind after his daily employment was over, he was wont frequently to prevail upon Schalken to accompany him home, and by his presence to dispel, in some degree, the gloom of his otherwise solitary supper. One evening, the painter and his pupil were sitting by the fire, having accomplished a comfortable supper, and had yielded to that silent pensiveness sometimes induced by the process of digestion, when their reflections were disturbed by a loud sound at the street door, as if occasioned by some person rushing forcibly and repeatedly against it. A domestic had run without delay to ascertain the cause of the disturbance, and they heard him twce or thrice interrogate the applicant for admission, but without producing an answer or any cessation of the sounds. They heard him then open the hall door, and immediately there followed a light and rapid tread upon the staircase. Schalken laid his hand on his sword, and advanced towards the door. It opened before he reached it, and Rose rushed into the room. She looked wild and haggard, and pale with exhaustion and terror, but her dress surprised them as much as even her unexpected appearance. It consisted of a kind of white woollen wrapper, made close about the neck, and descending to the very ground. It was much deranged and travel-soiled. The poor creature had hardly entered the chamber when she fell senseless on the floor. With some difficulty they succeeded in reviving her, and on recovering her senses, she instantly exclaimed, in a tone of eager, terrified impatience :

"Wine, wine, quickly, or I'm lost."

Much alarmed at the strange agitation in which the call was made, they at once administered to her wishes. and she drank some wine with a haste and eagerness which surprised them. She had hardly swallowed it, when she exclaimed, with the same urgency :

"Food, food, at once, or I perish."

A considerable fragment of a roast joint was upon the table, and Schalken immediately proceeded to cut some, but he was anticipated, for no sooner had she become aware of its presence, than she darted at it with the rapacity of a vulture, and, seizing it in her hands, she tore off the flesh with her teeth, and swallowed it. When the paroxysm of hunger had been a little appeased, she appeared suddenly to become aware how strange her conduct had been, or it may have been that other more agitating thoughts recurred to her mind, for she began to weep bitterly and to wring her hands.

"Oh, send for a minister of God," said she; "I am not safe till he comes; send for him speedily."

Gerard Douw despatched a messenger instantly, and prevailed on his niece to allow him to surrender his bedchamber to her use; he also persuaded her to retire to it at once and to rest; her consent was extorted upon the condition that they would not leave her for a moment.

"Oh that the holy man were here," she said; "he can deliver me – the dead and the living can never be one – God has forbidden it."

With these mysterious words she surrendered herself to their guidance, and they proceeded to the chamber which Gerard Douw had assigned to her use.

"Do not, do not leave me for a moment," said she; "I am lost for ever if you do."

Gerard Douw's chamber was approached through a spacious apartment, which they were now about to enter. Gerard Douw and Schalken each carried a wax candle, so that a sufficient degree of light was cast upon all surrounding objects. They were now entering the large chamber, which, as I have said, communicated with Douw's apartment, when Rose suddenly stopped, and, in a whisper which seemed to thrill with horror, she said :

"Oh, God! he is here, he is here; see, see, there he goes."

She pointed towards the door of the inner room, and Schalken thought he saw a shadowy and ill-defined form gliding into that apartment. He drew his sword, and, raising the candle so as to throw its light with increased distinctness upon the objects in the room, he entered the chamber into which the shadow had glided. No figure was there – nothing but the furniture which belonged to the room, and yet he could not be deceived as to the fact that something had moved before them into the chamber. A sickening dread came upon him, and the cold perspiration broke out in heavy drops upon his forehead; nor was he more composed, when he heard the increased urgency, the agony of entreaty, with which Rose implored them not to leave her for a moment.

"I saw him," said she; "he's here. I cannot be deceived – I know him – he's by me – he is with me – he's in the room;

then, for God's sake, as you would save me, do not stir from beside me."

They at length prevailed upon her to lie down upon the bed, where she continued to urge them to stay by her. She frequently uttered incoherent sentences, repeating, again and again, "the dead and the living cannot be one – God has forbidden it"; and then again, "rest to the wakeful – sleep to the sleep-walkers". These and such mysterious and broken sentences, she continued to utter until the clergyman arrived. Gerard Douw began to fear, naturally enough, that the poor girl, owing to terror or ill-treatment, had become deranged, and he half-suspected, by the suddenness of her appearance, and the unseasonableness of the hour, and, above all, from the wildness and terror of her manner, that she had made her escape from some place of confinement for lunatics, and was in immediate fear of pursuit. He resolved to summon medical advice, as soon as the mind of his niece had been in some measure set at rest by the offices of the clergyman whose attendance she had so earnestly desired; and until this object had been attained, he did not venture to put any questions to her which might possibly, by reviving painful or horrible recollections, increase her agitation. The clergyman soon arrived – a man of ascetic countenance and venerable age – one whom Gerard Douw respected much, forasmuch as he was a veteran polemic, though one, perhaps, more dreaded as a combatant than beloved as a Christian – of pure morality, subtle brain, and frozen heart. He entered the chamber which communicated with that in which Rose reclined, and immediately on his arrival, she requested him to pray for her, as for one who lay in the hands of Satan, and who could hope for deliverance – only from heaven.

That our readers may distinctly understand all the circumstances of the event which we are about imperfectly to describe, it is necessary to state the relative positions of the parties who were engaged in it. The old clergyman and

Schalken were in the ante-room of which we have already spoken; Rose lay in the inner chamber, the door of which was open; and by the side of the bed, at her urgent desire, stood her guardian; a candle burned in the bedchamber, and three were lighted in the outer apartment. The old man now cleared his voice as if about to commence, but before he had time to begin, a sudden gust of air blew out the candle which served to illuminate the room in which the poor girl lay, and she, with hurried alarm, exclaimed :

"Godfrey, bring in another candle; the darkness is unsafe."

Gerard Douw, forgetting for the moment her repeated injunctions, in the immediate impulse, stepped from the bedchamber into the other, in order to supply what she desired.

"Oh God! do not go, dear uncle," shrieked the unhappy girl – and at the same time she sprang from the bed, and darted after him, in order, by her grasp, to detain him. But the warning came too late, for scarcely had he passed the threshold, and hardly had his niece had time to utter the startling exclamation, when the door which divided the two rooms closed violently after him, as if swung to by a strong blast of wind. Schalken and he both rushed to the door, but their united and desperate efforts could not avail so much as to shake it. Shriek after shriek burst from the inner chamber, with all the piercing loudness of despairing terror. Schalken and Douw applied every energy and strained every nerve to force open the door; but all in vain. There was no sound of struggling from within, but the screams seemed to increase in loudness, and at the same time they heard the bolts of the latticed window withdrawn, and the window itself grated upon the sill as if thrown open. One *last* shriek, so long and piercing and agonized as to be scarcely human, swelled from the room, and suddenly there followed a death-like silence. A light step was heard crossing the floor, as if from the bed to the window; and almost at the same instant the door gave way, and, yielding to the pressure of the external applicants, they were nearly precipitated into the room. It was empty. The window was open, and Schalken sprang to a chair and gazed out upon the street and canal below. He saw no form, but he beheld, or thought he beheld, the waters of the broad canal beneath settling ring after ring in heavy circular ripples, as if a moment before disturbed by the immersion of some large and heavy mass.

No trace of Rose was ever after discovered, nor was anything certain respecting her mysterious wooer detected or even suspected – no clue whereby to trace the intricacies of the labyrinth and to arrive at a distinct conclusion was to be found. But an incident occurred which, though it will not be received by our rational readers as at all approaching to evidence upon the matter, nevertheless produced a strong and a lasting impression upon the mind of Schalken. Many years after the events which we have detailed, Schalken, then remotely situated, received an intimation of his father's death, and of his intended burial upon a fixed day in the church of Rotterdam. It was necessary that a very considerable journey should be performed by the funeral procession, which, as it will be readily believed, was not very numerously attended. Schalken with difficulty arrived in Rotterdam late in the day upon which the funeral was appointed to take place. It had not then arrived. Evening closed in, and still it did not appear.

Schalken strolled down to the church – he found it open – notice of the arrival of the funeral had been given, and the vault in which the body was to be laid had been opened. The officer, who is analogous to our sexton, on seeing a well-dressed gentleman, whose object was to attend the expected funeral, pacing the aisle of the church, hospitably invited him to share with him the comforts of a blazing wood fire, which, as was his custom in winter time upon such occasions, he had kindled in the hearth of a chamber which communicated, by a flight of steps, with the vault below. In this chamber Schalken and his entertainer seated themselves, and the sexton, after some fruitless attempts to engage his guest in conversation, was obliged to apply himself to his tobacco-pipe and can, to solace his solitude. In spite of his grief and cares, the fatigues of a rapid journey of nearly, forty hours gradually overcame the mind and body of Godfrey Schalken and he sank into a deep sleep, from which he was awakened by someone's shaking him gently by the shoulder. He first thought that the old sexton had called him, but *he* was no longer in the room. He roused himself, and as soon as he could clearly see what was around him, he perceived a female form, clothed in a kind of light robe of muslin, part of which was so disposed as to act as a veil, and in her hand she carried a lamp. She was moving rather away from him and towards the flight of steps which conducted towards the vaults. Schalken felt a vague alarm at the sight of this figure, and at the same time an irresistible impulse to follow its guidance. He followed it towards the vaults, but when it reached the head of the stairs, he paused – the figure paused also, and, turning gently round, displayed, by the light of the lamp it carried, the face and features of his first love, Rose Velderkaust. There was nothing horrible, or even sad, in the countenance. On the contrary, it wore the same arch smile which used to enchant the artist long before in his happy days. A feeling of awe and of interest, too intense to be resisted, prompted him to follow the spectre, if spectre it were. She descended the stairs – he followed – and, turning to the left, through a narrow passage, she led him, to his infinite surprise, into what appeared to be an old-fashioned Dutch apartment, such as the pictures of Gerard Douw have served to immortalize. Abundance of costly antique furniture was disposed about the room, and in one corner stood a four-post bed, with heavy black cloth curtains around it; the figure frequently turned towards him with the same arch smile; and when she came to the side of the bed, she drew the curtains, and, by the light of the lamp, which she held towards its contents, she disclosed to the horror-stricken painter, sitting bolt upright in bed, the livid and demoniac form of Vanderhausen. Schalken had hardly seen him, when he fell senseless upon the floor, where he lay until discovered, on the next morning, by persons employed in closing the passages into the vaults. He was lying in a cell of considerable size, which had not been disturbed for a long time, and he had fallen beside a large coffin, which was supported upon small stone pillars, a security against the attacks of vermin.

To his dying day Schalken was satisfied of the reality of the vision which he had witnessed, and he has left behind him a curious evidence of the impression which it wrought upon his fancy, in a painting executed shortly after the event we have narrated, and which is valuable as exhibiting not only the peculiarities which have made Schalken's pictures sought after, but even more so as presenting a portrait as close and faithful as one taken from memory can be, of his early love, Rose Velderkaust, whose mysterious fate must ever remain a matter of speculation. The picture represents a chamber of antique masonry, such as might be found in most old cathedrals, and is lighted faintly by a lamp carried in the hand of a female figure, such as we have above attempted to describe; and in the background, and to the left of him who examines the painting, there stands the form of a man apparently aroused from sleep, and by his attitude, his hand being laid upon his sword, exhibiting considerable alarm; this last figure is illuminated only by the expiring glare of a wood or charcoal fire. The whole production exhibits a beautiful specimen of that artful and singular distribution of light and shade which has rendered the name of Schalken immortal among the artists of his country. This tale is traditionary, and the reader will easily perceive by our studiously omitting to heighten many points of the narrative, when a little additional colouring might have added effect to the recital, that we have desired to lay before him, not a figment of the brain, but a curious tradition connected with, and belonging to, the biography of a famous artist.

The Ghost and the Bone-Setter

IN looking over the papers of my late valued and respected friend, Francis Purcell, who for nearly fifty years discharged the arduous duties of a parish priest in the south of Ireland, I met with the following document. It is one of many such; for he was a curious and industrious collector of old local traditions – a commodity in which the quarter where he resided mightily abounded. The collection and arrangement of such legends was, as long as I can remember him, his hobby; but I had never learned that his love of the marvellous and whimsical had carried him so far as to prompt him to commit the results of his inquiries to writing, until, in the character of residuary legatee, his will put me in possession of all his manuscript papers. To such as may think the composing of such productions as these inconsistent with the character and habits of a country priest, it is necessary to observe, that there did exist a race of priests – those of the old school, a race now nearly extinct – whose education abroad tended to produce in them tastes more literary than have yet been evinced by the *alumni* of Maynooth.

It is perhaps necessary to add that the superstition illustrated by the following story, namely, that the corpse last buried is obliged, during his juniority of internment, to supply his brother tenants of the churchyard in which he lies, with fresh water to allay the burning thirst of purgatory, is prevalent throughout the south of Ireland.

The writer can vouch for a case in which a respectable and wealthy farmer, on the borders of Tipperary, in tenderness to the corns of his departed helpmate, enclosed in her coffin two pair of brogues, a light and a heavy, the one for dry, the other for sloppy weather; seeking thus to mitigate the fatigues of her inevitable perambulations in procuring water and administering it to the thirsty souls of purgatory. Fierce and desperate conflicts have ensued in the case of two funeral parties approaching the same churchyard together, each endeavouring to secure to his own dead priority of sepulture, and a consequent immunity from the tax levied upon the pedestrian powers of the lastcomer. An instance not long since occurred, in which one of two such

arties, through fear of losing to their deceased friend this in-
stimable advantage, made their way to the churchyard by a
hort cut, and, in violation of one of their strongest prejudices,
ctually threw the coffin over the wall, lest time should be lost
n making their entrance through the gate. Innumerable in-
tances of the same kind might be quoted, all tending to show
ow strongly among the peasantry of the south this superstition
s entertained. However, I shall not detain the reader further
ry any prefatory remarks, but shall proceed to lay before him the
ollowing:

*Extracts from the MS. Papers of the late Rev. Francis Purcell, of
Drumcoolagh.*

I tell the following particulars, as nearly as I can recollect them, in
he words of the narrator. It may be necessary to observe that he was
vhat is termed a well-spoken man, having for a considerable time
nstructed the ingenious youth of his native parish in such of the
iberal arts and sciences as he found it convenient to profess – a cir-
:umstance which may account for the occurrence of several big
vords in the course of this narrative, more distinguished for eupho-
iious effect than for correctness of application. I proceed then,
vithout further preface, to lay before you the wonderful adventures
if Terry Neil.

'Why, thin, 'tis a quare story, an' as thrue as you're sittin'
here; and I'd make bould to say there isn't a boy in the seven
parishes could tell it better nor crickther than myself, for 'twas
my father himself it happened to, an' many's the time I heerd
it out iv his own mouth; an' I can say, an' I'm proud av that
same, my father's word was as incredible as any squire's oath
in the counthry; and so signs an' if a poor man got into any
unlucky throuble, he was the boy id go into the court an' prove;
but that doesn't signify – he was as honest and as sober a man,
barrin' he was a little bit too partial to the glass, as you'd find in
a day's walk; an' there wasn't the likes of him in the counthry
round for nate labourin' an' *baan* diggin'; and he was mighty
handy entirely for carpenther's work, and mendin' ould

spude-threes, an' the likes i' that. An' so he tuk up with bon
settin', as was most nathural, for none of them could come up
him in mendin' the leg iv a stool or a table; an' sure, there nev
was a bonesetter got so much custom – man an' child, young a
ould – there never was such breakin' and mendin' of bon
known in the memory of man. Well, Terry Neil – for that wz
my father's name – began to feel his heart growin' light, an
his purse heavy; an' he took a bit iv a farm in Squire Phelim
ground, just undher the ould castle, an' a pleasant little spot
was; an' day, an' mornin' poor crathurs not able to put a foc
to the ground, with broken arms and broken legs, id be comir
ramblin' in from all quarters to have their bones spliced up
Well, yer honour, all this was as well as well could be; but it wa
customary when Sir Phelim id go anywhere out iv the country
for some iv the tinants to sit up to watch in the ould castle, jus
for a kind of compliment to the ould family – an' a might
unplisant compliment it was for the tinants, for there wasn'
a man of them but knew there was something quare about th
ould castle. The neighbours had it, that the squire's ould grand
father, as good a gintleman – God be with him – as I heer'd, a
ever stood in shoe-leathern use to keep walkin' about in th
middle iv the night, ever sinst he bursted a bloodvessel pullin
out a cork out iv a bottle, as you or I might be doin', and wil
too, plase God – but that doesn't signify. So, as I was sayin', th
ould squire used to come down out of the frame, where hi:
picthur was hung up, and to break the bottles and glasses –
God be marciful to us all – an' dthrink all he could come at –
an' small blame to him for that same; and then if any of the
family id be comin' in, he id be up again in his place, looking
as quite an' as innocent as if he didn't know anything about it
– the mischievous ould chap.

'Well, your honour, as I was sayin', one time the family up
at the castle was stayin' in Dublin for a week or two; and so, as
usual, some of the tinants had to sit up in the castle, and the
third night it kem to my father's turn. "Oh, tare an' ouns!"
says he unto himself, "an' must I sit up all night, and that
ould vagabone of a sperit, glory be to God,' says he, 'serenadin'

hrough the house, an' doin' all sorts iv mischief?" However, here was no gettin' aff, and so he put a bould face on it, an' he vent up at nightfall with a bottle of pottieen, and another of oly wather.

'It was rainin' smart enough, an' the evenin' was darksome nd gloomy, when my father got in; and what with the rain he ot, and the holy wather he sprinkled on himself, it wasn't long ill he had to swally a cup iv the pottieen, to keep the cowld out v his heart. It was the ould steward, Lawrence Connor, that pened the door – and he an' my father wor always very great. io when he seen who it was, an' my father tould him how it vas his turn to watch in the castle, he offered to sit up along vith him; and you may be sure my father wasn't sorry for that ame. So says Larry:

'' We'll have a bit iv fire in the parlour," says he.

'"An' why not in the hall?' says my father, for he knew that he squire's picthur was hung in the parlour.

'"No fire can be lit in the hall," says Lawrence, "for there's n ould jackdaw's nest in the chimney."

'"Oh thin," says my father, "let us stop in the kitchen, for t's very unproper for the likes iv me to be sittin' in the parlour," ays he.

'"Oh, Terry, that can't be," says Lawrence; "if we keep up- he ould custom at all, we may as well keep it up properly," says 1e.

'"Divil sweep the ould custom!" says my father – to him- elf, do ye mind, for he didn't like to let Lawrence see that he vas more afeard himself.

'"Oh, very well," says he. "I'm agreeable, Lawrence," says 1e; and so down they both wint to the kitchen, until the fire id be lit in the parlour – an' that same wasn't long doing'.

'Well, your honour, they soon wint up again, an' sat down nighty comfortable by the parlour fire, and they beginned to :alk, an' to smoke, an' to dhrink a small taste iv the pottieen; and, moreover, they had a good rousin' fire o' bogwood and :urf, to warm their shins over.

'Well, sir, as I was sayin' they kep' convarsin' and smokin' together most agreeable, until Lawrence beginn'd to get sleepy as was but nathural for him, for he was an ould sarvint man, and was used to a great dale iv sleep.

'"Sure it's impossible," says my father, "it's gettin' sleepy you are?"

' "Oh, divil a tasten" says Larry; "I'm only shuttin' my eyes," says he, to keep out the parfume o' the tibacky smoke that's makin' them wather," says he. "So don't you mind other people's business," says he, stiff enough, for he had a mighty high stomach av his own (rest his sowl), "and go on," says he, "with your story, for I'm listening", says he, shuttin' down his eyes.

'Well, when my father seen spakin' was no use, he went on with his story. By the same token, it was the story of Jim Sooli van and his ould goat he was tellin' —an' a plisant story it is - an' there was so much divarsion in it, that it was enough to waken a dormouse, let alone to prevint a Christian goin' asleep But, faix, the way my father tould it, I believe there never was the likes heerd sinst nor before, for he bawled out every word av it, as if the life was fairly lavin' him, thrying to keep ould Larry awake; but, faix, it was no use, for the hoorsness came an him, an' before he kem to the end of his story Larry O'Con nor beginned to snore like a bagpipes.

'"Oh, blur an' agres," says my father, "isn't this a hard case," says he, "that ould villain, lettin' on to be my friend and to go asleep this way, an' us both in the very room with a sperit," says he. "The crass o' Christ about us!" says he and with that he was goin' to shake Lawrence to waken him but he just remimbered if he roused him, that he'd surely go off to his bed, an' lave him complately alone, an' that id be by far worse.

' "Oh thin," says my father, "I'll not disturb the poor boy It id be neither friendly nor good-nathured," says he, "to tor mint him while he is asleep," says he; "only I wish I was the same way, myself," says he.

'An' with that he beginned to walk up an' down, an' sayin' his prayers, until he worked himself into a sweat, savin' your

56

presence. But it was all no good; so he dthrunk about a pint of perits, to compose his mind.

'"Oh," says he, "I wish to the Lord I was as asy in my mind is Larry there, Maybe," says he, "if I thried I could go sleep"; an' with that he pulled a big armchair close beside Lawrence, an' settled himself in it as well as he could.

'But there was one quare thing I forgot to tell you. He couldn't help, in spite av himself, lookin' now an' thin at the picthur, an' he immediately obsarved that the eyes av it was follyin' him about, an' starin' at him, an' winkin' at him, wheriver he wint. "Oh," says he, when he seen that, "it's a poor chance I have," says he; "an' bad luck was with me that day I kem into this unforthunate place," says he. "But any way here's no use in bein' freckened now," says he; "for if I am to lie, I may as well parspire undaunted," says he.

'Well, your honour, he thried to keep himself quite an' asy, an' he thought two or three times he might have wint asleep, but for the way the storm was groanin' and creakin' through the great heavy branches outside, an' whistlin' through the ould chimleys iv the castle. Well, afther one great roarin' blast v the wind, you'd think the walls iv the castle was just goin' to fall, quite an' clane, with the shakin' iv it. All av a suddint the storm stopt, as silent an' as quite as if it was a July evenin'. Well, your honour, it wasn't stopped blowin' for three minnites, before he thought he hard a sort iv a noise over the chimley-piece; an' with that my father just opened his eyes the smallest taste in life, an' sure enough he seen the ould square gettin' out iv the picthur, for all the world as if he was throwin' aff his ridin' coat, until he stept out clane an' complate, out av the chimley-piece, an' thrun himself down an the floor. Well, the slieveen ould chap – an' my father thought it was the dirtiest turn iv all – before he beginned to do anything out iv the way, he stopped for a while to listen wor they both asleep; an' as soon as he thought all was quite, he put out his hand and tuk hould iv the whisky bottle, an' dthrank at laste a pint iv it. Well, your honour, when he tuk his turn out iv it, he settled it back mighty cute entirely, in the very same spot it was in before. An' he beginned to walk up an' down the room, lookin' as sober an' as solid as if he never done the likes at all. An' whinever he went apast my father, he thought he felt a great scent of brim-stone, an' it was that that freckened him entirely; for he knew it was brimstone that was burned in hell, savin' your presence. At any rate, he often heerd it from Father Murphy, an' he had a right to know what belonged to it – he's dead since, God rest him. Well, your honour, my father was asy enough until the sperit kem past him; so close, God be marciful to us all, that the smell iv the sulphur tuk the breath clane out iv him; an' with that he tuk such a fit iv coughin', that it al-a-most shuk him out iv the chair he was sittin' in.

'"Ho, ho!" says the squire, stoppin' short about two steps aff, and turnin' round facin' my father, "is it you that's in it? – an' how's all with you, Terry Neil?"

'"At your honour's service," says my father (as well as the fright id let him, for he was more dead than alive), "an' it's proud I am to see your honour tonight," says he.

'"Terence," says the squire, "you're a respectable man" (an' it was thrue for him), "an industhrious, sober man, an' an example of inebriety to the whole parish," says he.

'"Thank your honour," says my father, gettin' courage, "you were always a civil spoken gintleman. God rest your honour."

'"*Rest* my honour?" says the sperit (fairly gettin' red in the face with the madness), "Rest my honour?" says he. "Why, you ignorant spalpeen," says he, "you mane, niggarly igno-ramush," says he, "where did you leave your manners?" says he. "If I *am* dead, it's no fault iv mine," says he; "an' it's not to be thrun in my teeth at every hand's turn, by the likes iv you," says he, stampin' his foot an the flure, that you'd think the boords id smash undher him.

'"Oh," says my father, "I'm only a foolish, ignorant poor man," says he.

' "You're nothing else," says the squire: "but any way," says he, "it's not to be listenin' to your gosther, nor convarsin' with the likes iv you, that I came *up* – down I mane," says he – (an'

58

as little as the mistake was, my father tuk notice iv it).
'Listen to me now, Terence Neil," says he: "I was always a
good masther to Pathrick Neil, your grandfather," says he.

'"'Tis thrue for your honour," says my father.

'"And, moreover, I think I was always a sober, riglar gintle-
nan," says the squire.

'"That's your name, sure enough," says my father (though
t was a big lie for him, but he could not help it).

'"Well," says the sperit, "although I was as sober as most
nen – at laste as most gintlemin," says he; "an' though I was
it different pariods a most extempory Christian, and most
:haritable and inhuman to the poor," says he; "for all that I'm
10t as asy where I am now," says he, "as I had a right to ex-
)ect," says he.

'"An' more's the pity," says my father. Maybe your honour
d wish to have a word with Father Murphy?"

'"Hould your tongue, you misherable bliggard," says the
:quire, "it's not iv my sowl I'm thinkin' – an' I wondther
/ou'd have the impitence to talk to a gintleman consarnin' his
owl; and when I want *that* fixed," says he, slappin' his thigh,
'I'll go to them that knows what belongs to the likes," says he.
'It's not my sowl," says he, sittin' down opposite my father;
'it's not my sowl that's annoyin' me most – I'm unasy on my
:ight leg," says he, "that I bruk at Glenvarloch cover the day
: killed black Barney."

'My father found out afther, it was a favourite horse that
ell undher him, afther leapin' the big fence that runs along by
he glin.

'"I hope," says my father, "your honour's not unasy about
he killin' iv him?"

'"Hould your tongue, ye fool," said the squire, "an' I'll tell
/ou why I'm unasy on my leg," says he. "In the place, where
: spend most iv my time," says he, "except the little leisure I
1ave for lookin' about me here," says he, "I have to walk a
;reat dale more than I was ever used to," says he, "and by far
nore than is good for me either," says he; "for I must tell you,"
ays he, "the people where I am is ancommonly fond iv cowld

wather, for there is nothin' betther to be had; an', moreover, the weather is hotter than is altogether plisant," says he; "and I'm appinted," says he, "to assist in carrin' the wather, an' gets a mighty poor share iv it myself," says he, "an' a mighty throublesome, wearin' job it is, I can tell you," says he; "for they're all iv them surprisingly dthry, an' dthrinks it as fast as my legs can carry it," says he; "but what kills me entirely," says he, "is the wakeness in my leg," says he, "an' I want you to give it a pull or two to bring it to shape," says he, "and that's the long an' the short iv it," says he.

'"Oh, plase your honour," says my father (for he didn't like to handle the sperit at all), "I wouldn't have the impidence to do the likes to your honour," says he; "It's only to poor crathurs like myself I'd do it to," says he.

'"None iv your blarney," says the square. "Here's my leg," says he, cockin' it up to him − "pull it for the bare life," says he; "an' if you don't, by the immortial powers I'll not lave a bone in your carcish I'll not powdher," says he.

'When my father heerd that, he seen there was no use in purtendin', so he tuk hould iv the leg, an' he kep' pullin' an' pullin', till the sweat. God bless us, beginned to pour down his face.

'"Pull, you devil " says the squire.

'"At your sarvice, your honour," says my father.

'"Pull harder," says the squire.

'My father pulled like the divil.

'"I'll take a little sup," says the squire, rachin' over his hand to the bottle, "to keep up my courage," says he, lettin' an to be very wake in himself intirely. But, as cute as he was, he was out here, for he tuk the wrong one. "Here's to your good health, Terence," says he; "an' now pull like the very divil." An' with that he lifted the bottle of holy wather, but it was hardly to his mouth, whin he let a screech out, you'd think the room id fairly split with it, an' made one chuck that sent the leg clane aff his body in my father's hands. Down wint the squire over the table, an' bang wint my father half-way across the room on his back, upon the flure. Whin he kem to himself the cheerful mornin' sun was shinin' through the windy shutthers, an' he was lying flat an his back, with the leg iv one of the great ould chairs pulled clane out iv the socket an' tight in his hand, pintin' up to the ceilin', an' ould Larry fast asleep, an' snorin' as loud as ever. My father wint that mornin' to Father Murphy, an' from that to the day of his death, he never neglected confission nor mass, an' what he tould was betther believed that he spake av it but seldom. An', as for the squire, that is the sperit, whether it was that he did not like his liquor, or by rason iv the loss iv his leg, he was never known to walk agin.'

THE SPECTRE LOVERS

There lived some fifteen years since in a small and ruinous house, little better than a hovel, an old woman who was reported to have considerably exceeded her eightieth year, and who rejoiced in the name of Alice, or popularly, Ally Moran. Her society was not much courted, for she was neither rich, nor, as the reader may suppose, beautiful. In addition to a lean cur and a cat she had one human companion, her grandson, Peter Brien, whom, with laudable goodnature, she had supported from the period of his orphanage down to that of my story, which finds him in his twentieth year. Peter was a goodnatured slob of a fellow, much more addicted to wrestling, dancing, and love-making, than to hard work, and fonder of whiskey punch than good advice. His grandmother had a high opinion of his accomplishments, which indeed was but natural, and also of his genius, for Peter had of late years begun to apply his mind to politics; and as it was plain that he had a mortal hatred of honest labour, his grandmother predicted, like a true fortune-teller, that he was born to marry an heiress, and Peter himself (who had no mind to forego his freedom even on such terms) that he was destined to find a pot of gold. Upon one point both agreed, that being unfitted by the peculiar bias of his genius for work, he was to acquire the immense fortune to which his merits entitled him by means of a pure run of good luck. This solution of Peter's future had the double effect of reconciling both himself and his grandmother to his idle courses, and also of maintaining that even flow of hilarious spirits which made him everywhere welcome, and which was in truth the natural result of his consciousness of approaching affluence.

It happened one night that Peter had enjoyed himself to a very late hour with two or three choice spirits near Palmerstown. They had talked politics and love, sung songs, and told stories, and, above all, had swallowed, in the chastened disguise of punch, at least a pint of good whiskey, every man.

It was considerably past one o'clock when Peter bid his companions goodbye, with a sigh and a hiccough, and lighting his pipe set forth on his solitary homeward way.

The bridge of Chapelizod was pretty nearly the midway point of his night march, and from one cause or another his progress was rather slow, and it was past two o'clock by the time he found himself leaning over its old battlements, and looking up the river, over whose winding current and wooded banks the soft moonlight was falling.

The cold breeze that blew lightly down the stream was grateful to him. It cooled his throbbing head, and he drank it in at his hot lips. The scene, too, had, without his being well sensible of it, a secret fascination. The village was sunk in the profoundest slumber, not a mortal stirring, not a sound afloat, a soft haze covered it all, and the fairy moonlight hovered over the entire landscape.

In a state between rumination and rapture, Peter continued to lean over the battlements of the old bridge, and as he did so he saw, or fancied he saw, emerging one after another along the river bank in the little gardens and enclosures in the rear of the street of Chapelizod, the queerest little white-washed huts and cabins he had ever seen there before. They had not been there that evening when he passed the bridge on the way to his merry tryst. But the most remarkable thing about it was the odd way in which these quaint little cabins showed themselves. First he saw one or two of them just with the corner of his eye, and when he looked full at them, strange to say, they faded away and disappeared. Then another and another came in view, but all in the same coy way, just appearing and gone again before he could well fix his gaze upon them; in a little while, however, they began to bear a fuller gaze, and he found, as it seemed to himself, that he was able by an effort of attention to fix the vision for a longer and a longer time, and when they waxed faint and nearly vanished, he had the power of recalling them into light and substance, until at last their vacillating indistinctness became less and less, and they assumed a permanent place in the moonlit landscape.

'Be the hokey,' said Peter, lost in amazement, and dropping his pipe into the river unconsciously, 'them is the quarist bits iv mud cabins I ever seen, growing up like musharoons in the dew of an evening, and poppin' up here and down again there, and up again in another place, like so many white rabbits in a warren; and there they stand at last as firm and fast as if they were there from the Deluge; bedad it's enough to make a man a'most believe in the fairies.'

This latter was a large concession from Peter, who was a bit of a free-thinker, and spoke contemptuously in his ordinary conversation of that class of agencies.

Having treated himself to a long last stare at these mysterious fabrics, Peter prepared to pursue his homeward way; having crossed the bridge and passed the mill, he arrived at the corner of the main-street of the little town, and casting a careless look up the Dublin road, his eye was arrested by a most unexpected spectacle.

This was no other than a column of foot-soldiers, marching with perfect regularity towards the village, and headed by an officer on horseback. They were at the far side of the turnpike, which was closed; but much to his perplexity he perceived that they marched on through it without appearing to sustain the least check from that barrier.

On they came at a slow march; and what was most singular in the matter was, that they were drawing several cannons along with them; some held ropes, others spoked the wheels, and others again marched in front of the guns and behind them, with muskets shouldered, giving a stately character of parade and regularity to this, as it seemed to Peter, most unmilitary procedure.

It was owing either to some temporary defect in Peter's vision, or to some illusion attendant upon mist and moonlight, or perhaps to some other cause, that the whole procession had a certain waving and vapoury character which perplexed and tasked his eyes not a little. It was like the pictured pageant of a phantasmagoria reflected upon smoke. It was as if every breath disturbed it; sometimes it was blurred, sometimes obliterated; now here, now there. Sometimes, while the upper part was quite distinct, the legs of the column would nearly fade away or vanish outright, and then again they would come out into clear relief, marching on with measured tread, while the cocked hats and shoulders grew, as it were, transparent, and all but disappeared.

Notwithstanding these strange optical fluctuations however, the column continued steadily to advance. Peter crossed the street from the corner near the old bridge, running on tip-toe, and with his body stooped to avoid observation, and took up a position upon the raised footpath in the shadow of the houses, where, as the soldiers kept the middle of the road, he calculated that he might, himself undetected, see them distinctly enough as they passed.

'What the div—, what on airth,' he muttered, checking the irreligious ejaculation with which he was about to start, for certain queer misgivings were hovering about his heart, notwithstanding the factitious courage of the whiskey bottle. 'What on airth is the manin' of all this? Is it the French that's landed at last to give us a hand and help us in airnest to this blessed repale? If it is not them, I simply ask who the div—, I mane who on airth are they, for such sogers as them I never seen before in my born days?'

By this time the foremost of them were quite near, and truth to say they were the queerest soldiers he had ever seen in the course of his life. They wore long gaiters and leather breeches, three-cornered hats, bound with silver lace, long blue coats, with scarlet facings and linings, which latter were shewn by a fastening which held together the two opposite corners of the skirt behind; and in front the breasts were in like manner connected at a single point, where and below which they sloped back, disclosing a long-flapped waistcoat of snowy whiteness; they had very large, long cross-belts, and wore enormous pouches of white leather hung extraordinarily low, and on each of which a little silver star was glittering. But what struck him as most grotesque and outlandish in their costume was their extraordinary display of shirt-frill in front, and of ruffle about their wrists, and the strange manner in which their hair was frizzled out and powdered under their hats, and clubbed up into great rolls behind. But one of the party was mounted. He rode a tall white horse, with high action and arching neck; he had a snow-white feather in his three-cornered hat, and his coat was shimmering all over with a profusion of silver lace. From these circumstances Peter concluded that he must be the commander of the detachment, and examined him as he passed attentively. He was a slight, tall man, whose legs did not half fill his leather breeches, and he appeared to be at the wrong side of sixty. He had a shrunken, weather-beaten, mulberry-coloured face, carried a large black patch over one eye, and turned neither to the right nor to the left, but rode on at the head of his men, with a grim, military inflexibility.

The countenances of these soldiers, officers as well as men, seemed all full of trouble, and, so to speak, scared and wild. He watched in vain for a single contented or comely face. They had, one and all, a melancholy and hang-dog look; and as they passed by, Peter fancied that the air grew cold and thrilling.

He had seated himself upon a stone bench, from which, staring with all his might, he gazed upon the grotesque and noiseless procession as it filed by him. Noiseless it was; he could neither hear the jingle of accoutrements, the tread of feet, nor the rumble of the wheels; and when the old colonel turned his horse a little, and made as though he were giving the word of command, and a trumpeter, with a swollen blue nose and white feather fringe round his hat, who was walking beside him, turned about and put his bugle to his lips, still Peter heard nothing, although it was plain the sound had reached the soldiers, for they instantly changed their front to three abreast.

'Botheration!' muttered Peter, 'is it deaf I'm growing?'

But that could not be, for he heard the sighing of the breeze and the rush of the neighbouring Liffey plain enough.

'Well,' said he, in the same cautious key, 'by the piper, this bangs Banagher fairly! It's either the Frinch army that's in it, come to take the town iv Chapelizod by surprise, an' makin' no noise for feard iv wakenin' the inhabitants; or else it's—it's—what it's—somethin' else. But, tundher-an-ouns, what's gone wid Fitzpatrick's shop across the way?'

The brown, dingy stone building at the opposite side of the street looked newer and cleaner than he had been used to see it; the front door of it stood open, and a sentry, in the same grotesque uniform, with shouldered musket, was pacing noiselessly to and fro before it. At the angle of this building, in like manner, a wide gate (of which Peter had no recollection whatever) stood open, before which, also, a similar sentry was gliding, and into this gateway the whole column gradually passed, and Peter finally lost sight of it.

'I'm not asleep; I'm not dhramin',' said he, rubbing his eyes, and stamping slightly on the pavement, to assure himself that he was wide awake. 'It is a quare business, whatever it is; an' it's not alone that, but everything about the town looks strange to me. There's Tresham's house new painted, bedad, an' them flowers in the windies! An' Delany's house, too, that had not a whole pane of glass in it this morning, and scarce a slate on the roof of it! It is not possible it's what it's dhrunk I am. Sure there's the big tree, and not a leaf of it changed since I passed, and the stars overhead, all right. I don't think it is in my eyes it is.'

And so looking about him, and every moment finding or fancying new food for wonder, he walked along the pavement, intending, without further delay, to make his way home.

But his adventures for the night were not concluded. He had nearly reached the angle of the short lane that leads up to the church, when for the first time he perceived that an officer, in the uniform he had just seen, was walking before, only a few yards in advance of him.

The officer was walking along at an easy, swinging gait, and carried his sword under his arm, and was looking down on the pavement with an air of reverie.

In the very fact that he seemed unconscious of Peter's presence, and disposed to keep his reflections to himself, there was something reassuring. Besides, the reader must please to remember that our hero had a *quantum sufficit* of good punch before his adventure commenced, and was thus fortified against those qualms and terrors under which, in a more reasonable state of mind, he might not impossibly have sunk.

The idea of the French invasion revived in full power in Peter's fuddled imagination, as he pursued the nonchalant swagger of the officer.

'Be the powers iv Moll Kelly, I'll ax him what it is,' said Peter, with a sudden accession of rashness. 'He may tell me or not, as he plases, but he can't be offinded, anyhow.'

With this reflection having inspired himself, Peter cleared his voice and began—

'Captain!' said he, 'I ax your pardon, captain, an' maybe you'd be so condescindin' to my ignorance as to tell me, if it's plasin' to yer honour, whether your honour is not a Frinchman, if it's plasin' to you.'

This he asked, not thinking that, had it been as he suspected, not one word of his question in all probability would have been intelligible to the person he addressed. He was, however, understood, for the officer answered him in English, at the same time slackening his pace and moving a little to the side of the pathway, as if to invite his interrogator to take his place beside him.

'No; I am an Irishman,' he answered.

'I humbly thank your honour,' said Peter, drawing nearer —for the affability and the nativity of the officer encouraged him—'but maybe your honour is in the *sarvice* of the King of France?'

'I serve the same King as you do,' he answered, with a sorrowful significance which Peter did not comprehend at the time; and, interrogating in turn, he asked, 'But what calls you forth at this hour of the day?'

'The *day*, your honour!—the night, you mane.'

'It was always our way to turn night into day, and we keep to it still,' remarked the soldier. 'But, no matter, come up here to my house; I have a job for you, if you wish to earn some money easily. I live here.'

As he said this, he beckoned authoritatively to Peter, who followed almost mechanically at his heels, and they turned up a little lane near the old Roman Catholic chapel, at the end of which stood, in Peter's time, the ruins of a tall, stone-built house.

Like everything else in the town, it had suffered a metamorphosis. The stained and ragged walls were now erect, perfect, and covered with pebble-dash; window-panes glittered coldly in every window; the green hall-door had a bright brass knocker on it. Peter did not know whether to believe his previous or his present impressions; seeing is believing, and Peter could not dispute the reality of the scene. All the records of his memory seemed but the images of a tipsy dream. In a trance of astonishment and perplexity, therefore, he submitted himself to the chances of his adventure.

The door opened, the officer beckoned with a melancholy air of authority to Peter, and entered. Our hero followed him into a sort of hall, which was very dark, but he was guided by the steps of the soldier, and, in silence, they ascended the stairs. The moonlight, which shone in at the lobbies, showed an old, dark wainscoting, and a heavy, oak banister. They passed by closed doors at different landing-places, but all was dark and silent as, indeed, became that late hour of the night.

Now they ascended to the topmost floor. The captain paused for a minute at the nearest door, and, with a heavy groan, pushing it open, entered the room. Peter remained at the threshold. A slight female form in a sort of loose, white robe, and with a great deal of dark hair hanging loosely about her, was standing in the middle of the floor, with her back towards them.

The soldier stopped short before he reached her, and said, in a voice of great anguish, 'Still the same, sweet bird— sweet bird! still the same.' Whereupon, she turned suddenly, and threw her arms about the neck of the officer, with a gesture of fondness and despair, and her frame was agitated as if by a burst of sobs. He held her close to his breast in silence; and honest Peter felt a strange terror creep over him, as he witnessed these mysterious sorrows and endearments.

'Tonight, tonight—and then ten years more—ten long years—another ten years.'

The officer and the lady seemed to speak these words together; her voice mingled with his in a musical and fearful wail, like a distant summer wind, in the dead hour of night, wandering through ruins. Then he heard the officer say, alone, in a voice of anguish—

'Upon me be it all, for ever, sweet birdie, upon me.'

And again they seemed to mourn together in the same soft and desolate wail, like sounds of grief heard from a great distance.

Peter was thrilled with horror, but he was also under a strange fascination; and an intense and dreadful curiosity held him fast.

The moon was shining obliquely into the room, and through the window Peter saw the familiar slopes of the Park, sleeping mistily under its shimmer. He could also see the furniture of the room with tolerable distinctness—the old balloon-backed chairs, a four-post bed in a sort of recess, and a rack against the wall, from which hung some military clothes and accoutrements; and the sight of all these homely objects reassured him somewhat, and he could not help feeling unspeakably curious to see the face of the girl whose long hair was streaming over the officer's epaulet.

Peter, accordingly, coughed, at first slightly, and afterward more loudly, to recall her from her reverie of grief; and, apparently, he succeeded; for she turned round, as did her companion, and both, standing hand in hand, gazed upon him fixedly. He thought he had never seen such large, strange eyes in all his life; and their gaze seemed to chill the very air around him, and arrest the pulses of his heart. An eternity of misery and remorse was in the shadowy faces that looked upon him.

If Peter had taken less whisky by a single thimbleful, it is probable that he would have lost heart altogether before these figures, which seemed every moment to assume a more marked and fearful, though hardly definable, contrast to ordinary human shapes.

'What is it you want with me?' he stammered.

'To bring my lost treasure to the churchyard,' replied the lady, in a silvery voice of more than mortal desolation.

The word 'treasure' revived the resolution of Peter, although a cold sweat was covering him, and his hair was bristling with horror; he believed, however, that he was on the brink of fortune, if he could but command nerve to brave the interview to its close.

'And where,' he gasped, 'is it hid—where will I find it?'

They both pointed to the sill of the window, through which the moon was shining at the far end of the room, and the soldier said—

'Under that stone.'

Peter drew a long breath, and wiped the cold dew from his face, preparatory to passing to the window, where he expected to secure the reward of his protracted terrors. But looking steadfastly at the window, he saw the faint image of a new-born child sitting upon the sill in the moonlight, with its little arms stretched toward him, and a smile so heavenly as he never beheld before.

At sight of this, strange to say, his heart entirely failed him, he looked on the figures that stood near, and beheld them gazing on the infantine form with a smile so guilty and distorted, that he felt as if he were entering alive among the scenery of hell, and shuddering, he cried in an irrepressible agony of horror—

'I'll have nothing to say with you, and nothing to do with you; I don't know what yez are or what yez want iv me, but let me go this minute, every one of yez, in the name of God.'

With these words there came a strange rumbling and sighing about Peter's ears; he lost sight of everything, and felt that peculiar and not unpleasant sensation of falling softly, that sometimes supervenes in sleep, ending in a dull shock. After that he had neither dream nor consciousness till he wakened, chill and stiff, stretched between two piles of old rubbish, among the black and roofless walls of the ruined house.

We need hardly mention that the village had put on its wonted air of neglect and decay, or that Peter looked around him in vain for traces of those novelties which had so puzzled and distracted him upon the previous night.

'Ay, ay,' said his grandmother, removing her pipe, as he ended his description of the view from the bridge, 'sure enough I remember myself, when I was a slip of a girl, these little white cabins among the gardens by the river side. The artillery sogers that was married, or had not room in the barracks, used to be in them, but they're all gone long ago.'

'The Lord be merciful to us!' she resumed, when he had described the military procession, 'it's often I seen the regiment marchin' into the town, jist as you saw it last night, acushla. Oh, voch, but it makes my heart sore to think iv them days; they were pleasant times, sure enough; but is not it terrible, avick, to think its what it was the ghost of the rigiment you seen? The Lord betune us an' harm, for it was nothing else, as sure as I'm sittin' here.'

When he mentioned the peculiar physiognomy and figure of the old officer who rode at the head of the regiment—

'*That*,' said the old crone, dogmatically, 'was ould Colonel Grimshaw, the Lord presarve us! he's buried in the church-yard iv Chapelizod, and well I remember him, when I was a young thing, an' a cross ould floggin' fellow he was wid the men, an' a devil's boy among the girls—rest his soul!'

'Amen!' said Peter; 'it's often I read his tombstone myself; but he's a long time dead.'

'Sure, I tell you he died when I was no more nor a slip iv a girl—the Lord betune us and harm!'

'I'm afeard it is what I'm not long for this world myself, afther seeing such a sight as that,' said Peter, fearfully.

'Nonsinse, avourneen,' retorted his grandmother, indig-nantly, though she had herself misgivings on the subject; 'sure there was Phil Doolan, the ferryman, that seen black Ann Scanlan in his own boat, and what harm ever kem of it?'

Peter proceeded with his narrative, but when he came to the description of the house, in which his adventure had had so sinister a conclusion, the old woman was at fault.

'I know the house and the ould walls well, an' I can remember the time there was a roof on it, and the doors an' windows in it, but it had a bad name about being haunted, but by who, or for what, I forget intirely.'

'Did you ever hear was there goold or silver there?' he inquired.

'No, no, avick, don't be thinking about the likes; take a fool's advice, and never go next or near them ugly black walls again the longest day you have to live; an' I'd take my davy, it's what it's the same word the priest himself I'd be afther sayin' to you if you wor to ax his raverence consarnin' it, for it's plain to be seen it was nothing good you seen there, and there's neither luck nor grace about it.'

Peter's adventure made no little noise in the neighbour-hood, as the reader may well suppose; and a few evenings after it, being on an errand to old Major Vandeleur, who lived in a snug old-fashioned house, close by the river, under a perfect bower of ancient trees, he was called on to relate the story in the parlour.

The Major was, as I have said, an old man; he was small, lean, and upright, with a mahogany complexion, and a wooden inflexibility of face; he was a man, besides, of few words, and if *he* was old, it follows plainly that his mother was older still. Nobody could guess or tell *how* old, but it was admitted that her own generation had long passed away, and that she had not a competitor left. She had French blood in her veins, and although she did not retain her charms quite so well as Ninon de l'Enclos, she was in full possession of all her mental activity, and talked quite enough for herself and the Major.

'So, Peter,' she said, 'you have seen the dear, old Royal Irish again in the streets of Chapelizod. Make him a tumbler of punch, Frank; and Peter, sit down, and while you take it let us have the story.'

Peter accordingly, seated near the door, with a tumbler of the nectarian stimulant steaming beside him, proceeded with marvellous courage, considering they had no light but the uncertain glare of the fire, to relate with minute particularity his awful adventure. The old lady listened at first with a smile of goodnatured incredulity; her cross-examination touching the drinking-bout at Palmerstown had been teazing, but as the narrative proceeded she became attentive, and at length absorbed, and once or twice she uttered ejaculations of pity or awe. When it was over, the old lady looked with a somewhat sad and stern abstraction on the table, patting her cat assiduously meanwhile, and then suddenly looking upon her son, the Major, she said—

'Frank, as sure as I live he has seen the wicked Captain Devereux.'

The Major uttered an inarticulate expression of wonder.

'The house was precisely that he has described. I have told you the story often, as I heard it from your dear grandmother, about the poor young lady he ruined, and the dreadful suspicion about the little baby. *She*, poor thing, died in that house heart-broken, and you know he was shot shortly after in a duel.'

This was the only light that Peter ever received respecting his adventure. It was supposed, however, that he still clung to the hope that treasure of some sort was hidden about the old house, for he was often seen lurking about its walls, and at last his fate overtook him, poor fellow, in the pursuit; for climbing near the summit one day, his holding gave way, and he fell upon the hard uneven ground, fracturing a leg and a rib, and after a short interval died, and he, like the other heroes, lies buried in the little churchyard of Chapelizod.

FOOTSTEPS IN THE LOBBY

* * *

I went to my room early that night, but I was too miserable to sleep. At about twelve o'clock, feeling very nervous, I determined to call my cousin Emily, who slept in the next room, which communicated with mine by a second door. By this private entrance I found my way into her chamber, and without difficulty persuaded her to return to my room and sleep with me. We accordingly lay down together—she undressed, and I with my clothes on—for I was every moment walking up and down the room, and felt too nervous and miserable to think of rest or comfort. Emily was soon fast asleep, and I lay awake, fervently longing for the first pale gleam of morning, reckoning every stroke of the old clock with an impatience which made every hour appear like six.

It must have been about one o'clock when I thought I heard a slight noise at the partition door between Emily's room and mine, as if caused by somebody's turning the key in the lock. I held my breath, and the same sound was repeated at the second door of my room—that which opened upon the lobby—the sound was here distinctly caused by the revolution of the bolt in the lock, and it was followed by a slight pressure upon the door itself, as if to ascertain the security of the lock. The person, whoever it might be, was probably satisfied, for I heard the old boards of the lobby creak and strain, as if under the weight of somebody moving cautiously over them.

My sense of hearing became unnaturally, almost painfully acute. I suppose the imagination added distinctness to sounds vague in themselves. I thought that I could actually hear the breathing of the person who was slowly returning down the lobby; at the head of the staircase there appeared to occur a pause; and I could distinctly hear two or three sentences hastily whispered; the steps then descended the stairs with apparently less caution. I now ventured to walk quickly and lightly to the lobby door, and attempted to open it; but it was indeed fast locked upon the outside, as was also the other. I now felt that the dreadful hour was come; but one desperate expedient remained—it was to awaken Emily, and by our united strength, to attempt to force the partition door, which was slighter than the other, and through this to pass to the lower part of the house, whence it might be possible to escape to the grounds, and forth to the village.

I returned to the bedside, and shook Emily, but in vain; nothing that I could do availed to produce from her more than a few incoherent words—it was a death-like sleep. She had certainly drunk of some narcotic, as had I probably also, in spite of all the caution with which I had examined everything presented to us to eat or drink. I now attempted, with as little noise as possible, to force first one door, then the other—but all in vain. I believe no strength could have effected my object, for both doors opened inwards. I therefore collected whatever movables I could carry thither, and piled them against the doors, so as to assist me in whatever attempts I should make to resist the entrance of those without. I then returned to the bed and endeavoured again, but fruitlessly, to awaken my cousin. It was not sleep, it was torpor, lethargy, death. I knelt down and prayed with an agony of earnestness; and then seating myself upon the bed, I awaited my fate with a kind of terrible tranquillity.

I heard a faint clanking sound from the narrow court below, as if caused by the scraping of some iron instrument against stones or rubbish. I at first determined not to disturb the calmness which

I now felt, by uselessly watching the proceedings of those who sought my life; but as the sounds continued, the horrible curiosity which I felt overcame every other emotion, and I determined, at all hazards, to gratify it. I therefore crawled upon my knees to the window, so as to let the smallest portion of my head appear above the sill.

The moon was shining with an uncertain radiance upon the antique grey buildings, and obliquely upon the narrow court beneath, one side of which was therefore clearly illuminated, while the other was lost in obscurity, the sharp outlines of the old gables, with their nodding clusters of ivy, being at first alone visible. Whoever or whatever occasioned the noise which had excited my curiosity, was concealed under the shadow of the dark side of the quadrangle. I placed my hand over my eyes to shade them from the moonlight, which was so bright as to be almost dazzling, and, peering into the darkness, I first dimly, but afterwards gradually, almost with full distinctness, beheld the form of a man engaged in digging what appeared to be a rude hole close under the wall. Some implements, probably a shovel and pickaxe, lay beside him, and to these he every now and then applied himself as the nature of the ground required. He pursued his task rapidly, and with as little noise as possible.

'So,' thought I, as shovelful after shovelful the dislodged rubbish mounted into a heap, 'they are digging the grave in which, before two hours pass, I must lie, a cold, mangled corpse. I am *theirs*—I cannot escape.' I felt as if my reason was leaving me. I started to my feet, and in mere despair I applied myself again to each of the two doors alternately. I strained every nerve and sinew, but I might as well have attempted, with my single strength, to force the building itself from its foundation. I threw myself madly upon the ground, and clasped my hands over my eyes as if to shut out the horrible images which crowded upon me.

The paroxysm passed away. I prayed once more with the bitter, agonised fervour of one who feels that the hour of death is present and inevitable. When I arose I went once more to the window and looked out, just in time to see a shadowy figure glide stealthily along the wall. The task was finished. The catastrophe of the tragedy must soon be accomplished. I determined now to defend my life to the last; and that I might be able to do so with some effect, I searched the room for something which might serve as a weapon;

but either through accident, or from an anticipation of such a possibility, everything which might have been made available for such a purpose had been carefully removed. I must thus die tamely and without an effort to defend myself.

A thought suddenly struck me—might it not be possible to escape through the door, which the assassin must open in order to enter the room? I resolved to make the attempt. I felt assured that the door through which ingress to the room would be effected was that which opened upon the lobby. It was the more direct way, besides being, for obvious reasons, less liable to interruption than the other. I resolved then to place myself behind a projection of the wall, whose shadow would serve fully to conceal me, and when the door should be opened, and before they should have discovered the identity of the occupant of the bed, to creep noiselessly from the room, and then to trust to Providence for escape. In order to facilitate this scene, I removed all the lumber which I had heaped against the door; and I had nearly completed my arrangements, when I perceived the room suddenly darkened by the close approach of some shadowy object to the window. On turning my eyes in that direction, I observed at the top of the casement, as if suspended from above, first the feet, then the legs, then the body, and at length the whole figure of a man present itself.

It was Edward T——n. He appeared to be guiding his descent so as to bring his feet upon the centre of the stone block which occupied the lower part of the window; and having secured his footing upon this, he kneeled down and began to gaze into the room. As the moon was gleaming into the chamber, and the bed curtains were drawn, he was able to distinguish the bed itself and its contents. He appeared satisfied with his scrutiny, for he looked up and made a sign with his hand, upon which the rope by which his descent had been effected was slackened from above, and he proceeded to disengage it from his waist: this accomplished, he applied his hands to the window-frame, which must have been ingeniously contrived for the purpose, for with apparently no resistance the whole frame, containing casement and all, slipped from its position in the wall, and was by him lowered into the room. The cold night waved the bed-curtains, and he paused for a moment—all was still again—and he stepped in upon the floor of the room. He held in his hand what appeared to be a steel instrument, shaped something like a hammer, but larger and sharper at the extremities. This he held rather behind him, while, with three long *tip-toe* strides, he brought himself to the bedside.

I felt that the discovery must now be made, and held my breath in momentary expectation of the execration in which he would vent his surprise and disappointment. I closed my eyes—there was a pause—but it was a short one. I heard two dull blows, given in rapid succession: a quivering sigh, and the long-drawn, heavy breathing of the sleeper was for ever suspended. I unclosed my eyes, and saw the murderer fling the quilt across the head of his victim: he then, with the instrument of death still in his hand, proceeded to the lobby door, upon which he tapped sharply twice or thrice—a quick step was then heard approaching, and a voice whispered something from without—Edward answered, with a kind of chuckle, 'Her ladyship is past complaining; unlock the door, in the devil's name, unless you're afraid to come in, and help me to lift the body out of the window.' The key was turned in the lock—the door opened—and my uncle entered the room.

I have told you already that I had placed myself under the shade of a projection of the wall, close to the door. I had instinctively shrunk down cowering towards the ground on the entrance of Edward through the window. When my uncle entered the room, he and his son both stood so very close to me that his hand was every moment upon the point of touching my face. I held my breath, and remained motionless as death.

'You had no interruption from the next room?' said my uncle.

'No,' was the brief reply.

'Secure the jewels, Ned; the French harpy must not lay her claws upon them. You've a steady hand, by G—; not much blood—eh?'

'Not twenty drops,' replied his son, 'and those on the quilt.'

'I'm glad it's over,' whispered my uncle again; 'we must lift the—the *thing* through the window, and lay the rubbish over it.'

They then turned to the bedside, and, winding the bed-clothes round the body, carried it between them slowly to the window, and, exchanging a few brief words with someone below, they shoved it over the window sill, and I heard it fall heavily on the ground underneath.

'I'll take the jewels,' said my uncle; 'there are two caskets in the lower drawer.'

He proceeded, with an accuracy which, had I been more at ease, would have furnished me with matter of astonishment, to lay his hand upon the very spot where my jewels lay; and having possessed himself of them, he called to his son—

'Is the rope made fast above?'

'I'm not a fool—to be sure it is,' replied he.

They then lowered themselves from the window. I now rose lightly and cautiously, scarcely daring to breathe, from my place of concealment, and was creeping towards the door, when I heard my cousin's voice, in a sharp whisper, exclaim, 'Scramble up again; G—d d—n you, you've forgot to lock the door;' and I perceived, by the straining of the rope which hung from above, that the mandate was instantly obeyed.

Not a second was to be lost. I passed through the door, which was only closed, and moved as rapidly as I could, consistently with stillness, along the lobby. Before I had gone many yards I heard the door through which I had just passed double locked on the inside. I glided down the stairs in terror, lest, at every corner, I should meet the murderer or one of his accomplices. I reached the hall, and listened for a moment to ascertain whether all was silent around; no sound was audible; the parlour windows opened on the park, and through one of them I might, I thought, easily effect my escape. Accordingly, I hastily entered; but, to my consternation, a candle was burning in the room, and by its light I saw a figure seated at the dinner-table, upon which lay glasses, bottles, and the other accompaniments of a drinking party.

There was no other means of escape, so I advanced with a firm step and collected mind to the window. I noiselessly withdrew the bars and unclosed the shutters—I pushed open the casement, and, without waiting to look behind me, I ran with my utmost speed, scarcely feeling the ground under me, down the avenue, taking care to keep upon the grass which bordered it. I did not for a moment slack my speed, and I had now gained the centre point between the park gate and the mansion-house—here the avenue made a wider circuit, and in order to avoid delay, I directed my way across the smooth sward round which the pathway wound, intending, at the opposite side of the flat, at a point which I distinguished by a group of old birch trees, to enter again upon the beaten track, which was from thence tolerably direct to the gate.

I had, with my utmost speed, got about halfway across this broad flat when the rapid treading of a horse's hoofs struck upon my ear. My heart swelled in my bosom, as though I would smother. The clattering of galloping hoofs approached—I was pursued— they were now upon the sward on which I was running—there was not a bush or a bramble to shelter me—and, as if to render escape altogether desperate, the moon, which had hitherto been obscured, at this moment shone forth with a broad clear light, which made every object distinctly visible. The sounds were now close behind me. I felt my knees bending under me, with the sensation which torments one in dreams. I reeled—I stumbled— I fell—and at the same instant the cause of my alarm wheeled past me at full gallop. It was one of the young fillies which pastured loose about the park, whose frolics had thus all but maddened me with terror.

I scrambled to my feet, and rushed on with weak but rapid steps, my sportive companion still galloping round and round me with many a frisk and fling, until, at length, more dead than alive, I reached the avenue gate and crossed the stile, I scarce knew how. I ran through the village, in which all was silent as the grave, until my progress was arrested by the hoarse voice of a sentinel, who cried, 'Who goes there?' I felt that I was now safe. I turned in the direction of the voice, and fell fainting at the soldier's feet.

When I came to myself I was sitting in a miserable hovel, sur- rounded by strange faces, all bespeaking curiosity and compassion. Many soldiers were in it also; indeed, as I afterwards found, it was employed as a guard-room by a detachment of troops quartered for that night in the town. In a few words I informed their officer of the circumstances which had occurred, describing also the appear- ance of the persons engaged in the murder; and he, without loss of time, proceeded to the mansion-house of Carrickleigh, taking with him a number of his men. But the villains had discovered their mistake, and had effected their escape, before the arrival of the military.

Deep and fervent as must always be my gratitude to Heaven for my deliverance, effected by a chain of providential occur- rences, the failing of a single link of which must have insured my destruction, I was long before I could look back upon it with other feelings than those of bitterness, almost of agony. My cousin, the only being that had ever really loved me, my nearest dearest friend, ever ready to sympathise, to counsel, and to assist—the gayest, the gentlest, the warmest heart—the only creature on earth that cared for me—*her* life had been the price of my deliverance; and I then uttered the wish—which no event of my long and sorrowful life has taught me to recall—that she had been spared, and that in her stead *I* were mouldering in the grave forgotten and at rest.

Madam Crowl's Ghost

Twenty years have passed since we last saw Mrs
Joliffe's tall slim figure. She is now past seventy, and
can't have many milestones more to count on the journey that will bring her to her long home. The hair has
grown white as snow, that is parted under her cap, over
her shrewd, but kindly face. But her figure is still
straight, and her step light and active.

She has taken of late years to the care of adult in-
valids, having surrendered to younger hands the little
people who inhabit cradles, and crawl on all-fours.

Those who remember that good-natured face among the earliest that emerge from the darkness of nonentity, and who owe to her their first lessons in the accomplishment of walking, and a delighted appreciation of their first babblings and earliest teeth, have 'spired up' into tall lads and lasses, now. Some of them shew streaks of white by this time, in brown locks, 'the bonny gouden' hair, that she was so proud to brush and shew to admiring mothers, who are seen no more on the green of Golden Friars, and whose names are traced now on the flat grey stones in the churchyard.

So the time is ripening some, and searing others; and the saddening and tender sunset hour has come; and it is evening with the kind old north-country dame, who nursed pretty Laura Mildmay, who now stepping into the room, smiles so gladly, and throws her arms round the old woman's neck, and kisses her twice.

'Now, this is so lucky!' said Mrs Jenner, 'you have just come in time to hear a story.'

'Really! That's delightful.'

'Na, na, od wite it! no story, ouer true for that, I sid it a wi my aan eyen. But the barn here, would not like, at these hours, just goin' to her bed, to hear tell of freets and boggarts.'

'Ghosts? The very thing of all others I should most likely to hear of.'

'Well, dear,' said Mrs Jenner, 'if you are not afraid, sit ye down here, with us.'

'She was just going to tell me all about her first engagement to attend a dying old woman,' says Mrs Jenner, 'and of the ghost she saw there. Now, Mrs Jolliffe, make your tea first, and then begin.'

The good woman obeyed, and having prepared a cup of that companionable nectar, she sipped a little, drew her brows slightly together to collect her thoughts, and then looked up with a wondrous solemn face to begin.

Good Mrs Jenner, and the pretty girl, each gazed with eyes of solemn expectation in the face of the old woman, who seemed to gather awe from the recollections she was summoning.

The old room was a good scene for such a narrative, with the oak-wainscoting, quaint, and clumsy furniture, the heavy beams that crossed its ceiling, and the tall four-post bed, with dark curtains, within which you might imagine what shadows you please.

Mrs Jolliffe cleared her voice, rolled her eyes slowly round, and began her tale in these words:

MADAM CROWL'S GHOST

'I'm an ald woman now, and I was but thirteen, my last birthday, the night I came to Applewale House. My aunt was the housekeeper there, and a sort o' one-horse carriage was down at Lexhoe waitin' to take me and my box up to Applewale.

'I was a bit frightened by the time I got to Lexhoe, and when I saw the carriage and horse, I wished myself back again with my mother at Hazelden. I was crying when I got into the "shay" – that's what we used to call it – and old John Mulbery that drove it, and was a good-natured fellow, bought me a handful of apples at the Golden Lion to cheer me up a bit; and he told me that there was a currant-cake, and tea, and pork chops, waiting for me, all hot, in my aunt's room at the great house. It was a fine moonlight night, and I eat the apples, lookin' out o' the shay winda.

'It's a shame for gentlemen to frighten a poor foolish child like I was. I sometimes think it might be tricks.

There was two on 'em on the tap o' the coach beside me. And they began to question me after nightfall, when the moon rose, where I was going to. Well, I told them it was to wait on Dame Arabella Crowl, of Applewale House, near by Lexhoe.

' "Ho, then," says one of them, "you'll not be long there!"

'And I looked at him as much as to say "Why not?" for I had spoken out when I told them where I was goin', as if 'twas something clever I hed to say.

' "Because," says he, "and don't you for your life tell no one, only watch her and see – she's possessed by the devil, and more an half a ghost. Have you got a Bible?"

' "Yes, sir," says I. For my mother put my little Bible in my box, and I knew it was there: and by the same token, though the print's too small for my ald eyes, I have it in my press to this hour.

'As I looked up at him saying "Yes, sir," I thought I saw him winkin' at his friend; but I could not be sure.

' "Well," says he, 'be sure you put it under your bolster every night, it will keep the ald girl's claws aff ye."

'And I got such a fright when he said that, you wouldn't fancy! And I'd a liked to ask him a lot about the ald lady, but I was too shy, and he and his friend began talkin' together about their own consarns, and dowly enough I got down, as I told ye, at Lexhoe. My heart sank as I drove into the dark avenue. The trees stand very thick and big, as ald as the ald house almost, and four people, with their arms out and finger-tips touchin', barely girds round some of them.

- 'Well my neck was stretched out o' the winda, looking for the first view o' the great house; and all at once we pulled up in front of it.

'A great white-and-black house it is, wi' great black beams across and right up it, and gables lookin' out, as white as a sheet, to the moon, and the shadows o' the trees, two or three up and down in front, you could count the leaves on them, and all the little diamond-shaped windapanes, glimmering on the great hall winda, and great shutters, in the old fashion, hinged on the wall outside, boulted across all the rest o' the windas in front, for there was but three or four servants, and the old lady in the house, and most o' t'rooms was locked up.

'My heart was in my mouth when I sid the journey was over, and this the great house afoore me, and I sa near my aunt that I never sid till noo, and Dame Crowl, that I was come to wait upon, and was afeared on already.

'My aunt kissed me in the hall, and brought me to her room. She was tall and thin, wi' a pale face and black eyes, and long thin hands wi' black mittins on. She was past fifty, and her word was short; but her word was law. I hev no complaints to make of her; but she was a hard woman, and I think she would hev bin kinder to me if I had bin her sister's child in place of her brother's. But all that's o' no consequence noo.

The squire – his name was Mr Chevenix Crowl, he was Dame Crowl's grandson – came down there, by way of seeing that the old lady was well treated, about twice or thrice in the year. I sid him but twice all the time I was at Applewale House.

'I can't say but she was well taken care of, notwithstanding; but that was because my aunt and Meg Wyvern, that was her maid, had a conscience, and did their duty by her.

'Mrs Wyvern – Meg Wyvern my aunt called her to

herself, and Mrs Wyvern to me – was a fat, jolly lass of fifty, a good height and a good breadth, always good-humoured and walked slow. She had fine wages, but she was a bit stingy, and kept all her fine clothes under lock and key, and wore, mostly, a twilled chocolate cotton, wi' red and yellow and green sprigs and balls on it, and it lasted wonderful.

'She never gave me nout, not the vally o' a brass thimble, all the time I was there; but she was good-humoured, and always laughin', and she talked no end o' proas over her tea; and seeing me sa sackless and dowly, she rouscd me up wi' her laughin' and stories; and I think I liked her better than my aunt – children is so taken wi' a bit o' fun or a story – though my aunt was very good to me, but a hard woman about some things, and silent always.

'My aunt took me into her bed-chamber, that I might rest myself a bit while she was settin' the tea in her room. But first, she patted me on the shouther, and said I was a tall lass o' my years, and had spired up well, and asked me if I could do plain work and stitchin'; and she looked in my face, and said I was like my father, her brother, that was dead and gone, and she hoped I was a better Christian and wad na du a' that lids (would not do anything of that sort).

'It was a hard sayin' the first time I set foot in her room, I thought.

'When I went into the next room, the housekeeper's room – very comfortable, yak (oak) all round – there was a fine fire blazin', away, wi' coal, and peat, and wood, all in a low together, and tea on the table, and hot cake, and smokin' meat; and there was Mrs Wyvern, fat, jolly, and talkin' away, more in an hour than my aunt would in a year.

'While I was still at my tea my aunt went upstairs to see Madam Crowl.

' "She's agone up to see that old Judith Squailes is awake," says Mrs Wyvern. "Judith sits with Madam Crowl when me and Mrs Shutters" – that was my aunt's name – "is away. She's troublesome old lady. Ye'll hev to be sharp wi' her, or she'll be into the fire, or out o' t' winda. She goes on wires, she does, old though she be."

' "How old, ma'am?" says I.

' "Ninety-three her last birthday, and that's eight months gone," says she; and she laughed. "And don't be askin' questions about her before your aunt – mind, I tell ye; just take her as you find her, and that's all."

' "And what's to be my business about her, please, ma'am?" says I.

' "About the old lady? Well," says she, "your aunt, Mrs Shutters, will tell you that; but I suppose you'll hev to sit in the room with your work, and see she's at no mischief, and let her amuse herself with her things on the table, and get her food or drink as she calls for it, and keep her out o' mischief, and ring the bell hard if she's troublesome."

' "Is she deaf, ma'am?'

' "No, nor blind," says she; "as sharp as a needle, but she's gone quite aupy, and can't remember nout rightly; and Jack the Giant Killer, or Goody Twoshoes will please her as well as the king's court, or the affairs of the nation."

' "And what did the little girl go away for, ma'am, that went on Friday last? My aunt wrote to my mother she was to go."

' "Yes; she's gone."

' "What for?" says I again.

' "She didn't answer Mrs Shutters, I do suppose," says she. "I don't know. Don't be talkin'; your aunt can't abide a talkin' child."

' "And please, ma'am, is the old lady well in health?" says I.

' "It ain't no harm to ask that," says she. "She's torflin a bit lately, but better this week past, and I dare say she'll last out her hundred years yet. Hish! Here's your aunt coming down the passage."

'In comes my aunt, and begins talkin' to Mrs Wyvern, and I, beginnin' to feel more comfortable and at home like, and was walkin' about the room lookin' at this thing and at that. There was pretty old china things on the cupboard, and pictures again the wall; and there was a door open in the wainscot, and I sees a queer old leathern jacket, wi' straps and buckles to it, and sleeves as long as the bed-post hangin' up inside.

' "What's that you're at child?" says my aunt, sharp enough, turning about when I thought she least minded. "What's that in your hand?"

' "This, ma'am?" says I, turning about with the leathern jacket. 'I don't know what it is, ma'am."

'Pale as she was, the red came up in her cheeks, and her eyes flashed wi' anger, and I think only she had half a dozen steps to take, between her and me, she'd a gev me a sizzup. But she did gie me a shake by the shouther, and she plucked the thing out o' my hand, and says she, "While ever you stay here, don't ye meddle wi' nout that don't belong to ye," and she hung it up on the pin that was there, and shut the door wi' a bang and locked it fast.

'Mrs Wyvern was liftin' up her hands and laughin', all this time, quietly, in her chair, rolling herself a bit in it, as she used when she was kinkin'.

'The tears was in my eyes, and she winked at my aunt, and says she, dryin' her own eyes that was wet wi' the laughin', "Tut, the child meant no harm – come here to me, child. It's only a pair o' crutches for lame ducks, and ask us no questions mind, and we'll tell ye no lies; and come here and sit down, and drink a mug o' beer before ye go to your bed."

'My room, mind ye, was upstairs, next to the old lady's, and Mrs Wyvern's bed was near hers in her room, and I was to be ready at call, if need be.

'The old lady was in one of her tantrums that night and part of the day before. She used to take fits o' the sulks. Sometimes she would not let them dress her, and at other times she would not let them take her clothes off. She was a great beauty, they said, in her day. But there was no one about Applewale that remembered her in her prime. And she was dreadful fond o' dress, and had thick silks, and stiff satins, and velvets, and laces, and all sorts, enough to set up seven shops at the least. All her dresses was old-fashioned and queer, but worth a fortune.

'Well, I went to my bed. I lay for a while awake; for a' things was new to me; and I think the tea was in my nerves, too, for I wasn't used to it, except now and then on a holiday, or the like. And I heard Mrs Wyvern talkin', and I listened with my hand to my ear; but I could not hear Mrs Crowl, and I don't think she said a word.

'There was great care took of her. The people of Applewale knew that when she died they would every one get the sack; and their situations was well paid and easy.

'The doctor came twice a week to see the old lady, and you may be sure they all did as he bid them. One

93

thing was the same every time; they were never to cross or frump her, any way, but to humour and please her in everything.

'So she lay in her clothes all that night, and next day, not a word she said, and I was at my needlework all that day, in my own room, except when I went down to my dinner.

'I would a liked to see the ald lady, and even to hear her speak. But she might as well a' bin in Lunnon a' the time for me.

'When I had my dinner my aunt sent me out for a walk for an hour. I was glad when I came back, the trees was so big, and the place so dark and lonesome, and 'twas a cloudy day, and I cried a deal, thinkin' of home, while I was walkin' alone there. That evening, the candles bein' alight, I was sittin' in my room, and the door was open into Madam Crowl's chamber, where my aunt was. It was, then, for the first time I heard what I suppose was the ald lady talking.

'It was a queer noise like, I couldn't well say which, a bird, or a beast, only it had a bleatin' sound in it, and was very small.

'I pricked my ears to hear all I could. But I could not make out one word she said. And my aunt answered:

' "The evil one can't hurt no one, ma'am, bout the Lord permits."

'Then the same queer voice from the bed says something more that I couldn't make head nor tail on.

'And my aunt med answer again: "Let them pull faces, ma'am, and say what they will; if the Lord be for us, who can be against us?"

'I kept listenin' with my ear turned to the door, holdin' my breath, but not another word or sound came in from the room. In about twenty minutes, as I was sittin' by the table, lookin' at the pictures in the old Aesop's Fables, I was aware o' something moving at the door, and lookin' up I sid my aunt's face lookin' in at the door, and her hand raised.

'"Hish!" says she, very soft, and comes over to me on tiptoe, and she says in a whisper: "Thank God, she's asleep at last, and don't ye make no noise till I come back, for I'm goin' down to take my cup o' tea, and I'll be back i' noo – me and Mrs Wyvern, and she'll be sleepin' in the room, and you can run down when we come up, and Judith will gie ye yaur supper in my room."

'And with that she goes.

'I kep' looking at the picture-book, as before, listenin' every noo and then, but there was no sound, not a breath, that I could hear; an' I began whisperin' to the pictures and talkin' to myself to keep my heart up, for I was growin' feared in that big room.

'And at last up I got, and began walkin' about the room, lookin' at this and peepin' at that, to amuse my mind, ye'll understand. And at last what sud I do but peeps into Madam Crowl's bedchamber.

'A grand chamber it was, wi' a great four-poster, wi' flowered silk curtains as tall as the ceilin', and foldin' down on the floor, and drawn close all round. There was a lookin'-glass, the biggest I ever sid before, and the room was a blaze o' light. I counted twenty-two wax candles, all alight. Such was her fancy, and no one dared say her nay.

'I listened at the door, and gaped and wondered all round. When I heard there was not a breath, and did not see so much as a stir in the curtains, I took heart, and walked into the room on tiptoe, and looked round again. Then I takes a keek at myself in the big glass;

95

and at last it came in my head, 'Why couldn't I ha' a keek at the ald lady herself in the bed?''

'Ye'd think me a fule if ye knew half how I longed to see Dame Crowl, and I thought to myself if I didn't peep now I might wait many a day before I got so gude a chance again.

'Well, my dear, I came to the side o' the bed, the curtains bein' close, and my heart a'most failed me. But I took courage, and I slips my finger in between the thick curtains, and then my hand. So I waits a bit, but all was still as death. So, softly, softly I draws the curtain, and there, sure enough, I sid before me, stretched out like the painted lady on the tomb-stean in Lexhoe Church, the famous Dame Crowl, of Applewale House. There she was, dressed out. You never sid the like in they days. Satin and silk, and scarlet and green, and gold and pint lace; by Jen! 'twas a sight! A big powdered wig, half as high as herself, was a-top o' her head, and, wow! – was ever such wrinkles? – and her old baggy throat all powdered, white, and her cheeks rouged, and mouse-skin eyebrows, that Mrs Wyvern used to stick on, and there she lay proud and stark, wi' a pair o' clocked silk hose on, and heels to her shoon as tall as nine-pins. Lawk! But her nose was crooked and thin, and half the whites o' her eyes was open. She used to stand, dressed as she was, gigglin' and dribblin' before the lookin-' glass, wi' a fan in her hand and a big nosegay in her bodice. Her wrinkled little hands was stretched down by her sides, and such long nails, all cut into points, I never sid in my days. Could it even a bin the fashion for grit fowk to wear their fingernails so?

'Well, I think ye'd a-bin frightened yourself if ye'd a sid such a sight. I couldn't let go the curtain, nor move an inch, nor take my eyes off her; my very heart stood still. And in an instant she opens her eyes and up she sits, and spins herself round, and down wi' her, wi' a clack on her two tall heels on the floor, facin' me, ogglin' in my face wi' her two great glassy eyes, and a wicked simper wi' her wrinkled lips, and lang fause teeth.

'Well, a corpse is a natural thing: but this was the dreadfullest sight I ever sid. She had her fingers straight out pointin' at me, and her back was crooked, round again wi' age. Says she:

' "Ye little limb! what for did ye say I killed the boy? I'll tickle ye till ye're stiff!"

'If I'd a thought an instant, I'd a turned about and run. But I couldn't take my eyes off her, and I backed from her as soon as I could; and she came clatterin' after like a thing on wires, with her fingers pointing to my throat, and she makin' all the time a sound with her tongue like zizz-zizz-zizz.

'I kept backin' and backin' as quick as I could, and her fingers was only a few inches away from my throat, and I felt I'd lose my wits if she touched me.

'I went back this way, right into the corner, and I gev a yellock, ye'd think saul and body was partin', and that minute my aunt, from the door, calls out wi' a blare, and the ald lady turns round on her, and I turns about, and ran through my room, and down the stairs, as hard as my legs could carry me.

'I cried hearty, I can tell you, when I got down to the housekeeper's room. Mrs Wyvern laughed a deal when I told her what happened. But she changed her key when she heard the ald lady's words.

' "Say them again," says she.

'So I told her.

' "Ye little limb! What for did ye say I killed the boy? I'll tickle ye'till ye're stiff."

' "And did ye say she killed a boy?" says she.

' "Not I, ma'am," says I.

Judith was always up with me, after that, when the two elder women was away from her. I would a jumped out at winda, rather than stay alone in the same room wi' her.

'It was about a week after, as well as I can remember, Mrs Wyvern, one day when me and her was alone, told me a thing about Madam Crowl that I did not know before.

'She being young and a great beauty, full seventy year before, had married Squire Crowl, of Applewale. But he was a widower, and had a son about nine years old.

'There never was tale or tidings of this boy after one mornin'. No one could say where he went to. He was alowed too much liberty, and used to be off in the morning, one day, to the keeper's cottage and breakfast wi' him, and away to the warren, and not home, mayhap, till evening; and another time down to the lake, and bathe there, and spend the day fishing' there, or paddlin' about in the boat. Well, no one could say what was gone wi' him; only this, that his hat was found by the lake, under a haathorn that grows thar to this day, and 'twas thought he was drowned bathin'. And the squire's son, by his second marriage, with this Madam Crowl that lived sa dreadful lang, came in far the estates. It was his son, the ald lady's grandson, Squire Chevenix Crowl, that owned the estates at the time I came to Applewale.

'There was a deal o' talk lang before my aunt's time about it; and 'twas said the stepmother knew more than she was like to let out. And she managed her husband, the ald squire, wi' her whiteheft and flatteries. And as the boy was never seen more, in course of time the thing died out of fowks' minds.

'I'm goin' to tell ye noo about what I sid wi' my own een.

'I was not there six months, and it was winter time, when the ald lady took her last sickness.

'The doctor was afeard she might a took a fit o' madness, as she did fifteen years before, and was buckled up, many a time, in a strait-waistcoat, which was the very leathern jerkin I sid in the closet, off my aunt's room.

'Well, she didn't. She pined, and windered, and went off, torflin', torflin', quiet enough, till a day or two before her flittin', and then she took to rabblin', and sometimes skirlin' in the bed, ye'd think a robber had a knife to her throat, and she used to work out o' the bed, and not being strong enough, then, to walk or stand, she'd fall on the flure, wi' her ald wizened hands stretched before her face, and skirlin' still for mercy.

'Ye may guess I didn't go into the room, and I used to be shiverin' in my bed wi' fear, at her skirlin' and scrafflin' on the flure, and blarin' out words that id make your skin turn blue.

'My aunt, and Mrs Wyvern, and Judith Squailes, and a woman from Lexhoe, was always about her. At last she took fits, and they wore her out.

'T' sir was there, and prayed for her; but she was past praying with. I suppose it was right, but none could think there was much good in it, and sa at lang last she made her flittin', and a' was over, and old Dame Crowl was shrouded and coffined, and Squire Chevenix was wrote for. But he was away in France, and the delay was sa lang, that t' sir and doctor both agreed it would not du to keep her langer out o' her place, and no one cared but just them two, and my aunt and the rest o' us, from Applewale, to go to the buryin'. So the old lady of Applewale was laid in the vault under Lexhoe Church; and we lived up at the great house till such time as the squire should come to tell his will about us, and pay off such as he chose to discharge.

'I was put into another room, two doors away from what was Dame Crowl's chamber, after her death, and this thing happened the night before Squire Chevenix came to Applewale.

'The room I was in now was a large square chamber, covered wi' yak pannels, but unfurnished except for my bed, which had no curtains to it, and a chair and a table, or so, that looked nothing at all in such a big room. And the big looking-glass, that the old lady used to keek into and admire herself from head to heel, now that there was na mair o' that wark, was put out of the way, and stood against the wall in my room, for there was shiftin' o' many things in her chamber ye may suppose, when she came to be coffined.

'The news had come that day that the squire was to be down next morning at Applewale; and not sorry was I, for I thought I was sure to be sent home again to my mother. And right glad was I, and I was thinkin' of a' at hame, and my sister Janet, and the kitten and the pymag, and Trimmer the tike, and all the rest, and I go sa fidgetty, I couldn't sleep, and the clock struck twelve, and me wide awake, and the room as dark as pick. My back was turned to the door, and my eyes towards the wall opposite.

'Well, it could na be a full quarter past twelve, when

I sees a lightin' on the wall befoore me, as if something took fire behind, and the shadas o' the bed, and the chair, and my gown, that was hangin' from the wall, was dancin' up and down on the ceilin' beams and the yak pannels; and I turns my head ower my shouther quick, thinkin' something muss a gone a' fire.

'And what sud I see, by Jen! but the likeness o' the ald beldame, bedizened out in her satins and velvets, on her dead body, simperin', wi' her eyes as wide as saucers, and her face like the fiend himself. 'Twas a red light that rose about her in a fuffin low, as if her dress round her feet was blazin'. She was drivin' on right for me, wi' her ald shrivelled hands crooked as if she was goin' to claw me. I could not stir, but she passed me straight by, wi' a blast o' cald air, and I slid. her, at the wall, in the alcove as my aunt used to call it, which was a recess where the state bed used to stand in ald times wi' a door open wide, and her hands gropin' in at somethin' was there. I never sid that door befoore. And she turned round to me, like a thing on a pivot, flyrin', and all at once the room was dark, and I standin' at the far side o' the bed; I don't know how I got there, and I found my tongue at last, and if I did na blare a yellock, rennin' down the gallery and almost pulled Mrs Wyvern's door off t' hooks, and frighted her half out o' wits.

'Ye may guess I did na sleep that night; and with the first light, down wi' me to my aunt, as fast as my two legs cud carry me.

'Well my aunt did na frump or flite me, as I thought she would, but she held me by the hand, and looked hard in my face all the time. And she telt me not to be feared; and says she:

' "Hed the appearance a key in its hand?"

' "Yes," says I, bringin' it to mind, "a big key in a queer brass handle."

' "Stop a bit," says she, lettin' go ma hand, and openin' the cupboard-door. "Was it like this?" says she, takin' one out in her fingers, and showing it to me, with a dark look in my face.

' "That was it," says I, quick enough.

' "Are ye sure?" she says, turnin' it round.

' "Sart," says I, and I felt like I was gain' to faint when I sid it.

' "Well, that will do, child," says she, saftly thinkin', and she locked it up again.

' "The squire himself will be here today, before twelve o'clock, and ye must tell him all about it," says she, thinkin', "and I suppose I'll be leavin' soon, and so the best thing for the present is, that ye should go home this afternoon, and I'll look out another place for you when I can."

'Fain was I, ye may guess, at that word.

'My aunt packed up my things for me, and the three pounds that was due to me, to bring home, and Squire Crowl himself came down to Applewale that day, a handsome man, about thirty years ald. It was the second time I sid him. But this was the first time he spoke to me.

'My aunt talk wi' him in the housekeeper's room, and I don't know what they said. I was a bit feared on the squire, he bein' a great gentleman down in Lexhoe, and I darn't go near till I was called. And says he, smilin':

' "What's a' this ye a sen, child? it mun be a dream, for ye know there's na sic a thing as a bo or a freet in a' the world. But whatever it was, ma little maid, sit ye down and tell all about it from first to last."

'Well, so soon as I made an end, he thought a bit, and says he to my aunt:

' "I mind the place well. In old Sir Olivur's time lame Wyndel told me there was a door in that recess, to the left, where the lassie dreamed she saw my grandmother open it. He was past eighty when he told me that, and I but a boy. It's twenty year sen. The plate and jewels used to be kept there, long ago, before the iron closet was made in the arras chamber, and he told me the key had a brass handle, and this ye say was found in the bottom o' the kist where she kept her old fans. Now, would not it be a queer thing if we found some spoons or diamonds forgot there? Ye mun come up wi' us, lassie, and point to the very spot."

'Loth was I, and my heart in my mouth, and fast I held by my aunt's hand as I stept into that awsome room, and showed them both how she came and passed me by, and the spot where she stood, and where the door seemed to open.

'There was an ald empty press against the wall then, and shoving it aside, sure enough there was the tracing of a door in the wainscot, and a keyhole stopped with wood, and planed across as smooth as the rest, and the joining of the door all stopped wi' putty the colour o' yak, and, but for the hinges that showed a bit when the press was shoved aside, ye would not consayt there was a door there at all.

' "Ha!" says he, wi' a queer smile, "this looks like it."

'It took some minutes wi' a small chisel and hammer to pick the bit o' wood out o' the keyhole. The key fitted, sure enough, and, wi' a strang twist and a lang skreak, the boult went back and he pulled the door open.

'There was another door inside, stranger than the

first, but the lacks was gone, and it opened easy. Inside was a narrow floor and walls and vault o' brick; we could not see what was in it, for 'twas dark as pick.

'When my aunt had lighted the candle, the squire held it up and stept in.

'My aunt stood on tiptoe tryin' to look over his shouther, and I did na see nout.

'"Ha! ha!" says the squire, steppin' backward. "What's that? Gi' ma the poker – quick!" says he to my aunt. And as she went to the hearth I peeps beside his arm, and I sid squat down in the far corner a monkey or a flayin' on the chest, or else the maist shrivelled up, wizzened ald wife that ever was sen on yearth.

'"By Jen!" says my aunt, as puttin' the poker in his hand, she keeked by his shouther, and sid the ill-favoured thing, "hae a care, sir, what ye're doin'. Back wi' ye, and shut to the door!"

'But in place o' that he steps in saftly, wi' the poker pointed like a swoord, and he gies it a poke, and down it a' tumbles together, head and a', in a heap o' bayans and dust, little meyar an' a hatful.

''Twas the bayans o' a child; a' the rest went to dust at a touch. They said nout for a while, but he turns round the skull, as it lay on the floor.

'Young as I was, I consayted I knew well enough what they was thinkin' on.

'"A dead cat!" says he, pushin' back and blowin' out the can'le, and shuttin' to the door. "We'll come back, you and me, Mrs Shutters, and look on the shelves by-and-by. I've other matters first to speak to ye about; and this little girl's goin' hame, ye say. She has her wages, and I mun mak' her a present," says he, pattin' my shouther wi' his hand.

'And he did gimma a goud pound and I went aff to

Lexhoe about an hour after, and sa hame by the stage-coach, and fain was I to be at hame again; and I never sid Dame Crowl o' Applewale, God be thanked, either in appearance or in dream, at-efter. But when I was grown to be a woman, my aunt spent a day and night wi' me at Littleham, and she telt me there was no doubt it was the poor little boy that was missing sa lang sen, that was shut up to die thar in the dark by that wicked beldame, whar his skirls, or his prayers, or his thumpin' cud na be heard, and his hat was left by the water's edge, whoever did it, to mak' belief he was drowned. The clothes, at the first touch, a' ran into a snuff o' dust in the cell whar the bayans was found. But there was a handful o' jet buttons, and a knife with a green heft, together wi' a couple o' pennies the poor little fella had in his pocket, I suppose, when he was decoyed in thar, and sid his last o' the light. And there was, amang the squire's papers, a copy o' the notice that was prented after he was lost, when the ald squire thought he might'a run away, or bin took by gipsies, and it said he had a green-hefted knife wi' him, and that his buttons were o' cut jet. Sa that is a' I hev to say consarnin' ald Dame Crowl, o' Applewale House.'

THE BULLY OF CHAPELIZOD

About thirty years ago there lived in the town of Chapelizod an ill-conditioned fellow of herculean strength, well
known throughout the neighbourhood by the title of Bully
Larkin. In addition to his remarkable physical superiority,
this fellow had acquired a degree of skill as a pugilist
which alone would have made him formidable. As it was,
he was the autocrat of the village, and carried not the
sceptre in vain. Conscious of his superiority, and perfectly
secure of impunity, he lorded it over his fellows in a spirit
of cowardly and brutal insolence, which made him hated
even more profoundly than he was feared.

Upon more than one occasion he had deliberately forced
quarrels upon men whom he had singled out for the
exhibition of his savage prowess; and in every encounter
his overmatched antagonist had received an amount of
'punishment' which edified and appalled the spectators,
and in some instances left ineffaceable scars and lasting
injuries after it.

Bully Larkin's pluck had never been fairly tried. For,
owing to his prodigious superiority in weight, strength, and
skill, his victories had always been certain and easy; and in
proportion to the facility with which he uniformly smashed
an antagonist, his pugnacity and insolence were inflamed.
He thus became an odious nuisance in the neighbourhood,
and the terror of every mother who had a son, and of every
wife who had a husband who possessed a spirit to resent
insult, or the smallest confidence in his own pugilistic
capabilities.

Now it happened that there was a young fellow named Ned Moran – better known by the soubriquet of 'Long Ned', from his slender, lathy proportions – at that time living in the town. He was, in truth, a mere lad, nineteen years of age, and fully twelve years younger than the stalwart bully. This, however, as the reader will see, secured for him no exemption from the dastardly provocations of the ill-conditioned pugilist. Long Ned, in an evil hour, had thrown eyes of affection upon a certain buxom damsel, who, notwithstanding Bully Larkin's amorous rivalry, inclined to reciprocate them.

I need not say how easily the spark of jealousy, once kindled, is blown into a flame, and how naturally, in a coarse and ungoverned nature, it explodes in acts of violence and outrage.

'The bully' watched his opportunity, and contrived to provoke Ned Moran, while drinking in a public-house with a party of friends, into an altercation, in the course of which he failed not to put such insults upon his rival as manhood could not tolerate. Long Ned, though a simple, good-natured sort of fellow, was by no means deficient in spirit, and retorted in a tone of defiance which edified the more timid, and gave his opponent the opportunity he secretly coveted.

Bully Larkin challenged the heroic youth, whose pretty face he had privately consigned to the mangling and bloody discipline he was himself so capable of administering. The quarrel, which he had himself contrived to get up, to a certain degree covered the ill blood and malignant premeditation which inspired his proceedings, and Long Ned, being full of generous ire and whisky punch, accepted the gauge of battle on the instant. The whole party, accompanied by a mob of idle men and boys, and in short by all who could snatch a moment from the call of business, proceeded in slow procession through the old gate into the Phoenix Park, and mounting the hill overlooking the town, selected near its summit a level spot on which to decide the quarrel.

The combatants stripped, and a child might have seen in the contrast presented by the slight, lank form and limbs of the lad, and the muscular and massive build of his veteran antagonist, how desperate was the chance of poor Ned Moran.

'Seconds' and 'bottle-holders' – selected of course for their love of the game – were appointed, and 'the fight' commenced.

I will not shock my readers with a description of the cool-blooded butchery that followed. The result of the combat was what anybody might have predicted. At the eleventh round, poor Ned refused to 'give in'; the brawny pugilist, unhurt, in good wind, and pale with concentrated and as yet unslaked revenge, had the gratification of seeing his opponent seated upon his second's knee, unable to hold his head, his left arm disabled; his face a bloody, swollen, and shapeless mass; his breast scarred and bloody, and his whole body panting and quivering with rage and exhaustion.

'Give in, Ned, my boy,' cried more than one of the bystanders.

'Never, never,' shrieked he, with a voice hoarse and choking.

Time being 'up', his second placed him on his feet again. Blinded with his own blood, panting and staggering, he presented but a helpless mark for the blows of his stalwart opponent. It was plain that a touch would have been sufficient to throw him to the earth. But Larkin had no notion of letting him off so easily. He closed with him without striking a blow (the effect of which, prematurely dealt, would have been to bring him at once to the ground, and so put an end to the combat), and getting his battered and almost senseless head under his arm, fast in that peculiar 'fix' known to the fancy pleasantly by the name of 'chancery', he held him firmly, while with monotonous and brutal strokes he beat his fist, as it seemed, almost into his face. A cry of 'shame' broke from the crowd, for it was plain that the beaten man was now insensible, and supported only by the herculean arm of the bully. The round and the fight ended by his hurling him upon the ground, falling upon him at the same time with his knee upon his chest.

The bully rose, wiping the perspiration from his white face with his blood-stained hands, but Ned lay stretched and motionless upon the grass. It was impossible to get him upon his legs for another round. So he was carried down, just as he was, to the pond which then lay close to the old Park gate, and his head and body were washed beside it. Contrary to the belief of all he was not dead. He was carried home, and after some months to a certain extent recovered. But he never held up his head again, and before the year was over he had died of consumption. Nobody could doubt how the disease had been induced, but there was no actual proof to connect the cause and effect, and the ruffian Larkin escaped the vengeance of the law. A strange retribution, however, awaited him.

After the death of Long Ned, he became less quarrelsome than before, but more sullen and reserved. Some said 'he took it to heart', and others, that his conscience was not at ease about it. Be this as it may, however, his health did not suffer by reason of his presumed agitation, nor was his worldy prosperity marred by the blasting curses with which poor Moran's enraged mother pursued him, on the contrary, he had rather risen in the world, and obtained regular and well-remunerated employment from the Chief Secretary's gardener, at the other side of the Park. He still lived in Chapelizod, whither, on the close of his day's work, he used to return across the Fifteen Acres.

It was about three years after the catastrophe we have mentioned, and late in the autumn, when, one night, contrary to his habit, he did not appear at the house where he lodged, neither had he been seen anywhere, during the evening, in the village. His hours of return had been so very regular, that his absence excited considerable surprise, though, of course, no actual alarm, and, at the usual hour, the house was closed for the night, and the absent lodger consigned to the mercy of the elements, and the care of his presiding star. Early in the morning, however, he was found lying in a state of utter helplessness upon the slope immediately overlooking the Chapelizod gate. He had been smitten with a paralytic stroke : his right side was dead; and it was many weeks before he had recovered his speech sufficiently to make himself at all understood.

He then made the following relation : he had been detained, it appeared, later than usual, and darkness had closed before he commenced his homeward walk across the Park. It was a moonlit night, but masses of ragged clouds were slowly drifting across the heavens. He had not encountered a human figure, and no sounds but the softened rush of the wind sweeping through bushes and hollows met his ear. These wild and monotonous sounds, and the utter solitude which surrounded him, did not, however, excite any of those uneasy sensations which are ascribed to superstition, although he said he did feel depressed, or, in his own phraseology, 'lonesome'. Just as he crossed the brow of the hill which shelters the town of Chapelizod, the moon shone out for some moments with unclouded lustre, and his eye, which happened to wander by the shadowy enclosure which lay at the foot of the slope, was arrested by the sight of a human figure climbing, with all the haste of one pursued, over the churchyard wall, and running up the steep ascent directly towards him. Stories of 'resurrectionists' crossed his recollection, as he observed this suspicious-looking figure. But he began, momentarily, to be aware with a sort of fearful instinct which he could not explain, that the running figure was directing his steps, with a sinister purpose, towards himself.

The form was that of a man with a loose coat about him, which, as he ran, he disengaged, and as well as Larkin could see, for the moon was again wading in clouds, threw from him. The figure thus advanced until within some two score yards of him, it arrested its speed, and approached with a loose, swaggering gait. The moon again shone out bright and clear, and, gracious God! what was the spectacle before him? He saw as distinctly as if he had been presented there in the flesh, Ned Moran, himself, stripped naked from the waist upward, as if for pugilistic combat, and drawing towards him in silence. Larkin would have shouted, prayed, cursed, fled across the Park, but he was absolutely powerless; the apparition stopped within a few steps, and leered on him with a ghastly mimicry of the defiant stare with which pugilists strive to cow one another before combat. For a time, which he could not so much as conjecture, he was held in the fascination of that unearthly gaze, and at last the thing, whatever it was, on a sudden swaggered close up to him with extended palms. With an impulse of horror, Larkin put out his hand to keep the figure off, and their palms touched – at least, so he believed – for a thrill of unspeakable agony, running through his arm, pervaded his entire frame, and he fell senseless to the earth.

Though Larkin lived for many years after, his punishment was terrible. He was incurably maimed; and being unable to work, he was forced, for existence, to beg alms of those who had once feared and flattered him. He suffered, too, increasingly, under his own horrible interpretation of the preternatural encounter which was the beginning of all his miseries. It was vain to endeavour to shake his faith in the reality of the apparition, and equally vain, as some compassionately did, to try to persuade him that the greeting with which his vision closed was intended, while inflicting a temporary trial, to signify a compensating reconciliation.

'No, no,' he used to say, 'all won't do. I know the meaning of it well enough; it is a challenge to meet him in the other world – in Hell, where I am going – that's what it means, and nothing else.'

And so, miserable and refusing comfort, he lived on for some years, and then died, and was buried in the same narrow churchyard which contains the remains of his victim.

I need hardly say, how absolute was the faith of the honest inhabitants, at the time when I heard the story, in the reality of the preternatural summons which, through the portals of terror, sickness and misery, had summoned Bully Larkin to his long, last home, and that, too, upon the very ground on which he had signalized the guiltiest triumph of his violent and vindictive career.

BORRHOMEO THE ASTROLOGER

At the period of the famous plague of Milan in 1630, a frenzy of superstition seized upon the population high and low. Old prophecies of a diabolical visitation reserved for their city, in that particular year of grace, prepared the way for this wild panic of the imagination. When the plague broke out, terror seems to have acted to a degree scarcely paralleled upon the fancy or the credulity of the people. Excitement in very many cases produced absolutely the hallucinations of madness. Persons deposed, in the most solemn and consistent terms, to having themselves witnessed diabolical processions, spoken with an awful impersonation of Satan, and been solicited amidst scenes and personages altogether supernatural, to lend their human agency to the nefarious designs of the fiend, by consenting to disseminate by certain prescribed means, the virus of the pestilence.

Some of the stories related of persons possessed by these awful fancies are in print; and by no means destitute of a certain original and romantic horror. That which I am about to tell, however, has, I believe, never been printed. At all events I saw it only in MSS., sewed up in vellum, with a psaltery and half-a-dozen lives of saints, in the library of the old Dominican monastery which stands about two leagues to the north-east of the city. With your permission I am about to give you the best translation I was able to make of this short but odd story, of the truth of which, judging from the company in which I found it, the honest monks entertained no sort of doubt. You are to remember that all sorts of tales of wonder were at that time flying about and believed in Milan, and that many of these were authenticated in such a way as to leave no doubt as to the *bona fides* of those who believed themselves to have been eye-witnesses of what they told. Monks and country padres of course believed; but so did men who stood highest in the church, and who, unless fame belied them, believed little else.

In the year of our Lord, 1630, when Satan, by divine permission, appearing among us in person, afflicted our beautiful city of Milan with a pestilence unheard of in its severity, there lived in the *Strada Piana*, which has lately been pulled down, an astrologer calling himself Borrhomeo. Some say he came from Perrugia, others from Venice; I know not. He it was who first predicted, in the year of our Lord, 1628, by means of his art, that the pale comet which then appeared would speedily be followed, not by war or by famine, but by pestilence; which accordingly came to pass. Beside his skill in astrology, which was wonderful, he was profoundly versed in alchymy. He was a man great in stature, and strong, though old in years, and with a most reverent beard. But though seemingly austere in his life, it is said that he was given up, in secret, to enormous wickedness.

Having shut himself up in his house for more than a month, with his furnace and crucibles (truly he had made repeated and near approaches to the grand arcanum) he had arrived, as he supposed, at the moment of projection.

He collects the powder and tries it on molten lead; it was a failure. He was too wise to be angry; the long pursuit of his art had taught him patience. But while he is pondering in a profound and gloomy reverie, a retort, which he had forgotten in the furnace, explodes.

He sees in the smoke a pale young man, dressed in mourning, with black hair, and viewing him with a sad and reproachful countenance.

Borrhomeo, who lived among chimæras, is not utterly overcome, as another man might be, and confronts him, amazed, indeed, but not terrified.

The stranger shook his head like a holy young confessor, who hears an evil shrift; and says he, rather sternly – 'Borrhomeo! Beware of covetousness which is idolatry. On this sordid pursuit which you call a science, have you wasted your days on earth and your peace hereafter.'

'Young man,' says the alchymist, too much struck by the manner and reproof of the stranger to ask himself how he came there – 'Wealth is power to do good as well as evil. To seek it is, therefore, an ambition as honourable as any other.'

'We both know why you seek it, and how you would employ it,' answers the young man gravely.

The old man's face flushed with anger at this rebuke, and he looked down frowningly to the table whereon lay the book of his spells. But he bethought him this must be a good spirit, and he was abashed. Nevertheless, he roused his courage, and shook his white mane back, and was on the point of answering sternly, when the young man said with a melancholy smile –

'Besides, you will never discover the grand arcanum – the *elixir vitæ*, or the philosopher's stone.'

His words, which were as soft as snow flakes, fell like an iron mace upon the heart of the seer.

'Perhaps not,' said the astrologer frigidly.

'Not perhaps,' said the stranger.

'At all events, young man – for as such you appear – and I know what spirits seek who take that shape, the science has its charms for me; and when the pleasures of the young are as harmless as the amusements of the aged I'll hear you question mine.'

'You know not what spirit you are of. As for me, I am contrite and humble – well I may,' says the stranger faintly with a sigh. 'Besides, what you have pursued in vain, and will never by your own researches find, I have discovered.'

'What! the—'

'Yes, the tincture that can prolong life to virtual immortality, and the dust that can change that lead into gold; but I care for neither.'

'Why, young man, if this be true,' says Borrhomeo in a rapture of wonder, 'you stand before me an angel of wisdom, in power and immortality like a god!'

'No,' says the stranger, 'a long-lived fellow, with a long purse – that's all.'

'All? Everything?' cries the old man. 'Will you, will you—'

'Yes, sir, you shall see,' says the young man in black. 'Give me that crucible. It is all a matter of proportions. Water, clay, and air are the material of all the vegetable world – the flowers and forests, the wines and the fruits – the seed is both the laboratory and the chemist, and knows how, with the sun's help, to apportion and combine.'

While he said this with the abstracted manner of one whose mind is mazed in a double reverie while his hands work out some familiar problem, he tumbled over the alchymist's papers, and unstopped and stopped his bottles of crystals, precipitates, and elixirs, taking a little from this and a little from that, and throwing all into a small gold cup that stood on the table, but like a juggler, he moved those bottles so deftly that the quick eyes and retentive soul of the old man vainly sought to catch or keep the order of the process. When he had done there was hardly a thimbleful.

'Is that it?' whispered the old man, twinkling with greedy eyes.

'No,' said the stranger, with a sly smile, 'there is one very simple ingredient which you have forgotten.'

He took a large, flat, oval gold box, with some hair set under a crystal in the lid of it, and looking at it for a moment, he seemed to sigh. He tapped it like a snuff box – there was within it a powder like vermilion, and on the inside of the lid, in the centre, was the small enamel portrait of a beautiful but sinister female face. The features were so very beautiful, and the expression so strangely blended with horror, that it fixed the gaze of the old man for a moment; and – was it illusion? – he thought he saw the face steadily dilating as if it would gradually fill the lid of the box, and even expand to human dimensions.

'Yes,' said the stranger as, having taken some of the red powder, he shut the cover down again with a snap, 'she was beautiful, and her lineaments are still clear and bright – nothing like darkness to keep them from fading, and so the poor little miniature is again in prison;' and he dropped the box back into his pocket.

Then he took two iron ladles, and heating in the one his powder to a white heat, and bidding the alchymist melt a pellet of lead in the other, and pour it into the ladle which held the powder, there arose a beautiful purple fire in the bottom of it, with an intense fringe of green and yellow; and when it subsided there was a little nut of gold there of the bigness of the leaden pellet.

The fiery eyes of the alchymist almost leaped from their sockets into the iron cup, and he could have clasped his marvellous visitor round the knees and worshipped him.

'And now,' says the stranger very gently and earnestly, 'in return for satisfying your curiosity, I ask only your solemn promise to prosecute this dread science no more. Ha! you'll not give it. Take, then, my warning, and remember the wages of this knowledge is sorrow.'

'But won't you tell me how to commute – and – and – you have not produced the elixir,' the old man cried.

''Tis folly – and, as I've told you, worse – a snare,' answered the young man, sighing heavily. 'I came not to satisfy but to rebuke your dangerous though fruitless frenzy. Besides, I hear my friend still pacing the street. Hark! he taps at the window.'

Then came a sharp rattle as of a cane tapping angrily on the window.

The young man bowed, smiling sadly, and somehow got himself away, though without hurry, yet so quickly that the old man could not reach the door till after it had closed and he was gone.

'Oaf that I am!' cried the astrologer, losing patience and stamping on the ground. 'How have I let him go? He hesitated – he would have yielded – his scruples, benevolent perhaps, I could have quieted – and yet in the very crisis I was tongue-tied and motionless, and let him go!'

He pushed open the little window, from which he observed the street, and thought he saw the stranger walking round the corner, conversing with a little hunchback in a red cloak, and followed by an ugly dog.

At sight of the great white head and beard, and the fierce features of the alchymist, bleared and tanned in the smoke of his furnace, people stopped and looked. So he withdrew, and in haste got him ready for the street, waiting for no refreshment, though he had fasted long; for he had the strength as well as the stature of a giant, and forth he went.

By this time the twilight had passed into night. He had his mantle about him, and his rapier and dagger – for the streets were dangerous – and a feather in his cap, and his white beard hidden behind the fold of his cloak. So he might have passed for a tall soldier of the guard.

The pestilence kept people much within doors, and the streets more solitary than was customary. He had walked through the town two hours and more, before he met with anything to speak of. Then – lo! – on a sudden, near the Fountain of the Lion – it being then moonlight – he discovers, in a solitude, the figure of his visitor, standing with the hunchback and the dog, which he knew by its ungainly bones, and its carrying its huge head so near the ground.

So he shouts along the silent street, 'Stay a moment, *signor*,' and he mends his pace.

But they were parting company there, it seemed, and away went the deformed, with his unsightly beast at his heels, and this way came the youth in black.

So standing full in his way, and doffing his cap, and throwing back his cloak, that his snowy beard and head might appear, and the stranger recognize him when he drew nigh, he cried, 'Borrhomeo implores thee to take pity on his ignorance.'

'What! still mad?' said the young man. 'This man will waste the small remnant of his years in godless search after gold and immortality; better he should know all, and feel their vanity.'

'Better a thousand times!' cried the old man, in ecstasy.

'There is in this city, *signor*, at this time, in great secrecy, the master who taught me,' says the youth, 'the master of all alchymists. Many centuries since he found out the *elixir vitæ*. From him I've learned the few secrets that I know, and without his leave I dare not impart them. If you desire it, I will bring you before him; but, once in his presence, you cannot recede, and his conditions you must accept.'

'All, all, with my whole heart. But some reasonable pleasures—'

'With your pleasures he will not interfere; he cannot change your heart,' said the young man, with one of his heavy sighs; 'but you know what gold is, and what the elixir is, and power and immortality are not to be had for nothing.'

'Lead on, *signor*, I'm ready,' cries the old man, whose face flushed, and his eyes burned with the fires of an evil rapture.

'Take my hand,' said the young man, more stern and pale than he had yet appeared. So he did, and his conductor seized it with a cold grip, and they walked swiftly on.

Now he led him through several streets, and on their way Borrhomeo passes his notary, and, lingering a moment, asks him whether he has a bond, signed by a certain merchant, with whom he had contracted for a loan. The notary, who was talking to another, says, suddenly, to that other:

'Per Baccho! I've just called to mind a matter that must be looked after for Signor Borrhomeo;' and he called him a nickname, which incensed the astrologer, who struck him a lusty box upon the ear.

'There's a humming in my ear tonight,' said the notary, going into his house; 'I hope it is no sign of the plague.'

So on they walked, side by side, till they reached the shop of a vintner of no good repute. It was well known to Borrhomeo – a house of evil resort, where the philosopher sometimes stole, disguised, by night, to be no longer a necromancer, but a man, and, so, from a man to become a beast.

They passed through the shop. The host, with a fat pale face, and a villainous smile, was drawing wine, which a handsome damsel was waiting to take away with her. He kissed her as she paid, and she gave him a cuff on his fat white chops, and laughed.

'What's become of Signor Borrhomeo,' said the girl, 'that he never comes here now?'

'Why, here he is!' cries Borrhomeo, with a saturnine smile, and he slaps his broad palm on her shoulder.

But the girl only shrugged, with a little shiver, and said, 'What a chill down my back – they're walking over my grave now.' [The Italian phrase here is very nearly equivalent.]

'Why they neither hear nor see me!' said the astrologer, amazed.

They went into the inner room, where guests used to sit and drink. But the plague had stopped all that, and the room was empty.

'He's in there,' said the young man; 'you'll see him presently.'

Borrhomeo was filled with an awful curiosity. He knew the room, he thought, well; and there never had been, he thought, a door where the young man had pointed; but there was now a drapery there like what covers a doorway, and it swelled and swayed slowly in the wind.

'Some centuries?' said the astrologer, looking on the dark drapery. 'Geber, perhaps, or Alfarabi . . .'

'It matters not a pin's point what his name is; you'll call him "my lord", simply; and – observe – we alchymists are a potent order, and it behoves you to keep your word with us.'

'I will be true,' said Borrhomeo.

'And use the powers you gain, beneficently,' repeated his guide.

'I'm but a sinner. I will strive, with only an exception, in favour of such things as make wealth and life worth having,' answered the philosopher.

'See, take this, and do as I bid you,' said the youth, giving him a thin round film of human skin.

[How the honest monk who wrote the tale, or even Borrhomeo himself, knew this and many other matters he describes, 'tis for him to say.]

'Breathe on it,' said he.

And when he did so he made him stretch it to the size of a sheet of paper, which he did quite easily.

'Now cover your face with it as with a napkin.'

So he did.

''Twill do; give it to me. It is but a picture. See.'

And it slowly shrank until its disc was just the same as that of the lady's miniature in the lid of the box over which he fixed it.

Borrhomeo beheld his own picture.

'Every adept has his portrait here,' said the young man. 'So good a likeness is always pleasant; but these have a power beside, and establish a sympathy between their originals and their possessor which secures discipline and silence.'

'How does it work?' asked Borrhomeo.

'Have I not been your good angel?' said the young man, sitting before him. He extends his legs – pushing out his feet, and letting his chin sink on his chest – he fixes his eyes upon him with a horrible and sarcastic glare, and one of his feet contracts and divides into a goatish stump.

Borrhomeo would have burst into a yell, but he could not.

'It is a nightmare, is it not?' said the stranger, who seemed delighted to hold him, minute after minute, in that spell. At last the shoe and hose that seemed to have shrunk apart like burning parchment, closed over the goatish shin and hoof; and rising, he shook him by the shoulder. With a gasp, the astrologer started to his feet.

'There, I told you it was a nightmare, or – or what you please. I could not have done it but through the picture. You see how fast we have you. You must for once resemble a Christian, Borrhomeo, and with us deal truly and honestly.'

'You've promised me the *elixir vitæ*,' the old man said, fearful lest the secret should escape him.

'And you shall have it. Go, bring a cup of wine. He'll not see you, nor the wine, nor the cup.'

So he brought a cup of Falernian, which he loved the best.

'There's fifty years of life for every drop,' said the youth.

'Let me live a thousand years, to begin with,' cries Borrhomeo.

'Beware. You'll tire of it!'

'Nay. Give me the twenty drops.'

So he took the cup, and measured the drops; and as they fell, the wine was agitated with a gentle simmer all over, and threw out ring after ring of purple, green, and gold. And Borrhomeo drank it, and sucked in the last drop in ecstasy, and cried out, blaspheming, with joy and sensual delight: 'And I'm to have this secret, too.'

'This and all others when you claim them,' said the young man. 'See, 'tis time,' he added.

And Borrhomeo saw that the great misshapen dog he had seen in the street, was sniffing by the stranger's feet.

When they went into the inner room there was a large table, and many men at either side; and at the head a gigantic man, with a face like the face of a beast, but the flesh was as of a man. Borrhomeo quaked in his presence.

'I am aware of what hath passed, Borrhomeo,' he said. 'The condition is this: You take this vial, and with the fluid it contains and the sponge trace the letter S on every door of every church and religious house within the walls of Milan. The dog will go with you.'

It was a fiend in dog's shape, says the monkish writer; and had Borrhomeo failed in his task would have torn him in pieces.

So Borrhomeo, that old arch villain, undertook this office cheerfully, well knowing what its purpose was. For it was a thing notorious, that Satan was himself in a bodily, though phantasmal, shape seen before in Milan, and that he had tempted others to a like fascinorous action; but, happily for their souls, in vain. The Stygian satellites of the fiend had power to smear the door of every unconsecrated house in Milan with that pestilential virus, as, indeed, the citizens with their own eyes, when first the plague broke out, beheld upon their own doors. But they could not defile the church gates, nor the doors of the monasteries; and according to the conditions under which their infernal malice is bound, they could in nowise effect it save by the hand of one who was baptized, which, to the baleful abuse of that holy sacrament, the wretch, Borrhomeo, had been.

He did his accursed and murderous office well and fearlessly. His reward: mammon and indefinite long life. The hell-dog by his side compelling him, and the belief in his invisibility making him confident withal. But therein was shown forth to all the world the craft of the fiend, and the just judgment of heaven; for he was plainly seen in the very act by the Sexton of the Church of St Mary of the Passion, and by the Pastor of the convent of St Justina of Padua, and the same officer of the Olivetans of St Victor. So, finding in the morning the only too plain and fatal traces of what he had been doing, with a mob at their heels, who would have had his life but for the guard, they arrested him in his house next morning, and the mob breaking in, smashed all the instruments of his infernal art, and would have burnt the house had they been allowed.

He being duly arraigned was, according to law, put to the torture, and forthwith confessed all the particulars I have related. So he was cast into a dungeon to await execution, which secretly he dreaded not, being confident in the efficacy of the elixir he had swallowed.

He was not to be put to death by decapitation. It was justly thought too honourable for so sordid a miscreant. He was sentenced to be hanged, and after hanging a day and a night he was to be laid in an open grave outside the gate on the Roman road, and there impaled, and after three days' exposure to be covered in, and so committed to the keeping of the earth, no more to groan under his living enormities.

The night before his execution, thinking deeply on the virtue of the elixir, and having assured himself, by many notable instances, which he easily brought to remembrance, that they could not deprive him, even by this severity, of his life, he lifted up his eyes and beheld the young man, in mourning suit, whose visit had been his ruin, standing near him in the cell.

This slave of Satan affected a sad countenance at first; and said he, 'We are cast down, Borrhomeo, by reason of thy sentence.'

'But we've cheated them,' answers he, pretending, maybe, more confidence than he had; 'they can't kill me.'

'That's certain,' rejoins the fiend.

'I shall live for a thousand years,' says he.

'Ay, you must continue to live for full one thousand years; 'tis a fair term – is it not?'

'A great deal may be done in that time,' says the old man, while beads of perspiration covered his puckered forehead, and he thought that, perhaps, he might cheat *him* too, and make his peace with heaven. 'They can't hang me,' says Borrhomeo.

'Oh! yes, they will certainly hang you; but, then, you'll live through it.'

'Ay, the elixir,' cried the prisoner.

'Thus stands the case: when an ordinary man is hanged he dies outright; but you can't die.'

'No – ha, ha! – I can't die!'

'Therefore, when you are hanged, you feel, think, hear, and soforth during the process.'

'St Anthony! But then 'tis only an hour – one hour of agony – and it ends.'

'You are to hang for a whole day and night,' continued the fiend, 'but that don't signify. Then when they take you down, you continue to feel, hear, think, and, if they leave your eyes open, to see, just as usual.'

'Why, yes, certainly, I'm alive,' cries Borrhomeo.

'Yes, alive, quite alive, although you appear to be dead,' says the dæmon with a smile.

'Ay; but what's the best moment to make my escape?' says Borrhomeo.

'Escape! why, you *have* escaped. They can't kill you. No one can kill you, until your time is out. Then you know they lay you in an open grave and impale you.'

'What! ah, ha!' roared the old sinner, 'you are jesting.'

'Hush! depend upon it they will go through with it.'

The old man shook in every joint.

'Then, after three days and nights, they bury you,' said his visitor.

'I'll lose my life, or I'll break from them!' shouts the gigantic astrologer.

'But you can't lose your life, and you can't break from them,' says the fiend, softly.

'Why not? Oh! blessed saints! I'm stronger than you think.'

'Ay, muscle, bones – you are an old giant!'

'Surely,' cries the old man, 'and the terror of a dead man rising; ha! don't you see? They fly before me, and so I escape.'

'But you can't rise.'

'Say – say in heaven's name what you mean,' thundered old Borrhomeo.

'Do you remember, *signor*, that nightmare, as we jocularly called it, at the sign of the "Red Hat"?'

'Yes.'

'Well, a man who, having swallowed the *elixir vitæ*, suffers that sort of shock which in other mortals is a violent death, is afflicted during the remainder of his period of life, whether he be decapitated, or dismembered, or is laid unmutilated in the grave, with that sort of catalepsy, which you experienced for a minute – a catalepsy that does not relax or intermit. For that reason you ought to have carefully avoided this predicament.'

''Tis a lie,' roared the old man, and he ground his teeth. '*That's* not living.'

'You'll find, upon my honour, that it *is* living,' answered the fiend, with a gentle smile, and withdrawing from the cell.

Borrhomeo told all this to a priest, not under seal of confession, but to induce him to plead for his life. But the good man, seeing he had already made himself the liegeman and accomplice of Satan, refused. Nor would his intercession have prevailed in any wise.

So Borrhomeo was hanged, impaled, and buried, according to his sentence; and it came to pass that fourteen years afterwards, that grave was opened in making a great drain from the group of houses thereby, and Borrhomeo was found just as he was laid therein, in no wise decayed, but fresh and sound, which, indeed, showed that there did remain in him that sort of life which was supposed to ward off the common consequences of death.

So he was thrown into a great pit and, with many curses,

covered in with stones and earth, where his stupendous punishment proceeds.

Get thee hence, Satan.

Authentic Narrative of a Haunted House

Within the last eight years – the precise date I purposely omit. – I was ordered by my physician, my health being in an unsatisfactory state, to change my residence to one upon the sea-coast; and accordingly, I took a house for a year in a fashionable watering-place, at a moderate distance from the city in which I had previously resided, and connected with it by a railway.

Winter was setting in when my removal thither was decided upon; but there was nothing whatever dismal or depressing in the change. The house I had taken was to all appearance, and in point of convenience, too, quite a modern one. It formed one in a cheerful row, with small gardens in front, facing the sea, and commanding sea air and sea views in perfection. In the rear it had coach-house and stable, and between them and the house a considerable grass-plot, with some flower-beds, interposed.

Our family consisted of my wife and myself, with three children, the eldest about nine years old, she and the next in age being girls; and the youngest, between six and seven, a boy. To these were added six servants, whom, although for certain reasons I decline giving their real names, I shall indicate, for the sake of clearness, by arbitrary ones. There was a nurse, Mrs. Southerland; a nursery-maid, Ellen Page; the cook, Mrs. Greenwood; and the housemaid, Ellen Faith; a butler, whom I shall call Smith, and his son, James, about two-and-twenty.

We came out to take possession at about seven o'clock in the evening; every thing was comfortable and cheery; good fires lighted, the rooms neat and airy, and a general air of preparation and comfort, highly conducive to good spirits and pleasant anticipations.

The sitting-rooms were large and cheerful, and they and the bed-rooms more than ordinarily lofty, the kitchen and servants' rooms, on the same level, were well and comfortably furnished, and had, like the rest of the house, an air of recent painting and fitting up, and a completely modern character, which imparted a very cheerful air of cleanliness and convenience.

There had been just enough of the fuss of settling agreeably to occupy us, and to give a pleasant turn to our thoughts after we had retired to our rooms. Being an invalid, I had a small bed to myself – resigning the four-poster to my wife. The candle was extinguished, but a night-light was burning. I was coming up stairs, and she, already in bed, had just dismissed her maid, when we were both startled by a wild scream from her room; I found her in a state of the extremest agitation and terror. She insisted that she had seen an unnaturally tall figure come beside her bed and stand there. The light was too faint to enable her to define any thing respecting this apparition, beyond the fact of her having most distinctly seen such a shape, colourless from the insufficiency of the light to disclose more than its dark outline.

We both endeavoured to re-assure her. The room once more looked so cheerful in the candlelight, that we were quite uninfluenced by the contagion of her terrors. The movements and voices of the servants down stairs still getting things into their places and completing our comfortable arrangements, had also their effect in steeling us against any such influence, and we set the whole thing down as a dream, or an imperfectly-seen outline of the bed-curtains. When, however, we were alone, my wife reiterated, still in great agitation, her clear assertion that she had most positively seen, being at the time as completely awake as ever she was, precisely what she had described to us. And in this conviction she continued perfectly firm.

A day or two after this, it came out that our servants were under an apprehension that, somehow or other, thieves had established a secret mode of access to the lower part of the house. The butler, Smith, had seen an ill-looking woman in his room on the first night of our arrival; and he and other servants constantly saw, for many days subsequently, glimpses of a retreating figure, which corresponded with that so seen by him, passing through a passage which led to a back area in which were some coal-vaults.

This figure was seen always in the act of retreating, its back turned, generally getting round the corner of the passage into the area, in a stealthy and hurried way, and, when closely followed, imperfectly seen again entering one of the coal-vaults, and when pursued into it, nowhere to be found.

The idea of any thing supernatural in the matter had, strange to say, not yet entered the mind of any one of the servants. They had heard some stories of smugglers having secret passages into houses, and using their means of access for purposes of pillage, or with a view to frighten superstitious people out of houses which they needed for their own objects, and a suspicion of similar practices here, caused them extreme uneasiness. The apparent anxiety also manifested by this retreating figure to escape observation, and her always appearing to make her egress at the same point, favoured this romantic hypothesis. The men, however, made a most careful examination of the back area, and of the coal-vaults, with a view to discover some mode of egress, but entirely without success. On the contrary, the result was, so far as it went, subversive of the theory; solid masonry met them on every hand.

I called the man, Smith, up, to hear from his own lips the particulars of what he had seen; and certainly his report was very curious. I give it as literally as my memory enables me:—

His son slept in the same room, and was sound asleep; but he lay awake, as men sometimes will on a change of bed, and having many things on his mind. He was lying with his face towards the wall, but observing a light and some little stir in the room, he turned round in his bed, and saw the figure of a woman, squalid, and ragged in dress; her figure rather low and broad; as well as I recollect, she had something – either a cloak or shawl – on, and wore a bonnet. Her back was turned, and she appeared to be searching or rummaging for something on the floor, and, without appearing to observe him, she turned in doing so towards him. The light, which was more like the intense glow of a coal, as he described it, being of a deep red colour, proceeded from the hollow of her hand, which she held beside her head, and he saw her perfectly distinctly. She appeared middle-aged, was deeply pitted with the smallpox, and blind of one eye. His phrase in describing her general appearance was, that she was "a miserable, poor-looking creature".

He was under the impression that she must be the woman who had been left by the proprietor in charge of the house, and who had that evening, after having given up the keys, remained for some little time with the female servants. He coughed, therefore, to apprize her of his presence, and turned again towards the wall. When he again looked round she and the light were gone; and odd as was her method of lighting herself in her search, the circumstances excited neither uneasiness nor curiosity in his mind, until he discovered next morning that the woman in question had left the house long before he had gone to his bed.

I examined the man very closely as to the appearance of the person who had visited him, and the result was what I have described. It struck me as an odd thing, that even then, considering how prone to superstition persons in his rank of life usually are, he did not seem to suspect any thing supernatural in the occurrence; and, on the contrary, was thoroughly persuaded that his visitant was a living person, who had got into the house by some hidden entrance.

On Sunday, on his return from his place of worship, he told me that, when the service was ended, and the congregation making their way slowly out, he saw the very woman in the crowd, and kept his eye upon her for several minutes, but such was the crush, that all his efforts to reach her were unavailing, and when he got into the open street she was gone. He was quite positive as to his having distinctly seen her, however, for several minutes, and scouted the possibility of any mistake as to identity; and fully impressed with the substantial and living reality of his visitant, he was very much provoked at her having escaped him. He made inquiries also in the neighbourhood, but could procure no information, nor hear of any other persons having seen any woman corresponding with his visitant.

The cook and the housemaid occupied a bedroom on the kitchen floor. It had whitewashed walls, and they were actually terrified by the appearance of the shadow of a woman passing and repassing across the side wall opposite to their beds. They suspected that this had been going on much longer than they were aware, for its presence was discovered by a sort of accident, its movements happening to take a direction in distinct contrariety to theirs.

This shadow always moved upon one particular wall, returning after short intervals, and causing them extreme terror. They placed the candle, as the most obvious specific, so close to the infested wall, that the flame all but touched it; and believed for some time that they had effectually got rid of this annoyance; but one night, notwithstanding this arrangement of the light, the shadow returned, passing and repassing, as heretofore, upon the same wall, although their only candle was burning within an inch of it, and it was obvious that no substance capable of casting such a shadow could have interposed; and, indeed, as they described it, light, and appeared, as I have said, in manifest defiance of the laws of optics.

I ought to mention that the housemaid was a particularly fearless sort of person, as well as a very honest one; and her companion, the cook, a scrupulously religious woman, and both agreed in every particular in their relation of what occurred.

Meanwhile, the nursery was not without its annoyances, though as yet of a comparatively trivial kind. Sometimes, at night, the handle of the door was turned hurriedly as if by a person trying to come in, and at others a knocking was made at it. These sounds occurred after the children had settled to sleep, and while the nurse still remained awake. Whenever she called to know "who is there," the sounds ceased; but several times, and particularly at first, she was under the impression that they were caused by her mistress, who had come to see the children, and thus impressed she had got up and opened the door, expecting to see her, but discovering only darkness, and receiving no answer to her inquiries.

With respect to this nurse, I must mention that I believe no more perfectly trustworthy servant was ever employed in her capacity; and, in addition to her integrity, she was remarkably gifted with sound common sense.

One morning, I think about three or four weeks after our arrival, I was sitting at the parlour window which looked to the front, when I saw the little iron door which admitted into the small garden that lay between the window where I was sitting and the public road, pushed open by a woman who so exactly answered the description given by Smith of the woman who had visited his room on the night of his arrival as instantaneously to impress me with the conviction that she must be the identical person. She was a square, short woman, dressed in soiled and tattered clothes, scarred and pitted with smallpox, and blind of an eye. She stepped hurriedly into the little enclosure, and peered from a distance of a few yards into the room where I was sitting. I felt that now was the moment to clear the matter up; but there was something stealthy in the manner and look of the woman which convinced me that I must not appear to notice her until her retreat was fairly cut off. Unfortunately, I was suffering from a lame foot, and could not reach the bell as quickly as I wished. I made all the haste I could, and rang violently to bring up the servant Smith. In the short interval that intervened, I observed the woman from the window, who having in a leisurely way, and with a kind of scrutiny, looked along the front windows of the house, passed quickly out again, closing the gate after her, and followed a lady who was walking along the footpath at a quick pace, as if with the intention of begging from her. The moment the man entered I told him – "the blind woman you described to me has this instant followed a lady in that direction, try to overtake her." He was, if possible, more eager than I in the chase, but returned in a short time after a vain pursuit, very hot, and utterly disappointed. And, thereafter, we saw her face no more.

All this time, and up to the period of our leaving the house, which was not for two or three months later, there occurred at intervals the only phenomenon in the entire series having any resemblance to what we hear described of "Spiritualism." This was a knocking, like a soft hammering with a wooden mallet, as it seemed in the timbers between the bedroom ceilings and the roof. It had this special peculiarity, that it was always rythmical, and, I think, invariably, the emphasis upon the last stroke. It would sound rapidly "one, two, three, *four* – one, two, three, *four*;" or "one, two, *three* – one, two, *three*," and sometimes "one, *two* – one, *two*," &c., and this, with intervals and resumptions, monotonously for hours at a time.

At first this caused my wife, who was a good deal confined to her bed, much annoyance; and we sent to our neighbours to inquire if any hammering or carpentering was going on in their houses, but were informed that nothing of the sort was taking place. I have myself heard it frequently, always in the same inaccessible part of the house, and with the same monotonous emphasis. One odd thing about it was, that on my wife's calling out, as she used to do when it became more than usually troublesome, "stop that noise", it was invariably arrested for a longer or shorter time.

Of course none of these occurrences were ever mentioned in hearing of the children. They would have been, no doubt, like most children, greatly terrified had they heard any thing of the matter, and known that their elders were unable to account for what was passing; and their fears would have made them wretched and troublesome.

They used to play for some hours every day in the back garden – the house forming one end of this oblong inclosure, the stable and coach-house the other, and two parallel walls of considerable height the sides. Here, as it afforded a perfectly safe playground, they were frequently left quite to themselves; and in talking over their days' adventures, as children will, they happened to mention a woman, or rather the woman, for they had long grown familiar with her appearance, whom they used to see in the garden while they were at play. They assumed that she came in and went out at the stable door, but they never actually saw her enter or depart. They merely saw a figure – that of a very poor woman, soiled and ragged – near the stable wall, stooping over the ground, and apparently grubbing in the loose clay in search of something. She did not disturb, or appear to observe them; and they left her in undisturbed possession of her nook of ground. When seen it was always in the same spot, and similarly occupied; and the description they gave of her general appearance – for they never saw her face – corresponded with that of the one-eyed woman whom Smith, and subsequently as it seemed, I had seen.

The other man, James, who looked after a mare which I had purchased for the purpose of riding exercise, had, like every one else in the house, his little trouble to report, though it was not much. The stall in which, as the most comfortable, it was decided to place her, she peremptorily declined to enter. Though a very docile and gentle little animal, there was no getting her into it. She would snort and rear, and, in fact, do or suffer any thing rather than set her hoof in it. He was fain, therefore, to place her in another. And on several occasions he found her there, exhibiting all the equine symptoms of extreme fear. Like the rest of us, however, this man was not troubled in the particular case with any superstitious qualms. The mare had evidently been frightened; and he was puzzled to find out how, or by whom, for the stable was well-secured, and had, I am nearly certain, a lock-up yard outside.

One morning I was greeted with the intelligence that robbers had certainly got into the house in the night; and that one of them had actually been seen in the nursery. The witness, I found, was my eldest child, then, as I have said, about nine years of age. Having awoke in the night, and lain awake for some time in her bed, she heard the handle of the door turn, and a person whom she distinctly saw – for it was a light night, and the window-shutters unclosed – but whom she had never seen before, stepped in on tiptoe, and with an appearance of great caution. He was a rather small man, with a very red face; he wore an oddly cut frock coat, the collar of which stood up, and trousers, rough and wide, like those of a sailor, turned up at the ankles, and either short boots or clumsy shoes, covered with mud. This man listened beside the nurse's bed, which stood next the door, as if to satisfy himself that she was sleeping soundly; and having done so for some seconds, he began to move cautiously in a diagonal line, across the room to the chimney-piece, where he stood for a while, and so resumed his tiptoe walk, skirting the wall, until he reached a chest of drawers, some of which were open, and into which he looked, and began to rummage in a hurried way, as the child supposed, making search for something worth taking away. He then passed on to the window, where was a dressing-table, at which he also stopped, turning over the things upon it, and standing for some time at the window as if looking out, and then resuming his walk by the side wall opposite to that by which he had moved up to the window, he returned in the same way toward the nurse's bed, so as to reach it at the foot. With its side to the end wall, in which was the door, was placed the little bed in which lay my eldest child, who watched his proceedings with the extremest terror. As he drew near she instinctively moved herself in the bed, with her head and shoulders to the wall, drawing up her feet; but he passed by without appearing to observe, or, at least, to care for her presence. Immediately after the nurse turned in her bed as if about to waken; and when the child, who had drawn the clothes about her head, again ventured to peep out, the man was gone.

The child had no idea of her having seen any thing more formidable than a thief. With the prowling, cautious, and noiseless manner of proceeding common to such marauders, the air and movements of the man whom she had seen entirely corresponded. And on hearing her perfectly distinct and consistent account, I could myself arrive at no other conclusion than that a stranger had actually got into the house. I had, therefore, in the first instance, a most careful examination made to discover any traces of an entrance having been made by any window into the house. The doors had been found barred and locked as usual; but no sign of any thing of the sort was discernible. I then had the various articles – plate, wearing apparel, books, &c., counted; and after having conned over and reckoned up every thing, it became quite clear that nothing whatever had been removed from the house, nor was there the slightest indication of any thing having been so much as disturbed there. I must here state that this child was remarkably clear, intelligent, and observant; and that her description of the man, and of all that had occurred, was most exact, and as detailed as the want of perfect light rendered possible.

I felt assured that an entrance had actually been effected into the house, though for what purpose was not easily to be conjectured. The man, Smith, was equally confident upon this point; and his theory was that the object was simply to frighten us out of the house by making us believe it haunted; and he was more than ever anxious and on the alert to discover the conspirators. It often since appeared to me odd. Every year, indeed, more odd, as this cumulative case of the marvellous becomes to my mind more and more inexplicable – that underlying my sense of mystery and puzzle, was all along the quiet assumption that all these occurrences were one way or another referable to natural causes. I could not account for them, indeed, myself; but during the whole period I inhabited that house, I never once felt, though much alone, and often up very late at night, any of those tremors and thrills which every one has at times experienced when situation and the hour are favourable. Except the cook and housemaid, who were plagued with the shadow I mentioned crossing and recrossing upon the bedroom wall, we all, without exception, experienced the same strange sense of security, and regarded these phenomena rather with a perplexed sort of interest and curiosity, than with any more unpleasant sensations.

The knockings which I have mentioned at the nursery door, preceded generally by the sound of a step on the lobby, meanwhile continued. At that time (for my wife, like myself, was an invalid) two eminent physicians, who came out occasionally by rail, were attending us. These gentlemen were at first only amused, but ultimately interested, and very much puzzled by the occurrences which we described. One of them, at last, recommended that a candle should be kept burning upon the lobby. It was in fact a recurrence to an old woman's recipe against ghosts – of course it might be serviceable, too, against impostors; at all events, seeming, as I have said, very much interested and puzzled, he advised it, and it was tried. We fancied that it was successful; for there was an interval of quiet for, I think, three or four nights. But after that, the noises – the footsteps on the lobby – the knocking at the door, and the turning of the handle recommenced in full force, notwithstanding the light upon the table outside; and these particular phenomena became only more perplexing than ever.

The alarm of robbers and smugglers gradually subsided after a week or two; but we were again to hear news from the nursery. Our second little girl, then between seven and eight years of age, saw in the night time – she alone being awake – a young woman, with black, or very dark hair, which hung loose, and with a black cloak on, standing near the middle of the floor, opposite the hearthstone, and fronting the foot of her bed. She appeared quite unobservant of the children and nurse sleeping in the room. She was very pale, and looked, the child said, both "sorry and frightened," and with something very peculiar and terrible about her eyes, which made the child conclude that she was dead. She was looking, not at, but in the direction of the child's bed, and there was a dark streak across her throat, like a scar with blood upon it. This figure was not motionless; but once or twice turned slowly, and without appearing to be conscious of the presence of the child, or the other occupants of the room, like a person in vacancy or abstraction. There was on this occasion a night-light burning in the chamber; and the child saw, or thought she saw, all these particulars with the most perfect distinctness. She got her head under the bed-clothes; and although a good many years have passed since then, she cannot recall the spectacle without feelings of peculiar horror.

One day, when the children were playing in the back garden, I asked them to point out to me the spot where they were accustomed to see the woman who occasionally showed herself as I have described, near the stable wall. There was no division of opinion as to this precise point, which they indicated in the most distinct and confident way. I suggested that, perhaps, something might be hidden there in the ground; and advised them digging a hole there with their little spades, to try for it. Accordingly, to work they went, and by my return in the evening they had grubbed up a piece of a jawbone, with several teeth in it. The bone was very much decayed, and ready to crumble to pieces, but the teeth were quite sound. I could not tell whether they were human grinders; but I showed the fossil to one of the physicians I have mentioned, who came out the next evening, and he pronounced them human teeth. The same conclusion was come to a day or two later by the other medical man. It appears to me now, on reviewing the whole matter, almost unaccountable that, with such evidence before me, I should not have got in a labourer, and had the spot effectually dug and searched. I can only say, that so it was. I was quite satisfied of the moral truth of every word that had been related to me, and which I have here set down with scrupulous accuracy. But I experienced an apathy, for which neither then nor afterwards did I quite know how to account. I had a vague, but immovable impression that the whole affair was referable to natural agencies. It was not until some time after we had left the house, which, by-the-by, we afterwards found had had the reputation of being haunted before we had come to live in it, that on reconsideration I discovered the serious difficulty of accounting satisfactorily for all that had occurred upon ordinary principles. A great deal we might arbitrarily set down to imagination. But even in so doing there was, *in limine*, the oddity, not to say improbability, of so many different persons having nearly simultaneously suffered from different spectral and other illusions during the short period for which we had occupied that house, who never before, nor so far as we learned, afterwards were troubled by any fears or fancies of the sort. There were other things, too, not to be so accounted for. The odd knockings in the roof I frequently heard myself.

There were also, which I before forgot to mention, in the daytime, rappings at the doors of the sitting-rooms, which constantly deceived us; and it was not till our "come in" was unanswered, and the hall or passage outside the door was discovered to be empty, that we learned that whatever else caused them, human hands did not. All the persons who reported having seen the different persons or appearances here described by me, were just as confident of having literally and distinctly seen them, as I was of having seen the hard-featured woman with the blind eye, so remarkably corresponding with Smith's description.

About a week after the discovery of the teeth, which were found, I think, about two feet under the ground, a friend, much advanced in years, and who remembered the town in which we had now taken up our abode, for a very long time, happened to pay us a visit. He good-humouredly pooh-poohed the whole thing; but at the same time was evidently curious about it. "We might construct a sort of story," said I (I am giving, of course, the substance and purport, not the exact words, of our dialogue), "and assign to each of the three figures who appeared their respective parts in some dreadful tragedy enacted in this house. The male figure represents the murderer; the ill-looking, one-eyed woman his accomplice, who, we will suppose, buried the body where she is now so often seen grubbing in the earth, and where the human teeth and jawbone have so lately been disinterred; and the young woman with dishevelled tresses, and black cloak, and the bloody scar across her throat, their victim. A difficulty, however, which I cannot get over, exists in the cheerfulness, the great publicity, and the evident very recent date of the house." "Why, as to that," said he, "the house is *not* modern; it and those beside it formed an old government store, altered and fitted up recently as you see. I remember it well in my young days, fifty years ago, before the town had grown out in this direction, and a more entirely lonely spot, or one more fitted for the commission of a secret crime, could not have been imagined."

I have nothing to add, for very soon after this my physician pronounced a longer stay unnecessary for my health, and we took our departure for another place of abode. I may add, that although I have resided for considerable periods in many other houses, I never experienced any annoyances of a similar kind elsewhere; neither have I made (stupid dog! you will say), any inquiries respecting either the antecedents or subsequent history of the house in which we made so disturbed a sojourn. I was content with what I knew, and have here related as clearly as I could, and I think it a very pretty puzzle as it stands.

The drunkard's dream

'All this *he* told with some confusion and
Dismay, the usual consequence of dreams
Of the unpleasant kind, with none at hand
To expound their vain and visionary gleams,
I've known some odd ones which seemed really planned
Prophetically, as that which one deems
"A strange coincidence," to use a phrase
By which such things are settled nowadays.'
BYRON

Dreams! What age, or what country of the world, has not felt
and acknowledged the mystery of their origin and end? I have
thought not a little upon the subject, seeing it is one which has
been often forced upon my attention, and sometimes strangely
enough; and yet I have never arrived at anything which at all
appeared a satisfactory conclusion. It does appear that a mental
phenomenon so extraordinary cannot be wholly without its use.
We know, indeed, that in the olden times it has been made the

organ of communication between the Deity and His creatures; and when, as I have seen, a dream produces upon a mind, to all appearance hopelessly reprobate and depraved, an effect so powerful and so lasting as to break down the inveterate habits, and to reform the life of an abandoned sinner, we see in the result, in the reformation of morals which appeared incorrigible, in the reclamation of a human soul which seemed to be irretrievably lost, something more than could be produced by a mere chimera of the slumbering fancy, something more than could arise from the capricious images of a terrified imagination; but once presented, we behold in all these things, and in their tremendous and mysterious results, the operation of the hand of God. And while Reason rejects as absurd the superstition which will read a prophecy in every dream, she may, without violence to herself, recognize, even in the wildest and most incongruous of the wanderings of a slumbering intellect, the evidences and the fragments of a language which may be spoken, which *has* been spoken, to terrify, to warn, and to command. We have reason to believe too, by the promptness of action which in the age of the prophets followed all intimations of this kind, and by the strength of conviction and strange permanence of the effects resulting from certain dreams in latter times, which effects we ourselves may have witnessed, that when this medium of communication has been employed by the Deity, the evidences of His presence have been unequivocal. My thoughts were directed to this subject, in a manner to leave a lasting impression upon my mind, by the events which I shall now relate, the statement of which, however extraordinary, is nevertheless *accurately correct.*

About the year 17—, having been appointed to the living of C—h, I rented a small house in the town, which bears the same name: one morning in the month of November, I was awakened before my usual time by my servant, who bustled into my bedroom for the purpose of announcing a sick call. As the Catholic

Church holds her last rites to be totally indispensable to the safety of the departing sinner, no conscientious clergyman can afford a moment's unnecessary delay, and in little more than five minutes I stood ready cloaked and booted for the road, in the small front parlour, in which the messenger, who was to act as my guide, awaited my coming. I found a poor little girl crying piteously near the door, and after some slight difficulty I ascertained that her father was either dead or just dying.

'And what may be your father's name, my poor child?' said I. She held down her head, as if ashamed. I repeated the question, and the wretched little creature burst into floods of tears still more bitter than she had shed before. At length, almost provoked by conduct which appeared to me so unreasonable, I began to lose patience, spite of the pity which I could not help feeling towards her, and I said rather harshly:

'If you will not tell me the name of the person to whom you would lead me, your silence can arise from no good motive, and I might be justified in refusing to go with you at all.'

'Oh, don't say that – don't say that!' cried she. 'Oh, sir, it was that I was afeard of when I would not tell you – I was afeard, when you heard his name, you would not come with me; but it is no use hidin' it now – it's Pat Connell, the carpenter, your honour.'

She looked in my face with the most earnest anxiety, as if her very existence depended upon what she should read there; but I relieved her at once. The name, indeed, was most unpleasantly familiar to me; but however fruitless my visits and advice might have been at another time, the present was too fearful an occasion to suffer my doubts of their utility or my reluctance to reattempt what appeared a hopeless task to weigh even against the slightest chance that a consciousness of his imminent danger might produce in him a more docile and tractable disposition. Accordingly I told the child to lead the way, and followed her in silence. She hurried rapidly through the long narrow street which forms the great thoroughfare of the town. The darkness of the hour, rendered still deeper by the close approach of the old-fashioned houses, which lowered in tall obscurity on either side of the way; the damp, dreary chill which renders the advance of morning peculiarly cheerless, combined with the object of my walk, to visit the death-bed of a presumptuous sinner, to endeavour, almost against my own conviction, to infuse a hope into the heart of a dying reprobate – a drunkard but too probably perishing under the conse-quences of some mad fit of intoxication; all these circumstances united served to enhance the gloom and solemnity of my feel-ings, as I silently followed my little guide, who with quick steps traversed the uneven pavement of the main street. After a walk of about five minutes she turned off into a narrow lane, of that obscure and comfortless class which is to be found in almost all small old-fashioned towns, chill, without ventilation, reeking with all manner of offensive effluviae, and lined by dingy, smoky, sickly and pent-up buildings, frequently not only in a wretched but in a dangerous condition.

'Your father has changed his abode since I last visited him, and, I am afraid, much for the worse,' said I.

'Indeed he has, sir; but we must not complain,' replied she. 'We have to thank God that we have lodging and food, though it's poor enough, it is, your honour.'

Poor child! thought I, how many an older head might learn wisdom from thee – how many a luxurious philosopher, who is skilled to preach but not to suffer, might not thy patient words put to the blush! The manner and language of this child were alike above her years and station; and, indeed, in all cases in which the cares and sorrows of life have anticipated their usual date, and have fallen, as they sometimes do, with melancholy prematurity to the lot of childhood, I have observed the result to have proved uniformly the same. A young mind, to which joy and indulgence have been strangers, and to which suffering and self-denial have been familiarized from the first, acquires a solidity and an elevation which no other discipline could have bestowed, and which, in the present case, communicated a striking but mournful peculiarity to the manners, even to the voice, of the child. We paused before a narrow, crazy door, which she opened by means of a latch, and we forthwith began to ascend the steep and broken stairs which led upwards to the sick man's room.

As we mounted flight after flight towards the garret-floor, I heard more and more distinctly the hurried talking of many voices. I could also distinguish the low sobbing of a female. On arriving upon the uppermost lobby these sounds became fully audible.

'This way, your honour,' said my little conductress; at the same time, pushing open a door of patched and half-rotten plank, she admitted me into the squalid chamber of death and misery. But one candle, held in the fingers of a scared and haggard-looking child, was burning in the room, and that so dim that all was twilight or darkness except within its immediate influence. The general obscurity, however, served to throw into prominent and startling relief the death-bed and its occupant. The light was nearly approximated to, and fell with horrible clearness upon, the blue and swollen features of the drunkard. I did not think it possible that a human countenance could look so terrific. The lips were black and drawn apart; the teeth were firmly set; the eyes a little unclosed, and nothing but the whites appearing. Every feature was fixed and livid, and the whole face wore a ghastly and rigid expression of despairing terror such as I never saw equalled. His hands were crossed upon his breast, and firmly clenched; while, as if to add to the corpse-like effect of the whole, some white cloths, dipped in water, were wound about the forehead and temples.

As soon as I could remove my eyes from this horrible spectacle, I observed my friend Dr D—, one of the most humane of a humane profession, standing by the bedside. He had been attempting, but unsuccessfully, to bleed the patient, and had now applied his finger to the pulse.

'Is there any hope?' I inquired in a whisper.

A shake of the head was the reply. There was a pause while he continued to hold the wrist; but he waited in vain for the throb of life – it was not there: and when he let go the hand, it fell stiffly back into its former position upon the other.

'The man is dead,' said the physician, as he turned from the bed where the terrible figure lay.

Dead! thought I, scarcely venturing to look upon the tremendous and revolting spectacle. Dead! without an hour for repentance, even a moment for reflection; dead! without the rites which even the best should have. Is there a hope for him? The glaring eyeball, the grinning mouth, the distorted brow – that unutterable look in which a painter would have sought to embody the fixed despair of the nethermost hell. These were my answer.

The poor wife sat at a little distance, crying as if her heart would break – the younger children clustered round the bed, looking with wondering curiosity upon the form of death never seen before.

When the first tumult of uncontrollable sorrow had passed away, availing myself of the solemnity and impressiveness of the scene, I desired the heart-stricken family to accompany me in prayer, and all knelt down while I solemnly and fervently repeated some of those prayers which appeared most applicable to the occasion. I employed myself thus in a manner which, I trusted, was not unprofitable, at least to the living, for about ten minutes; and having accomplished my task, I was the first to arise.

I looked upon the poor, sobbing, helpless creatures who knelt so humbly around me, and my heart bled for them. With a natural transition I turned my eyes from them to the bed in which the body lay; and, great God! what was the revulsion, the horror which I experienced on seeing the corpse-like, terrific thing seated half upright before me; the white cloths which had been wound about the head had now partly slipped from their position, and were hanging in grotesque festoons about the face and shoulders, while the distorted eyes leered from amid them—

'A sight to dream of, not to tell.'

I stood actually riveted to the spot. The figure nodded its head and lifted its arm, I thought, with a menacing gesture. A thousand confused and horrible thoughts at once rushed upon my mind. I had often read that the body of a presumptuous sinner, who, during life, had been the willing creature of every satanic impulse, after the human tenant had deserted it, had been known to become the horrible sport of demoniac possession.

I was roused from the stupefaction of terror in which I stood, by the piercing scream of the mother, who now, for the first time, perceived the change which had taken place. She rushed towards the bed, but stunned by the shock, and overcome by the conflict of violent emotions, before she reached it she fell prostrate upon the floor.

I am perfectly convinced that had I not been startled from the torpidity of horror in which I was bound by some powerful and arousing stimulant, I should have gazed upon this unearthly apparition until I had fairly lost my senses. As it was, however, the spell was broken – superstition gave way to reason: the man whom all believed to have been actually dead was living!

Dr D— was instantly standing by the bedside, and upon examination he found that a sudden and copious flow of blood had taken place from the wound which the lancet had left; and this, no doubt, had effected his sudden and almost preternatural restoration to an existence from which all thought he had been for ever removed. The man was still speechless, but he seemed to understand the physician when he forbid his repeating the painful and fruitless attempts which he made to articulate, and he at once resigned himself quietly into his hands.

I left the patient with leeches upon his temples, and bleeding freely, apparently with little of the drowsiness which accompanies apoplexy; indeed, Dr D— told me that he had never before witnessed a seizure which seemed to combine the symptoms of so many kinds, and yet which belonged to none of the recognized classes; it certainly was not apoplexy, catalepsy, nor *delirium tremens*, and yet it seemed, in some degree, to partake of the properties of all. It was strange, but stranger things are coming.

During two or three days Dr D— would not allow his patient to converse in a manner which could excite or exhaust him, with anyone; he suffered him merely as briefly as possible to express his immediate wants. And it was not until the fourth day after my early visit, the particulars of which I have just detailed, that it was thought expedient that I should see him, and then only because it appeared that his extreme importunity and impatience to meet me were likely to retard his recovery more than the mere exhaustion attendant upon a short conversation could possibly do; perhaps, too, my friend entertained some hope that if by holy confession his patient's bosom were eased of the perilous stuff which no doubt oppressed it, his recovery would be more assured and rapid. It was then, as I have said, upon the fourth day after my first professional call, that I found myself once more in the dreary chamber of want and sickness.

The man was in bed, and appeared low and restless. On my entering the room he raised himself in the bed, and muttered, twice or thrice:

'Thank God! Thank God!'

I signed to those of his family who stood by to leave the

room, and took a chair beside the bed. So soon as we were alone, he said, rather doggedly:

'There's no use in telling me of the sinfulness of bad ways – I know it all. I know where they lead to – I seen everything about it with my own eyesight, as plain as I see you.' He rolled himself in the bed, as if to hide his face in the clothes; and then suddenly raising himself, he exclaimed with startling vehemence: 'Look, sir! there is no use in mincing the matter: I'm blasted with the fires of hell; I have been in hell. What do you think of that? In hell – I'm lost for ever – I have not a chance. I am damned already – damned – damned!'

The end of this sentence he actually shouted. His vehemence was perfectly terrific; he threw himself back, and laughed, and sobbed hysterically. I poured some water into a tea-cup, and gave it to him. After he had swallowed it, I told him if he had anything to communicate, to do so as briefly as he could, and in a manner as little agitating to himself as possible; threatening at the same time, though I had no intention of doing so, to leave him at once, in case he again gave way to such passionate excitement.

'It's only foolishness,' he continued, 'for me to try to thank you for coming to such a villain as myself at all. It's no use for me to wish good to you, or to bless you; for such as me has no blessings to give.'

I told him that I had but done my duty, and urged him to proceed to the matter which weighed upon his mind. He then spoke nearly as follows:

'I came in drunk on Friday night last, and got to my bed here; I don't remember how. Sometime in the night it seemed to me I wakened, and feeling uneasy in myself, I got up out of the bed. I wanted the fresh air; but I would not make a noise to open the window, for fear I'd waken the crathurs. It was very dark and troublesome to find the door; but at last I did get it, and I groped my way out, and went down as asy as I could. I felt quite sober, and I counted the steps one after another, as I was going down, that I might not stumble at the bottom.

'When I came to the first landing-place – God be about us always! – the floor of it sunk under me, and I went down – down – down, till the senses almost left me. I do not know how long I was falling, but it seemed to me a great while. When I came rightly to myself at last, I was sitting near the top of a great table; and I could not see the end of it, if it had any, it was so far off. And there was men beyond reckoning, sitting down all along by it, at each side, as far as I could see at all. I did not know at first was it in the open air; but there was a close smothering feel in it that was not natural. And there was a kind of light that my eyesight never saw before, red and unsteady; and I did not see for a long time where it was coming from, until I looked straight up, and then I seen that it came from great balls of blood-coloured fire that were rolling high over head with a sort of rushing, trembling sound, and I perceived that they shone on the ribs of a great roof of rock that was arched overhead instead of the sky. When I seen this, scarce knowing what I did, I got up, and I said, "I have no right to be here; I must go." And the man that was sitting at my left hand only smiled, and said, "Sit down again; you can *never* leave this place." And his voice was weaker than any child's voice I ever heard; and when he was done speaking he smiled again.

'Then I spoke out very loud and bold, and I said, "In the name of God, let me out of this bad place." And there was a great man that I did not see before, sitting at the end of the table that I was near; and he was taller than twelve men, and his face was very proud and terrible to look at. And he stood up and stretched out his hand before him; and when he stood up, all that was there, great and small, bowed down with a sighing sound, and a dread came on my heart, and he looked at me, and I could not speak; I felt I was his own, to do what he liked with, for I knew at once who he was; and he said, "If you promise to return, you may depart for a season"; and the voice he spoke with was terrible and mournful, and the echoes of it went rolling and swelling down the endless cave, and mixing with the trembling of the fire overhead; so that when he sat down there was a sound after him, all through the place, like the roaring of a furnace, and I said, with all the strength I had, "I promise to come back – in God's name let me go!"

'And with that I lost the sight and the hearing of all that was there, and when my senses came to me again, I was sitting in the bed with the blood all over me, and you and the rest praying around the room.'

Here he paused and wiped away the chill drops of horror which hung upon his forehead.

I remained silent for some moments. The vision which he had just described struck my imagination not a little, for this was long before Vathek and the 'Hall of Eblis' had delighted the world; and the description which he gave had, as I received it, all the attractions of novelty beside the impressiveness which always belongs to the narration of an *eye-witness*, whether in the body or in the spirit, of the scenes which he describes. There was something, too, in the stern horror with which the man related these things, and in the incongruity of his description, with the vulgarly received notions of the great place of punishment, and of its presiding spirit, which struck my mind with awe, almost with fear. At length he said, with an expression of horrible, imploring earnestness, which I shall never forget— 'Well, sir, is there any hope; is there any chance at all? or, is my soul pledged and promised away for ever? is it gone out of my power? must I go back to the place?'

In answering him, I had no easy task to perform; for however clear might be my internal conviction of the groundlessness of his fears, and however strong my scepticism respecting the reality of what he had described, I nevertheless felt that his impression to the contrary, and his humility and terror resulting from it, might be made available as no mean engines in the work of his conversion from profligacy, and of his restoration to decent habits, and to religious feeling.

I therefore told him that he was to regard his dream rather in the light of a warning than in that of a prophecy; that our salvation depended not upon the word or deed of a moment, but upon the habits of a life; that, in fine, if he at once discarded his idle companions and evil habits, and firmly adhered to a sober, industrious, and religious course of life, the powers of darkness might claim his soul in vain, for that there were higher and firmer pledges than human tongue could utter, which promised salvation to him who should repent and lead a new life.

I left him much comforted, and with a promise to return upon the next day. I did so, and found him much more cheerful and without any remains of the dogged sullenness which I suppose had arisen from his despair. His promises of amendment were given in that tone of deliberate earnestness, which belongs to deep and solemn determination; and it was with no small delight that I observed, after repeated visits, that his good resolutions, so far from failing, did but gather strength by time; and when I saw that man shake off the idle and debauched companions, whose society had for years formed alike his amusement and his ruin, and revive his long discarded habits of industry and sobriety, I said within myself, there is something more in all this than the operation of an idle dream.

One day, sometime after his perfect restoration to health, I was surprised on ascending the stairs, for the purpose of visiting this man, to find him busily employed in nailing down some planks upon the landing-place, through which, at the commencement of his mysterious vision, it seemed to him that he had sunk. I perceived at once that he was strengthening the floor with a view to securing himself against such a catastrophe, and could scarcely forbear a smile as I bid 'God bless his work'.

He perceived my thoughts, I suppose, for he immediately said:

'I can never pass over that floor without trembling. I'd leave this house if I could, but I can't find another lodging in the town so cheap, and I'll not take a better till I've paid off all my debts, please God; but I could not be asy in my mind till I made it as safe as I could. You'll hardly believe me, your honour, that while I'm working, maybe a mile away, my heart is in a flutter the whole way back, with the bare thoughts of the two little steps I have to walk upon this bit of a floor. So it's no wonder, sir, I'd try to make it sound and firm with any idle timber I have.'

I applauded his resolution to pay off his debts, and the steadiness with which he pursued his plans of conscientious economy, and passed on.

Many months elapsed, and still there appeared no alteration in his resolutions of amendment. He was a good workman, and with his better habits he recovered his former extensive and profitable employment. Everything seemed to promise comfort and respectability. I have little more to add, and that shall be told quickly. I had one evening met Pat Connell, as he returned from his work, and as usual, after a mutual, and on his side respectful salutation, I spoke a few words of encouragement and approval. I left him industrious, active, healthy – when next I saw him, not three days after, he was a corpse.

The circumstances which marked the event of his death were somewhat strange – I might say fearful. The unfortunate man had accidentally met an early friend just returned, after a long absence, and in a moment of excitement, forgetting everything in the warmth of his joy, he yielded to his urgent invitation to accompany him into a public-house, which lay close by the spot where the encounter had taken place. Connell, however, previously to entering the room, had announced his determination to take nothing more than the strictest temperance would warrant.

But oh! who can describe the inveterate tenacity with which a drunkard's habits cling to him through life? He may repent — he may reform – he may look with actual abhorrence upon his past profligacy; but amid all this reformation and compunction, who can tell the moment in which the base and ruinous propensity may not recur, triumphing over resolution, remorse, shame, everything, and prostrating its victim once more in all that is destructive and revolting in that fatal vice?

The wretched man left the place in a state of utter intoxication. He was brought home nearly insensible, and placed in his bed, where he lay in the deep calm lethargy of drunkenness. The younger part of the family retired to rest much after their usual hour; but the poor wife remained up sitting by the fire, too much grieved and shocked at the occurrence of what she had so little expected, to settle to rest; fatigue, however, at length overcame her, and she sank gradually into an uneasy slumber. She could not tell how long she had remained in this state, when she awakened, and immediately on opening her eyes, she perceived by the faint red light of the smouldering turf embers, two persons, one of whom she recognized as her husband, noiselessly gliding out of the room.

'Pat, darling, where are you going?' said she. There was no answer – the door closed after them; but in a moment she was startled and terrified by a loud and heavy crash, as if some ponderous body had been hurled down the stair. Much alarmed, she started up, and going to the head of the staircase, she called repeatedly upon her husband, but in vain. She returned to the room, and with the assistance of her daughter, whom I had occasion to mention before, she succeeded in finding and lighting a candle, with which she hurried again to the head of the staircase.

At the bottom lay what seemed to be a bundle of clothes, heaped together, motionless, lifeless – it was her husband. In going down the stair, for what purpose can never now be known, he had fallen helplessly and violently to the bottom, and coming head foremost, the spine at the neck had been dislocated by the shock, and instant death must have ensued. The body lay upon that landing-place to which his dream had referred. It is scarcely worth endeavouring to clear up a single point in a narrative where all is mystery; yet I could not help suspecting that the second figure which had been seen in the room by Connell's wife on the night of his death, might have been no other than his own shadow. I suggested this solution of the difficulty; but she told me that the unknown person had been considerably in advance of the other, and on reaching the door, had turned back as if to communicate something to his companion. It was then a mystery.

Was the dream verified? – whither had the disembodied spirit sped? – who can say? We know not. But I left the house of death that day in a state of horror which I could not describe. It seemed to me that I was scarce awake. I heard and saw everything as if under the spell of a nightmare. The coincidence was terrible.

AN ACCOUNT OF SOME STRANGE DISTURBANCES IN AUNGIER STREET

from DUBLIN UNIVERSITY MAGAZINE, 1853

It is not worth telling, this story of mine—at least, not worth writing. Told, indeed, as I have sometimes been called upon to tell it, to a circle of intelligent and eager faces, lighted up by a good after-dinner fire on a winter's evening, with a cold wind rising and wailing outside, and all snug and cosy within, it has gone off—though I say it, who should not—indifferent well. But it is a venture to do as you would have me. Pen, ink, and paper are cold vehicles for the marvellous, and a " reader " decidedly a more critical animal than a " listener." If, however, you can induce your friends to read it after nightfall, and when the fireside talk has run for a while on thrilling tales of shapeless terror ; in short, if you will secure me the *mollia tempora fandi*, I will go to my work, and say my say, with better heart. Well, then, these conditions presupposed, I shall waste no more words, but tell you simply how it all happened.

My cousin (Tom Ludlow) and I studied medicine together. I think he would have succeeded, had he stuck to the profession; but he preferred the Church, poor fellow, and died early, a sacrifice to contagion, contracted in the noble discharge of his duties. For my present purpose, I say enough of his character when I mention that he was of a sedate but frank and cheerful nature; very exact in his observance of truth, and not by any means like myself—of an excitable or nervous temperament.

My Uncle Ludlow—Tom's father—while we were attending lectures, purchased three or four old houses in Aungier Street, one of which was unoccupied. *He* resided in the country, and Tom proposed that we should take up our abode in the untenanted house, so long as it should continue unlet; a move which would accomplish the double end of settling us nearer alike to our lecture-rooms and to our amusements, and of relieving us from the weekly charge of rent for our lodgings.

Our furniture was very scant—our whole equipage remarkably modest and primitive; and, in short, our arrangements pretty nearly as simple as those of a bivouac. Our new plan was, therefore, executed almost as soon as conceived. The front drawing-room was our sitting-room. I had the bedroom over it, and Tom the back bedroom on the same floor, which nothing could have induced me to occupy.

The house, to begin with, was a very old one. It had been, I believe, newly fronted about fifty years before; but with this exception, it had nothing modern about it. The agent who bought it and looked into the titles for my uncle, told me that it was sold, along with much other forfeited property, at Chichester House, I think, in 1702; and had belonged to Sir Thomas Hacket, who was Lord Mayor of Dublin in James II's time. How old it was *then*, I can't say; but, at all events, it had seen years and changes enough to have contracted all that mysterious and saddened air, at once exciting and depressing, which belongs to most old mansions.

There had been very little done in the way of modernising details; and, perhaps, it was better so; for there was something queer and by-gone in the very walls and ceilings—in the shape of doors and windows—in the odd diagonal site of the chimney-pieces—in the beams and ponderous cornices—not to mention the singular solidity of all the woodwork, from the banisters to the window-frames, which hopelessly defied disguise, and would have emphatically proclaimed their antiquity through any conceivable amount of modern finery and varnish.

An effort had, indeed, been made, to the extent of papering the drawing-rooms ; but, somehow the paper looked raw and out of keeping ; and the old woman, who kept a little dirt-pie of a shop in the lane, and whose daughter—a girl of two and fifty—was our solitary handmaid, coming in at sunrise, and chastely receding again as soon as she had made all ready for tea in our state apartment ;—this woman, I say, remembered it, when old Judge Horrocks (who, having earned the reputation of a particularly " hanging judge," ended by hanging himself, as the coroner's jury found, under an impulse of " temporary insanity," with a child's skipping-rope, over the massive old banisters) resided there, entertaining good company, with fine venison and rare old port. In those halcyon days, the drawing-rooms were hung with gilded leather, and, I dare say, cut a good figure, for they were really spacious rooms.

The bedrooms were wainscoted, but the front one was not gloomy ; and in it the cosiness of antiquity quite overcame its sombre associations. But the back bedroom, with its two queerly-placed melancholy windows, staring vacantly at the foot of the bed, and with the shadowy recess to be found in most old houses in Dublin, like a large ghostly closet, which, from congeniality of temperament, had amalgamated with the bedchamber, and dissolved the partition. At night-time, this " alcove "—as our " maid " was wont to call it—had, in my eyes, a specially sinister and suggestive character. Tom's distant and solitary candle glimmered vainly into its darkness. *There* it was always overlooking him—always itself impenetrable. But this was only part of the effect. The whole room was, I can't tell how, repulsive to me. There was, I suppose, in its proportions and features, a latent discord—a certain mysterious and indescribable relation, which jarred indistinctly upon some secret sense of the fitting and the safe, and raised indefinable suspicions and apprehensions of the imagination. On the whole, as I began by saying, nothing could have induced me to pass a night alone in it.

I had never pretended to conceal from poor Tom my superstitious weakness ; and he, on the other hand, most unaffectedly ridiculed my tremors. The sceptic was, however, destined to receive a lesson, as you shall hear.

We had not been very long in occupation of our respective dormitories, when I began to complain of uneasy nights and disturbed sleep. I was, I suppose, the more impatient under this annoyance, as I was usually a sound sleeper, and by no means prone to nightmares. It was now, however, my destiny, instead of enjoying my customary repose, every night to " sup full of horrors." After a preliminary course of disagreeable and frightful dreams, my troubles took a definite form, and the same vision, without an appreciable variation in a single detail, visited me at least (on an average) every second night in the week.

Now, this dream, nightmare, or infernal illusion—which you please—of which I was the miserable sport, was on this wise :—

I saw, or thought I saw, with the most abominable distinctness, although at the time in profound darkness, every article of furniture and accidental arrangement of the chamber in which I lay. This, as you know, is incidental to ordinary nightmare. Well, while in this clairvoyant condition, which seemed but the lighting up of the theatre in which was to be exhibited the monotonous tableau of horror, which made my nights insupportable, my attention invariably became, I know not why, fixed upon the windows opposite the foot of my bed ; and, uniformly with the same effect, a sense of dreadful anticipation always took slow but sure possession of me. I became somehow conscious of a sort of horrid but undefined preparation going forward in some unknown quarter, and by some unknown agency, for my torment ; and, after an interval, which always seemed to me of the same length, a picture suddenly flew up to the window, where it remained fixed, as if by an electrical attraction, and my discipline of horror then commenced, to last perhaps for hours. The picture thus mysteriously glued to the window-panes, was the portrait of an old man, in a crimson flowered silk dressing-gown, the folds of which I could now describe, with a countenance embodying a strange mixture of intellect, sensuality, and power, but withal sinister and full of malignant omen. His nose was hooked, like the beak of a vulture ; his eyes large, grey, and prominent, and lighted up with a more than mortal cruelty and coldness. These features were surmounted by a crimson velvet cap, the hair that peeped from under which was white with age, while the eyebrows retained their original blackness. Well I remember every line, hue, and shadow of that stony countenance, and well I may ! The gaze of this hellish visage was fixed upon me, and mine returned it with the inexplicable fascination of nightmare, for what appeared to me to be hours of agony. At last—

" The cock he crew, away then flew "

the fiend who had enslaved me through the awful watches of the night ; and, harassed and nervous, I rose to the duties of the day.

I had—I can't say exactly why, but it may have been from the exquisite anguish and profound impressions of unearthly horror, with which this strange phantasmagoria was associated—an insurmountable antipathy to describing the exact nature of my nightly troubles to my friend and comrade. Generally, however, I told him that I was haunted by abominable dreams ; and, true to the imputed materialism of medicine, we put our heads together to dispel my horrors, not by exorcism, but by a tonic.

I will do this tonic justice, and frankly admit that the accursed portrait began to intermit its visits under its influence. What of that ? Was this singular apparition—as full of character as of terror—therefore the creature of my fancy, or the invention of my poor stomach ? Was it, in short, *subjective* (to borrow the technical slang of the day) and not the palpable aggression and intrusion of an external agent ? That, good friend, as we will both admit, by no means follows. The evil spirit, who enthralled my senses in the shape of that portrait, may have been just as near me, just as energetic, just as malignant, though I saw him not. What means the whole moral code of revealed religion regarding the due keeping of our own bodies, soberness, temperance, etc. ? here is an obvious connexion between the material and the invisible ; the healthy tone of the system, and its unimpaired energy, may, for aught we can tell, guard us against influences which would otherwise render life itself terrific. The mesmerist and the electro-biologist will fail upon an average with nine patients out of ten—so may the evil spirit. Special conditions of the corporeal system are indispensable to the production of certain spiritual phenomena. The operation succeeds sometimes—sometimes fails—that is all.

I found afterwards that my would-be sceptical companion had his troubles too. But of these I knew nothing yet. One night, for a wonder, I was sleeping soundly, when I was roused by a step on the lobby outside my room, followed by the loud clang of what turned out to be a large brass candlestick, flung with all his force by poor Tom Ludlow over the banisters, and rattling with a rebound down the second flight of stairs ; and almost concurrently with this, Tom burst open my door, and bounced into my room backwards, in a state of extraordinary agitation.

I had jumped out of bed and clutched him by the arm before I had any distinct idea of my own whereabouts. There we were—in our shirts—standing before the open door—staring through the great old banister opposite, at the lobby window, through which the sickly light of a clouded moon was gleaming.

" What's the matter, Tom? What's the matter with you? What the devil's the matter with you, Tom? " I demanded, shaking him with nervous impatience.

He took a long breath before he answered me, and then it was not very coherently.

" It's nothing, nothing at all—did I speak ?—what did I say ?—where's the candle, Richard? It's dark ; I—I had a candle ! "

" Yes, dark enough," I said ; " but what's the matter ?—what is it ?—why don't you speak, Tom ?—have you lost your wits ?—what is the matter ? "

" The matter ?—oh, it is all over. It must have been a dream—nothing at all but a dream—don't you think so ? It could not be anything more than a dream."

" Of *course*," said I, feeling uncommonly nervous, " it *was* a dream."

" I thought," he said, " there was a man in my room, and—and I jumped out of bed ; and—and—where's the candle ? "

" In your room, most likely," I said, " shall I go and bring it ? "

" No ; stay here—don't go ; it's no matter—don't, I tell you ; it was all a dream. Bolt the door, Dick ; I'll stay here with you—I feel nervous. So, Dick, like a good fellow, light your candle and open the window—I am in a *shocking state*."

I did as he asked me, and robing himself like Granuaile in one of my blankets, he seated himself close beside my bed.

Everybody knows how contagious is fear of all sorts, but more especially that particular kind of fear under which poor Tom was at that moment labouring. I would not have heard, nor I believe would he have recapitulated, just at that moment, for half the world, the details of the hideous vision which had so unmanned him.

" Don't mind telling me anything about your nonsensical dream, Tom," said I, affecting contempt, really in a panic ; " let us talk about something else ; but it is quite plain that this dirty old house disagrees with us both, and hang me if I stay here any longer, to be pestered with indigestion and—and—bad nights, so we may as well look out for lodgings—don't you think so?—at once."

Tom agreed, and, after an interval, said—

"I have been thinking, Richard, that it is a long time since I saw my father, and I have made up my mind to go down to-morrow and return in a day or two, and you can take rooms for us in the meantime."

I fancied that this resolution, obviously the result of the vision which had so profoundly scared him, would probably vanish next morning with the damps and shadows of night. But I was mistaken. Off went Tom at peep of day to the country, having agreed that so soon as I had secured suitable lodgings, I was to recall him by letter from his visit to my Uncle Ludlow.

Now, anxious as I was to change my quarters, it so happened, owing to a series of petty procrastinations and accidents, that nearly a week elapsed before my bargain was made and my letter of recall on the wing to Tom; and, in the meantime, a trifling adventure or two had occurred to your humble servant, which, absurd as they now appear, diminished by distance, did certainly at the time serve to whet my appetite for change considerably.

A night or two after the departure of my comrade, I was sitting by my bedroom fire, the door locked, and the ingredients of a tumbler of hot whisky-punch upon the crazy spider-table; for, as the best mode of keeping the

> "*Black spirits and white,*
> *Blue spirits and grey,*"

with which I was environed, at bay, I had adopted the practice recommended by the wisdom of my ancestors, and "kept my spirits up by pouring spirits down." I had thrown aside my volume of Anatomy, and was treating myself by way of a tonic, prepara-tory to my punch and bed, to half-a-dozen pages of the *Spectator*, when I heard a step on the flight of stairs descending from the attics. It was two o'clock, and the streets were as silent as a church-yard—the sounds were, therefore, perfectly distinct. There was a slow, heavy tread, characterised by the emphasis and deliberation of age, descending by the narrow staircase from above; and, what made the sound more singular, it was plain that the feet which produced it were perfectly bare, measuring the descent with some-thing between a pound and a flop, very ugly to hear.

I knew quite well that my attendant had gone away many hours before, and that nobody but myself had any business in the house. It was quite plain also that the person who was coming downstairs had no intention whatever of concealing his movements ; but, on the contrary, appeared disposed to make even more noise, and proceed more deliberately, than was at all necessary. When the step reached the foot of the stairs outside my room, it seemed to stop ; and I expected every moment to see my door open spontaneously, and give admission to the original of my detested portrait. I was, however, relieved in a few seconds by hearing the descent renewed, just in the same manner, upon the staircase leading down to the drawing-rooms, and thence, after another pause, down the next flight, and so on to the hall, whence I heard no more.

Now, by the time the sound had ceased, I was wound up, as they say, to a very unpleasant pitch of excitement. I listened, but there was not a stir. I screwed up my courage to a decisive experiment—opened my door, and in a stentorian voice bawled over the banisters, " Who's there ? " There was no answer, but the ringing of my own voice through the empty old house,—no renewal of the movement ; nothing, in short, to give my unpleasant sensations a definite direction. There is, I think, something most disagreeably disenchanting in the sound of one's own voice under such circumstances, exerted in solitude and in vain. It redoubled my sense of isolation, and my misgivings increased on perceiving that the door, which I certainly thought I had left open, was closed behind me ; in a vague alarm, lest my retreat should be cut off, I got again into my room as quickly as I could, where I remained in a state of imaginary blockade, and very uncomfortable indeed, till morning.

Next night brought no return of my barefooted fellow-lodger ; but the night following, being in my bed, and in the dark—somewhere, I suppose, about the same hour as before, I distinctly heard the old fellow again descending from the garrets.

This time I had had my punch, and the *morale* of the garrison was consequently excellent. I jumped out of bed, clutched the poker as I passed the expiring fire, and in a moment was upon the lobby. The sound had ceased by this time—the dark and chill were discouraging ; and, guess my horror, when I saw, or thought I saw, a black monster, whether in the shape of a man or a bear I could not say, standing, with its back to the wall, on the lobby, facing me, with a pair of great greenish eyes shining dimly out. Now, I must be frank, and confess that the cupboard which displayed our plates and cups stood just there, though at the moment I did not recollect it. At the same time I must honestly say, that making every allowance for an excited imagination, I never could satisfy myself that I was made the dupe of my own fancy in this matter ; for this apparition, after one or two shiftings of shape, as if in the act of incipient transformation, began, as it seemed on second thoughts, to advance upon me in its original form. From an instinct of terror rather than of courage, I hurled the poker, with all my force, at its head ; and to the music of a horrid crash made my way into my room, and double-locked the door. Then, in a minute more, I heard the horrid bare feet walk down the stairs, till the sound ceased in the hall, as on the former occasion.

. If the apparition of the night before was an ocular delusion of my fancy sporting with the dark outlines of our cupboard, and if its horrid eyes were nothing but a pair of inverted teacups, I had, at all events, the satisfaction of having launched the poker with admirable effect, and in true " fancy " phrase, " knocked its two daylights into one," as the commingled fragments of my tea-service testified. I did my best to gather comfort and courage from these evidences ; but it would not do. And then what could I say of those horrid bare feet, and the regular tramp, tramp, tramp, which measured the distance of the entire staircase through the solitude of my haunted dwelling, and at an hour when no good influence was stirring ? Confound it !—the whole affair was abominable. I was out of spirits, and dreaded the approach of night.

It came, ushered ominously in with a thunder-storm and dull torrents of depressing rain. Earlier than usual the streets grew silent ; and by twelve o'clock nothing but the comfortless pattering of the rain was to be heard.

I made myself as snug as I could. I lighted *two* candles instead of one. I forswore bed, and held myself in readiness for a sally, candle in hand ; for, *coute qui coute*, I was resolved to *see* the being, if visible at all, who troubled the nightly stillness of my mansion. I was fidgety and nervous and, tried in vain to interest myself with my books. I walked up and down my room, whistling in turn martial and hilarious music, and listening ever and anon for the dreaded noise. I sate down and stared at the square label on the solemn and reserved-looking black bottle, until " FLANAGAN & CO.'S BEST OLD MALT WHISKY " grew into a sort of subdued accompaniment to all the fantastic and horrible speculations which chased one another through my brain.

Silence, meanwhile, grew more silent, and darkness darker. I listened in vain for the rumble of a vehicle, or the dull clamour of a distant row. There was nothing but the sound of a rising wind, which had succeeded the thunder-storm that had travelled over the Dublin mountains quite out of hearing. In the middle of this great city I began to feel myself alone with nature, and Heaven knows what beside. My courage was ebbing. Punch, however, which makes beasts of so many, made a man of me again—just in time to hear with tolerable nerve and firmness the lumpy, flabby, naked feet deliberately descending the stairs again.

I took a candle, not without a tremor. As I crossed the floor I tried to extemporise a prayer, but stopped short to listen, and never finished it. The steps continued. I confess I hesitated for some seconds at the door before I took heart of grace and opened it. When I peeped out the lobby was perfectly empty—there was no monster standing on the staircase ; and as the detested sound ceased, I was reassured enough to venture forward nearly to the banisters. Horror of horrors ! within a stair or two beneath the spot where I stood the unearthly tread smote the floor. My eye caught something in motion ; it was about the size of Goliath's foot—it was grey, heavy, and flapped with a dead weight from one step to another. As I am alive, it was the most monstrous grey rat I ever beheld or imagined.

Shakespeare says—" Some men there are cannot abide a gaping pig, and some that are mad if they behold a cat." I went well-nigh out of my wits when I beheld this *rat* ; for, laugh at me as you may, it fixed upon me, I thought, a perfectly human expression of malice ; and, as it shuffled about and looked up into my face almost from between my feet, I saw, I could swear it—I felt it then, and know it now, the infernal gaze and the accursed countenance of my old friend in the portrait, transfused into the visage of the bloated vermin before me.

I bounced into my room again with a feeling of loathing and horror I cannot describe, and locked and bolted my door as if a lion had been at the other side. D——n him or *it* ; curse the portrait and its original ! I felt in my soul that the rat—yes, the *rat*, the RAT I had just seen, was that evil being in masquerade, and rambling through the house upon some infernal night lark.

Next morning I was early trudging through the miry streets ; and, among other transactions, posted a peremptory note recalling Tom. On my return, however, I found a note from my absent " chum," announcing his intended return next day. I was doubly rejoiced at this, because I had succeeded in getting rooms ; and because the change of scene and return of my comrade were rendered specially pleasant by the last night's half ridiculous half horrible adventure.

I slept extemporaneously in my new quarters in Digges' Street that night, and next morning returned for breakfast to the haunted mansion, where I was certain Tom would call immediately on his arrival.

I was quite right—he came ; and almost his first question referred to the primary object of our change of residence.

" Thank God," he said with genuine fervour, on hearing that all was arranged. " On *your* account I am delighted. As to myself, I assure you that no earthly consideration could have induced me ever again to pass a night in this disastrous old house."

" Confound the house ! " I ejaculated, with a genuine mixture of fear and detestation, " we have not had a pleasant hour since we came to live here " ; and so I went on, and related incidentally my adventure with the plethoric old rat.

" Well, if that were *all*," said my cousin, affecting to make light of the matter, " I don't think I should have minded it very much."

" Ay, but its eye—its countenance, my dear Tom," urged I ; " if you had seen *that*, you would have felt it might be *anything* but what it seemed."

" I am inclined to think the best conjurer in such a case would be an able-bodied cat," he said, with a provoking chuckle.

" But let us hear your own adventure," I said tartly.

At this challenge he looked uneasily round him. I had poked up a very unpleasant recollection.

" You shall hear it, Dick ; I'll tell it to you," he said. " Begad, sir, I should feel quite queer, though, telling it *here*, though we are too strong a body for ghosts to meddle with just now."

Though he spoke this like a joke, I think it was serious calculation. Our Hebe was in a corner of the room, packing our cracked delf tea and dinner-services in a basket. She soon suspended operations, and with mouth and eyes wide open became an absorbed listener. Tom's experiences were told nearly in these words :—

" I saw it three times, Dick—three distinct times ; and I am perfectly certain it meant me some infernal harm. I was, I say, in danger—in *extreme* danger ; for, if nothing else had happened, my reason would most certainly have failed me, unless I had escaped so soon. Thank God. I *did* escape.

" The first night of this hateful disturbance, I was lying in the attitude of sleep, in that lumbering old bed. I hate to think of it. I was really wide awake, though I had put out my candle, and was lying as quietly as if I had been asleep ; and although accidentally restless, my thoughts were running in a cheerful and agreeable channel.

" I think it must have been two o'clock at least when I thought I heard a sound in that—that odious dark recess at the far end of the bedroom. It was as if someone was drawing a piece of cord slowly along the floor, lifting it up, and dropping it softly down again in coils. I sate up once or twice in my bed, but could see nothing, so I concluded it must be mice in the wainscot. I felt no emotion graver than curiosity, and after a few minutes ceased to observe it.

" While lying in this state, strange to say ; without at first a suspicion of anything supernatural, on a sudden I saw an old man, rather stout and square, in a sort of roan-red dressing-gown, and with a black cap on his head, moving stiffly and slowly in a diagonal direction, from the recess, across the floor of the bedroom, passing my bed at the foot, and entering the lumber-closet at the left. He had something under his arm ; his head hung a little at one side ; and merciful God ! when I saw his face."

Tom stopped for a while, and then said—

" That awful countenance, which living or dying I never can forget, disclosed what he was. Without turning to the right or left, he passed beside me, and entered the closet by the bed's head.

" While this fearful and indescribable type of death and guilt was passing, I felt that I had no more power to speak or stir than if I had been myself a corpse. For hours after it had disappeared, I was too terrified and weak to move. As soon as daylight came, I took courage, and examined the room, and especially the course which the frightful intruder had seemed to take, but there was not a vestige to indicate anybody's having passed there ; no sign of any disturbing agency visible among the lumber that strewed the floor of the closet.

" I now began to recover a little. I was fagged and exhausted, and at last, overpowered by a feverish sleep. I came down late ; and finding you out of spirits, on account of your dreams about the portrait, whose *original* I am now certain disclosed himself to me, I did not care to talk about the infernal vision. In fact, I was trying to persuade myself that the whole thing was an illusion, and I did not like to revive in their intensity the hated impressions of the past night—or, to risk the constancy of my scepticism, by recounting the tale of my sufferings.

" It required some nerve, I can tell you, to go to my haunted chamber next night, and lie down quietly in the same bed," continued Tom. " I did so with a degree of trepidation, which, I am not ashamed to say, a very little matter would have sufficed to stimulate to downright panic. This night, however, passed off quietly enough, as also the next ; and so too did two or three more. I grew more confident, and began to fancy that I believed in the theories of spectral illusions, with which I had at first vainly tried to impose upon my convictions.

" The apparition had been, indeed, altogether anomalous. It had crossed the room without any recognition of my presence : I had not disturbed *it*, and *it* had no mission to *me*. What, then, was the imaginable use of its crossing the room in a visible shape at all ? Of course it might have *been* in the closet instead of *going* there, as easily as it introduced itself into the recess without entering the chamber in a shape discernible by the senses. Besides, how the deuce *had* I seen it ? It was a dark night ; I had no candle ; there was no fire ; and yet I saw it as distinctly, in colouring and outline, as ever I beheld human form ! A cataleptic dream would explain it all ; and I was determined that a dream it should be.

" One of the most remarkable phenomena connected with the practice of mendacity is the vast number of deliberate lies we tell ourselves, whom, of all persons, we can least expect to deceive. In all this, I need hardly tell you, Dick, I was simply lying to myself, and did not believe one word of the wretched humbug. Yet I went on, as men will do, like persevering charlatans and impostors, who tire people into credulity by the mere force of reiteration ; so I hoped to win myself over at last to a comfortable scepticism about the ghost.

" He had not appeared a second time—that certainly was a comfort ; and what, after all, did I care for him, and his queer old toggery and strange looks ? Not a fig ! I was nothing the worse for having seen him, and a good story the better. So I tumbled into bed, put out my candle, and, cheered by a loud drunken quarrel in the back lane, went fast asleep.

" From this deep slumber I awoke with a start. I knew I had had a horrible dream ; but what it was I could not remember. My heart was thumping furiously ; I felt bewildered and feverish ; I sate up in the bed and looked about the room. A broad flood of moonlight came in through the curtainless window ; everything was as I had last seen it ; and though the domestic squabble in the back lane was, unhappily for me, allayed, I yet could hear a pleasant fellow singing, on his way home, the then popular comic ditty called, ' Murphy Delany.' Taking advantage of this diversion I lay down again, with my face towards the fireplace, and closing my eyes, did my best to think of nothing else but the song, which was every moment growing fainter in the distance :—

> ' 'Twas Murphy Delany, so funny and frisky,
> Stept into a shebeen shop to get his skin full ;
> He reeled out again pretty well lined with whiskey,
> As fresh as a shamrock, as blind as a bull.'

" The singer, whose condition I dare say resembled that of his hero, was soon too far off to regale my ears any more ; and as his music died away, I myself sank into a doze, neither sound nor refreshing. Somehow the song had got into my head, and I went meandering on through the adventures of my respectable fellow-countryman, who, on emerging from the ' shebeen shop,' fell into a river, from which he was fished up to be ' sat upon ' by a coroner's jury, who having learned from a ' horse-doctor ' that he was ' dead as a door-nail, so there was an end,' returned their verdict accordingly, just as he returned to his senses, when an angry altercation and a pitched battle between the body and the coroner winds up the lay with due spirit and pleasantry.

" Through this ballad I continued with a weary monotony to plod, down to the very last line, and then *da capo*, and so on, in my uncomfortable half-sleep, for how long, I can't conjecture. I found myself at last, however, muttering, ' *dead* as a door-nail, so there was an end ' ; and something like another voice within me, seemed to say, very faintly, but sharply, ' dead ! dead ! *dead !* and may the Lord have mercy on your soul ! " and instantaneously I was wide awake, and staring right before me from the pillow.

"Now—will you believe it, Dick?—I saw the same accursed figure standing full front, and gazing at me with its stony and fiendish countenance, not two yards from the bedside."

Tom stopped here, and wiped the perspiration from his face. I felt very queer. The girl was as pale as Tom ; and, assembled as we were in the very scene of these adventures, we were all, I dare say, equally grateful for the clear daylight and the resuming bustle out of doors.

"For about three seconds only I saw it plainly ; then it grew indistinct ; but, for a long time, there was something like a column of dark vapour where it had been standing between me and the wall ; and I felt sure that he was still there. After a good while, this appearance went too. I took my clothes downstairs to the hall, and dressed there, with the door half open ; then went out into the street, and walked about the town till morning, when I came back, in a miserable state of nervousness and exhaustion. I was such a fool, Dick, as to be ashamed to tell you how I came to be so upset. I thought you would laugh at me ; especially as I had always talked philosophy, and treated *your* ghosts with contempt. I concluded you would give me no quarter ; and so kept my tale of horror to myself.

"Now, Dick, you will hardly believe me, when I assure you, that for many nights after this last experience, I did not go to my room at all. I used to sit up for a while in the drawing-room after you had gone up to your bed ; and then steal down softly to the hall-door, let myself out, and sit in the ' Robin Hood ' tavern until the last guest went off ; and then I got through the night like a sentry, pacing the streets till morning.

"For more than a week I never slept in bed. I sometimes had a snooze on a form in the ' Robin Hood,' and sometimes a nap in a chair during the day ; but regular sleep I had absolutely none.

"I was quite resolved that we should get into another house ; but I could not bring myself to tell you the reason, and I somehow put it off from day to day, although my life was, during every hour of this procrastination, rendered as miserable as that of a felon with the constables on his track. I was growing absolutely ill from this wretched mode of life.

"One afternoon I determined to enjoy an hour's sleep upon your bed. I hated mine ; so that I had never, except in a stealthy visit every day to unmake it, lest Martha should discover the secret of my nightly absence, entered the ill-omened chamber.

" As ill-luck would have it, you had locked your bedroom, and taken away the key. I went into my own to unsettle the bedclothes, as usual, and give the bed the appearance of having been slept in. Now, a variety of circumstances concurred to bring about the dreadful scene through which I was that night to pass. In the first place, I was literally overpowered with fatigue, and longing for sleep ; in the next place, the effect of this extreme exhaustion upon my nerves resembled that of a narcotic, and rendered me less susceptible than, perhaps I should in any other condition have been, of the exciting fears which had become habitual to me. Then again, a little bit of the window was open, a pleasant freshness pervaded the room, and, to crown all, the cheerful sun of day was making the room quite pleasant. What was to prevent my enjoying an hour's nap *here* ? The whole air was resonant with the cheerful hum of life, and the broad matter-of-fact light of day filled every corner of the room.

" I yielded—stifling my qualms—to the almost overpowering temptation ; and merely throwing off my coat, and loosening my cravat, I lay down, limiting myself to *half*-an-hour's doze in the unwonted enjoyment of a feather bed, a coverlet, and a bolster.

" It was horribly insidious ; and the demon, no doubt, marked my infatuated preparations. Dolt that I was, I fancied, with mind and body worn out for want of sleep, and an arrear of a full week's rest to my credit, that such measure as *half*-an-hour's sleep, in such a situation, was possible. My sleep was death-like, long, and dreamless.

" Without a start or fearful sensation of any kind, I waked gently, but completely. It was, as you have good reason to remember, long past midnight—I believe, about two o'clock. When sleep has been deep and long enough to satisfy nature thoroughly, one often wakens in this way, suddenly, tranquilly, and completely.

" There was a figure seated in that lumbering, old sofa-chair, near the fireplace. Its back was rather towards me, but I could not be mistaken ; it turned slowly round, and, merciful heavens ! there was the stony face, with its infernal lineaments of malignity and despair, gloating on me. There was now no doubt as to its consciousness of my presence, and the hellish malice with which it was animated, for it arose, and drew close to the bedside. There was a rope about its neck, and the other end, coiled up, it held stiffly in its hand.

" My good angel nerved me for this horrible crisis. I remained for some seconds transfixed by the gaze of this tremendous phantom. He came close to the bed, and appeared on the point of mounting upon it. The next instant I was upon the floor at the far side, and in a moment more was, I don't know how, upon the lobby.

" But the spell was not yet broken ; the valley of the shadow of death was not yet traversed. The abhorred phantom was before me there ; it was standing near the banisters, stooping a little, and with one end of the rope round its own neck, was poising a noose at the other, as if to throw over mine ; and while engaged in this baleful pantomime, it wore a smile so sensual, so unspeakably dreadful, that my senses were nearly overpowered. I saw and remember nothing more, until I found myself in your room.

" I had a wonderful escape, Dick—there is no disputing *that*— an escape for which, while I live, I shall bless the mercy of heaven. No one can conceive or imagine what it is for flesh and blood to stand in the presence of such a thing, but one who has had the terrific experience. Dick, Dick, a shadow has passed over me—a chill has crossed my blood and marrow, and I will never be the same again—never, Dick—never ! "

Our handmaid, a mature girl of two-and-fifty, as I have said, stayed her hand, as Tom's story proceeded, and by little and little drew near to us, with open mouth, and her brows contracted over her little, beady black eyes, till stealing a glance over her shoulder now and then, she established herself close behind us. During the relation, she had made various earnest comments, in an under-tone ; but these and her ejaculations, for the sake of brevity and simplicity, I have omitted in my narration.

" It's often I heard tell of it," she now said, " but I never believed it rightly till now—though, indeed, why should not I ? Does not my mother, down there in the lane, know quare stories, God bless us, beyant telling about it ? But you ought not to have slept in the back bedroom. She was loath to let me be going in and out of that room even in the day time, let alone for any Christian to spend the night in it ; for sure she says it was his own bedroom."

" *Whose* own bedroom ? " we asked, in a breath.

" Why, *his*—the ould Judge's—Judge Horrock's, to be sure, God rest his sowl " ; and she looked fearfully round.

" Amen ! " I muttered. " But did he die there ? "

" Die there ! No, not quite *there*," she said. " Shure, was not it over the banisters he hung himself, the ould sinner, God be merciful to us all? and was not it in the alcove they found the handles of the skipping-rope cut off, and the knife where he was settling the cord, God bless us, to hang himself with? It was his housekeeper's daughter owned the rope, my mother often told me, and the child never throve after, and used to be starting up out of her sleep, and screeching in the night time, wid dhrames and frights that cum an her; and they said how it was the speerit of the ould Judge that was tormentin' her; and she used to be roaring and yelling out to hould back the big ould fellow with the crooked neck; and then she'd screech ' Oh, the master! the master! he's stampin' at me, and beckoning to me! Mother, darling, don't let me go!' And so the poor crathure died at last, and the docthers said it was wather on the brain, for it was all they could say."

" How long ago was all this? " I asked.

" Oh, then, how would I know? " she answered. " But it must be a wondherful long time ago, for the housekeeper was an ould woman, with a pipe in her mouth, and not a tooth left, and better nor eighty years ould when my mother was first married; and they said she was a rale buxom, fine-dressed woman when the ould Judge come to his end; an', indeed, my mother's not far from eighty years ould herself this day; and what made it worse for the unnatural ould villain, God rest his soul, to frighten the little girl out of the world the way he did, was what was mostly thought and believed by everyone. My mother says how the poor little crathure was his own child; for he was by all accounts an ould villain every way, an' the hangin'est judge that ever was known in Ireland's ground."

" From what you said about the danger of sleeping in that bed-room," said I, " I suppose there were stories about the ghost having appeared there to others."

" Well, there *was* things said—quare things, surely," she answered, as it seemed, with some reluctance. " And why would not there? Sure was it not up in that same room he slept for more than twenty years? and was it not in the *alcove* he got the rope ready that done his own business at last, the way he done many a betther man's in his lifetime?—and was not the body lying in the same bed after death, and put in the coffin there, too, and carried out to his grave from it in Pether's churchyard, after the coroner was done? But there was quare stories—my mother has them all—about how one Nicholas Spaight got into trouble on the head of it."

" And what did they say of this Nicholas Spaight ? " I asked.

" Oh, for that matther, it's soon told," she answered.

And she certainly did relate a very strange story, which so piqued my curiosity, that I took occasion to visit the ancient lady, her mother, from whom I learned many very curious particulars. Indeed, I am tempted to tell the tale, but my fingers are weary, and I must defer it. But if you wish to hear it another time, I shall do my best.

When we had heard the strange tale I have *not* told you, we put one or two further questions to her about the alleged spectral visitations, to which the house had, ever since the death of the wicked old Judge, been subjected.

" No one ever had luck in it," she told us. " There was always cross accidents, sudden deaths, and short times in it. The first that tuck it was a family—I forget their name—but at any rate there was two young ladies and their papa. He was about sixty, and a stout healthy gentleman as you'd wish to see at that age. Well, he slept in that unlucky back bedroom ; and, God between us an' harm ! sure enough he was found dead one morning, half out of the bed, with his head as black as a sloe, and swelled like a puddin', hanging down near the floor. It was a fit, they said. He was as dead as a mackerel, and so *he* could not say what it was ; but the ould people was all sure that it was nothing at all but the ould Judge, God bless us ! that frightened him out of his senses and his life together.

" Some time after there was a rich old maiden lady took the house. I don't know which room *she* slept in, but she lived alone ; and at any rate, one morning, the servants going down early to their work, found her sitting on the passage-stairs, shivering and talkin' to herself, quite mad ; and never a word more could any of *them* or her friends get from her ever afterwards but, ' Don't ask me to go, for I promised to wait for him.' They never made out from her who it was she meant by *him*, but of course those that knew all about the ould house were at no loss for the meaning of all that happened to her.

" Then afterwards, when the house was let out in lodgings, there was Micky Byrne that took the same room, with his wife and three little children ; and sure I heard Mrs. Byrne myself telling how the children used to be lifted up in the bed at night, she could not see by what mains ; and how they were starting and screeching every hour, just all as one as the housekeeper's little girl that died, till at last one night poor Micky had a dhrop in him, the way he used now and again ; and what do you think in the middle of the night he thought he heard a noise on the stairs, and being in liquor, nothing less id do him but out he must go himself to see what was wrong. Well, after that, all she ever heard of him was himself sayin', ' Oh, God ! ' and a tumble that shook the very house ; and there, sure enough, he was lying on the lower stairs, under the lobby, with his neck smashed double undher him, where he was flung over the banisters."

Then the handmaiden added—

" I'll go down to the lane, and send up Joe Gavvey to pack up the rest of the taythings, and bring all the things across to your new lodgings."

And so we all sallied out together, each of us breathing more freely, I have no doubt, as we crossed that ill-omened threshold for the last time.

Now, I may add thus much, in compliance with the immemorial usage of the realm of fiction, which sees the hero not only through his adventures, but fairly out of the world. You must have perceived that what the flesh, blood, and bone hero of romance proper is to the regular compounder of fiction, this old house of brick, wood, and mortar is to the humble recorder of this true tale. I, therefore, relate, as in duty bound, the catastrophe which ultimately befell it, which was simply this—that about two years subsequently to my story it was taken by a quack doctor, who called himself Baron Duhlstoerf, and filled the parlour windows with bottles of indescribable horrors preserved in brandy, and the newspapers with the usual grandiloquent and mendacious advertisements. This gentleman among his virtues did not reckon sobriety, and one night, being overcome with much wine, he set fire to his bed curtains, partially burned himself, and totally consumed the house. It was afterwards rebuilt, and for a time an undertaker established himself in the premises.

I have now told you my own and Tom's adventures, together with some valuable collateral particulars ; and having acquitted myself of my engagement, I wish you a very good night, and pleasant dreams.

NARRATIVE OF THE GHOST
OF A HAND

I'm sure she believed every word she related, for old Sally was veracious. But all this was worth just so much as such talk commonly is—marvels, fabulæ, what our ancestors called winter's tales —which gathered details from every narrator, and dilated in the act of narration. Still it was not quite for nothing that the house was held to be haunted. Under all this smoke there smouldered just a little spark of truth—an authenticated mystery, for the solution of which some of my readers may possibly suggest a theory, though I confess I can't.

Miss Rebecca Chattesworth, in a letter dated late in the autumn of 1753, gives a minute and curious relation of occurrences in the Tiled House, which, it is plain, although at starting she protests against all such fooleries, she has heard with a peculiar sort of interest, and relates it certainly with an awful sort of particularity.

I was for printing the entire letter, which is really very singular as well as characteristic. But my publisher meets me with his *veto* ; and I believe he is right. The worthy old lady's letter *is*, perhaps, too long ; and I must rest content with a few hungry notes of its tenor.

That year, and somewhere about the 24th October, there broke out a strange dispute between Mr. Alderman Harper, of High Street, Dublin, and my Lord Castlemallard, who, in virtue of his cousinship to the young heir's mother, had undertaken for him the management of the tiny estate on which the Tiled or Tyled House—for I find it spelt both ways—stood.

This Alderman Harper had agreed for a lease of the house for his daughter, who was married to a gentleman named Prosser. He furnished it and put up hangings, and otherwise went to considerable expense. Mr. and Mrs. Prosser came there sometime in June, and after having parted with a good many servants in the interval, she made up her mind that she could not live in the house, and her father waited on Lord Castlemallard, and told him plainly that he would not take out the lease because the house was subjected to annoyances which he could not explain. In plain terms, he said it was haunted, and that no servants would live there more than a few weeks, and that after what his son-in-law's family had suffered there, not only should he be excused from taking a lease of it, but that the house itself ought to be pulled down as a nuisance and the habitual haunt of something worse than human malefactors.

Lord Castlemallard filed a bill in the Equity side of the Exchequer to compel Mr. Alderman Harper to perform his contract, by taking out the lease. But the Alderman drew an answer, supported by no less than seven long affidavits, copies of all which were furnished to his lordship, and with the desired effect ; for rather than compel him to place them upon the file of the court, his lordship struck, and consented to release him.

I am sorry the cause did not proceed at least far enough to place upon the files of the court the very authentic and unaccountable story which Miss Rebecca relates.

The annoyances described did not begin till the end of August, when, one evening, Mrs. Prosser, quite alone, was sitting in the twilight at the back parlour window, which was open, looking out into the orchard, and plainly saw a hand stealthily placed upon the stone window-sill outside, as if by some one beneath the window, at her right side, intending to climb up. There was nothing but the hand, which was rather short but handsomely formed, and white and plump, laid on the edge of the window-sill ; and it was not a very young hand, but one aged, somewhere about forty, as she conjectured. It was only a few weeks before that the horrible robbery at Clondalkin had taken place, and the lady fancied that the hand was that of one of the miscreants who was now about to scale the windows of the Tiled House. She uttered a loud scream and an ejaculation of terror, and at the same moment the hand was quietly withdrawn.

Search was made in the orchard, but no indications of any person's having been under the window, beneath which, ranged along the wall, stood a great column of flower-pots, which it seemed must have prevented any one's coming within reach of it.

The same night there came a hasty tapping, every now and then, at the window of the kitchen. The women grew frightened, and the servant-man, taking fire-arms with him, opened the back-door, but discovered nothing. As he shut it, however, he said, "a thump came on it," and a pressure as of somebody striving to force his way in, which frightened *him* ; and though the tapping went on upon the kitchen window panes, he made no further explorations.

About six o'clock on the Saturday evening following, the cook, "an honest, sober woman, now aged nigh sixty years," being alone in the kitchen, saw, on looking up, it is supposed, the same fat but aristocratic-looking hand, laid with its palm against the glass, near the side of the window, and this time moving slowly up and down, pressed all the while against the glass, as if feeling carefully for some inequality in its surface. She cried out, and said something like a prayer on seeing it. But it was not withdrawn for several seconds after.

After this, for a great many nights, there came at first a low, and afterwards an angry rapping, as it seemed with a set of clenched knuckles at the back-door. And the servant-man would not open it, but called to know who was there ; and there came no answer, only a sound as if the palm of the hand was placed against it, and drawn slowly from side to side with a sort of soft, groping motion.

All this time, sitting in the back parlour, which, for the time, they used as a drawing-room, Mr. and Mrs. Prosser were disturbed by rappings at the window, sometimes very low and furtive, like a clandestine signal, and at others sudden and so loud as to threaten the breaking of the pane.

This was all at the back of the house, which looked upon the orchard as you know. But on a Tuesday night, at about half-past nine, there came precisely the same rapping at the hall-door, and went on, to the great annoyance of the master and terror of his wife, at intervals, for nearly two hours.

After this, for several days and nights, they had no annoyance whatsoever, and began to think that the nuisance had expended itself. But on the night of the 13th September, Jane Easterbrook, an English maid, having gone into the pantry for the small silver bowl in which her mistress's posset was served, happening to look up at the little window of only four panes, observed through an augur-hole which was drilled through the window frame, for the admission of a bolt to secure the shutter, a white pudgy finger —first the tip, and then the two first joints introduced, and turned about this way and that, crooked against the inside, as if in search of a fastening which its owner designed to push aside.

When the maid got back into the kitchen, we are told "she fell into ' a swounde,' and was all the next day very weak."

Mr. Prosser being, I've heard, a hard-headed and conceited sort of fellow, scouted the ghost, and sneered at the fears of his family. He was privately of opinion that the whole affair was a practical joke or a fraud, and waited an opportunity of catching the rogue *flagrante delicto*. He did not long keep this theory to himself, but let it out by degrees with no stint of oaths and threats, believing that some domestic traitor held the thread of the conspiracy.

Indeed it was time something were done ; for not only his servants, but good Mrs. Prosser herself, had grown to look unhappy and anxious. They kept at home from the hour of sunset, and would not venture about the house after night-fall, except in couples.

The knocking had ceased for about a week ; when one night, Mrs. Prosser being in the nursery, her husband, who was in the parlour, heard it begin very softly at the hall-door. The air was quite still, which favoured his hearing distinctly. This was the first time there had been any disturbance at that side of the house, and the character of the summons was changed.

Mr. Prosser, leaving the parlour-door open, it seems, went quietly into the hall. The sound was that of beating on the outside of the stout door, softly and regularly, "with the flat of the hand." He was going to open it suddenly, but changed his mind ; and went back very quietly, and on to the head of the kitchen stair, where was a "strong closet" over the pantry, in which he kept his firearms, swords, and canes.

Here he called his man-servant, whom he believed to be honest, and, with a pair of loaded pistols in his own coat-pockets, and giving another pair to him, he went as lightly as he could, followed by the man, and with a stout walking-cane in his hand, forward to the door.

Everything went as Mr. Prosser wished. The besieger of his house, so far from taking fright at their approach, grew more impatient ; and the sort of patting which had aroused his attention at first assumed the rhythm and emphasis of a series of doubleknocks.

Mr. Prosser, angry, opened the door with his right arm across, cane in hand. Looking, he saw nothing ; but his arm was jerked up oddly, as it might be with the hollow of a hand, and something passed under it, with a kind of gentle squeeze. The servant neither saw nor felt anything, and did not know why his master looked back so hastily, cutting with his cane, and shutting the door with so sudden a slam.

From that time Mr. Prosser discontinued his angry talk and swearing about it, and seemed nearly as averse from the subject as the rest of his family. He grew, in fact, very uncomfortable, feeling an inward persuasion that when, in answer to the summons, he had opened the hall-door, he had actually given admission to the besieger.

He said nothing to Mrs. Prosser, but went up earlier to his bedroom, " where he read a while in his Bible, and said his prayers." I hope the particular relation of this circumstance does not indicate its singularity. He lay awake a good while, it appears ; and, as he supposed, about a quarter past twelve he heard the soft palm of a hand patting on the outside of the bedroom-door, and then brushed slowly along it.

Up bounced Mr. Prosser, very much frightened, and locked the door, crying, " Who's there ? " but receiving no answer, but the same brushing sound of a soft hand drawn over the panels, which he knew only too well.

In the morning the housemaid was terrified by the impression of a hand in the dust of the "little parlour" table, where they had been unpacking delft and other things the day before. The print of the naked foot in the sea-sand did not frighten Robinson Crusoe half so much. They were by this time all nervous, and some of them half-crazed, about the hand.

Mr. Prosser went to examine the mark, and, made light of it, but, as he swore afterwards, rather to quiet his servants than from any comfortable feeling about it in his own mind ; however, he had them all, one by one, into the room, and made each place his or her hand, palm downward, on the same table, thus taking a similar impression from every person in the house, including himself and his wife ; and his "affidavit" deposed that the formation of the hand so impressed differed altogether from those of the living inhabitants of the house, and corresponded with that of the hand seen by Mrs. Prosser and by the cook.

Whoever or whatever the owner of that hand might be, they all felt this subtle demonstration to mean that it was declared he was no longer out of doors, but had established himself in the house.

And now Mrs. Prosser began to be troubled with strange and

horrible dreams, some of which as set out in detail, in Aunt Rebecca's long letter, are really very appalling nightmares. But one night, as Mr. Prosser closed his bedchamber-door, he was struck somewhat by the utter silence of the room, there being no sound of breathing, which seemed unaccountable to him, as he knew his wife was in bed, and his ears were particularly sharp.

There was a candle burning on a small table at the foot of the bed, besides the one he held in one hand, a heavy ledger, connected with his father-in-law's business being under his arm. He drew the curtain at the side of the bed, and saw Mrs. Prosser lying, as for a few seconds he mortally feared, dead, her face being motionless, white, and covered with a cold dew ; and on the pillow, close beside her head, and just within the curtains, was, as he first thought, a toad—but really the same fattish hand, the wrist resting on the pillow, and the fingers extended towards her temple.

Mr. Prosser, with a horrified jerk, pitched the ledger right at the curtains, behind which the owner of the hand might be supposed to stand. The hand was instantaneously and smoothly snatched away, the curtains made a great wave, and Mr. Prosser got round the bed in time to see the closet-door, which was at the other side, pulled to by the same white, puffy hand, as he believed.

He drew the door open with a fling, and stared in : but the closet was empty, except for the clothes hanging from the pegs on the wall, and the dressing-table and looking-glass facing the windows. He shut it sharply, and locked it, and felt for a minute, he says, " as if he were like to lose his wits " ; then, ringing at the bell, he brought the servants, and with much ado they recovered Mrs. Prosser from a sort of " trance," in which, he says, from her looks, she seemed to have suffered " the pains of death " : and Aunt Rebecca adds, " from what she told me of her visions, with her own lips, he might have added, ' and of hell also.' "

But the occurrence which seems to have determined the crisis was the strange sickness of their eldest child, a little boy aged between two and three years. He lay awake, seemingly in paroxysms of terror, and the doctors who were called in, set down the symptoms to incipient water on the brain. Mrs. Prosser used to sit up with the nurse, by the nursery fire, much troubled in mind about the condition of her child.

His bed was placed sideways along the wall, with its head against the door of a press or cupboard, which, however. did not shut quite close. There was a little valance, about a foot deep, round the top of the child's bed, and this descended within some ten or twelve inches of the pillow on which it lay.

They observed that the little creature was quieter whenever they took it up and held it on their laps. They had just replaced him, as he seemed to have grown quite sleepy and tranquil, but he was not five minutes in his bed when he began to scream in one of his frenzies of terror ; at the same moment the nurse, for the first time, detected, and Mrs. Prosser equally plainly saw, following the direction of *her* eyes, the real cause of the child's sufferings.

Protruding through the aperture of the press, and shrouded in the shade of the valance, they plainly saw the white fat hand, palm downwards, presented towards the head of the child. The mother uttered a scream, and snatched the child from its little bed, and she and the nurse ran down to the lady's sleeping-room, where Mr. Prosser was in bed, shutting the door as they entered ; and they had hardly done so, when a gentle tap came to it from the outside.

There is a great deal more, but this will suffice. The singularity of the narrative seems to me to be this, that it describes the ghost of a hand, and no more. The person to whom that hand belonged never once appeared ; nor was it a hand separated from a body, but only a hand so manifested and introduced that its owner was always, by some crafty accident, hidden from view.

In the year 1819, at a college breakfast, I met a Mr. Prosser—a thin, grave, but rather chatty old gentleman, with very white hair drawn back into a pigtail—and he told us all, with a concise particularity, a story of his cousin, James Prosser, who, when an infant, had slept for some time in what his mother said was a haunted nursery in an old house near Chapelizod, and who, whenever he was ill, over-fatigued, or in anywise feverish, suffered all through his life as he had done from a time he could scarce remember, from a vision of a certain gentleman, fat and pale, every curl of whose wig, every button and fold of whose laced clothes, and every feature and line of whose sensual, benignant, and unwholesome face, was as minutely engraven upon his memory as the dress and lineaments of his own grandfather's portrait, which hung before him every day at breakfast, dinner, and supper.

Mr. Prosser mentioned this as an instance of a curiously monotonous, individualised, and persistent nightmare, and hinted the extreme horror and anxiety with which his cousin, of whom he spoke in the past tense as " poor Jemmie," was at any time induced to mention it.

I hope the reader will pardon me for loitering so long in the Tiled House, but this sort of lore has always had a charm for me ; and people, you know, especially old people, will talk of what most interests themselves, too often forgetting that others may have had more than enough of it.

———

CARMILLA

from IN A GLASS DARKLY

Richard Bentley, 1872

PROLOGUE

Upon a paper attached to the Narrative which follows, Doctor Hesselius has written a rather elaborate note, which he accompanies with a reference to his Essay on the strange subject which the MS. illuminates.

This mysterious subject he treats, in that Essay, with his usual learning and acumen, and with remarkable directness and condensation. It will form but one volume of the series of that extraordinary man's collected papers.

As I publish the case, in this volume, simply to interest the "laity," I shall forestall the intelligent lady, who relates it, in nothing ; and, after due consideration, I have determined, therefore, to abstain from presenting any *précis* of the learned Doctor's reasoning, or extract from his statement on a subject which he describes as " involving, not improbably, some of the profoundest arcana of our dual existence, and its intermediates."

I was anxious, on discovering this paper, to re-open the correspondence commenced by Doctor Hesselius, so many years before, with a person so clever and careful as his informant seems to have been. Much to my regret, however, I found that she had died in the interval.

She, probably, could have added little to the Narrative which she communicates in the following pages, with, so far as I can pronounce, such a conscientious particularity.

CHAPTER I

AN EARLY FRIGHT

In Styria, we, though by no means magnificent people, inhabit a castle, or schloss. A small income, in that part of the world, goes a great way. Eight or nine hundred a year does wonders. Scantily enough ours would have answered among wealthy people at home. My father is English, and I bear an English name, although I never saw England. But here, in this lonely and primitive place, where everything is so marvellously cheap, I really don't see how ever so much more money would at all materially add to our comforts, or even luxuries.

My father was in the Austrian service, and retired upon a pension and his patrimony, and purchased this feudal residence, and the small estate on which it stands, a bargain.

Nothing can be more picturesque or solitary. It stands on a slight eminence in a forest. The road, very old and narrow, passes in front of its drawbridge, never raised in my time, and its moat, stocked with perch, and sailed over by many swans, and floating on its surface white fleets of water-lilies.

Over all this the schloss shows its many-windowed front ; its towers, and its Gothic chapel.

The forest opens in an irregular and very picturesque glade before its gate, and at the right a steep Gothic bridge carries the road over a stream that winds in deep shadow through the wood.

I have said that this is a very lonely place. Judge whether I say truth. Looking from the hall door towards the road, the forest in which our castle stands extends fifteen miles to the right, and twelve to the left. The nearest inhabited village is about seven of your English miles to the left. The nearest inhabited schloss of any historic associations, is that of old General Spielsdorf, nearly twenty miles away to the right.

I have said " the nearest *inhabited* village," because there is, only three miles westward, that is to say in the direction of General Spielsdorf's schloss, a ruined village, with its quaint little church, now roofless, in the aisle of which are the mouldering tombs of the proud family of Karnstein, now extinct, who once owned the equally-desolate château which, in the thick of the forest, overlooks the silent ruins of the town.

Respecting the cause of the desertion of this striking and melancholy spot, there is a legend which I shall relate to you another time.

I must tell you now, how very small is the party who constitute the inhabitants of our castle. I don't include servants, or those dependants who occupy rooms in the buildings attached to the schloss. Listen, and wonder ! My father, who is the kindest man on earth, but growing old ; and I, at the date of my story, only nineteen. Eight years have passed since then. I and my father constituted the family at the schloss. My mother, a Styrian lady, died in my infancy, but I had a good-natured governess, who had been with me from, I might almost say, my infancy. I could not remember the time when her fat, benignant face was not a familiar picture in my memory. This was Madame Perrodon, a native of Berne, whose care and good nature in part supplied to me the loss of my mother, whom I do not even remember, so early I lost her. She made a third at our little dinner party. There was a fourth, Mademoiselle De Lafontaine, a lady such as you term, I believe, a " finishing governess." She spoke French and German, Madame Perrodon French and broken English, to which my father and I added English, which, partly to prevent its becoming a lost language among us, and partly from patriotic motives, we spoke every day. The consequence was a Babel, at which strangers used to laugh, and which I shall make no attempt to reproduce in this narrative. And there were two or three young lady friends besides, pretty nearly of my own age, who were occasional visitors, for longer or shorter terms ; and these visits I sometimes returned.

These were our regular social resources ; but of course there were chance visits from " neighbours " of only five or six leagues' distance. My life was, notwithstanding, rather a solitary one, I can assure you.

My gouvernantes had just so much control over me as you might conjecture such sage persons would have in the case of a rather spoiled girl, whose only parent allowed her pretty nearly her own way in everything.

The first occurrence in my existence, which produced a terrible impression upon my mind, which, in fact, never has been effaced, was one of the very earliest incidents of my life which I can recollect. Some people will think it so trifling that it should not be recorded here. You will see, however, by-and-by, why I mention it. The nursery, as it was called, though I had it all to myself, was a large room in the upper story of the castle, with a steep oak roof. I can't have been more than six years old, when one night I awoke, and looking round the room from my bed, failed to see the nursery-maid. Neither was my nurse there ; and I thought myself alone. I was not frightened, for I was one of those happy children who are studiously kept in ignorance of ghost stories, of fairy tales, and of all such lore as makes us cover up our heads when the door creaks suddenly, or the flicker of an expiring candle makes the shadow of a bed-post dance upon the wall, nearer to our faces. I was vexed and insulted at finding myself, as I conceived, neglected, and I began to whimper, preparatory to a hearty bout of roaring ; when to my surprise, I saw a solemn, but very pretty face looking at me from the side of the bed. It was that of a young lady who was kneeling, with her hands under the coverlet. I looked at her with a kind of pleased wonder, and ceased whimpering. She caressed me with her hands, and lay down beside me on the bed, and drew me towards her, smiling ; I felt immediately delightfully soothed, and fell asleep again. I was wakened by a sensation as if two needles ran into my breast very deep at the same moment, and I cried loudly. The lady started back, with her eyes fixed on me, and then slipped down upon the floor, and, as I thought, hid herself under the bed.

I was now for the first time frightened, and I yelled with all my might and main. Nurse, nursery-maid, housekeeper, all came running in, and hearing my story, they made light of it, soothing me all they could meanwhile. But, child as I was, I could perceive that their faces were pale with an unwonted look of anxiety, and I saw them look under the bed, and about the room, and peep under tables and pluck open cupboards ; and the housekeeper whispered to the nurse : " Lay your hand along that hollow in the bed ; some one *did* lie there, so sure as you did not ; the place is still warm."

I remember the nursery-maid petting me, and all three examining my chest, where I told them I felt the puncture, and pronouncing that there was no sign visible that any such thing had happened to me.

The housekeeper and the two other servants who were in charge of the nursery, remained sitting up all night ; and from that time a servant always sat up in the nursery until I was about fourteen.

I was very nervous for a long time after this. A doctor was called in, he was pallid and elderly. How well I remember his long saturnine face, slightly pitted with small-pox, and his chestnut wig. For a good while, every second day, he came and gave me medicine, which of course I hated.

The morning after I saw this apparition I was in a state of terror, and could not bear to be left alone, daylight though it was, for a moment.

I remember my father coming up and standing at the bedside, and talking cheerfully, and asking the nurse a number of questions, and laughing very heartily at one of the answers ; and patting me on the shoulder, and kissing me, and telling me not to be frightened, that it was nothing but a dream and could not hurt me.

But I was not comforted, for I knew the visit of the strange woman was *not* a dream ; and I was *awfully* frightened.

I was a little consoled by the nursery-maid's assuring me that it was she who had come and looked at me, and lain down beside me in the bed, and that I must have been half-dreaming not to have known her face. But this, though supported by the nurse, did not quite satisfy me.

I remember, in the course of that day, a venerable old man, in a black cassock, coming into the room with the nurse and house-keeper, and talking a little to them, and very kindly to me ; his face was very sweet and gentle, and he told me they were going to pray, and joined my hands together, and desired me to say, softly, while they were praying, " Lord, hear all good prayers for us, for Jesus' sake." I think these were the very words, for I often repeated them to myself, and my nurse used for years to make me say them in my prayers.

I remember so well the thoughtful sweet face of that white-haired old man, in his black cassock, as he stood in that rude, lofty, brown room, with the clumsy furniture of a fashion three hundred years old, about him, and the scanty light entering its shadowy atmosphere through the small lattice. He kneeled, and the three women with him, and he prayed aloud with an earnest quavering voice for, what appeared to me, a long time. I forget all my life preceding that event, and for some time after it is all obscure also ; but the scenes I have just described stand out vivid as the isolated pictures of the phantasmagoria surrounded by darkness.

CHAPTER II

A GUEST

I am now going to tell you something so strange that it will require all your faith in my veracity to believe my story. It is not only true, nevertheless, but truth of which I have been an eye-witness.

It was a sweet summer evening, and my father asked me, as he sometimes did, to take a little ramble with him along that beautiful forest vista which I have mentioned as lying in front of the schloss.

" General Spielsdorf cannot come to us so soon as I had hoped," said my father, as we pursued our walk.

He was to have paid us a visit of some weeks, and we had expected his arrival next day. He was to have brought with him a young lady, his niece and ward, Mademoisُlle Rheinfeldt, whom I had never seen, but whom I had heard described as a very charming girl, and in whose society I had promised myself many happy days. I was more disappointed than a young lady living in a town, or a bustling neighbourhood can possibly imagine. This visit, and the new acquaintance it promised, had furnished my day dream for many weeks.

" And how soon does he come ? " I asked.

" Not till autumn. Not for two months, I dare say," he answered. " And I am very glad now, dear, that you never knew Mademoiselle Rheinfeldt."

" And why ? " I asked, both mortified and curious.

" Because the poor young lady is dead," he replied. " I quite forgot I had not told you, but you were not in the room when I received the General's letter this evening."

I was very much shocked. General Spielsdorf had mentioned in his first letter, six or seven weeks before, that she was not so well as he would wish her, but there was nothing to suggest the remotest suspicion of danger.

" Here is the General's letter," he said, handing it to me. " I am afraid he is in great affliction ; the letter appears to me to have been written very nearly in distraction."

We sat down on a rude bench, under a group of magnificent lime trees. The sun was setting with all its melancholy splendour behind the sylvan horizon, and the stream that flows beside our home, and passes under the steep old bridge I have mentioned, wound through many a group of noble trees, almost at our feet, reflecting in its current the fading crimson of the sky. General Spielsdorf's letter was so extraordinary, so vehement, and in some places so self-contradictory, that I read it twice over—the second time aloud to my father—and was still unable to account for it, except by supposing that grief had unsettled his mind.

It said, " I have lost my darling daughter, for as such I loved her. During the last days of dear Bertha's illness I was not able to write to you. Before then I had no idea of her danger. I have lost

her, and now learn *all*, too late. She died in the peace of innocence, and in the glorious hope of a blessed futurity. The fiend
who betrayed our infatuated hospitality has done it all. I thought
I was receiving into my house innocence, gaiety, a charming
companion for my lost Bertha. Heavens ! what a fool have I been !
I thank God my child died without a suspicion of the cause of her
sufferings. She is gone without so much as conjecturing the
nature of her illness, and the accursed passion of the agent of all
this misery. I devote my remaining days to tracking and extinguishing a monster. I am told I may hope to accomplish my
righteous and merciful purpose. At present there is scarcely a
gleam of light to guide me. I curse my conceited incredulity, my
despicable affectation of superiority, my blindness, my obstinacy
—all—too late. I cannot write or talk collectedly now. I am distracted. So soon as I shall have a little recovered, I mean to devote
myself for a time to enquiry, which may possibly lead me as far as
Vienna. Some time in the autumn, two months hence, or earlier if
I live, I will see you—that is, if you permit me ; I will then tell
you all that I scarce dare put upon paper now. Farewell. Pray
for me, dear friend."

In these terms ended this strange letter. Though I had never
seen Bertha Rheinfeldt, my eyes filled with tears at the sudden
intelligence ; I was startled, as well as profoundly disappointed.

The sun had now set, and it was twilight by the time I had
returned the General's letter to my father.

It was a soft clear evening, and we loitered, speculating upon
the possible meanings of the violent and incoherent sentences
which I had just been reading. We had nearly a mile to walk
before reaching the road that passes the schloss in front, and by
that time the moon was shining brilliantly. At the drawbridge we
met Madame Perrodon and Mademoiselle De Lafontaine, who
had come out, without their bonnets, to enjoy the exquisite
moonlight.

We heard their voices gabbling in animated dialogue as we
approached. We joined them at the drawbridge, and turned about
to admire with them the beautiful scene.

The glade through which we had just walked lay before us. At
our left the narrow road wound away under clumps of lordly
trees, and was lost to sight amid the thickening forest. At the right
the same road crosses the steep and picturesque bridge, near which
stands a ruined tower, which once guarded that pass ; and beyond

the bridge an abrupt eminence rises, covered with trees, and showing in the shadow some grey ivy-clustered rocks.

Over the sward and low grounds, a thin film of mist was stealing like smoke, marking the distances with a transparent veil ; and here and there we could see the river faintly flashing in the moon-light.

No softer, sweeter scene could be imagined. The news I had just heard made it melancholy ; but nothing could disturb its character of profound serenity, and the enchanted glory and vagueness of the prospect.

My father, who enjoyed the picturesque, and I, stood looking in silence over the expanse beneath us. The two good governesses, standing a little way behind us, discoursed upon the scene, and were eloquent upon the moon.

Madame Perrodon was fat, middle-aged, and romantic, and talked and sighed poetically. Mademoiselle De Lafontaine—in right of her father, who was a German, assumed to be psycho-logical, metaphysical, and something of a mystic—now declared that when the moon shone with a light so intense it was well known that it indicated a special spiritual activity. The effect of the full moon in such a state of brilliancy was manifold. It acted on dreams, it acted on lunacy, it acted on nervous people ; it had marvellous physical influences connected with life. Mademoiselle related that her cousin, who was mate of a merchant ship, having taken a nap on deck on such a night, lying on his back, with his face full in the light of the moon, had awakened, after a dream of an old woman clawing him by the cheek, with his features horribly drawn to one side ; and his countenance had never quite recovered its equilibrium.

" The moon, this night," she said, " is full of odylic and magnetic influence—and see, when you look behind you at the front of the schloss, how all its windows flash and twinkle with that silvery splendour, as if unseen hands had lighted up the rooms to receive fairy guests."

There are indolent states of the spirits in which, indisposed to talk ourselves, the talk of others is pleasant to our listless ears ; and I gazed on, pleased with the tinkle of the ladies' con-versation.

" I have got into one of my moping moods to-night," said my father, after a silence, and quoting Shakespeare, whom, by way of keeping up our English, he used to read aloud, he said :—

> " ' *In truth I know not why I am so sad :*
> *It wearies me ; you say it wearies you ;*
> *But how I got it—came by it.*'

" I forget the rest. But I feel as if some great misfortune were hanging over us. I suppose the poor General's afflicted letter has had something to do with it."

At this moment the unwonted sound of carriage wheels and many hoofs upon the road, arrested our attention.

They seemed to be approaching from the high ground overlooking the bridge, and very soon the equipage emerged from that point. Two horsemen first crossed the bridge, then came a carriage drawn by four horses, and two men rode behind.

It seemed to be the travelling carriage of a person of rank ; and we were all immediately absorbed in watching that very unusual spectacle. It became, in a few moments, greatly more interesting, for just as the carriage had passed the summit of the steep bridge, one of the leaders, taking fright, communicated his panic to the rest, and, after a plunge or two, the whole team broke into a wild gallop together, and dashing between the horsemen who rode in front, came thundering along the road towards us with the speed of a hurricane.

The excitement of the scene was made more painful by the clear, long-drawn screams of a female voice from the carriage window.

We all advanced in curiosity and horror ; my father in silence, the rest with various ejaculations of terror.

Our suspense did not last long. Just before you reach the castle drawbridge, on the route they were coming, there stands by the roadside a magnificent lime tree, on the other stands an ancient stone cross, at sight of which the horses, now going at a pace that was perfectly frightful, swerved so as to bring the wheel over the projecting roots of the tree.

I knew what was coming. I covered my eyes, unable to see it out, and turned my head away ; at the same moment I heard a cry from my lady-friends, who had gone on a little.

Curiosity opened my eyes, and I saw a scene of utter confusion. Two of the horses were on the ground, the carriage lay upon its side, with two wheels in the air ; the men were busy removing the traces, and a lady, with a commanding air and figure had got out, and stood with clasped hands, raising the handkerchief that was in them every now and then to her eyes. Through the carriage door was now lifted a young lady, who appeared to be lifeless. My dear old father was already beside the elder lady, with his hat in his hand, evidently tendering his aid and the resources of his schloss. The lady did not appear to hear him, or to have eyes for anything but the slender girl who was being placed against the slope of the bank.

I approached ; the young lady was apparently stunned, but she was certainly not dead. My father, who piqued himself on being something of a physician, had just had his fingers to her wrist and assured the lady, who declared herself her mother, that her pulse, though faint and irregular, was undoubtedly still distinguishable. The lady clasped her hands and looked upward, as if in a momentary transport of gratitude ; but immediately she broke out again in that theatrical way which is, I believe, natural to some people.

She was what is called a fine-looking woman for her time of life, and must have been handsome ; she was tall, but not thin, and dressed in black velvet, and looked rather pale, but with a proud and commanding countenance, though now agitated strangely.

" Was ever being so born to calamity ? " I heard her say, with clasped hands, as I came up. " Here am I, on a journey of life and death, in prosecuting which to lose an hour is possibly to lose all. My child will not have recovered sufficiently to resume her route for who can say how long. I must leave her ; I cannot, dare not, delay. How far on, sir, can you tell, is the nearest village ? I must leave her there ; and shall not see my darling, or even hear of her till my return, three months hence."

I plucked my father by the coat, and whispered earnestly in his ear, " Oh ! papa, pray ask her to let her stay with us—it would be so delightful. Do, pray."

" If Madame will entrust her child to the care of my daughter and of her good gouvernante, Madame Perrodon, and permit her to remain as our guest, under my charge, until her return, it will confer a distinction and an obligation upon us, and we shall treat her with all the care and devotion which so sacred a trust deserves."

" I cannot do that, sir, it would be to task your kindness and chivalry too cruelly," said the lady, distractedly.

" It would, on the contrary, be to confer on us a very great kindness at the moment when we most need it. My daughter has just been disappointed by a cruel misfortune, in a visit from which she had long anticipated a great deal of happiness. If you confide this young lady to our care it will be her best consolation. The nearest village on your route is distant, and affords no such inn as you could think of placing your daughter at ; you cannot allow her to continue her journey for any considerable distance without danger. If, as you say, you cannot suspend your journey, you must part with her to-night, and nowhere could you do so with more honest assurances of care and tenderness than here."

There was something in this lady's air and appearance so distinguished, and even imposing, and in her manner so engaging, as to impress one, quite apart from the dignity of her equipage, with a conviction that she was a person of consequence.

By this time the carriage was replaced in its upright position, and the horses, quite tractable, in the traces again.

The lady threw on her daughter a glance which I fancied was not quite so affectionate as one might have anticipated from the beginning of the scene ; then she beckoned slightly to my father and withdrew two or three steps with him out of hearing ; and talked to him with a fixed and stern countenance, not at all like that with which she had hitherto spoken.

I was filled with wonder that my father did not seem to perceive the change, and also unspeakably curious to learn what it could be that she was speaking, almost in his ear, with so much earnestness and rapidity.

Two or three minutes at most, I think, she remained thus employed, then she turned, and a few steps brought her to where her daughter lay, supported by Madame Perrodon. She kneeled beside her for a moment and whispered, as Madame supposed, a little benediction in her ear ; then hastily kissing her, she stepped into her carriage, the door was closed, the footmen in stately liveries jumped up behind, the outriders spurred on, the postilions cracked their whips, the horses plunged and broke suddenly into a furious canter that threatened soon again to become a gallop, and the carriage whirled away, followed at the same rapid pace by the two horsemen in the rear.

CHAPTER III

WE COMPARE NOTES

We followed the *cortège* with our eyes until it was swiftly lost to sight in the misty wood ; and the very sound of the hoofs and wheels died away in the silent night air.

Nothing remained to assure us that the adventure had not been an illusion for a moment but the young lady, who just at that moment opened her eyes. I could not see, for her face was turned from me, but she raised her head, evidently looking about her, and I heard a very sweet voice ask complainingly, " Where is mamma ? "

Our good Madame Perrodon answered tenderly, and added some comfortable assurances.

I then heard her ask :

" Where am I ? What is this place ? " and after that she said, " I don't see the carriage ; and Matska, where is she ? "

Madame answered all her questions in so far as she understood them ; and gradually the young lady remembered how the mis-adventure came about, and was glad to hear that no one in, or in attendance on, the carriage was hurt ; and on learning that her mamma had left her here, till her return in about three months, she wept.

I was going to add my consolations to those of Madame Perro-don when Mademoiselle De Lafontaine placed her hand upon my arm, saying :

" Don't approach, one at a time is as much as she can at present converse with ; a very little excitement would possibly overpower her now."

As soon as she is comfortably in bed, I thought, I will run up to her room and see her.

My father in the meantime had sent a servant on horseback for the physician, who lived about two leagues away ; and a bed-room was being prepared for the young lady's reception.

The stranger now rose, and leaning on Madame's arm, walked slowly over the drawbridge and into the castle gate.

In the hall the servants waited to receive her, and she was con-ducted forthwith to her room.

The room we usually sat in as our drawing-room is long, having four windows, that looked over the moat and drawbridge, upon the forest scene I have just described.

It is furnished in old carved oak, with large carved cabinets, and the chairs are cushioned with crimson Utrecht velvet. The walls are covered with tapestry, and surrounded with great gold frames, the figures being as large as life, in ancient and very curious costume, and the subjects represented are hunting, hawking, and generally festive. It is not too stately to be extremely comfortable ; and here we had our tea, for with his usual patriotic leanings he insisted that the national beverage should make its appearance regularly with our coffee and chocolate.

We sat here this night, and with candles lighted, were talking over the adventure of the evening.

Madame Perrodon and Mademoiselle De Lafontaine were both of our party. The younger stranger had hardly lain down in her bed when she sank into a deep sleep ; and those ladies had left her in the care of a servant.

" How do you like our guest ? " I asked, as soon as Madame entered. " Tell me all about her ? "

" I like her extremely," answered Madame, " she is, I almost think, the prettiest creature I ever saw ; about your age, and so gentle and nice."

" She is absolutely beautiful," threw in Mademoiselle, who had peeped for a moment into the stranger's room.

" And such a sweet voice ! " added Madame Perrodon.

" Did you remark a woman in the carriage, after it was set up again, who did not get out," inquired Mademoiselle, " but only looked from the window ? "

No, we had not seen her.

Then she described a hideous black woman, with a sort of coloured turban on her head, who was gazing all the time from the carriage window, nodding and grinning derisively towards the ladies, with gleaming eyes and large white eye-balls, and her teeth set as if in fury.

" Did you remark what an ill-looking pack of men the servants were ? " asked Madame.

" Yes," said my father, who had just come in, " ugly, hang-dog looking fellows, as ever I beheld in my life. I hope they mayn't rob the poor lady in the forest. They are clever rogues, however ; they got everything to rights in a minute."

" I dare say they are worn out with too long travelling," said Madame. " Besides looking wicked, their faces were so strangely lean, and dark, and sullen. I am very curious, I own ; but I dare say the young lady will tell us all about it to-morrow, if she is sufficiently recovered."

"I don't think she will," said my father, with a mysterious smile, and a little nod of his head, as if he knew more about it than he cared to tell us.

This made me all the more inquisitive as to what had passed between him and the lady in the black velvet, in the brief but earnest interview that had immediately preceded her departure.

We were scarcely alone, when I entreated him to tell me. He did not need much pressing.

"There is no particular reason why I should not tell you. She expressed a reluctance to trouble us with the care of her daughter, saying she was in delicate health, and nervous, but not subject to any kind of seizure—she volunteered that—nor to any illusion ; being, in fact, perfectly sane."

"How very odd to say all that ! " I interpolated. "It was so unnecessary."

"At all events it *was* said," he laughed, "and as you wish to know all that passed, which was indeed very little, I tell you. She then said, ' I am making a long journey of *vital* importance '— she emphasized the word— 'rapid and secret ; I shall return for my child in three months ; in the meantime, she will be silent as to who we are, whence we come, and whither we are travelling.' That is all she said. She spoke very pure French. When she said the word ' secret,' she paused for a few seconds, looking sternly, her eyes fixed on mine. I fancy she makes a great point of that. You saw how quickly she was gone. I hope I have not done a very foolish thing, in taking charge of the young lady."

For my part, I was delighted. I was longing to see and talk to her ; and only waiting till the doctor should give me leave. You who live in towns, can have no idea how great an event the intro- duction of a new friend is, in such a solitude as surrounded us.

The doctor did not arrive till nearly one o'clock ; but I could no more have gone to my bed and slept, than I could have overtaken, on foot, the carriage in which the princess in black velvet had driven away.

When the physician came down to the drawing-room, it was to report very favourably upon his patient. She was now sitting up, her pulse quite regular, apparently perfectly well. She had sus- tained no injury, and the little shock to her nerves had passed away quite harmlessly. There could be no harm certainly in my seeing her, if we both wished it ; and, with this permission, I sent, forthwith, to know whether she would allow me to visit her for a few minutes in her room.

The servant returned immediately to say that she desired nothing more.

You may be sure I was not long in availing myself of this permission.

Our visitor lay in one of the handsomest rooms in the schloss. It was, perhaps a little stately. There was a sombre piece of tapestry opposite the foot of the bed, representing Cleopatra with the asp to her bosom ; and other solemn classic scenes were displayed, a little faded, upon the other walls. But there was gold carving, and rich and varied colour enough in the other decorations of the room, to more than redeem the gloom of the old tapestry.

There were candles at the bed side. She was sitting up ; her slender pretty figure enveloped in the soft silk dressing-gown, embroidered with flowers, and lined with thick quilted silk, which her mother had thrown over her feet as she lay upon the ground.

What was it that, as I reached the bed side and had just begun my little greeting, struck me dumb in a moment, and made me recoil a step or two from before her ? I will tell you.

I saw the very face which had visited me in my childhood at night, which remained so fixed in my memory, and on which I had for so many years so often ruminated with horror, when no one suspected of what I was thinking.

It was pretty, even beautiful ; and when I first beheld it, wore the same melancholy expression.

But this almost instantly lighted into a strange fixed smile of recognition.

There was a silence of fully a minute, and then at length *she* spoke ; *I* could not.

" How wonderful ! " she exclaimed. " Twelve years ago, I saw your face in a dream, and it has haunted me ever since."

" Wonderful indeed ! " I repeated, overcoming with an effort the horror that had for a time suspended my utterances. " Twelve years ago, in vision or reality, *I* certainly saw you. I could not forget your face. It has remained before my eyes ever since."

Her smile had softened. Whatever I had fancied strange in it, was gone, and it and her dimpling cheeks were now delightfully pretty and intelligent.

I felt reassured, and continued more in the vein which hospitality indicated, to bid her welcome, and to tell her how much pleasure her accidental arrival had given us all, and especially what a happiness it was to me.

I took her hand as I spoke. I was a little shy, as lonely people are, but the situation made me eloquent, and even bold. She pressed my hand, she laid hers upon it, and her eyes glowed, as, looking hastily into mine, she smiled again, and blushed.

She answered my welcome very prettily. I sat down beside her, still wondering ; and she said :

" I must tell you my vision about you ; it is so very strange that you and I should have had, each of the other so vivid a dream, that each should have seen, I you and you me, looking as we do now, when of course we both were mere children. I was a child about six years old, and I awoke from a confused and troubled dream, and found myself in a room, unlike my nursery, wainscoted clumsily in some dark wood, and with cupboards and bedsteads, and chairs, and benches placed about it. The beds were, I thought, all empty, and the room itself without any one but myself in it ; and I, after looking about me for some time, and admiring especially an iron candlestick, with two branches, which I should certainly know again, crept under one of the beds to reach the window ; but, as I got from under the bed, I heard someone crying ; and looking up, while I was still upon my knees, I saw *you* —most assuredly you—as I see you now ; a beautiful young lady, with golden hair and large blue eyes, and lips—your lips—you, as you are here. Your looks won me ; I climbed on the bed and put my arms about you, and I think we both fell asleep. I was aroused by a scream ; you were sitting up screaming. I was frightened, and slipped down upon the ground, and, it seemed to me, lost consciousness for a moment ; and when I came to myself, I was again in my nursery at home. Your face I have never forgotten since. I could not be misled by mere resemblance. You *are* the lady whom I then saw."

It was now my turn to relate my corresponding vision, which I did, to the undisguised wonder of my new acquaintance.

" I don't know which should be most afraid of the other," she said, again smiling. " If you were less pretty I think I should be very much afraid of you, but being as you are, and you and I both so young, I feel only that I have made your acquaintance twelve years ago, and have already a right to your intimacy ; at all events, it does seem as if we were destined, from our earliest childhood, to be friends. I wonder whether you feel as strangely drawn towards me as I do to you ; I have never had a friend— shall I find one now ? " She sighed, and her fine dark eyes gazed passionately on me.

Now the truth is, I felt rather unaccountably towards the beautiful stranger. I did feel, as she said, " drawn towards her," but there was also something of repulsion. In this ambiguous feeling, however, the sense of attraction immensely prevailed. She interested and won me ; she was so beautiful and so indescribably engaging.

I perceived now something of languor and exhaustion stealing over her, and hastened to bid her good-night.

" The doctor thinks," I added, " that you ought to have a maid to sit up with you to-night ; one of ours is waiting, and you will find her a very useful and quiet creature."

" How kind of you, but I could not sleep, I never could with an attendant in the room. I shan't require any assistance—and, shall I confess my weakness, I am haunted with a terror of robbers. Our house was robbed once, and two servants murdered, so I always lock my door. It has become a habit—and you look so kind I know you will forgive me. I see there is a key in the lock."

She held me close in her pretty arms for a moment and whispered in my ear, " Good-night, darling, it is very hard to part with you, but good-night ; to-morrow, but not early, I shall see you again."

She sank back on the pillow with a sigh, and her fine eyes followed me with a fond and melancholy gaze, and she murmured again, " Good-night, dear friend."

Young people like, and even love, on impulse. I was flattered by the evident, though as yet undeserved, fondness she showed me. I liked the confidence with which she at once received me. She was determined that we should be very dear friends.

Next day came and we met again. I was delighted with my companion ; that is to say, in many respects.

Her looks lost nothing in daylight—she was certainly the most beautiful creature I had ever seen, and the unpleasant remembrance of the face presented in my early dream, had lost the effect of the first unexpected recognition.

She confessed that she had experienced a similar shock on seeing me, and precisely the same faint antipathy that had mingled with my admiration of her. We now laughed together over our momentary horrors.

CHAPTER IV

I told you that I was charmed with her in most particulars.

There were some that did not please me so well.

She was above the middle height of women. I shall begin by describing her. She was slender, and wonderfully graceful. Except that her movements were languid—*very* languid—indeed, there was nothing in her appearance to indicate an invalid. Her complexion was rich and brilliant ; her features were small and beautifully formed ; her eyes large, dark, and lustrous ; her hair was quite wonderful, I never saw hair so magnificently thick and long when it was down about her shoulders ; I have often placed my hands under it, and laughed with wonder at its weight. It was exquisitely fine and soft, and in colour a rich very dark brown, with something of gold. I loved to let it down, tumbling with its own weight, as, in her room, she lay back in her chair talking in her sweet low voice, I used to fold and braid it, and spread it out and play with it. Heavens ! If I had but known all !

I said there were particulars which did not please me. I have told you that her confidence won me the first night I saw her ; but I found that she exercised with respect to herself, her mother, her history, everything in fact connected with her life, plans, and people, an ever-wakeful reserve. I dare say I was unreasonable, perhaps I was wrong ; I dare say I ought to have respected the solemn injunction laid upon my father by the stately lady in black velvet. But curiosity is a restless and unscrupulous passion, and no one girl can endure, with patience, that her's should be baffled by another. What harm could it do anyone to tell me what I so ardently desired to know ? Had she no trust in my good sense or honour ? Why would she not believe me when I assured her, so solemnly, that I would not divulge one syllable of what she told me to any mortal breathing.

There was a coldness, it seemed to me, beyond her years, in her smiling melancholy persistent refusal to afford me the least ray of light.

I cannot say we quarrelled upon this point, for she would not quarrel upon any. It was, of course, very unfair of me to press her, very ill-bred, but I really could not help it ; and I might just as well have let it alone.

What she did tell me amounted, in my unconscionable estimation—to nothing.

It was all summed up in three very vague disclosures.

First.—Her name was Carmilla.

Second.—Her family was very ancient and noble.

Third.—Her home lay in the direction of the west.

She would not tell me the name of her family, nor their armorial bearings, nor the name of their estate, nor even that of the country they lived in.

You are not to suppose that I worried her incessantly on these subjects. I watched opportunity, and rather insinuated than urged my enquiries. Once or twice, indeed, I did attack her more directly. But no matter what my tactics, utter failure was invariably the result. Reproaches and caresses were all lost upon her. But I must add this, that her evasion was conducted with so pretty a melancholy and deprecation, with so many, and even passionate declarations of her liking for me, and trust in my honour, and with so many promises, that I should at last know all, that I could not find it in my heart long to be offended with her.

She used to place her pretty arms about my neck, draw me to her, and laying her cheek to mine, murmur with her lips near my ear, " Dearest, your little heart is wounded ; think me not cruel because I obey the irresistible law of my strength and weakness ; if your dear heart is wounded, my wild heart bleeds with yours. In the rapture of my enormous humiliation I live in your warm life, and you shall die—die, sweetly die—into mine. I cannot help it ; as I draw near to you, you, in your turn, will draw near to others, and learn the rapture of that cruelty, which yet is love ; so, for a while, seek to know no more of me and mine, but trust me with all your loving spirit."

And when she had spoken such a rhapsody, she would press me more closely in her trembling embrace, and her lips in soft kisses gently glow upon my cheek.

Her agitations and her language were unintelligible to me.

From these foolish embraces, which were not of very frequent occurrence, I must allow, I used to wish to extricate myself ; but my energies seemed to fail me. Her murmured words sounded like a lullaby in my ear, and soothed my resistance into a trance, from which I only seemed to recover myself when she withdrew her arms.

In these mysterious moods I did not like her. I experienced a strange tumultuous excitement that was pleasurable, ever and anon, mingled with a vague sense of fear and disgust. I had no distinct thoughts about her while such scenes lasted, but I was conscious of a love growing into adoration, and also of abhorrence. This I know is paradox, but I can make no other attempt to explain the feeling.

I now write, after an interval of more than ten years, with a trembling hand, with a confused and horrible recollection of certain occurrences and situations, in the ordeal through which I was unconsciously passing ; though with a vivid and very sharp remembrance of the main current of my story. But, I suspect, in all lives there are certain emotional scenes, those in which our passions have been most wildly and terribly roused, that are of all others the most vaguely and dimly remembered.

Sometimes after an hour of apathy, my strange and beautiful companion would take my hand and hold it with a fond pressure, renewed again and again ; blushing softly, gazing in my face with languid and burning eyes, and breathing so fast that her dress rose and fell with the tumultuous respiration. It was like the ardour of a lover ; it embarrassed me ; it was hateful and yet overpowering ; and with gloating eyes she drew me to her, and her hot lips travelled along my cheek in kisses ; and she would whisper, almost in sobs, " You are mine, you *shall* be mine, and you and I are one for ever." Then she has thrown herself back in her chair, with her small hands over her eyes, leaving me trembling.

" Are we related," I used to ask ; " what can you mean by all this ? I remind you perhaps of some one whom you love ; but you must not, I hate it ; I don't know you—I don't know myself when you look so and talk so."

She used to sigh at my vehemence, then turn away and drop my hand.

Respecting these very extraordinary manifestations I strove in vain to form any satisfactory theory—I could not refer them to affectation or trick. It was unmistakably the momentary breaking out of suppressed instinct and emotion. Was she, notwithstanding her mother's volunteered denial, subject to brief visitations of insanity ; or was there here a disguise and a romance ? I had read in old story books of such things. What if a boyish lover had found his way into the house, and sought to prosecute his suit in masquerade, with the assistance of a clever old adventuress. But here were many things against this hypothesis, highly interesting as it was to my vanity.

I could boast of no little attentions such as masculine gallantry delights to offer. Between these passionate moments there were long intervals of common-place, of gaiety, of brooding melancholy, during which, except that I detected her eyes so full of melancholy fire, following me, at times I might have been as nothing to her. Except in these brief periods of mysterious excitement her ways were girlish ; and there was always a languor about her, quite incompatible with a masculine system in a state of health.

In some respects her habits were odd. Perhaps not so singular in the opinion of a town lady like you, as they appeared to us rustic people. She used to come down very late, generally not till one o'clock, she would then take a cup of chocolate, but eat nothing ; we then went out for a walk, which was a mere saunter, and she seemed, almost immediately, exhausted, and either returned to the schloss or sat on one of the benches that were placed, here and there, among the trees. This was a bodily languor in which her mind did not sympathise. She was always an animated talker, and very intelligent.

She sometimes alluded for a moment to her own home, or mentioned an adventure or situation, or an early recollection, which indicated a people of strange manners, and described customs of which we knew nothing. I gathered from these chance hints that her native country was much more remote than I had at first fancied.

As we sat thus one afternoon under the trees a funeral passed us by. It was that of a pretty young girl, whom I had often seen, the daughter of one of the rangers of the forest. The poor man was walking behind the coffin of his darling ; she was his only child, and he looked quite heartbroken. Peasants walking two-and-two came behind, they were singing a funeral hymn.

I rose to mark my respect as they passed, and joined in the hymn they were very sweetly singing.

My companion shook me a little roughly, and I turned surprised. She said brusquely, " Don't you perceive how discordant that is ? "

" I think it is very sweet, on the contrary," I answered, vexed at the interruption, and very uncomfortable, lest the people who composed the little procession should observe and resent what was passing.

I resumed, therefore, instantly, and was again interrupted. " You pierce my ears," said Carmilla, almost angrily, and stopping her ears with her tiny fingers. " Besides, how can you tell that your religion and mine are the same ; your forms wound me, and I hate funerals. What a fuss ! Why, *you* must die—*everyone* must die ; and all are happier when they do. Come home."

" My father has gone on with the clergyman to the churchyard. I thought you knew she was to be buried to-day."

" *She ?* I don't trouble my head about peasants. I don't know who she is," answered Carmilla, with a flash from her fine eyes.

" She is the poor girl who fancied she saw a ghost a fortnight ago, and has been dying ever since, till yesterday, when she expired."

" Tell me nothing about ghosts. I shan't sleep to-night if you do."

" I hope there is no plague or fever coming ; all this looks very like it," I continued. " The swineherd's young wife died only a week ago, and she thought something seized her by the throat as she lay in her bed, and nearly strangled her. Papa says such horrible fancies do accompany some forms of fever. She was quite well the day before. She sank afterwards, and died before a week."

" Well, *her* funeral is over, I hope, and *her* hymn sung ; and our ears shan't be tortured with that discord and jargon. It has made me nervous. Sit down here, beside me ; sit close ; hold my hand ; press it hard—hard—harder."

We had moved a little back, and had come to another seat.

She sat down. Her face underwent a change that alarmed and even terrified me for a moment. It darkened, and became horribly livid ; her teeth and hands were clenched, and she frowned and compressed her lips, while she stared down upon the ground at her feet, and trembled all over with a continued shudder as irrepressible as ague. All her energies seemed strained to suppress a fit, with which she was then breathlessly tugging ; and at length a low convulsive cry of suffering broke from her, and gradually the hysteria subsided. " There ! That comes of strangling people with hymns ! " she said at last. " Hold me, hold me still. It is passing away."

And so gradually it did ; and perhaps to dissipate the sombre impression which the spectacle had left upon me, she became unusually animated and chatty ; and so we got home.

This was the first time I had seen her exhibit any definable symptoms of that delicacy of health which her mother had spoken of. It was the first time, also, I had seen her exhibit anything like temper.

Both passed away like a summer cloud ; and never but once afterwards did I witness on her part a momentary sign of anger. I will tell you how it happened.

She and I were looking out of one of the long drawing-room windows, when there entered the court-yard, over the draw-bridge, a figure of a wanderer whom I knew very well. He used to visit the schloss generally twice a year.

It was the figure of a hunchback, with the sharp lean features that generally accompany deformity. He wore a pointed black beard, and he was smiling from ear to ear, showing his white fangs. He was dressed in buff, black, and scarlet, and crossed with more straps and belts than I could count, from which hung all manner of things. Behind, he carried a magic-lantern, and two boxes, which I well knew, in one of which was a salamander, and in the other a mandrake. These monsters used to make my father laugh. They were compounded of parts of monkeys, parrots, squirrels, fish, and hedgehogs, dried and stitched together with great neatness and startling effect. He had a fiddle, a box of conjuring apparatus, a pair of foils and masks attached to his belt, several other mysterious cases dangling about him, and a black staff with copper ferrules in his hand. His companion was a rough spare dog, that followed at his heels, but stopped short, suspiciously at the drawbridge, and in a little while began to howl dismally.

In the meantime, the mountebank, standing in the midst of the court-yard, raised his grotesque hat, and made us a very cere-monious bow, paying his compliments very volubly in execrable French, and German not much better. Then, disengaging his fiddle, he began to scrape a lively air, to which he sang with a merry discord, dancing with ludicrous airs and activity, that made me laugh, in spite of the dog's howling.

Then he advanced to the window with many smiles and salutations, and his hat in his left hand, his fiddle under his arm, and with a fluency that never took breath, he gabbled a long advertisement of all his accomplishments, and the resources of the various arts which he placed at our service, and the curiosities and entertainments which it was in his power, at our bidding to display.

"Will your ladyships be pleased to buy an amulet against the oupire, which is going like the wolf, I hear, through these woods," he said, dropping his hat on the pavement. "They are dying of it right and left, and here is a charm that never fails ; only pinned to the pillow, and you may laugh in his face."

These charms consisted of oblong slips of vellum, with cabalistic ciphers and diagrams upon them.

Carmilla instantly purchased one, and so did I.

He was looking up, and we were smiling down upon him, amused ; at least, I can answer for myself. His piercing black eye, as he looked up in our faces, seemed to detect something that fixed for a moment his curiosity.

In an instant he unrolled a leather case, full of all manner of odd little steel instruments.

"See here, my lady," he said, displaying it, and addressing me, "I profess, among other things less useful, the art of dentistry. Plague take the dog ! " he interpolated. "Silence, beast ! He howls so that your ladyships can scarcely hear a word. Your noble friend, the young lady at your right, has the sharpest tooth—long, thin, pointed, like an awl, like a needle ; ha, ha ! With my sharp and long sight, as I look up, I have seen it distinctly ; now if it happens to hurt the young lady, and I think it must, here am I, here are my file, my punch, my nippers ; I will make it round and blunt, if her ladyship pleases ; no longer the tooth of a fish, but of a beautiful young lady as she is. Hey ? Is the young lady displeased ? Have I been too bold ? Have I offended her ? "

The young lady, indeed, looked very angry as she drew back from the window.

"How dares that mountebank insult us so ? Where is your father ? I shall demand redress from him. My father would have had the wretch tied up to the pump, and flogged with a cart-whip, and burnt to the bones with the castle brand ! "

She retired from the window a step or two, and sat down, and hardly lost sight of the offender, when her wrath subsided as suddenly as it had risen, and she gradually recovered her usual tone, and seemed to forget the little hunchback and his follies.

My father was out of spirits that evening. On coming in he told us that there had been another case very similar to the two fatal ones which had lately occurred. The sister of a young peasant on his estate, only a mile away, was very ill, had been, as she described it, attacked very nearly in the same way, and was now slowly but steadily sinking.

"All this," said my father, "is strictly referable to natural causes. These poor people infect one another with their superstitions, and so repeat in imagination the images of terror that have infested their neighbours."

"But that very circumstance frightens one horribly," said Carmilla.

"How so?" inquired my father.

"I am so afraid of fancying I see such things; I think it would be as bad as reality."

"We are in God's hands; nothing can happen without His permission, and all will end well for those who love Him. He is our faithful creator; He had made us all, and will take care of us."

"Creator! *Nature!*" said the young lady in answer to my gentle father. "And this disease that invades the country is natural. Nature. All things proceed from Nature—don't they? All things in the heaven, in the earth, and under the earth, act and live as Nature ordains? I think so."

"The doctor said he would come here to-day," said my father, after a silence. "I want to know what he thinks about it, and what he thinks we had better do."

"Doctors never did me any good," said Carmilla.

"Then you have been ill?" I asked.

"More ill than ever you were," she answered.

"Long ago?"

"Yes, a long time. I suffered from this very illness; but I forget all but my pain and weakness, and they were not so bad as are suffered in other diseases."

"You were very young then?"

"I dare say; let us talk no more of it. You would not wound a friend?" She looked languidly in my eyes, and passed her arm round my waist lovingly, and led me out of the room. My father was busy over some papers near the window.

"Why does your papa like to frighten us?" said the pretty girl, with a sigh and a little shudder.

"He doesn't, dear Carmilla, it is the very furthest thing from his mind."

"Are you afraid, dearest?"

" I should be very much if I fancied there was any real danger of my being attacked as those poor people were."

" You are afraid to die ? "

" Yes, every one is."

" But to die as lovers may—to die together, so that they may live together. Girls are caterpillars while they live in the world, to be finally butterflies when the summer comes ; but in the meantime there are grubs and larvæ, don't you see—each with their peculiar propensities, necessities and structure. So says Monsieur Buffon, in his big book, in the next room."

Later in the day the doctor came, and was closeted with papa for some time. He was a skilful man, of sixty and upwards, he wore powder, and shaved his pale face as smooth as a pumpkin. He and papa emerged from the room together, and I heard papa laugh, and say as they came out :

" Well, I do wonder at a wise man like you. What do you say to hippogriffs and dragons ? "

The doctor was smiling, and made answer, shaking his head—

" Nevertheless, life and death are mysterious states, and we know little of the resources of either."

And so they walked on, and I heard no more. I did not then know what the doctor had been broaching, but I think I guess it now.

CHAPTER V

A WONDERFUL LIKENESS

This evening there arrived from Gratz the grave, dark-faced son of the picture-cleaner, with a horse and cart laden with two large packing-cases, having many pictures in each. It was a journey of ten leagues, and whenever a messenger arrived at the schloss from our little capital of Gratz, we used to crowd about him in the hall, to hear the news.

This arrival created in our secluded quarters quite a sensation. The cases remained in the hall, and the messenger was taken charge of by the servants till he had eaten his supper. Then with assistants, and armed with hammer, ripping chisel, and turnscrew he met us in the hall, where we had assembled to witness the unpacking of the cases.

Carmilla sat looking listlessly on, while one after the other the old pictures, nearly all portraits, which had undergone the process of renovation, were brought to light. My mother was of an old Hungarian family, and most of these pictures, which were about to be restored to their places, had come to us through her.

My father had a list in his hand, from which he read, as the artist rummaged out the corresponding numbers. I don't know that the pictures were very good, but they were, undoubtedly very old, and some of them very curious also. They had, for the most part, the merit of being now seen by me, I may say, for the first time ; for the smoke and dust of time had all but obliterated them.

"There is a picture that I have not seen yet," said my father. "In one corner, at the top of it, is the name, as well as I could read, ' Marcia Karnstein,' and the date ' 1698 ' ; and I am curious to see how it has turned out."

I remembered it ; it was a small picture, about a foot and a half high, and nearly square, without a frame ; but it was so blackened by age that I could not make it out.

The artist now produced it, with evident pride. It was quite beautiful ; it was startling ; it seemed to live. It was the effigy of Carmilla !

"Carmilla, dear, here is an absolute miracle. Here you are, living, smiling, ready to speak, in this picture. Isn't it beautiful, papa ? And see, even the little mole on her throat."

My father laughed, and said "Certainly it is a wonderful likeness," but he looked away, and to my surprise seemed but little struck by it, and went on talking to the picture-cleaner, who was also something of an artist, and discoursed with intelligence about the portraits or other works, which his art had just brought into light and colour, while *I* was more and more lost in wonder the more I looked at the picture.

"Will you let me hang this picture in my room, papa ? " I asked.

"Certainly, dear," said he, smiling, " I'm very glad you think it so like. It must be prettier even than I thought it, if it is."

The young lady did not acknowledge this pretty speech, did not seem to hear it. She was leaning back in her seat, her fine eyes under their long lashes gazing on me in contemplation, and she smiled in a kind of rapture.

"And now you can read quite plainly the name that is written in the corner. It is not Marcia ; it looks as if it was done in gold. The name is Mircalla, Countess Karnstein, and this is a little coronet over it, and underneath A.D. 1698. I am descended from the Karnsteins ; that is, mamma was."

" Ah ! " said the lady, languidly, " so am I, I think, a very long descent, very ancient. Are there any Karnsteins living now ? "

" None who bear the name, I believe. The family were ruined, I believe, in some civil wars, long ago but the ruins of the castle are only about three miles away."

" How interesting ! " she said, languidly. " But see what beautiful moonlight ! " She glanced through the hall door, which stood a little open. " Suppose you take a little ramble round the court and look down at the road and river."

" It is so like the night you came to us," I said.

She sighed, smiling.

She rose, and each with her arm about the other's waist, we walked out upon the pavement.

In silence, slowly we walked down to the drawbridge, where the beautiful landscape opened before us.

" And so you were thinking of the night I came here ? " she almost whispered. " Are you glad I came ? "

" Delighted, dear Carmilla," I answered.

" And you ask for the picture you think like me, to hang in your room," she murmured with a sigh, as she drew her arm closer about my waist, and let her pretty head sink upon my shoulder.

" How romantic you are, Carmilla," I said. " Whenever you tell me your story, it will be made up chiefly of some one great romance."

She kissed me silently.

" I am sure, Carmilla, you have been in love ; that there is, at this moment, an affair of the heart going on."

" I have been in love with no one, and never shall," she whispered, " unless it should be with you."

How beautiful she looked in the moonlight !

Shy and strange was the look with which she quickly hid her face in my neck and hair, with tumultuous sighs, that seemed almost to sob, and pressed in mine a hand that trembled.

Her soft cheek was glowing against mine. " Darling, darling," she murmured, " I live in you ; and you would die for me, I love you so."

I started from her.

She was gazing on me with eyes from which all fire, all meaning had flown, and a face colourless and apathetic.

"Is there a chill in the air, dear?" she said drowsily. "I almost shiver; have I been dreaming? Let us come in. Come, come; come in."

"You look ill, Carmilla; a little faint. You certainly must take some wine," I said.

"Yes, I will. I'm better now. I shall be quite well in a few minutes. Yes, do give me a little wine," answered Carmilla, as we approached the door. "Let us look again for a moment; it is the last time, perhaps, I shall see the moonlight with you."

"How do you feel now, dear Carmilla? Are you really better?" I asked.

I was beginning to take alarm, lest she should have been stricken with the strange epidemic that they said had invaded the country about us.

"Papa, would be grieved beyond measure," I added, "if he thought you were ever so little ill, without immediately letting us know. We have a very skilful doctor near this, the physician who was with papa to-day."

"I'm sure he is. I know how kind you all are; but, dear child, I am quite well again. There is nothing ever wrong with me, but a little weakness. People say I am languid; I am incapable of exertion; I can scarcely walk as far as a child of three years old; and every now and then the little strength I have falters, and I become as you have just seen me. But after all I am very easily set up again; in a moment I am perfectly myself. See how I have recovered."

So, indeed, she had; and she and I talked a great deal, and very animated she was; and the remainder of that evening passed without any recurrence of what I called her infatuations. I mean her crazy talk and looks, which embarrassed, and even frightened me.

But there occurred that night an event which gave my thoughts quite a new turn, and seemed to startle even Carmilla's languid nature into momentary energy.

CHAPTER VI

A VERY STRANGE AGONY

When we got into the drawing-room, and had sat down to our coffee and chocolate, although Carmilla did not take any, she seemed quite herself again, and Madame, and Mademoiselle

De Lafontaine, joined us, and made a little card party, in the course of which papa came in for what he called his " dish of tea."

When the game was over he sat down beside Carmilla on the sofa, and asked her, a little anxiously, whether she had heard from her mother since her arrival.

She answered " No."

He then asked her whether she knew where a letter would reach her at present.

" I cannot tell," she answered, ambiguously, " but I have been thinking of leaving you ; you have been already too hospitable and too kind to me. I have given you an infinity of trouble, and I should wish to take a carriage to-morrow, and post in pursuit of her ; I know where I shall ultimately find her, although I dare not yet tell you."

" But you must not dream of any such thing," exclaimed my father, to my great relief. " We can't afford to lose you so, and I won't consent to your leaving us, except under the care of your mother, who was so good as to consent to your remaining with us till she should herself return. I should be quite happy if I knew that you heard from her ; but this evening the accounts of the progress of the mysterious disease that has invaded our neighbour-hood, grow even more alarming ; and my beautiful guest, I do feel the responsibility, unaided by advice from your mother, very much. But I shall do my best ; and one thing is certain, that you must not think of leaving us without her distinct direction to that effect. We should suffer too much in parting from you to consent to it easily."

" Thank you, sir, a thousand times for your hospitality," she answered, smiling bashfully. " You have all been too kind to me ; I have seldom been so happy in all my life before, as in your beautiful château, under your care, and in the society of your dear daughter."

So he gallantly, in his old-fashioned way, kissed her hand, smiling, and pleased at her little speech.

I accompanied Carmilla as usual to her room, and sat and chatted with her while she was preparing for bed.

" Do you think," I said, at length, " that you will ever confide fully in me ? "

She turned round smiling, but made no answer, only continued to smile on me.

" You won't answer that ? " I said. " You can't answer pleasantly ; I ought not to have asked you."

" You were quite right to ask me that, or anything. You do not
know how dear you are to me, or you could not think any confidence too great to look for. But I am under vows, no nun half so
awfully, and I dare not tell my story yet, even to you. The time is
very near when you shall know everything. You will think me
cruel, very selfish, but love is always selfish ; the more ardent the
more selfish. How jealous I am you cannot know. You must come
with me, loving me, to death ; or else hate me, and still come
with me, and *hating* me through death and after. There is no such
word as indifference in my apathetic nature."

" Now, Carmilla, you are going to talk your wild nonsense
again," I said hastily.

" Not I, silly little fool as I am, and full of whims and fancies ;
for your sake I'll talk like a sage. Were you ever at a ball ? "

" No ; how you do run on. What is it like ? How charming it
must be."

" I almost forget, it is years ago."

I laughed.

" You are not so old. Your first ball can hardly be forgotten
yet."

" I remember everything about it—with an effort. I see it all,
as divers see what is going on above them, through a medium,
dense, rippling, but transparent. There occurred that night what
has confused the picture, and made its colours faint. I was all but
assassinated in my bed, wounded *here*," she touched her breast,
" and never was the same since."

" Were you near dying ? "

" Yes, very—a cruel love—strange love, that would have taken
my life. Love will have its sacrifices. No sacrifice without blood.
Let us go to sleep now ; I feel so lazy. How can I get up just now
and lock my door ? "

She was lying with her tiny hands buried in her rich wavy hair,
under her cheek, her little head upon the pillow, and her glittering
eyes followed me wherever I moved, with a kind of shy smile that
I could not decipher.

I bid her good-night, and crept from the room with an uncomfortable sensation.

I often wondered whether our pretty guest ever said her prayers.
I certainly had never seen her upon her knees. In the morning she

never came down until long after our family prayers were over, and at night she never left the drawing-room to attend our brief evening prayers in the hall.

If it had not been that it had casually come out in one of our careless talks that she had been baptised, I should have doubted her being a Christian. Religion was a subject on which I had never heard her speak a word. If I had known the world better, this particular neglect or antipathy would not have so much surprised me.

The precautions of nervous people are infectious, and persons of a like temperament are pretty sure, after a time, to imitate them. I had adopted Carmilla's habit of locking her bed-room door, having taken into my head all her whimsical alarms about midnight invaders, and prowling assassins. I had also adopted her precaution of making a brief search through her room, to satisfy herself that no lurking assassin or robber was " ensconced."

These wise measures taken, I got into my bed and fell asleep. A light was burning in my room. This was an old habit, of very early date, and which nothing could have tempted me to dispense with.

Thus fortified I might take my rest in peace. But dreams come through stone walls, light up dark rooms, or darken light ones, and their persons make their exits and their entrances as they please, and laugh at locksmiths.

I had a dream that night that was the beginning of a very strange agony.

I cannot call it a nightmare, for I was quite conscious of being asleep. But I was equally conscious of being in my room, and lying in bed, precisely as I actually was. I saw, or fancied I saw, the room and its furniture just as I had seen it last, except that it was very dark, and I saw something moving round the foot of the bed, which at first I could not accurately distinguish. But I soon saw that it was a sooty-black animal that resembled a monstrous cat. It appeared to me about four or five feet long, for it measured fully the length of the hearth-rug as it passed over it ; and it continued to-ing and fro-ing with the lithe sinister restlessness of a beast in a cage. I could not cry out, although as you may suppose, I was terrified. Its pace was growing faster, and the room rapidly darker and darker, and at length so dark that I could no longer see anything of it but its eyes. I felt it spring lightly on the bed. The two broad eyes approached my face, and suddenly I felt a stinging pain as if two large needles darted, an inch or two apart, deep into my breast. I waked with a scream. The room was lighted by the candle that burnt there all through the night, and I saw a female figure standing at the foot of the bed, a little at the right side. It was in a dark loose dress, and its hair was down and covered its shoulders. A block of stone could not have been more still. There was not the slightest stir of respiration. As I stared at it, the figure appeared to have changed its place, and was now nearer the door ; then, close to it, the door opened, and it passed out.

I was now relieved, and able to breathe and move. My first thought was that Carmilla had been playing me a trick, and that I had forgotten to secure my door. I hastened to it, and found it locked as usual on the inside. I was afraid to open it—I was horrified. I sprang into my bed and covered my head up in the bed-clothes, and lay there more dead than alive till morning.

CHAPTER VII

DESCENDING

It would be vain my attempting to tell you the horror with which, even now, I recall the occurrence of that night. It was no such transitory terror as a dream leaves behind it. It seemed to deepen by time, and communicated itself to the room and the very furniture that had encompassed the apparition.

I could not bear next day to be alone for a moment. I should have told papa, but for two opposite reasons. At one time I thought he would laugh at my story, and I could not bear its being treated as a jest ; and at another, I thought he might fancy that I had been attacked by the mysterious complaint which had invaded our neighbourhood. I had myself no misgivings of the kind, and as he had been rather an invalid for some time, I was afraid of alarming him.

I was comfortable enough with my good-natured companions, Madame Perrodon, and the vivacious Mademoiselle Lafontaine. They both perceived that I was out of spirits and nervous, and at length I told them what lay so heavy at my heart.

Mademoiselle laughed, but I fancied that Madame Perrodon looked anxious.

" By-the-by," said Mademoiselle, laughing, " the long lime tree walk, behind Carmilla's bedroom window, is haunted ! "

" Nonsense ! " exclaimed Madame, who probably thought the theme rather inopportune, " and who tells that story, my dear ? "

" Martin says that he came up twice, when the old yard-gate was being repaired before sunrise, and twice saw the same female figure walking down the lime tree avenue."

" So he well might, as long as there are cows to milk in the river fields," said Madame.

" I dare say ; but Martin chooses to be frightened, and never did I see a fool *more* frightened."

" You must not say a word about it to Carmilla, because she can see down that walk from her room window," I interposed, " and she is, if possible, a greater coward than I."

Carmilla came down rather later than usual that day.

" I was so frightened last night," she said, so soon as we were together, " and I am sure I should have seen something dreadful if it had not been for that charm I bought from the poor little hunchback whom I called such hard names. I had a dream of something black coming round my bed, and I awoke in a perfect horror, and I really thought, for some seconds, I saw a dark figure near the chimney piece, but I felt under my pillow for my charm, and the moment my fingers touched it, the figure disappeared, and I felt quite certain, only that I had it by me, that something frightful would have made its appearance, and perhaps, throttled me, as it did those poor people we heard of."

" Well, listen to me," I began, and recounted my adventure, at the recital of which she appeared horrified.

" And had you the charm near you ? " she asked, earnestly.

" No, I had dropped it into a china vase in the drawing-room, but I shall certainly take it with me to-night, as you have so much faith in it."

At this distance of time I cannot tell you, or even understand, how I overcame my horror so effectually as to lie alone in my room that night. I remember distinctly that I pinned the charm to my pillow. I fell asleep almost immediately, and slept even more soundly than usual all night.

Next night I passed as well. My sleep was delightfully deep and dreamless. But I wakened with a sense of lassitude and melancholy which, however, did not exceed a degree that was almost luxurious.

" Well, I told you so," said Carmilla, when I described my quiet sleep, " I had such delightful sleep myself last night ; I pinned the charm to the breast of my nightdress. It was too far away the night before. I am quite sure it was all fancy, except the dreams. I used to think that evil spirits made dreams, but our doctor told me it is no such thing. Only a fever passing by, or some other malady, as they often do, he said, knocks at the door, and not being able to get in, passes on, with that alarm."

" And what do you think the charm is ? " said I.

" It has been fumigated or immersed in some drug, and is an antidote against the malaria," she answered.

" Then it acts only on the body ? "

" Certainly ; you don't suppose that evil spirits are frightened by bits of ribbon, or the perfumes of a druggist's shop ? No, these complaints, wandering in the air, begin by trying the nerves, and so infect the brain ; but before they can seize upon you, the antidote repels them. That I am sure is what the charm has done for us. It is nothing magical, it is simply natural."

I should have been happier if I could quite have agreed with Carmilla, but I did my best, and the impression was a little losing its force.

For some nights I slept profoundly ; but still every morning I felt the same lassitude, and a languor weighed upon me all day. I felt myself a changed girl. A strange melancholy was stealing over me, a melancholy that I would not have interrupted. Dim thoughts of death began to open, and an idea that I was slowly sinking took gentle, and, somehow, not unwelcome possession of me. If it was sad, the tone of mind which this induced was also sweet. Whatever it might be, my soul acquiesced in it.

I would not admit that I was ill, I would not consent to tell my papa, or to have the doctor sent for.

Carmilla became more devoted to me than ever, and her strange paroxysms of languid adoration more frequent. She used to gloat on me with increasing ardour the more my strength and spirits waned. This always shocked me like a momentary glare of insanity.

Without knowing it, I was now in a pretty advanced stage of the strangest illness under which mortal ever suffered. There was an unaccountable fascination in its earlier symptoms that more than reconciled me to the incapacitating effect of that stage of the malady. This fascination increased for a time, until it reached a certain point, when gradually a sense of the horrible mingled itself with it, deepening, as you shall hear, until it discoloured and perverted the whole state of my life.

The first change I experienced was rather agreeable. It was very near the turning point from which began the descent of Avernus.

Certain vague and strange sensations visited me in my sleep. The prevailing one was of that pleasant, peculiar cold thrill which we feel in bathing, when we move against the current of a river. This was soon accompanied by dreams that seemed interminable, and were so vague that I could never recollect their scenery and persons, or any one connected portion of their action. But they left an awful impression, and a sense of exhaustion, as if I had passed through a long period of great mental exertion and danger. After all these dreams there remained on waking a remembrance of having been in a place very nearly dark, and of having spoken to people whom I could not see ; and especially of one clear voice, of a female's, very deep, that spoke as if at a distance, slowly, and producing always the same sensation of indescribable solemnity and fear. Sometimes there came a sensation as if a hand was drawn softly along my cheek and neck. Sometimes it was as if warm lips kissed me, and longer and more lovingly as they reached my throat, but there the caress fixed itself. My heart beat faster, my breathing rose and fell rapidly and full drawn ; a sobbing, that rose into a sense of strangulation, supervened, and turned into a dreadful convulsion, in which my senses left me, and I became unconscious.

It was now three weeks since the commencement of this unaccountable state. My sufferings had, during the last week, told upon my appearance. I had grown pale, my eyes were dilated and darkened underneath, and the languor which I had long felt began to display itself in my countenance.

My father asked me often whether I was ill ; but, with an obstinacy which now seems to me unaccountable, I persisted in assuring him that I was quite well.

In a sense this was true. I had no pain, I could complain of no bodily derangement. My complaint seemed to be one of the imagination, or the nerves, and, horrible as my sufferings were, I kept them, with a morbid reserve, very nearly to myself.

It could not be that terrible complaint which the peasants call the oupire, for I had now been suffering for three weeks, and they were seldom ill for much more than three days, when death put an end to their miseries.

Carmilla complained of dreams and feverish sensations, but by no means of so alarming a kind as mine. I say that mine were extremely alarming. Had I been capable of comprehending my condition, I would have invoked aid and advice on my knees. The narcotic of an unsuspected influence was acting upon me, and my perceptions were benumbed.

I am going to tell you now of a dream that led immediately to an odd discovery.

One night, instead of the voice I was accustomed to hear in the dark, I heard one, sweet and tender, and at the same time terrible, which said, " Your mother warns you to beware of the assassin." At the same time a light unexpectedly sprang up, and I saw Carmilla, standing, near the foot of my bed, in her white night-dress, bathed, from her chin to her feet, in one great stain of blood.

I wakened with a shriek, possessed with the one idea that Carmilla was being murdered. I remember springing from my bed, and my next recollection is that of standing on the lobby, crying for help.

Madame and Mademoiselle came scurrying out of their rooms in alarm ; a lamp burned always on the lobby, and seeing me, they soon learned the cause of my terror.

I insisted on our knocking at Carmilla's door. Our knocking was unanswered. It soon became a pounding and an uproar. We shrieked her name but all was vain.

We all grew frightened, for the door was locked. We hurried back, in panic, to my room. There we rang the bell long and furiously. If my father's room had been at that side of the house, we would have called him up at once to our aid. But, alas ! he was quite out of hearing, and to reach him involved an excursion for which we none of us had courage.

Servants, however, soon came running up the stairs ; I had got on my dressing-gown and slippers meanwhile, and my com-panions were already similarly furnished. Recognising the voices of the servants on the lobby, we sallied out together ; and having renewed, as fruitlessly, our summons at Carmilla's door, I ordered the men to force the lock. They did so, and we stood, holding our lights aloft, in the doorway, and so stared into the room.

We called her by name ; but there was still no reply. We looked round the room. Everything was undisturbed. It was exactly in the state in which I left it on bidding her good night. But Carmilla was gone.

CHAPTER VIII

SEARCH

At sight of the room, perfectly undisturbed except for our violent entrance, we began to cool a little, and soon recovered our senses sufficiently to dismiss the men. It had struck Mademoiselle that possibly Carmilla had been wakened by the uproar at her door, and in her first panic had jumped from her bed, and hid herself in a press, or behind a curtain, from which she could not, of course, emerge until the major-domo and his myrmidons had withdrawn. We now recommenced our search, and began to call her by name again.

It was all to no purpose. Our perplexity and agitation increased. We examined the windows, but they were secured. I implored of Carmilla, if she had concealed herself, to play this cruel trick no longer—to come out, and to end our anxieties. It was all useless. I was by this time convinced that she was not in the room, nor in the dressing-room, the door of which was still locked on this side. She could not have passed it. I was utterly puzzled. Had Carmilla discovered one of those secret passages which the old housekeeper said were known to exist in the schloss, although the tradition of their exact situation had been lost. A little time would, no doubt, explain all—utterly perplexed as, for the present, we were.

It was past four o'clock, and I preferred passing the remaining hours of darkness in Madame's room. Daylight brought no solution of the difficulty.

The whole household, with my father at its head, was in a state of agitation next morning. Every part of the château was searched. The grounds were explored. Not a trace of the missing lady could be discovered. The stream was about to be dragged ; my father was in distraction ; what a tale to have to tell the poor girl's mother on her return. I, too, was almost beside myself, though my grief was quite of a different kind.

The morning was passed in alarm and excitement. It was now one o'clock, and still no tidings. I ran up to Carmilla's room, and found her standing at her dressing-table. I was astounded. I could not believe my eyes. She beckoned me to her with her pretty finger, in silence. Her face expressed extreme fear.

I ran to her in an ecstasy of joy ; I kissed and embraced her again and again. I ran to the bell and rang it vehemently, to bring others to the spot, who might at once relieve my father's anxiety.

"Dear Carmilla, what has become of you all this time? We have been in agonies of anxiety about you," I exclaimed. "Where have you been? How did you come back?"

"Last night has been a night of wonders," she said.

"For mercy's sake, explain all you can."

"It was past two last night," she said, "when I went to sleep as usual in my bed, with my doors locked, that of the dressing-room and that opening upon the gallery. My sleep was uninterrupted, and, so far as I know, dreamless; but I awoke just now on the sofa in the dressing-room there, and I found the door between the rooms open, and the other door forced. How could all this have happened without my being awakened? It must have been accompanied with a great deal of noise, and I am particularly easily wakened; and how could I have been carried out of my bed without my sleep having been interrupted, I whom the slightest stir startles?"

By this time, Madame, Mademoiselle, my father, and a number of the servants were in the room. Carmilla was, of course, overwhelmed with enquiries, congratulations, and welcomes. She had but one story to tell, and seemed the least able of all the party to suggest any way of accounting for what had happened.

My father took a turn up and down the room, thinking. I saw Carmilla's eye follow him for a moment with a sly, dark glance.

When my father had sent the servants away, Mademoiselle having gone in search of a little bottle of valerian and sal-volatile, and there being no one now in the room with Carmilla except my father, Madame, and myself, he came to her thoughtfully, took her hand very kindly, led her to the sofa, and sat down beside her.

"Will you forgive me, my dear, if I risk a conjecture, and ask a question?"

"Who can have a better right?" she said. "Ask what you please, and I will tell you everything. But my story is simply one of bewilderment and darkness. I know absolutely nothing. Put any question you please. But you know, of course, the limitations mamma has placed me under."

"Perfectly, my dear child. I need not approach the topics on which she desires our silence. Now, the marvel of last night consists in your having been removed from your bed and your room without being wakened, and this removal having occurred apparently while the windows were still secured, and the two doors locked upon the inside. I will tell you my theory, and first ask you a question."

Carmilla was leaning on her hand dejectedly ; Madame and I were listening breathlessly.

" Now, my question is this. Have you ever been suspected of walking in your sleep ? "

" Never since I was very young indeed."

" But you did walk in your sleep when you were young ? "

" Yes ; I know I did. I have been told so often by my old nurse."

My father smiled and nodded.

" Well, what has happened is this. You got up in your sleep, unlocked the door, not leaving the key, as usual, in the lock, but taking it out and locking it on the outside ; you again took the key out, and carried it away with you to some one of the five-and-twenty rooms on this floor, or perhaps upstairs or downstairs. There are so many rooms and closets, so much heavy furniture, and such accumulations of lumber, that it would require a week to search this old house thoroughly. Do you see, now, what I mean ? "

" I do, but not all," she answered.

" And how, papa, do you account for her finding herself on the sofa in the dressing-room, which we had searched so carefully ? "

" She came there after you had searched it, still in her sleep, and at last awoke spontaneously, and was as much surprised to find herself where she was as any one else. I wish all mysteries were as easily and innocently explained as yours, Carmilla," he said, laughing. " And so we may congratulate ourselves on the certainty that the most natural explanation of the occurrence is one that involves no drugging, no tampering with locks, no burglars, or poisoners, or witches—nothing that need alarm Carmilla, or any one else, for our safety."

Carmilla was looking charmingly. Nothing could be more beautiful than her tints. Her beauty was, I think enhanced by that graceful languor that was peculiar to her. I think my father was silently contrasting her looks with mine, for he said :—

" I wish my poor Laura was looking more like herself " ; and he sighed.

So our alarms were happily ended, and Carmilla restored to her friends.

CHAPTER IX

THE DOCTOR

As Carmilla would not hear of an attendant sleeping in her room, my father arranged that a servant should sleep outside her door so that she could not attempt to make another such excursion without being arrested at her own door.

That night passed quietly ; and next morning early, the doctor, whom my father had sent for without telling me a word about it, arrived to see me.

Madame accompanied me to the library ; and there the grave little doctor, with white hair and spectacles, whom I mentioned before, was waiting to receive me.

I told him my story, and as I proceeded he grew graver and graver.

We were standing, he and I, in the recess of one of the windows, facing one another. When my statement was over, he leaned with his shoulders against the wall, and with his eyes fixed on me earnestly with an interest in which was a dash of horror.

After a minute's reflection, he asked Madame if he could see my father.

He was sent for accordingly, and as he entered, smiling, he said :

" I dare say, doctor, you are going to tell me that I am an old fool for having brought you here ; I hope I am."

But his smile faded into shadow as the doctor, with a very grave face, beckoned him to him.

He and the doctor talked for some time in the same recess where I had just conferred with the physician. It seemed an earnest and argumentative conversation. The room is very large, and I and Madame stood together, burning with curiosity, at the further end. Not a word could we hear, however, for they spoke in a very low tone, and the deep recess of the window quite concealed the doctor from view, and very nearly my father, whose foot, arm, and shoulder only could we see ; and the voices were, I suppose, all the less audible for the sort of closet which the thick wall and window formed.

After a time my father's face looked into the room ; it was pale, thoughtful, and, I fancied, agitated.

" Laura, dear, come here for a moment. Madame, we shan't trouble you, the doctor says, at present."

Accordingly I approached, for the first time a little alarmed ;

for, although I felt very weak, I did not feel ill ; and strength, one always fancies, is a thing that may be picked up when we please.

My father held out his hand to me as I drew near, but he was looking at the doctor, and he said :

" It certainly *is* very odd ; I don't understand it quite. Laura, come here, dear ; now attend to Doctor Spielsberg, and recollect yourself."

" You mentioned a sensation like that of two needles piercing the skin, somewhere about your neck, on the night when you experienced your first horrible dream. Is there still any soreness ? "

" None at all," I answered.

" Can you indicate with your finger about the point at which you think this occurred ? "

" Very little below my throat—*here*," I answered.

I wore a morning dress, which covered the place I pointed to.

" Now you can satisfy yourself," said the doctor. " You won't mind your papa's lowering your dress a very little. It is necessary, to detect a symptom of the complaint under which you have been suffering."

I acquiesced. It was only an inch or two below the edge of my collar.

" God bless me !—so it is," exclaimed my father, growing pale.

" You see it now with your own eyes," said the doctor, with a gloomy triumph.

" What is it ? " I exclaimed, beginning to be frightened.

" Nothing, my dear young lady, but a small blue spot, about the size of the tip of your little finger ; and now," he continued, turning to papa, " the question is what is best to be done ? "

" Is there any danger ? " I urged, in great trepidation.

" I trust not, my dear," answered the doctor. " I don't see why you should not recover. I don't see why you should not begin *immediately* to get better. That is the point at which the sense of strangulation begins ? "

" Yes," I answered.

" And—recollect as well as you can—the same point was a kind of centre of that thrill which you described just now, like the current of a cold stream running against you ? "

" It may have been ; I think it was."

" Ay, you see ? " he added, turning to my father. " Shall I say a word to Madame ? "

" Certainly," said my father.

He called Madame to him, and said :

" I find my young friend here far from well. It won't be of any great consequence, I hope ; but it will be necessary that some steps be taken, which I will explain by-and-by ; but in the meantime, Madame, you will be so good as not to let Miss Laura be alone for one moment. That is the only direction I need give for the present. It is indispensable."

" We may rely upon your kindness, Madame, I know," added my father.

Madame satisfied him eagerly.

" And you, dear Laura, I know you will observe the doctor's direction."

" I shall have to ask your opinion upon another patient, whose symptoms slightly resemble those of my daughter, that have just been detailed to you—very much milder in degree, but I believe quite of the same sort. She is a young lady—our guest ; but as you say you will be passing this way again this evening, you can't do better than take your supper here, and you can then see her. She does not come down till the afternoon."

" I thank you," said the doctor. " I shall be with you, then, at about seven this evening."

And then they repeated their directions to me and to Madame, and with this parting charge my father left us, and walked out with the doctor ; and I saw them pacing together up and down between the road and the moat, on the grassy platform in front of the castle, evidently absorbed in earnest conversation.

The doctor did not return. I saw him mount his horse there, take his leave, and ride away eastward through the forest. Nearly at the same time I saw the man arrive from Dranfeld with the letters, and dismount and hand the bag to my father.

In the meantime, Madame and I were both busy, lost in conjecture as to the reasons of the singular and earnest direction which the doctor and my father had concurred in imposing. Madame, as she afterwards told me, was afraid the doctor apprehended a sudden seizure, and that, without prompt assistance, I might either lose my life in a fit, or at least be seriously hurt.

This interpretation did not strike me ; and I fancied perhaps luckily for my nerves, that the arrangement was prescribed simply to secure a companion, who would prevent my taking too much exercise, or eating unripe fruit, or doing any of the fifty foolish things to which young people are supposed to be prone.

About half-an-hour after, my father came in—he had a letter in his hand—and said :

" This letter had been delayed ; it is from General Spielsdorf. He might have been here yesterday, he may not come till to-morrow, or he may be here to-day."

He put the open letter into my hand ; but he did not look pleased, as he used when a guest, especially one so much loved as the General, was coming. On the contrary, he looked as if he wished him at the bottom of the Red Sea. There was plainly something on his mind which he did not choose to divulge.

" Papa, darling, will you tell me this ? " said I, suddenly laying my hand on his arm, and looking, I am sure, imploringly in his face.

" Perhaps," he answered, smoothing my hair caressingly over my eyes.

" Does the doctor think me very ill ? "

" No, dear ; he thinks, if right steps are taken, you will be quite well again, at least on the high road to a complete recovery, in a day or two," he answered, a little drily. " I wish our good friend, the General, had chosen any other time ; that is, I wish you had been perfectly well to receive him."

" But do tell me, papa," I insisted, " *what* does he think is the matter with me ? "

" Nothing ; you must not plague me with questions," he answered, with more irritation than I ever remember him to have displayed before ; and seeing that I looked wounded, I suppose, he kissed me, and added, " You shall know all about it in a day or two ; that is, all that *I* know. In the meantime, you are not to trouble your head about it."

He turned and left the room, but came back before I had done wondering and puzzling over the oddity of all this ; it was merely to say that he was going to Karnstein and had ordered the carriage to be ready at twelve, and that I and Madame should accompany him ; he was going to see the priest who lived near those picturesque grounds, upon business, and as Carmilla had never seen them, she could follow, when she came down, with Mademoiselle, who would bring materials for what you call a pic-nic, which might be laid for us in the ruined castle.

At twelve o'clock, accordingly, I was ready, and not long after, my father, Madame and I set out upon our projected drive. Passing the drawbridge we turn to the right, and follow the road over the steep Gothic bridge westward, to reach the deserted village and ruined castle of Karnstein.

No sylvan drive can be fancied prettier. The ground breaks into gentle hills and hollows, all clothed with beautiful wood, totally destitute of the comparative formality which artificial planting and early culture and pruning impart.

The irregularities of the ground often lead the road out of its course, and cause it to wind beautifully round the sides of broken hollows and the steeper sides of the hills, among varieties of ground almost inexhaustible.

Turning one of these points, we suddenly encountered our old friend, the General, riding towards us, attended by a mounted servant. His portmanteaus were following in a hired waggon, such as we term a cart.

The General dismounted as we pulled up, and, after the usual greetings, was easily persuaded to accept the vacant seat in the carriage, and send his horse on with his servant to the schloss.

CHAPTER X

BEREAVED

It was about ten months since we had last seen him ; but that time had sufficed to make an alteration of years in his appearance. He had grown thinner ; something of gloom and anxiety had taken the place of that cordial serenity which used to characterise his features. His dark blue eyes, always penetrating, now gleamed with a sterner light from under his shaggy grey eyebrows. It was not such a change as grief alone usually induces, and angrier passions seemed to have had their share in bringing it about.

We had not long resumed our drive, when the General began to talk, with his usual soldierly directness, of the bereavement, as he termed it, which he had sustained in the death of his beloved niece and ward ; and he then broke out in a tone of intense bitterness and fury, inveighing against the " hellish arts " to which she had fallen a victim, and expressing with more exasperation than piety, his wonder that Heaven should tolerate so monstrous an indulgence of the lusts and malignity of hell.

My father, who saw at once that something very extraordinary had befallen, asked him, if not too painful to him, to detail the circumstances which he thought justified the strong terms in which he expressed himself.

" I should tell you all with pleasure," said the General, " but you would not believe me."

" Why should I not ? " he asked.

" Because," he answered testily, " you believe in nothing but what consists with your own prejudices and illusions. I remember when I was like you, but I have learned better."

" Try me," said my father ; " I am not such a dogmatist as you suppose. Besides which, I very well know that you generally require proof for what you believe, and am, therefore, very strongly predisposed to respect your conclusions."

" You are right in supposing that I have not been led lightly into a belief in the marvellous—for what I have experienced *is* marvellous—and I have been forced by extraordinary evidence to credit that which ran counter, diametrically, to all my theories. I have been made the dupe of a preternatural conspiracy."

Notwithstanding his professions of confidence in the General's penetration, I saw my father, at this point, glance at the General, with, as I thought a marked suspicion of his sanity.

The General did not see it, luckily. He was looking gloomily and curiously into the glades and vistas of the woods that were opening before us.

" You are going to the Ruins of Karnstein ? " he said. " Yes, it is a lucky coincidence ; do you know I was going to ask you to bring me there to inspect them. I have a special object in exploring. There is a ruined chapel, isn't there, with a great many tombs of that extinct family ? "

" So there are—highly interesting," said my father. " I hope you are thinking of claiming the title and estates ? "

My father said this gaily, but the General did not recollect the laugh, or even the smile, which courtesy exacts for a friend's joke ; on the contrary, he looked grave and even fierce, ruminating on a matter that stirred his anger and horror.

" Something very different," he said, gruffly. " I mean to unearth some of those fine people. I hope, by God's blessing, to accomplish a pious sacrilege here, which will relieve our earth of certain monsters, and enable honest people to sleep in their beds without being assailed by murderers. I have strange things to tell you, my dear friend, such as I myself would have scouted as incredible a few months since."

My father looked at him again, but this time not with a glance of suspicion—with an eye, rather, of keen intelligence and alarm.

"The house of Karnstein," he said, "has been long extinct: a hundred years at least. My dear wife was maternally descended from the Karnsteins. But the name and title have long ceased to exist. The castle is a ruin; the very village is deserted; it is fifty years since the smoke of a chimney was seen there; not a roof left."

"Quite true. I have heard a great deal about that since I last saw you; a great deal that will astonish you. But I had better relate everything in the order in which it occurred," said the General. "You saw my dear ward—my child, I may call her. No creature could have been more beautiful and only three months ago none more blooming."

"Yes, poor thing! when I saw her last she certainly was quite lovely," said my father. "I was grieved and shocked more than I can tell you, my dear friend; I knew what a blow it was to you."

He took the General's hand, and they exchanged a kind pressure. Tears gathered in the old soldier's eyes. He did not seek to conceal them. He said:

"We have been very old friends; I knew you would feel for me, childless as I am. She had become an object of very dear interest to me, and repaid my care by an affection that cheered my home and made my life happy. That is all gone. The years that remain to me on earth may not be very long; but by God's mercy I hope to accomplish a service to mankind before I die, and to subserve the vengeance of Heaven upon the fiends who have murdered my poor child in the spring of her hopes and beauty!"

"You said, just now, that you intended relating everything as it occurred," said my father. "Pray do; I assure you that it is not mere curiosity that prompts me."

By this time we had reached the point at which the Drunstall road, by which the General had come, diverges from the road which we were travelling to Karnstein.

"How far is it to the ruins?" enquired the General, looking anxiously forward.

"About half a league," answered my father. "Pray let us hear the story you were so good as to promise."

CHAPTER XI

"With all my heart," said the General, with an effort ; and after a short pause in which to arrange his subject, he commenced one of the strangest narratives I ever heard.

"My dear child was looking forward with great pleasure to the visit you had been so good as to arrange for her to your charming daughter." Here he made me a gallant but melancholy bow. "In the meantime we had an invitation to my old friend the Count Carlsfeld, whose schloss is about six leagues to the other side of Karnstein. It was to attend the series of fêtes which, you remember, were given by him in honour of his illustrious visitor, the Grand Duke Charles."

"Yes ; and very splendid, I believe, they were," said my father.

"Princely ! But then his hospitalities are quite regal. He has Aladdin's lamp. The night from which my sorrow dates was devoted to a magnificent masquerade. The grounds were thrown open, the trees hung with coloured lamps. There was such a display of fireworks as Paris itself had never witnessed. And such music—music, you know, is my weakness—such ravishing music ! The finest instrumental band, perhaps, in the world, and the finest singers who could be collected from all the great operas in Europe. As you wandered through these fantastically illuminated grounds, the moon-lighted château throwing a rosy light from its long rows of windows, you would suddenly hear these ravishing voices stealing from the silence of some grove, or rising from boats upon the lake. I felt myself, as I looked and listened, carried back into the romance and poetry of my early youth.

"When the fireworks were ended, and the ball beginning, we returned to the noble suite of rooms that was thrown open to the dancers. A masked ball, you know, is a beautiful sight ; but so brilliant a spectacle of the kind I never saw before.

"It was a very aristocratic assembly. I was myself almost the only ' nobody ' present.

"My dear child was looking quite beautiful. She wore no mask. Her excitement and delight added an unspeakable charm to her features, always lovely. I remarked a young lady, dressed magnificently, but wearing a mask, who appeared to me to be observing my ward with extraordinary interest. I had seen her, earlier in the evening, in the great hall, and again, for a few minutes, walking near us, on the terrace under the castle windows, similarly employed. A lady, also masked, richly and gravely dressed, and with a stately air, like a person of rank, accompanied her as a chaperon. Had the young lady not worn a mask, I could, of course, have been much more certain upon the question whether she was really watching my poor darling. I am now well assured that she was.

" We were now in one of the *salons*. My poor dear child had been dancing, and was resting a little in one of the chairs near the door ; I was standing near. The two ladies I have mentioned had approached, and the younger took the chair next my ward ; while her companion stood beside me, and for a little time addressed herself, in a low tone, to her charge.

" Availing herself of the privilege of her mask she turned to me, and in the tone of an old friend, and calling me by my name, opened a conversation with me, which piqued my curiosity a good deal. She referred to many scenes where she had met me—at Court, and at distinguished houses. She alluded to little incidents which I had long ceased to think of, but which, I found, had only lain in abeyance in my memory, for they instantly started into life at her touch.

" I became more and more curious to ascertain who she was, every moment. She parried my attempts to discover very adroitly and pleasantly. The knowledge she showed of many passages in my life seemed to me all but unaccountable ; and she appeared to take a not unnatural pleasure in foiling my curiosity, and in seeing me flounder, in my eager perplexity, from one conjecture to another.

" In the meantime the young lady, whom her mother called by the odd name of Millarca, when she once or twice addressed her, had, with the same ease and grace, got into conversation with my ward.

" She introduced herself by saying that her mother was a very old acquaintance of mine. She spoke of the agreeable audacity which a mask rendered practicable ; she talked like a friend ; she admired her dress, and insinuated very prettily her admiration of her beauty. She amused her with laughing criticisms upon the people who crowded the ballroom, and laughed at my poor child's fun. She was very witty and lively when she pleased, and after a time they had grown very good friends, and the young stranger lowered her mask, displaying a remarkably beautiful face. I had never seen it before, neither had my dear child. But though it was new to us, the features were so engaging, as well as lovely, that it was impossible not to feel the attraction powerfully. My poor girl did so. I never saw anyone more taken with another at first sight, unless indeed, it was the stranger herself, who seemed quite to have lost her heart to her.

" In the meantime, availing myself of the licence of a masquerade, I put not a few questions to the elder lady.

" ' You have puzzled me utterly,' I said, laughing. ' Is that not enough ? won't you, now, consent to stand on equal terms, and do me the kindness to remove your mask ? '

" ' Can any request be more unreasonable ? ' she replied. ' Ask a lady to yield an advantage ! Beside, how do you know you should recognise me ? Years make changes.'

" ' As you see,' I said, with a bow, and, I suppose, a rather melancholy little laugh.

" ' As philosophers tell us,' she said ; ' and how do you know that a sight of my face would help you ? '

" ' I should take chance for that,' I answered. ' It is vain trying to make yourself out an old woman ; your figure betrays you.'

" ' Years, nevertheless, have passed since I saw you, rather since you saw me, for that is what I am considering. Millarca, there, is my daughter ; I cannot then be young, even in the opinion of people whom time has taught to be indulgent, and I may not like to be compared with what you remember me. You have no mask to remove. You can offer me nothing in exchange.'

" ' My petition is to your pity, to remove it.'

" ' And mine to yours, to let it stay where it is,' she replied.

" ' Well, then, at least you will tell me whether you are French or German ; you speak both languages so perfectly.'

" ' I don't think I shall tell you that, General ; you intend a surprise, and are meditating the particular point of attack.'

" ' At all events, you won't deny this,' I said, ' that being honoured by your permission to converse, I ought to know how to address you. Shall I say Madame la Comtesse ! '

" She laughed, and she would, no doubt, have met me with another evasion—if, indeed, I can treat any occurrence in an interview every circumstance of which was pre-arranged, as I now believe, with the profoundest cunning, as liable to be modified by accident.

" ' As to that,' she began ; but she was interrupted, almost as she opened her lips, by a gentleman, dressed in black, who looked particularly elegant and distinguished, with this drawback, that his face was the most deadly pale I ever saw, except in death. He was in no masquerade—in the plain evening dress of a gentleman ; and he said, without a smile, but with a courtly and unusually low bow :—

" ' Will Madame la Comtesse permit me to say á very few words which may interest her ? '

" The lady turned quickly to him, and touched her lip in token of silence ; she then said to me, ' Keep my place for me, General ; I shall return when I have said a few words.'

" And with this injunction, playfully given, she walked a little aside with the gentleman in black, and talked for some minutes, apparently very earnestly. They then walked away slowly together in the crowd, and I lost them for some minutes.

" I spent the interval in cudgelling my brains for conjecture as to the identity of the lady who seemed to remember me so kindly, and I was thinking of turning about and joining in the conversation between my pretty ward and the Countess's daughter, and trying whether, by the time she returned, I might not have a surprise in store for her, by having her name, title, château, and estates at my fingers' ends. But at this moment she returned, accompanied by the pale man in black, who said :

" ' I shall return and inform Madame la Comtesse when her carriage is at the door.'

" He withdrew with a bow."

CHAPTER XII

A PETITION

" ' Then we are to lose Madame. la Comtesse, but I hope only for a few hours,' I said, with a low bow.

" ' It may be that only, or it may be a few weeks. It was very unlucky his speaking to me just now as he did. Do you now know me ? "

" I assured her I did not.

" ' You shall know me,' she said, ' but not at present. We are older and better friends than, perhaps, you suspect. I cannot yet declare myself. I shall in three weeks pass your beautiful schloss about which I have been making enquiries. I shall then look in upon you for an hour or two, and renew a friendship which I never think of without a thousand pleasant recollections. This moment a piece of news has reached me like a thunderbolt. I must set out now, and travel by a devious route, nearly a hundred miles, with all the dispatch I can possibly make. My perplexities multiply. I am only deterred by the compulsory reserve I practise as to my name from making a very singular request of you. My poor child has not quite recovered her strength. Her horse fell with her, at a hunt which she had ridden out to witness, her nerves have not yet recovered the shock, and our physician says that she must on no account exert herself for some time to come. We came here, in consequence, by very easy stages—hardly six leagues a day. I must now travel day and night, on a mission of life and death—a mission the critical and momentous nature of which I shall be able to explain to you when we meet, as I hope we shall, in a few weeks, without the necessity of any concealment.'

" She went on to make her petition, and it was in the tone of a person from whom such a request amounted to conferring, rather than seeking a favour. This was only in manner, and, as it seemed, quite unconsciously. Than the terms in which it was expressed, nothing could be more deprecatory. It was simply that I would consent to take charge of her daughter during her absence.

" This was, all things considered, a strange, not to say, an audacious request. She in some sort disarmed me, by stating and admitting everything that could be urged against it, and throwing herself entirely upon my chivalry. At the same moment, by a fatality that seems to have predetermined all that happened, my poor child came to my side, and, in an undertone, besought me to invite her new friend, Millarca, to pay us a visit. She had just been sounding her, and thought, if her mamma would allow her, she would like it extremely.

" At another time I should have told her to wait a little, until, at least, we knew who they were. But I had not a moment to think in. The two ladies assailed me together, and I must confess the refined and beautiful face of the young lady, about which there was something extremely engaging, as well as the elegance and fire of high birth, determined me ; and quite overpowered, I submitted, and undertook, too easily, the care of the young lady, whom her mother called Millarca.

" The Countess beckoned to her daughter, who listened with grave attention while she told her, in general terms, how suddenly and peremptorily she had been summoned, and also of the arrangement she had made for her under my care, adding that I was one of her earliest and most valued friends.

" I made, of course, such speeches as the case seemed to call for, and found myself, on reflection, in a position which I did not half like.

" The gentleman in black returned, and very ceremoniously conducted the lady from the room.

" The demeanour of this gentleman was such as to impress me with the conviction that the Countess was a lady of very much more importance than her modest title alone might have led me to assume.

" Her last charge to me was that no attempt was to be made to learn more about her than I might have already guessed, until her return. Our distinguished host, whose guest she was, knew her reasons.

" ' But here,' she said, ' neither I nor my daughter could safely remain for more than a day. I removed my mask imprudently for a moment, about an hour ago, and, too late, I fancied you saw me. So I resolved to seek an opportunity of talking a little to you. Had I found that you *had* seen me, I should have thrown myself on your high sense of honour to keep my secret for some weeks. As it is, I am satisfied that you did not see me ; but if you now *suspect*, or, on reflection, *should* suspect, who I am, I commit myself, in like manner, entirely to your honour. My daughter will observe the same secrecy, and I well know that you will, from time to time, remind her, lest she should thoughtlessly disclose it.'

" She whispered a few words to her daughter, kissed her hurriedly twice, and went away, accompanied by the pale gentleman in black, and disappeared in the crowd.

" ' In the next room,' said Millarca, ' there is a window that looks upon the hall door. I should like to see the last of mamma, and to kiss my hand to her.'

" We assented, of course, and accompanied her to the window. We looked out, and saw a handsome old-fashioned carriage, with a troop of couriers and footmen. We saw the slim figure of the pale gentleman in black, as he held a thick velvet cloak, and placed it about her shoulders and threw the hood over her head. She nodded to him, and just touched his hand with hers. He bowed low repeatedly as the door closed, and the carriage began to move.

" ' She is gone,' said Millarca, with a sigh.

" ' She is gone,' I repeated to myself, for the first time—in the hurried moments that had elapsed since my consent—reflecting upon the folly of my act.

" ' She did not look up,' said the young lady, plaintively.

" ' The Countess had taken off her mask, perhaps, and did not care to show her face,' I said ; ' and she could not know that you were in the window.'

" She sighed and looked in my face. She was so beautiful that I relented. I was sorry I had for a moment repented of my hospitality, and I determined to make her amends for the unavowed churlishness of my reception.

" The young lady, replacing her mask, joined my ward in persuading me to return to the grounds, where the concert was soon to be renewed. We did so, and walked up and down the terrace that lies under the castle windows. Millarca became very intimate with us, and amused us with lively descriptions and stories of most of the great people whom we saw upon the terrace. I liked her more and more every minute. Her gossip, without being ill-natured, was extremely diverting to me, who had been so long out of the great world. I thought what life she would give to our sometimes lonely evenings at home.

" This ball was not over until the morning sun had almost reached the horizon. It pleased the Grand Duke to dance till then, so loyal people could not go away, or think of bed.

" We had just got through a crowded saloon, when my ward asked me what had become of Millarca. I thought she had been by my side, and she fancied she was by mine. The fact was, we had lost her.

" All my efforts to find her were vain. I feared that she had mistaken, in the confusion of a momentary separation from us, other people for her new friends, and had, possibly, pursued and lost them in the extensive grounds which were thrown open to us.

" Now, in its full force, I recognised a new folly in my having undertaken the charge of a young lady without so much as knowing her name ; and fettered as I was by promises, of the reasons for imposing which I knew nothing, I could not even point my enquiries by saying that the missing young lady was the daughter of the Countess who had taken her departure a few hours before.

" Morning broke. It was clear daylight before I gave up my search. It was not till near two o'clock next day that we heard anything of my missing charge.

" At about that time a servant knocked at my niece's door, to say that he had been earnestly requested by a young lady, who appeared to be in great distress, to make out where she could find the General Baron Spielsdorf and the young lady, his daughter, in whose charge she had been left by her mother.

" There could be no doubt, notwithstanding the slight inaccuracy, that our young friend had turned up ; and so she had. Would to Heaven we had lost her !

" She told my poor child a story to account for her having failed to recover us for so long. Very late, she said, she had got into the housekeeper's bedroom in despair of finding us, and had then fallen into a deep sleep which, long as it was, had hardly sufficed to recruit her strength after the fatigues of the ball.

" That day Millarca came home with us. I was only too happy, after all, to have secured so charming a companion for my dear girl."

CHAPTER XIII

THE WOOD-MAN

" There soon, however, appeared some drawbacks. In the first place, Millarca complained of extreme languor—the weakness that remained after her late illness—and she never emerged from her room till the afternoon was pretty far advanced. In the next place, it was accidentally discovered, although she always locked her door on the inside, and never disturbed the key from its place, till she admitted the maid to assist at her toilet, that she was undoubtedly sometimes absent from her room in the very early morning, and at various times later in the day, before she wished it to be understood that she was stirring. She was repeatedly seen from the windows of the schloss, in the first faint grey of the morning, walking through the trees, in an easterly direction, and looking like a person in a trance. This convinced me that she walked in her sleep. But this hypothesis did not solve the puzzle. How did she pass out from her room, leaving the door locked on the inside. How did she escape from the house without unbarring door or window ?

" In the midst of my perplexities, an anxiety of a far more urgent kind presented itself.

" My dear child began to lose her looks and health, and that in a manner so mysterious, and even horrible, that I became thoroughly frightened.

" She was at first visited by appalling dreams ; then, as she fancied, by a spectre, something resembling Millarca, sometimes in the shape of a beast, indistinctly seen, walking round the foot of the bed, from side to side. Lastly came sensations. One, not unpleasant, but very peculiar, she said, resembled the flow of an icy stream against her breast. At a later time, she felt something like a pair of large needles pierce her, a little below the throat, with a very sharp pain. A few nights after, followed a gradual and convulsive sense of strangulation ; then came unconsciousness."

I could hear distinctly every word the kind old General was saying, because by this time we were driving upon the short grass that spreads on either side of the road as you approach the roofless village which had not shown the smoke of a chimney for more than half a century.

You may guess how strangely I felt as I heard my own symptoms so exactly described in those which had been experienced by the poor girl who, but for the catastrophe which followed, would have been at that moment a visitor at my father's château. You may suppose, also, how I felt as I heard him detail habits and mysterious peculiarities which were, in fact, those of our beautiful guest, Carmilla !

A vista opened in the forest ; we were on a sudden under the chimneys and gables of the ruined village, and the towers and battlements of the dismantled castle, round which gigantic trees are grouped, overhung us from a slight eminence.

In a frightened dream I got down from the carriage, and in silence, for we had each abundant matter for thinking ; we soon mounted the ascent, and were among the spacious chambers, winding stairs, and dark corridors of the castle.

" And this was once the palatial residence of the Karnsteins ! " said the old General at length, as from a great window he looked out across the village, and saw the wide, undulating expanse of forest. " It was a bad family, and here its blood-stained annals were written," he continued. " It is hard that they should, after death, continue to plague the human race with their atrocious lusts. That is the chapel of the Karnsteins, down there."

He pointed down to the grey walls of the Gothic building, partly visible through the foliage, a little way down the steep. " And I hear the axe of a woodman," he added, " busy among the trees that surround it ; he possibly may give us the information of which I am in search, and point out the grave of Mircalla, Countess of Karnstein. These rustics preserve the local traditions of great families, whose stories die out among the rich and titled so soon as the families themselves become extinct."

"We have a portrait, at home, of Mircalla, the Countess Karnstein ; should you like to see it ? " asked my father.

"Time enough, dear friend," replied the General. "I believe that I have seen the original ; and one motive which has led me to you earlier than I at first intended, was to explore the chapel which we are now approaching."

"What ! see the Countess Mircalla," exclaimed my father ; " why, she has been dead more than a century ! "

"Not so dead as you fancy, I am told," answered the General.

"I confess, General, you puzzle me utterly," replied my father, looking at him, I fancied, for a moment with a return of the suspicion I detected before. But although there was anger and detestation, at times, in the old General's manner, there was nothing flighty.

"There remains to me," he said, as we passed under the heavy arch of the Gothic church—for its dimensions would have justified its being so styled—" but one object which can interest me during the few years that remain to me on earth, and that is to wreak on her the vengeance which, I thank God, may still be accomplished by a mortal arm."

"What vengeance can you mean ? " asked my father, in increasing amazement.

"I mean, to decapitate the monster," he answered, with a fierce flush, and a stamp that echoed mournfully through the hollow ruin, and his clenched hand was at the same moment raised, as if it grasped the handle of an axe, while he shook it ferociously in the air.

"What ! " exclaimed my father, more than ever bewildered.

"To strike her head off."

"Cut her head off ! "

"Aye, with a hatchet, with a spade, or with anything that can cleave through her murderous throat. You shall hear," he answered, trembling with rage. And hurrying forward he said :

"That beam will answer for a seat ; your dear child is fatigued ; let her be seated, and I will, in a few sentences, close my dreadful story."

The squared block of wood, which lay on the grass-grown pavement of the chapel, formed a bench on which I was very glad to seat myself, and in the meantime the General called to the woodman, who had been removing some boughs which leaned upon the old walls ; and, axe in hand, the hardy old fellow stood before us.

He could not tell us anything of these monuments ; but there was an old man, he said, a ranger of this forest, at present sojourning in the house of the priest, about two miles away, who could point out every monument of the old Karnstein family and, for a trifle, he undertook to bring him back with him, if we would lend him one of our horses, in little more than half-an-hour.

" Have you been long employed about this forest ? " asked my father of the old man.

" I have been a woodman here," he answered in his *patois*, " under the forester, all my days ; so has my father before me, and so on, as many generations as I can count up. I could show you the very house in the village here, in which my ancestors lived."

" How came the village to be deserted ? " asked the General.

" It was troubled by *revenants*, sir ; several were tracked to their graves, there detected by the usual tests, and extinguished in the usual way, by decapitation, by the stake, and by burning ; but not until many of the villagers were killed.

" But after all these proceedings according to law," he continued—" so many graves opened, and so many vampires deprived of their horrible animation—the village was not relieved. But a Moravian nobleman, who happened to be travelling this way, heard how matters were, and being skilled—as many people are in his country—in such affairs, he offered to deliver the village from its tormentor. He did so thus : There being a bright moon that night, he ascended, shortly after sunset, the tower of the chapel here, from whence he could distinctly see the churchyard beneath him ; you can see it from that window. From this point he watched until he saw the vampire come out of his grave, and place near it the linen clothes in which he had been folded, and glide away towards the village to plague its inhabitants.

" The stranger, having seen all this, came down from the steeple, took the linen wrappings of the vampire, and carried them up to the top of the tower, which he again mounted. When the vampire returned from his prowlings and missed his clothes, he cried furiously to the Moravian, whom he saw at the summit of the tower, and who, in reply beckoned him to ascend and take them. Whereupon the vampire, accepting his invitation, began to climb the steeple, and so soon as he had reached the battlements, the Moravian, with a stroke of his sword, clove his skull in twain, hurling him down to the churchyard, whither, descending by the winding stairs, the stranger followed and cut his head off, and next day delivered it and the body to the villagers, who duly impaled and burnt them.

" This Moravian nobleman had authority from the then head of the family to remove the tomb of Mircalla, Countess Karnstein, which he did effectually, so that in a little while its site was quite forgotten."

" Can you point out where it stood ? " asked the General, eagerly.

The forester shook his head and smiled.

" Not a soul living could tell you that now," he said ; " besides they say her body was removed ; but no one is sure of that either."

Having thus spoken, as time pressed, he dropped his axe and departed, leaving us to hear the remainder of the General's strange story.

CHAPTER XIV

THE MEETING

" My beloved child," he resumed, " was now growing rapidly worse. The physician who attended her had failed to produce the slightest impression upon her disease, for such I then supposed it to be. He saw my alarm, and suggested a consultation. I called in an abler physician, from Gratz. Several days elapsed before he arrived. He was a good and pious, as well as a learned man. Having seen my poor ward together, they withdrew to my library to confer and discuss. I, from the adjoining room, where I awaited their summons, heard these two gentlemen's voices raised in something sharper than a strictly philosophical discussion. I knocked at the door and entered, I found the old physician from Gratz maintaining his theory. His rival was combating it with undisguised ridicule, accompanied with bursts of laughter. This unseemly manifestation subsided and the altercation ended on my entrance.

" ' Sir,' said my first physician, ' my learned brother seems to think that you want a conjuror, and not a doctor.'

"'Pardon me,' said the old physician from Gratz, looking displeased, 'I shall state my own view of the case in my own way another time. I grieve, Monsieur le Général, that by my skill and science I can be of no use. Before I go I shall do myself the honour to suggest something to you.'

"He seemed thoughtful, and sat down at a table, and began to write. Profoundly disappointed, I made my bow, and as I turned to go, the other doctor pointed over his shoulder to his companion who was writing, and then, with a shrug, significantly touched his forehead.

"This consultation, then, left me precisely where I was. I walked out into the grounds, all but distracted. The doctor from Gratz, in ten or fifteen minutes, overtook me. He apologised for having followed me, but said that he could not conscientiously take his leave without a few words more. He told me that he could not be mistaken ; no natural disease exhibited the same symptoms ; and that death was already very near. There remained, however, a day, or possibly two, of life. If the fatal seizure were at once arrested, with great care and skill her strength might possibly return. But all hung now upon the confines of the irrevocable. One more assault might extinguish the last spark of vitality which is, every moment, ready to die.

"'And what is the nature of the seizure you speak of ?' I entreated.

"'I have stated all fully in this note, which I place in your hands, upon the distinct condition that you send for the nearest clergyman, and open my letter in his presence, and on no account read it till he is with you ; you would despise it else, and it is a matter of life and death. Should the priest fail you, then, indeed, you may read it.'

"He asked me, before taking his leave finally, whether I would wish to see a man curiously learned upon the very subject, which, after I had read his letter, would probably interest me above all others, and he urged me earnestly to invite him to visit him there ; and so took his leave.

"The ecclesiastic was absent, and I read the letter by myself. At another time, or in another case, it might have excited my ridicule. But into what quackeries will not people rush for a last chance, where all accustomed means have failed, and the life of a beloved object is at stake ?

"Nothing, you will say, could be more absurd than the learned man's letter. It was monstrous enough to have consigned him to a madhouse. He said that the patient was suffering from the visits of a vampire ! The punctures which she described as having occurred near the throat, were, he insisted, the insertion of those two long, thin, and sharp teeth which, it is well known, are peculiar to vampires ; and there could be no doubt, he added, as to the well-defined presence of the small livid mark which all concurred in describing as that induced by the demon's lips, and every symptom described by the sufferer was in exact conformity with those recorded in every case of a similar visitation.

" Being myself wholly sceptical as to the existence of any such portent as the vampire, the supernatural theory of the good doctor furnished, in my opinion, but another instance of learning and intelligence oddly associated with some hallucination. I was so miserable, however, that, rather than try nothing, I acted upon the instructions of the letter.

" I concealed myself in the dark dressing-room, that opened upon the poor patient's room, in which a candle was burning, and watched there till she was fast asleep. I stood at the door, peeping through the small crevice, my sword laid on the table beside me, as my directions prescribed, until, a little after one, I saw a large black object, very ill-defined, crawl, as it seemed to me, over the foot of the bed, and swiftly spread itself up to the poor girl's throat, where it swelled, in a moment, into a great, palpitating mass.

" For a few moments I had stood petrified. I now sprang forward, with my sword in my hand. The black creature suddenly contracted toward the foot of the bed, glided over it, and, standing on the floor about a yard below the foot of the bed, with a glare of skulking ferocity and horror fixed on me, I saw Millarca. Speculating I know not what, I struck at her instantly with my sword ; but I saw her standing near the door, unscathed. Horrified, I pursued, and struck again. She was gone ! and my sword flew to shivers against the door.

" I can't describe to you all that passed on that horrible night. The whole house was up and stirring. The spectre Millarca was gone. But her victim was sinking fast, and before the morning dawned, she died."

The old General was agitated. We did not speak to him. My father walked to some little distance, and began reading the inscriptions on the tombstones ; and thus occupied, he strolled into the door of a side chapel to prosecute his researches. The General leaned against the wall, dried his eyes, and sighed heavily. I was relieved on hearing the voices of Carmilla and Madame, who were at that moment approaching. The voices died away.

In this solitude, having just listened to so strange a story, connected, as it was, with the great and titled dead, whose monuments were mouldering among the dust and ivy round us, and every incident of which bore so awfully upon my own mysterious case—in this haunted spot, darkened by the towering foliage that rose on every side, dense and high above its noiseless walls—a horror began to steal over me, and my heart sank as I thought that my friends were, after all, not about to enter and disturb this triste and ominous scene.

The old General's eyes were fixed on the ground, as he leaned with his hand upon the basement of a shattered monument.

Under a narrow, arched doorway, surmounted by one of those demoniacal grotesques in which the cynical and ghastly fancy of old Gothic carving delights, I saw very gladly the beautiful face and figure of Carmilla enter the shadowy chapel.

I was just about to rise and speak, and nodded smiling, in answer to her peculiarly engaging smile ; when, with a cry, the old man by my side caught up the woodman's hatchet, and started forward. On seeing him a brutalised change came over her features. It was an instantaneous and horrible transformation, as she made a crouching step backwards. Before I could utter a scream, he struck at her with all his force, but she dived under his blow, and unscathed, caught him in her tiny grasp by the wrist. He struggled for a moment to release his arm, but his hand opened, the axe fell to the ground, and the girl was gone.

He staggered against the wall. His grey hair stood upon his head, and a moisture shone over his face, as if he were at the point of death.

The frightful scene had passed in a moment. The first thing I recollect after, is Madame standing before me, and impatiently repeating again and again, the question, " Where is Mademoiselle Carmilla ? "

I answered at length, " I don't know—I can't tell—she went there," and I pointed to the door through which Madame had just entered ; " only a minute or two since."

" But I have been standing there, in the passage, ever since Mademoiselle Carmilla entered ; and she did not return."

She then began to call " Carmilla " through every door and passage and from the windows, but no answer came.

"She called herself Carmilla?" asked the General, still agitated.

"Carmilla, yes," I answered.

"Aye," he said ; that is Millarca. That is the same person who long ago was called Mircalla, Countess Karnstein. Depart from this accursed ground, my poor child, as quickly as you can. Drive to the clergyman's house, and stay there till we come. Begone ! May you never behold Carmilla more ; you will not find her here."

CHAPTER XV

ORDEAL AND EXECUTION

As he spoke one of the strangest-looking men I ever beheld, entered the chapel at the door through which Carmilla had made her entrance and her exit. He was tall, narrow-chested, stooping, with high shoulders, and dressed in black. His face was brown and dried in with deep furrows ; he wore an oddly-shaped hat with a broad leaf. His hair, long and grizzled, hung on his shoulders. He wore a pair of gold spectacles, and walked slowly, with an odd shambling gait, and his face sometimes turned up to the sky, and sometimes bowed down toward the ground, seemed to wear a perpetual smile ; his long thin arms were swinging, and his lank hands, in old black gloves ever so much too wide for them, waving and gesticulating in utter abstraction.

"The very man ! " exclaimed the General, advancing with manifest delight. " My dear Baron, how happy I am to see you, I had no hope of meeting you so soon." He signed to my father, who had by this time returned, and leading the fantastic old gentleman, whom he called the Baron, to meet him. He introduced him formally, and they at once entered into earnest conversation. The stranger took a roll of paper from his pocket, and spread it on the worn surface of a tomb that stood by. He had a pencil case in his fingers, with which he traced imaginary lines from point to point on the paper, which from their often glancing from it, together, at certain points of the building, I concluded to be a plan of the chapel. He accompanied, what I may term his lecture, with occasional readings from a dirty little book, whose yellow leaves were closely written over.

They sauntered together down the side aisle, opposite to the spot where I was standing, conversing as they went ; then they began measuring distances by paces, and finally they all stood together, facing a piece of the side-wall, which they began to examine with great minuteness ; pulling off the ivy that clung over it, and rapping the plaster with the ends of their sticks, scraping here, and knocking there. At length they ascertained the existence of a broad marble tablet, with letters carved in relief upon it.

With the assistance of the woodman, who soon returned, a monumental inscription, and carved escutcheon, were disclosed. They proved to be those of the long lost monument of Mircalla, Countess Karnstein.

The old General, though not I fear given to the praying mood, raised his hands and eyes to heaven, in mute thanksgiving for some moments.

" To-morrow," I heard him say ; " the commissioner will be here, and the Inquisition will be held according to law."

Then turning to the old man with the gold spectacles, whom I have described, he shook him warmly by both hands and said :

" Baron, how can I thank you ? How can we all thank you ? You will have delivered this region from a plague that has scourged its inhabitants for more than a century. The horrible enemy, thank God, is at last tracked."

My father led the stranger aside, and the General followed. I knew that he had led them out of hearing, that he might relate my case, and I saw them glance often quickly at me, as the discussion proceeded.

My father came to me, kissed me again and again, and leading me from the chapel, said :

" It is time to return, but before we go home, we must add to our party the good priest, who lives but a little way from this ; and persuade him to accompany us to the schloss."

In this quest we were successful : and I was glad, being unspeakably fatigued when we reached home. But my satisfaction was changed to dismay, on discovering that there were no tidings of Carmilla. Of the scene that had occurred in the ruined chapel, no explanation was offered to me, and it was clear that it was a secret which my father for the present determined to keep from me.

The sinister absence of Carmilla made the remembrance of the scene more horrible to me. The arrangements for that night were singular. Two servants and Madame were to sit up in my room that night ; and the ecclesiastic with my father kept watch in the adjoining dressing-room.

The priest had performed certain solemn rites that night, the purport of which I did not understand any more than I comprehended the reason of this extraordinary precaution taken for my safety during sleep.

I saw all clearly a few days later.

The disappearance of Carmilla was followed by the discontinuance of my nightly sufferings.

You have heard, no doubt, of the appalling superstition that prevails in Upper and Lower Styria, in Moravia, Silesia, in Turkish Servia, in Poland, even in Russia ; the superstition, so we must call it, of the vampire.

If human testimony, taken with every care and solemnity, judicially, before commissions innumerable, each consisting of many members, all chosen for integrity and intelligence, and constituting reports more voluminous perhaps than exist upon any one other class of cases, is worth anything, it is difficult to deny, or even to doubt the existence of such a phenomenon as the vampire.

For my part I have heard no theory by which to explain what I myself have witnessed and experienced, other than that supplied by the ancient and well-attested belief of the country.

The next day the formal proceedings took place in the Chapel of Karnstein. The grave of the Countess Mircalla was opened ; and the General and my father recognized each his perfidious and beautiful guest, in the face now disclosed to view. The features, though a hundred and fifty years had passed since her funeral, were tinted with the warmth of life. Her eyes were open ; no cadaverous smell exhaled from the coffin. The two medical men, one officially present, the other on the part of the promoter of the enquiry, attested the marvellous fact, that there was a faint but appreciable respiration, and a corresponding action of the heart. The limbs were perfectly flexible, the flesh elastic ; and the leaden coffin floated with blood, in which to a depth of seven inches, the body lay immersed. Here then, were all the admitted signs and proofs of vampirism. The body, therefore, in accordance with the ancient practice, was raised, and a sharp stake driven through the heart of the vampire, who uttered a piercing shriek at the moment, in all respects such as might escape from a living person in the last agony. Then the head was struck off, and a torrent of blood flowed from the severed neck. The body and head were next placed on a pile of wood, and reduced to ashes, which were thrown upon the river and borne away, and that territory has never since been plagued by the visits of a vampire.

My father has a copy of the report of the Imperial Commission, with the signatures of all who were present at these proceedings, attached in verification of the statement. It is from this official paper that I have summarised my account of this last shocking scene.

CHAPTER XVI

CONCLUSION

I write all this you suppose with composure. But far from it ; I cannot think of it without agitation. Nothing but your earnest desire so repeatedly expressed, could have induced me to sit down to a task that has unstrung my nerves for months to come, and re-induced a shadow of the unspeakable horror which years after my deliverance continued to make my days and nights dreadful, and solitude insupportably terrific.

Let me add a word or two about that quaint Baron Vordenburg, to whose curious lore we were indebted for the discovery of the Countess Mircalla's grave.

He had taken up his abode in Gratz, where, living upon a mere pittance, which was all that remained to him of the once princely estates of his family, in Upper Styria, he devoted himself to the minute and laborious investigation of the marvellously authenticated tradition of vampirism. He had at his fingers' ends all the great and little works upon the subject. *Magia Posthuma, Phlegon de Mirabilibus, Augustinus de curâ pro Mortuis, Philosophicæ et Christianæ Cogitationes de Vampiris*, by John Christofer Herenberg ; and a thousand others, among which I remember only a few of those which he lent to my father. He had a voluminous digest of all the judicial cases, from which he had extracted a system of principles that appear to govern—some always, and others occasionally only—the condition of the vampire. I may mention, in passing, that the deadly pallor attributed to that sort of *revenants*, is a mere melodramatic fiction. They present, in the grave, and when they show themselves in human society, the appearance of healthy life. When disclosed to light in their coffins, they exhibit all the symptoms that are enumerated as those which proved the vampire-life of the long-dead Countess Karnstein.

How they escape from their graves and return to them for certain hours every day, without displacing the clay or leaving any trace of disturbance in the state of the coffin or the cerements, has always been admitted to be utterly inexplicable. The amphibious existence of the vampire is sustained by daily renewed slumber in the grave. Its horrible lust for living blood supplies the vigour of its waking existence. The vampire is prone to be fascinated with an engrossing vehemence, resembling the passion of love, by particular persons. In pursuit of these it will exercise inexhaustible patience and stratagem, for access to a particular object may be obstructed in a hundred ways. It will never desist until it has satiated its passion, and drained the very life of its coveted victim. But it will, in these cases, husband and protract its murderous enjoyment with the refinement of an epicure, and heighten it by the gradual approaches of an artful courtship. In these cases it seems to yearn for something like sympathy and consent. In ordinary ones it goes direct to its object, overpowers with violence, and strangles and exhausts often at a single feast.

The vampire is, apparently, subject, in certain situations, to special conditions. In the particular instance of which I have given you a relation, Mircalla seemed to be limited to a name which, if not her real one, should at least reproduce, without the omission or addition of a single letter, those, as we say, anagrammatically, which compose it. *Carmilla* did this ; so did *Millarca*.

My father related to the Baron Vordenburg, who remained with us for two or three weeks after the expulsion of Carmilla, the story about the Moravian nobleman and the vampire at Karnstein churchyard, and then he asked the Baron how he had discovered the exact position of the long-concealed tomb of the Countess Millarca. The Baron's grotesque features puckered up into a mysterious smile ; he looked down, still smiling on his worn spectacle-case and fumbled with it. Then looking up, he said :

" I have many journals, and other papers, written by that remarkable man ; the most curious among them is one treating of the visit of which you speak, to Karnstein. The tradition, of course, discolours and distorts a little. He might have been termed a Moravian nobleman, for he had changed his abode to that territory, and was, beside, a noble. But he was, in truth, a native of Upper Styria. It is enough to say that in very early youth he had been a passionate and favoured lover of the beautiful Mircalla, Countess Karnstein. Her early death plunged him into inconsolable grief. It is the nature of vampires to increase and multiply, but according to an ascertained and ghostly law.

" Assume, at starting, a territory perfectly free from that pest. How does it begin, and how does it multiply itself? I will tell you. A person, more or less wicked, puts an end to himself. A suicide, under certain circumstances, becomes a vampire. That spectre visits living people in their slumbers ; *they* die, and almost invariably, in the grave, develop into vampires. This happened in the case of the beautiful Mircalla, who was haunted by one of those demons. My ancestor, Vordenburg, whose title I still bear, soon discovered this, and in the course of the studies to which he devoted himself, learned a great deal more.

" Among other things, he concluded that suspicion of vampirism would probably fall, sooner or later, upon the dead Countess, who in life had been his idol. He conceived a horror, be she what she might, of her remains being profaned by the outrage of a posthumous execution. He has left a curious paper to prove that the vampire, on its expulsion from its amphibious existence, is projected into a far more horrible life ; and he resolved to save his once beloved Mircalla from this.

" He adopted the stratagem of a journey here, a pretended removal of her remains, and a real obliteration of her monument. When age had stolen upon him, and from the vale of years he looked back on the scenes he was leaving, he considered, in a different spirit, what he had done, and a horror took possession of him. He made the tracings and notes which have guided me to the very spot, and drew up a confession of the deception that he had practised. If he had intended any further action in this matter, death prevented him ; and the hand of a remote descendant has too late for many, directed the pursuit to the lair of the beast."

We talked a little more, and among other things he said was this :

" One sign of the vampire is the power of the hand. The slender hand of Mircalla closed like a vice of steel on the General's wrist when he raised the hatchet to strike. But its power is not confined to its grasp ; it leaves a numbness in the limb it seizes, which is slowly, if ever, recovered from."

The following Spring my father took me a tour through Italy. We remained away for more than a year. It was long before the terror of recent events subsided ; and to this hour the image of

Carmilla returns to memory with ambiguous alternations—sometimes the playful, languid, beautiful girl ; sometimes the writhing fiend I saw in the ruined church ; and often from a reverie I have started, fancying I heard the light step of Carmilla at the drawing-room door.

SIR DOMINICK'S BARGAIN

In the early autumn of the year 1838, business called me to the south of Ireland. The weather was delightful, the scenery and people were new to me, and sending my luggage on by the mail-coach route in charge of a servant, I hired a serviceable nag at a posting-house, and, full of the curiosity of an explorer, I commenced a leisurely journey of five-and-twenty miles on horseback, by sequestered cross-roads, to my place of destination. By bog and hill, by plain and ruined castle, and many a winding stream, my picturesque road led me.

I had started late, and having made little more than half my journey, I was thinking of making a short halt at the next convenient place, and letting my horse have a rest and a feed, and making some provision also for the comforts of his rider.

It was about four o'clock when the road, ascending a gradual steep, found a passage through a rocky gorge between the abrupt termination of a range of mountain to my left and a rocky hill, that rose dark and sudden at my right. Below me lay a little thatched village, under a long line of gigantic beech-trees, through the boughs of which the lowly chimneys sent up their thin turf-smoke. To my left, stretched away for miles, ascending the mountain range I have mentioned, a wild park, through whose sward and ferns the rock broke, time-worn and lichen-stained. This park was studded with straggling wood, which thickened to something like a forest, behind and beyond the little village I was approaching, clothing the irregular ascent of the hillsides with beautiful, and in some places discoloured foliage.

As you descend, the road winds slightly, with the grey park-wall, built of loose stone, and mantled here and there with ivy, at its left, and crosses a shallow ford ; and as I approached the village, through breaks in the woodlands, I caught glimpses of the long front of an old ruined house, placed among the trees, about half-way up the picturesque mountain-side.

The solitude and melancholy of this ruin piqued my curiosity, and when I had reached the rude thatched public-house, with the sign of St. Columbkill, with robes, mitre, and crozier displayed over its lintel, having seen to my horse and made a good meal myself on a rasher and eggs, I began to think again of the wooded park and the ruinous house, and resolved on a ramble of half an hour among its sylvan solitudes.

The name of the place, I found, was Dunoran ; and beside the gate a stile admitted to the grounds, through which, with a pensive enjoyment, I began to saunter towards the dilapidated mansion.

A long grass-grown road, with many turns and windings, led up to the old house, under the shadow of the wood.

The road, as it approached the house skirted the edge of a precipitous glen, clothed with hazel, dwarf-oak, and thorn, and the silent house stood with its wide-open hall-door facing this dark ravine, the further edge of which was crowned with towering forest ; and great trees stood about the house and its deserted court-yard and stables.

I walked in and looked about me, through passages overgrown with nettles and weeds ; from room to room with ceilings rotted, and here and there a great beam dark and worn, with tendrils of ivy trailing over it. The tall walls with rotten plaster were stained and mouldy, and in some rooms the remains of decayed wainscoting crazily swung to and fro. The almost sashless windows were darkened also with ivy, and about the tall chimneys the jackdaws were wheeling, while from the huge trees that overhung the glen in sombre masses at the other side, the rooks kept up a ceaseless cawing.

As I walked through these melancholy passages—peeping only into some of the rooms, for the flooring was quite gone in the middle, and bowed down toward the centre, and the house was very nearly un-roofed, a state of things which made the exploration a little critical—I began to wonder why so grand a house, in the midst of scenery so picturesque, had been permitted to go to decay ; I dreamed of the hospitalities of which it had long ago been the rallying place, and I thought what a scene of Redgauntlet revelries it might disclose at midnight.

The great staircase was of oak, which had stood the weather wonderfully, and I sat down upon its steps, musing vaguely on the transitoriness of all things under the sun.

Except for the hoarse and distant clamour of the rooks, hardly audible where I sat, no sound broke the profound stillness of the spot. Such a sense of solitude I have seldom experienced before. The air was stirless, there was not even the rustle of a withered leaf along the passage. It was oppressive. The tall trees that stood close about the building darkened it, and added something of awe to the melancholy of the scene.

In this mood I heard, with an unpleasant surprise, close to me, a voice that was drawling, and, I fancied, sneering, repeat the words : " Food for worms, dead and rotten ; God over all."

There was a small window in the wall, here very thick, which had been built up, and in the dark recess of this, deep in the shadow, I now saw a sharp-featured man, sitting with his feet dangling. His keen eyes were fixed on me, and he was smiling cynically, and before I had well recovered my surprise, he repeated the distich :

If death was a thing that money could buy,
The rich they would live, and the poor they would die.

" It was a grand house in its day, sir," he continued, " Dunoran House, and the Sarsfields. Sir Dominick Sarsfield was the last of the old stock. He lost his life not six foot away from where you are sitting."

As he thus spoke he let himself down, with a little jump, on to the ground.

He was a dark-faced, sharp-featured, little hunchback, and had a walking-stick in his hand, with the end of which he pointed to a rusty stain in the plaster of the wall.

" Do you mind that mark, sir ? " he asked.

" Yes," I said, standing up, and looking at it, with a curious anticipation of something worth hearing.

" That's about seven or eight feet from the ground, sir, and you'll not guess what it is."

" I dare say not," said I, " unless it is a stain from the weather."

" 'Tis nothing so lucky, sir," he answered, with the same cynical smile and a wag of his head, still pointing at the mark with his stick. " That's a splash of brains and blood. It's there this hundhred years ; and it will never leave it while the wall stands."

" He was murdered, then ? "

" Worse than that, sir," he answered.

" He killed himself, perhaps ? "

" Worse than that, itself, this cross between us and harm ! I'm oulder than I look, sir ; you wouldn't guess my years."

He became silent, and looked at me, evidently inviting a guess.

" Well, I should guess you to be about five-and-fifty."

He laughed, and took a pinch of snuff, and said :

" I'm that, your honour, and something to the back of it. I was seventy last Candlemas. You would not a' thought that, to look at me."

" Upon my word I should not ; I can hardly believe it even now. Still, you don't remember Sir Dominick Sarsfield's death ? " I said, glancing up at the ominous stain on the wall.

" No, sir, that was a long while before I was born. But my grandfather was butler here long ago, and many a time I heard tell how Sir Dominick came by his death. There was no masther in the great house ever sinst that happened. But there was two sarvants in care of it, and my aunt was one o' them ; and she kep' me here wid her till I was nine year old, and she was lavin' the place to go to Dublin ; and from that time it was let to go down. The wind sthript the roof, and the rain rotted the timber, and little by little, in sixty years' time, it kem to what you see. But I have a likin' for it still, for the sake of ould times ; and I never come this way but I take a look in. I don't think it's many more times I'll be turnin' to see the ould place, for I'll be undher the sod myself before long."

" You'll outlive younger people," I said.

And, quitting that trite subject, I ran on :

" I don't wonder that you like this old place ; it is a beautiful spot, such noble trees."

" I wish ye seen the glin when the nuts is ripe ; they're the sweetest nuts in all Ireland, I think," he rejoined, with a practical sense of the picturesque. " You'd fill your pockets while you'd be lookin' about you."

" These are very fine old woods," I remarked. " I have not seen any in Ireland I thought so beautiful."

" Eiah ! your honour, the woods about here is nothing to what they wor. All the mountains along here was wood when my father was a gossoon, and Murroa Wood was the grandest of them all. All oak mostly, and all cut down as bare as the road. Not one left here that's fit to compare with them. Which way did your honour come hither—from Limerick ? "

" No. Killaloe."

" Well, then, you passed the ground where Murroa Wood was in former times. You kem undher Lisnavourra, the steep knob of a hill about a mile above the village here. 'Twas near that Murroa Wood was, and 'twas there Sir Dominick Sarsfield first met the devil, the Lord between us and harm, and a bad meeting it was for him and his."

I had become interested in the adventure which had occurred in the very scenery which had so greatly attracted me, and my new acquaintance, the little hunchback, was easily entreated to tell me the story, and spoke thus, so soon as we had each resumed his seat :

It was a fine estate when Sir Dominick came into it ; and grand doings there was entirely, feasting and fiddling, free quarters for all the pipers in the counthry round, and a welcome for every one that liked to come. There was wine, by the hogshead, for the quality ; and potteen enough to set a town a-fire, and beer and cidher enough to float a navy, for the boys and girls, and the likes o' me. It was kep' up the best part of a month, till the weather broke, and the rain spoilt the sod for the moneen jigs, and the fair of Allybally Killudeen comin' on they wor obliged to give over their divarsion, and attind to the pigs.

But Sir Dominick was only beginnin' when they wor lavin' off. There was no way of gettin' rid of his money and estates he did not try—what with drinkin', dicin', racin', cards, and all soarts, it was not many years before the estates wor in debt, and Sir Dominick a distressed man. He showed a bold front to the world as long as he could ; and then he sould off his dogs, and most of his horses, and gev out he was going to thravel in France, and the like ; and so off with him for awhile ; and no one in these parts heard tale or tidings of him for two or three years. Till at last quite unexpected, one night there comes a rapping at the big kitchen window. It was past ten o'clock, and old Connor Hanlon, the butler, my grand-father, was sittin' by the fire alone, warming his shins over it. There was keen east wind blowing along the mountains that night, and whistling cowld enough through the tops of the trees, and soundin' lonesome through the long chimneys.

(And the story-teller glanced up at the nearest stack visible from his seat.)

So he wasn't quite sure of the knockin' at the window, and up he gets, and sees his master's face.

My grandfather was glad to see him safe, for it was a long time since there was any news of him ; but he was sorry, too, for it was a changed place and only himself and old Juggy Broadrick in charge of the house, and a man in the stables, and it was a poor thing to see him comin' back to his own like that.

He shook Con by the hand, and says he :

" I came here to say a word to you. I left my horse with Dick in the stable ; I may want him again before morning, or I may never want him."

And with that he turns into the big kitchen, and draws a stool, and sits down to take an air of the fire.

" Sit down, Connor, opposite me, and listen to what I tell you, and don't be afeard to say what you think."

He spoke all the time lookin' into the fire, with his hands stretched over it, and a tired man he looked.

" An why should I be afeard, Masther Dominick ? " says my grandfather. " Yourself was a good masther to me, and so was your father, rest his sould, before you, and I'll say the truth, and dar' the devil, and more than that, for any Sarsfield of Dunoran, much less yourself, and a good right I'd have."

" It's all over with me, Con," says Sir Dominick.

" Heaven forbid ! " says my grandfather.

" 'Tis past praying for," says Sir Dominick. " The last guinea's gone ; the ould place will follow it. It must be sold, and I'm come here, I don't know why, like a ghost to have a last look round me, and go off in the dark again."

And with that he tould him to be sure, in case he should hear of his death, to give the oak box, in the closet off his room, to his cousin, Pat Sarsfield, in Dublin, and the sword and pistols his grandfather carried in Aughrim, and two or three thrifling things of the kind.

And says he, " Con, they say if the divil gives you money over-night, you'll find nothing but a bagful of pebbles, and chips, and nutshells, in the morning. If I thought he played fair, I'm in the humour to make a bargain with him to-night."

" Lord forbid ! " says my grandfather, standing up, with a start and crossing himself.

" They say the country's full of men, listin' sogers for the King o' France. If I light on one o' them, I'll not refuse his offer. How contrary things goes ! How long is it since me and Captain Waller fought the jewel at New Castle ? "

" Six years, Masther Dominick, and ye broke his thigh with the bullet the first shot."

" I did, Con," says he, " and I wish, instead, he had shot me through the heart. Have you any whisky ? "

My grandfather took it out of the buffet, and the masther pours out some into a bowl, and drank it off.

" I'll go out and have a look at my horse," says he, standing up. There was sort of a stare in his eyes, as he pulled his riding-cloak about him, as if there was something bad in his thoughts.

" Sure, I won't be a minute running out myself to the stable, and looking after the horse for you myself," says my grandfather.

" I'm not goin' to the stable," says Sir Dominick ; " I may as well tell you, for I see you found it out already—I'm goin' across the deer-park ; if I come back you'll see me in an hour's time. But, anyhow, you'd better not follow me, for if you do I'll shoot you, and that 'id be a bad ending to our friendship."

And with that he walks down this passage here, and turns the key in the side door at that end of it, and out wid him on the sod into the moonlight and the cowld wind ; and my grandfather seen him walkin' hard towards the park-wall, and then he comes in and closes the door with a heavy heart.

Sir Dominick stopped to think when he got to the middle of the deer-park, for he had not made up his mind, when he left the house and the whisky did not clear his head, only it gev him courage.

He did not feel the cowld wind now, nor fear death, nor think much of anything, but the shame and fall of the old family.

And he made up his mind, if no better thought came to him between that and there, so soon as he came to Murroa Wood, he'd hang himself from one of the oak branches with his cravat.

It was a bright moonlight night, there was just a bit of a cloud driving across the moon now and then, but, only for that, as light a'most as day.

Down he goes, right for the wood of Murroa. It seemed to him every step he took was as long as three, and it was no time till he was among the big oak-trees with their roots spreading from one to another, and their branches stretching overhead like the timbers of a naked roof, and the moon shining down through them, and casting their shadows thick and twist abroad on the ground as black as my shoe.

He was sobering a bit by this time, and he slacked his pace, and he thought 'twould be better to list in the French king's army, and thry what that might do for him, for he knew a man might take his own life any time, but it would puzzle him to take it back again when he liked.

Just as he made up his mind not to make away with himself, what should he hear but a step clinkin' along the dry ground under the trees, and soon he sees a grand gentleman right before him comin' up to meet him.

He was a handsome young man like himself, and he wore a cocked-hat with gold-lace round it, such as officers wears on their coats, and he had on a dress the same as French officers wore in them times.

He stopped opposite Sir Dominick, and he cum to a standstill also.

The two gentlemen took off their hats to one another, and says the stranger :

" I am recruiting, sir," says he, " for my sovereign, and you'll find my money won't turn into pebbles, chips, and nutshells, by to-morrow."

At the same time he pulls out a big purse full of gold.

The minute he set eyes on that gentleman, Sir Dominick had his own opinion of him ; and at those words he felt the very hair standing up on his head.

" Don't be afraid," says he, " the money won't burn you. If it proves honest gold, and if it prospers with you, I'm willing to make a bargain. This is the last day of February," says he ; " I'll serve you seven years, and at the end of that time you shall serve me, and I'll come for you when the seven years is over, when the clock turns the minute between February and March ; and the first of March ye'll come away with me, or never. You'll not find me a bad master, any more than a bad servant. I love my own ; and I command all the pleasures and the glory of the world. The bargain dates from this day, and the lease is out at midnight on the last day I told you ; and in the year "—he told him the year, it was easy reckoned, but I forget it—" and if you'd rather wait," he says, " for eight months and twenty eight days, before you sign the writin', you may, if you meet me here. But I can't do a great deal for you in the mean time ; and if you don't sign then, all you get from me, up to that time, will vanish away, and you'll be just as you are to-night, and ready to hang yourself on the first tree you meet."

Well, the end of it was, Sir Dominick chose to wait, and he came back to the house with a big bag full of money, as round as your hat a'most.

My grandfather was glad enough, you may be sure, to see the master safe and sound again so soon. Into the kitchen he bangs again, and swings the bag o' money on the table ; and he stands up straight, and heaves up his shoulders like a man that has just got shut of a load ; and he looks at the bag, and my grandfather looks at him, and from him to it, and back again. Sir Dominick looked as white as a sheet, and says he :

" I don't know, Con, what's in it ; it's the heaviest load I ever carried."

He seemed shy of openin' the bag ; and he made my grandfather heap up a roaring fire of turf and wood, and then, at last, he opens it, and, sure enough, 'twas stuffed full o' golden guineas, bright and new, as if they were only that minute out o' the Mint.

Sir Dominick made my grandfather sit at his elbow while he counted every guinea in the bag.

When he was done countin', and it wasn't far from daylight when that time came, Sir Dominick made my grandfather swear not to tell a word about it. And a close secret it was for many a day after.

When the eight months and twenty-eight days were pretty near spent and ended, Sir Dominick returned to the house here with a troubled mind, in doubt what was best to be done, and no one alive but my grandfather knew anything about the matter, and he not half what had happened.

As the day drew near, towards the end of October, Sir Dominick grew only more and more troubled in mind,

One time he made up his mind to have no more to say to such things, nor to speak again with the like of them he met with in the wood of Murroa. Then, again, his heart failed him when he thought of his debts, and he not knowing where to turn. Then, only a week before the day, everything began to go wrong with him. One man wrote from London to say that Sir Dominick paid three thousand pounds to the wrong man, and must pay it over again ; another demanded a debt he never heard of before ; and another, in Dublin, denied the payment of a thundherin' big bill, and Sir Dominick could nowhere find the receipt, and so on, wid fifty other things as bad.

Well, by the time the night of the 28th of October came round, he was a'most ready to lose his senses with all the demands that was risin' up again him on all sides, and nothing to meet them but the help of the one dhreadful friend he had to depind on at night in the oak-wood down there below.

So there was nothing for it but to go through with the business that was begun already, and about the same hour as he went last, he takes off the little crucifix he wore round his neck, for he was a Catholic, and his gospel, and his bit o' the thrue cross that he had in a locket, for since he took the money from the Evil One he was growin' frightful in himself, and got all he could to guard him from the power of the devil. But to-night, for his life, he daren't take them with him. So he gives them into my grandfather's hands without a word, only he looked as white as a sheet o' paper ; and he takes his hat and sword, and telling my grandfather to watch for him, away he goes, to try what would come of it.

It was a fine still night, and the moon—not so bright, though, now as the first time—was shinin' over heath and rock, and down on the lonesome oak-wood below him.

His heart beat thick as he drew near it. There was not a sound, not even the distant bark of a dog from the village behind him. There was not a lonesomer spot in the country round, and if it wasn't for his debts and losses that was drivin' him on half mad, in spite of his fears for his soul and his hopes of paradise, and all his good angel was whisperin' in his ear, he would a' turned back, and sent for his clargy, and made his confession and his penance, and changed his ways, and led a good life, for he was frightened enough to have done a great dale.

Softer and slower he stept as he got, once more, in undher the big branches of the oak-threes ; and when he got in a bit, near where he met with the bad spirit before, he stopped and looked round him, and felt himself, every bit, turning as cowld as a dead man, and you may be sure he did not feel much betther when he seen the same man steppin' from behind the big tree that was touchin' his elbow a'most.

" You found the money good," says he, " but it was not enough. No matter, you shall have enough and to spare. I'll see after your luck, and I'll give you a hint whenever it can serve you ; and any time you want to see me you have only to come down here, and call my face to mind, and wish me present. You shan't owe a shilling by the end of the year, and you shall never miss the right card, the best throw, and the winning horse. Are you willing ? "

The young gentleman's voice almost stuck in his throat, and his hair was rising on his head, but he did get out a word or two to signify that he consented ; and with that the Evil One handed him a needle, and bid him give him three drops of blood from his arm ; and he took them in the cup of an acorn, and gave him a pen, and bid him write some words that he repeated, and that Sir Dominick did not understand, on two thin slips of parchment. He took one himself and the other he sunk in Sir Dominick's arm at the place where he drew the blood, and he chosed the flesh over it. And that's as true as you're sittin' there !

Well, Sir Dominick went home. He was a frightened man, and well he might be. But in a little time he began to grow aisier in his mind. Anyhow, he got out of debt very quick, and money came tumbling in to make him richer, and everything he took in hand prospered, and he never made a wager, or played a game, but he won ; and for all that, there was not a poor man on the estate that was not happier than Sir Dominick.

So he took again to his old ways ; for, when the money came back, all came back, and there were hounds and horses, and wine galore, and no end of company, and grand doin's, and divarsion, up here at the great house. And some said Sir Dominick was thinkin' of gettin' married ; and more said he wasn't. But, anyhow, there was somethin' troublin' him more than common, and so one night, unknownst to all, away he goes to the lonesome oak-wood. It was something, maybe, my grandfather thought was troublin' him about a beautiful young lady he was jealous of, and mad in love with her. But that was only guess.

Well, when Sir Dominick got into the wood this time, he grew more in dread than ever ; and he was on the point of turnin' and lavin' the place, when who should he see, close beside him, but my gentleman, seated on a big stone undher one of the trees. In place of looking the fine young gentleman in goold lace and grand clothes he appeared before, he was now in rags, he looked twice the size he had been, and his face smutted with soot, and he had a murtherin' big steel hammer, as heavy as a half-hundhred, with a handle a yard long, across his knees. It was so dark under the tree, he did not see him quite clear for some time.

He stood up, and he looked awful tall entirely. And what passed between them in that discourse my grandfather never heered. But Sir Dominick was as black as night afterwards, and hadn't a laugh for anything nor a word a'most for any one, and he only grew worse and worse, and darker and darker. And now this thing, whatever it was, used to come to him of its own accord, whether he wanted it or no ; sometimes in one shape, and sometimes in another, in lonesome places, and sometimes at his side by night when he'd be ridin' home alone, until at last he lost heart altogether and sent for the priest.

The priest was with him a long time, and when he heered the whole story, he rode off all the way for the bishop, and the bishop came here to the great house next day, and he gev Sir Dominick a good advice. He toult him he must give over dicin', and swearin', and drinkin', and all bad company, and live a vartuous steady life until the seven years bargain was out, and if the divil didn't come for him the minute afther the stroke of twelve the first morning of the month of March, he was safe out of the bargain. There was not more than eight or ten months to run now before the seven years wor out, and he lived all the time according to the bishop's advice, as strict as if he was " in retreat."

Well, you may guess he felt quare enough when the mornin' of the 28th of February came.

The priest came up by appointment, and Sir Dominick and his raverence wor together in the room you see there, and kep' up their prayers together till the clock struck twelve, and a good hour after, and not a sign of a disturbance, nor nothing came near them, and the priest slep' that night in the house in the room next Sir Dominick's, and all went over as comfortable as could be, and they shook hands and kissed like two comrades after winning a battle.

So, now, Sir Dominick thought he might as well have a pleasant evening, after all his fastin' and praying ; and he sent round to half a dozen of the neighbouring gentlemen to come and dine with him, and his raverence stayed and dined also, and a roarin' bowl o' punch they had, and no end o' wine, and the swearin' and dice, and cards and guineas changing hands, and songs and stories, that wouldn't do any one good to hear, and the priest slipped away, when he seen the turn things was takin', and it was not far from the stroke of twelve when Sir Dominick, sitting at the head of his table, swears, " this is the best first of March I ever sat down with my friends."

" It ain't the first o' March," says Mr. Hiffernan of Ballyvoreen. He was a scholard, and always kep' an almanack.

" What is it, then ? " says Sir Dominick, startin' up, and

dhroppin' the ladle into the bowl, and starin' at him as if he had two heads.

" 'Tis the twenty-ninth of February, leap year," says he. And just as they were talkin', the clock strikes twelve ; and my grandfather, who was half asleep in a chair by the fire in the hall, openin' his eyes, sees a short square fellow with a cloak on, and long black hair bushin' out from under his hat, standin' just there where you see the bit o' light shinin' again' the wall.

(My hunchbacked friend pointed with his stick to a little patch of red sunset light that relieved the deepening shadow of the passage.)

" Tell your master," says he, in an awful voice, like the growl of a baist, " that I'm here by appointment, and expect him downstairs this minute."

Up goes my grandfather, by these very steps you are sittin' on.

" Tell him I can't come down yet," says Sir Dominick, and he turns to the company in the room, and says he with a cold sweat shinin' on his face, " for God's sake, gentlemen, will any of you jump from the window and bring the priest here ? " One looked at another and no one knew what to make of it, and in the meantime, up comes my grandfather again, and says he, tremblin', " He says, sir, unless you go down to him, he'll come up to you."

" I don't understand this, gentlemen, I'll see what it means," says Sir Dominick, trying to put a face on it, and walkin' out o' the room like a man through the press-room, with the hangman waitin' for him outside. Down the stairs he comes, and two or three of the gentlemen peeping over the banisters, to see. My grandfather was walking six or eight steps behind him, and he seen the stranger take a stride out to meet Sir Dominick, and catch him up in his arms, and whirl his head against the wall, and wi' that the hall-doore flies open, and out goes the candles, and the turf and wood-ashes flyin' with the wind out o' the hall-fire, ran in a drift o' sparks along the floore by his feet.

Down runs the gintlemen. Bang goes the hall-doore. Some comes runnin' up, and more runnin' down, with lights. It was all over with Sir Dominick. They lifted up the corpse, and put its shoulders again' the wall ; but there was not a gasp left in him. He was cowld and stiffenin' already.

Pat Donovan was comin' up to the great house late that night and after he passed the little brook, that the carriage track up to the house crosses, and about fifty steps to this side of it, his dog, that was by his side, makes a sudden wheel, and springs over the wall, and sets up a yowlin' inside you'd hear a mile away ; and that minute two men passed him by in silence, goin' down from the house, one of them short and square, and the other like Sir Dominick in shape, but there was little light under the trees where he was, and they looked only like shadows ; and as they passed him by he could not hear the sound of their feet and he drew back to the wall frightened ; and when he got up to the great house, he found all in confusion, and the master's body, with the head smashed to pieces, lying just on *that spot.*

The narrator stood up and indicated with the point of his stick the exact site of the body, and, as I looked, the shadow deepened, the red stain of sunlight vanished from the wall, and the sun had gone down behind the distant hill of New Castle, leaving the haunted scene in the deep grey of darkening twilight.

So I and the story-teller parted, not without good wishes on both sides, and a little " tip " which seemed not unwelcome, from me.

It was dusk and the moon up by the time I reached the village, remounted my nag, and looked my last on the scene of the terrible legend of Dunoran.

The Strange Investigator

One of the strangest-looking men I ever beheld, entered the chapel at the door through which Carmilla had made her entrance and her exit. He was tall, narrow-chested, stooping, with high shoulders, and dressed in black. His face was brown and dried in with deep furrows; he wore an oddly-shaped hat with a broad leaf. His hair, long and grizzled, hung on his shoulders. He wore a pair of gold spectacles, and walked slowly, with an odd shambling gait, with his face sometimes turned up to the sky, and sometimes bowed down toward the ground, seemed to wear a per-petual smile; his long thin arms were swinging, and his lank hands, in old black gloves ever so much too wide for them, waving and gesticulating in utter abstraction.

'The very man!' exclaimed the General, advancing with manifest delight. 'My dear Baron, how happy I am to see you, I had no hope of meeting you so soon.' He signed to my father, who had by this time returned, and leading the fantastic old gentleman, whom he called the Baron, to meet him. He introduced him formally, and they at once entered into earnest conversation. The stranger took a roll of paper from his pocket, and spread it on the worn surface of a tomb that stood by. He had a pencil case in his fingers, with which he traced imaginary lines from point to point on the paper, which from their often glancing from it, together, at certain points of the building, I concluded to be a plan of the chapel. He accompanied, what I may term his lecture, with occasional readings from a dirty little book, whose yellow leaves were closely written over.

They sauntered together down the side aisle, opposite to the spot where I was standing, conversing as they went; then they began measuring distances by paces, and finally they all stood together, facing a piece of the side-wall, which they began to examine with great minuteness; pulling off the ivy that clung over it, and rapping the plaster with the ends of their sticks, scraping here, and knocking there. At length they ascertained the existence of a broad marble tablet, with letters carved in relief upon it.

With the assistance of the woodman, who soon returned, a monumental inscription, and carved escutcheon, were disclosed. They proved to be of those of the long lost monument of Mircalla, Countess Karnstein.

The old General, though not I fear given to the praying mood, raised his hands and eyes to heaven, in mute thanksgiving for some moments.

'Tomorrow,' I heard him say; 'the commissioner will be here, and the Inquisition will be held according to law.'

Then turning to the old man with the gold spectacles, whom I have described, he shook him warmly by both hands and said:

'Baron, how can I thank you? How can we all thank you? You will have delivered this region from a plague that has scourged its inhabitants for more than a century. The horrible enemy, thank God, is at last tracked.'

My father led the stranger aside, and the General followed. I knew that he had led them out of hearing, that he might relate my case, and I saw them glance often quickly at me, as the discussion proceeded.

My father came to me, kissed me again and again, and leading me from the chapel said:

'It is time to return, but before we go home, we must add to our party the good priest, who lives but a little way from this; and persuade him to accompany us to the schloss.'

In this quest we were successful: and I was glad, being unspeakably fatigued when we reached home. But my satisfaction was changed to dismay, on discovering that there were no tidings of Carmilla. Of the scene that had occurred in the ruined chapel, no explanation was offered to me, and it was clear that it was a secret which my father for the present determined to keep from me.

The sinister absence of Carmilla made the remembrance of the scene more horrible to me. The arrangements for that night were singular. Two servants and Madame were to sit up in my room that night; and the ecclesiastic with my father kept watch in the adjoining dressing-room.

The priest had performed certain solemn rites that night, the purport of which I did not understand any more than I comprehended the reason of this extraordinary precaution taken for my safety during sleep.

I saw all clearly a few days later.

The disappearance of Carmilla was followed by the discontinuance of my nightly sufferings.

You have heard, no doubt, of the appalling superstition that prevails in Upper and Lower Styria, in Moravia, Silesia, in Turkish Servia, in Poland, even in Russia; the superstition, so we must call it, of the vampire.

If human testimony, taken with every care and solemnity, judicially, before commissions innumerable, each consisting of many members, all chosen for integrity and intelligence, and constituting reports more voluminous perhaps that exist upon any one other class of cases, is worth anything, it is difficult to deny, or even to doubt the existence of such a phenomenon as the vampire.

For my part I have heard no theory by which to explain what I myself have witnessed and experienced, other than that supplied by the ancient and well-attested belief of the country.

The next day the formal proceedings took place in the Chapel of Karnstein. The grave of the Countess Mircalla was opened; and the General and my father recognized each his perfidious and beautiful guest, in the face now disclosed to view. The features, though a hundred and fifty years had passed since her funeral, were tinted with the warmth of life. Her eyes were open; no cadaverous smell exhaled from the coffin. The two medical men, one officially present, the other on the part of the promoter of the inquiry, attested the marvellous fact, that there was a faint, but appreciable respiration, and a corresponding action of the heart. The limbs were perfectly flexible, the flesh elastic; and the leaden coffin floated with blood, in which to a depth of seven inches, the body lay immersed. Here then, were all the admitted signs and proofs of vampirism. The body, therefore, in accordance with the ancient practice, was raised, and a sharp stake driven through the heart of the vampire, who uttered a piercing shriek at the moment, in all respects such as might escape from a living person in the last agony. Then the head was struck off, and a torrent of blood flowed from the severed neck. The body and head were next placed on a pile of wood, and reduced to ashes, which were thrown upon the river and borne away, and that territory has never since been plagued by the visits of a vampire.

My father has a copy of the report of the Imperial Commission, with the signatures of all who were present at these proceedings, attached in verification of the statement. It is from this official paper that I have summarized my account of this last shocking scene.

I write all this you suppose with composure. But far from it; I cannot think of it without agitation. Nothing but your earnest desire so repeatedly expressed, could have induced me to sit down to a task that has unstrung my nerves for months to come, and reinduced a shadow of the unspeakable horror which years after my deliverance continued to make my days and nights dreadful, and solitude insupportably terrific.

Let me add a word or two about that quaint Baron Vordenburg, to whose curious lore we were indebted for the discovery of the Countess Mircalla's grave.

He had taken up his abode in Gratz, where, living upon a mere pittance, which was all that remained to him of the once princely estates of his family, in Upper Styria, he devoted himself to the minute and laborious investigation of the marvellously authenticated tradition of vampirism. He had at his fingers' ends all the great and little works upon the subject. 'Magia Posthuma', 'Phlegon de Mirabilibus', 'Augustinus de curâ pro Mortuis', 'Philosophicæ et Christianæ Cogitantiones de Vampiris', by John Christofer Harenberg; and a thousand others, among which I remember only a few of those which he lent to my father. He had a voluminous digest of all the judicial cases, from which he had extracted a system of principles that appear to govern – some always, and others occasionally only – the condition of the vampire. I may mention, in passing, that the deadly pallor attributed to that sort of *revenants*, is a mere melodramatic fiction. They present, in the grave, and when they show themselves in human society, the appearance of healthy life. When disclosed to light in their coffins, they exhibit all the symptoms that are enumerated as those which proved the vampire life of the long-dead Countess Karnstein.

How they escape from their graves and return to them for certain hours every day, without displacing the clay or leaving any trace of disturbance in the state of the coffin or the cerements, has always been admitted to be utterly inexplicable. The amphibious existence of the vampire is sustained by daily renewed slumber in the grave. Its horrible lust for living blood supplies the vigour of its walking existence. The vampire is prone to be fascinated with an engrossing vehemence, resembling the passion of love, by particular persons. In pursuit of these it will exercise inexhaustible patience and stratagem, for access to a particular object may be obstructed in a hundred ways. It will never desist until it has satiated its passion, and drained the very life of its coveted victim. But it will, in these cases, husband and protract its murderous enjoyment with the refinement of an epicure, and heighten it by the gradual approaches of an artful courtship. In these cases it seems to yearn for something like sympathy and consent. In ordinary ones it goes direct to its object, overpowers with violence, and strangles and exhausts often at a single feast.

The vampire is, apparently, subject, in certain situations, to special conditions. In the particular instance of which I have given you a relation, Mircalla seemed to be limited to a name which, if not her real one, should at least reproduce, without the omission or addition of a single letter, those, as we say, anagrammatically, which compose it. *Carmilla* did this; so did *Millarca*.

My father related to the Baron Vordenburg, who remained with us for two or three weeks after the expulsion of Carmilla, the story about the Moravian nobleman and the vampire at Karnstein churchyard, and then he asked the Baron how he had discovered the exact position of the long-concealed tomb of the Countess Millarca? The Baron's grotesque features puckered up into a mysterious smile; he looked down, still smiling, on his worn spectacle-case and fumbled with it. Then looking up, he said:

'I have many journals, and other papers, written by that remarkable man; the most curious among them is one treating of the visit of which you speak, to Karnstein. The tradition, of course, discolours and distorts a little. He might have been termed a Moravian nobleman, for he had changed his abode to that territory, and was, beside, a noble. But he was, in truth, a native of Upper Styria. It is enough to say that in very early youth he had been a passionate and favoured lover of the beautiful Mircalla, Countess Karnstein. Her early death plunged him into inconsolable grief. It is the nature of vampires to increase and multiply, but according to an ascertained and ghostly law.

'Assume, at starting, a territory perfectly free from that pest. How does it begin, and how does it multiply itself? I will tell you. A person, more or less wicked, puts an end to himself. A suicide, under certain circumstances, becomes a vampire. That spectre visits living people in their slumbers; *they* die, and almost invariably, in the grave, develop into vampires. This happened in the case of the beautiful Mircalla, who was haunted by one of those demons. My ancestor, Vordenburg, whose title I still bear, soon discovered this, and in the course of the studies to which he devoted himself, learned a great deal more.

'Among other things, he concluded that suspicion of vampirism would probably fall, sooner or later, upon the dead Countess, who in life had been his idol. He conceived a horror, be she what she might, of her remains being profaned by the outrage of a posthumous execution. He has left a curious paper to prove that the vampire, on its expulsion from its amphibious existence, is projected into a far more horrible life; and he resolved to save his once beloved Mircalla from this.

'He adopted the stratagem of a journey here, a pretended removal of her remains, and a real obliteration of her monument. When age had stolen upon him, and from the vale of years he looked back on the scenes he was leaving, he considered, in a different spirit, what he had done; and a horror took possession of him. He made the tracings and notes which have guided me to the very spot, and drew up a confession of the deception that he had practised. If he had intended any further action in this matter, death prevented him; and the hand of a remote descendant has, too late for many, directed the pursuit to the lair of the beast.'

We talked a little more, and among other things he said was this:

'One sign of the vampire is the power of the hand. The slender hand of Mircalla closed like a vice of steel on the General's wrist when he raised the hatchet to strike. But its power is not confined to its grasp; it leaves a numbness in the limb it seizes, which is slowly, if ever, recovered from.'

The following Spring my father took me on a tour through Italy. We remained away for more than a year. It was long before the terror of recent events subsided; and to this hour the image of Carmilla returns to memory with ambiguous alternations – sometimes the playful, languid, beautiful girl; sometimes the writhing fiend I saw in the ruined church; and often from a reverie I have started, fancying I heard the light step of Carmilla at the drawing-room door.

WICKED CAPTAIN WALSHAWE

A very odd thing happened to my uncle, Mr. Watson, of Haddle-stone; and to enable you to understand it, I must begin at the beginning.

In the year 1822, Mr. James Walshawe, more commonly known as Captain Walshawe, died at the age of eighty-one years. The Captain in his early days, and so long as health and strength permitted, was a scamp of the active, intriguing sort; and spent his days and nights in sowing his wild oats, of which he seemed to have an inexhaustible stock.

Captain Walshawe was very well known in the neighbourhood of Wauling, and very generally avoided there. He had quitted the service in 1766, at the age of twenty-five, immediately previous to which period his debts had grown so troublesome that he was induced to extricate himself by running away with and marrying an heiress. He was quartered in Ireland, at Clonmel, where was a nunnery, in which, as pensioner, resided Miss O'Neill, or as she was called in the country, Peg O'Neill, the heiress.

Her situation was the only ingredient of romance in the affair, for the young lady was decidedly plain, though good-humoured looking, with that style of features which is termed potato; and in figure she was a little too plump, and rather short. But she was impressible; and the handsome young English lieutenant was too much for her monastic tendencies, and she eloped. They took up their abode at Wauling, in Lancashire.

Here the Captain amused himself after his fashion, sometimes running up, of course, on business to London. He spent her income, frightened her out of her wits, with oath and threats, and broke her heart.

Latterly she shut herself up pretty nearly altogether in her room. She had an old, rather grim, Irish servant-woman in attendance, Molly Doyle. This domestic was lean and religious, and the Captain knew instinctively she hated him; and he hated her in return, and often threatened to put her out of the house, and sometimes even to kick her out of the window.

Years passed away, and old Molly Doyle remained still in her original position. Perhaps he thought that there must be somebody there, and that he was not, after all, very likely to change for the better.

He tolerated another intrusion, too, and thought himself a paragon of patience and easy good-nature for so doing. A Roman Catholic clergyman, in a long black frock, with a low standing collar, and a little white muslin fillet round his neck—tall, sallow, with blue chin, and dark steady eyes—used to glide up and down the stairs, and through the passages; and the Captain sometimes met him in one place and sometimes in another. But by a caprice incident to such tempers he treated this cleric exceptionally, and even with a surly sort of courtesy, though he grumbled about his visits behind his back.

Well, the time came at last, when poor Peg O'Neill—in an evil hour Mrs. James Walshawe—must cry, and quake, and pray her last. The doctor came from Penlynden, and was just as vague as usual, but more gloomy, and for about a week came and went oftener. The cleric in the long black frock was also daily there. And at last came that last sacrament in the gates of death, when the sinner is traversing those dread steps that never can be retraced.

The Captain drank a great deal of brandy and water that night, and called in Farmer Dobbs, for want of better company, to drink with him; and told him all his grievances, and how happy he and 'the poor lady upstairs' might have been had it not been for liars, and pick-thanks, and tale-bearers, and the like, who came between them—meaning Molly Doyle—whom, as he waxed eloquent over his liquor, he came to curse and rail at by name, with more than his accustomed freedom. And he described his own natural character and amiability in such moving terms that he wept maudlin tears of sensibility over his theme; and when Dobbs was gone, drank some more grog, and took to railing and cursing again by himself; and then mounted the stairs unsteadily to see 'what the devil Doyle and the other —— old witches were about in poor Peg's room'.

When he pushed open the door, he found some half-dozen crones, chiefly Irish, from the neighbouring town of Hackleton, sitting over tea and snuff, etc., with candles lighted round the corpse, which was arrayed in a strangely cut robe of brown serge. She had secretly belonged to some order—I think the Carmelite, but I am not certain—and wore the habit in her coffin.

'What the d—— are you doing with my wife?' cried the Captain, rather thickly. 'How dare you dress her up in this—trumpery, you—you cheating old witch; and what's that candle doing in her hand?'

I think he was a little startled, for the spectacle was grisly enough. The dead lady was arrayed in this strange brown robe, and in her rigid fingers, as in a socket, with the large wooden heads and cross wound round it, burned a wax candle, shedding its white light over the sharp features of the corpse. Molly Doyle was not to be put down by the Captain, whom she hated, and accordingly, in her phrase, 'he got as good as he gave'. And the Captain's wrath waxed fiercer, and he plucked the wax taper from the dead hand, and was on the point of flinging it at the old serving-woman's head.

'The holy candle, you sinner!' cried she.

'I've a mind to make you eat it, you beast,' cried the Captain. But I think he had not known before what it was, for he subsided a little sulkily, and he stuffed his hand with the candle (quite extinct by this time) into his pocket, and said he:

'You know devilish well you had no business going on with y-y-your d—— witchcraft about my poor wife, without my leave —you do—and you'll please to take off that d—— brown pinafore, and get her decently into her coffin, and I'll pitch your devil's waxlight into the sink.'

And the Captain stalked out of the room.

'An' now her poor sowl's in prison, you wretch, be the mains o' ye; an' may yer own be shut into the wick o' that same candle, till it's burned out, ye savage.'

'I'd have you ducked for a witch, for twopence,' roared the Captain up the staircase, with his hand on the banisters, standing on the lobby. But the door of the chamber of death clapped angrily, and he went down to the parlour, where he examined the holy candle for a while, with a tipsy gravity, and then with something of that reverential feeling for the symbolic, which is not uncommon in rakes and scamps, he thoughtfully locked it up in a press, where were accumulated all sorts of obsolete rubbish— soiled packs of cards, disused tobacco-pipes, broken powder-flasks, his military sword, and a dusky bundle of the *Flash Songster* and other questionable literature.

Captain Walshawe reigned alone for many years at Wauling. He was too shrewd and too experienced by this time to run violently down the steep hill that leads to ruin. Forty years acted forcibly upon the gay Captain Walshawe. Gout supervened, and was no more conducive to temper than to enjoyment, and made his elegant hands lumpy at all the small joints, and turned them slowly into crippled claws. He grew stout when his exercise was interfered with, and ultimately almost corpulent. He suffered from what Mr. Holloway calls 'bad legs', and was wheeled about in a great leathern-back chair, and his infirmities went on accumulating with his years.

I am sorry to say, I never heard that he repented, or turned his thoughts seriously to the future. On the contrary, his talk grew fouler, and his fun ran upon his favourite sins, and his temper waxed more truculent. But he did not sink into dotage. Considering his bodily infirmities, his energies and his malignities, which were many and active, were marvellously little abated by time.

It was a peculiarity of Captain Walshawe, that he, by this time, hated nearly everybody. My uncle, Mr. Watson, of Haddlestone, was cousin to the Captain, and his heir at law. But my uncle had lent him money on mortgage of his estates and there had been a treaty to sell, and terms and a price were agreed upon, in 'articles' which the lawyers said were still in force.

I think the ill-conditioned Captain bore him a grudge for being richer than he, and would have liked to do him an ill turn. But it did not lie in his way; at least while he was living.

My Uncle Watson was a Methodist, and what they call a 'class leader'; and, on the whole, a very good man. He was now near fifty—grave, as beseemed his profession—somewhat dry—and a little severe, perhaps—but a just man.

A letter from the Penlynden doctor reached him at Haddlestone, announcing the death of the wicked old Captain; and suggesting his attendance at the funeral, and the expediency of his being on the spot to look after things at Wauling. The reasonableness of this striking my good uncle, he made his journey to the old house in Lancashire incontinently, and reached it in time for the funeral.

The day turning out awfully rainy and tempestuous, my uncle persuaded the doctor and the attorney to remain for the night at Wauling.

There was no will—the attorney was sure of that; for the Captain's enmities were perpetually shifting, and he could never quite make up his mind as to how best to give effect to a malignity whose direction was being constantly modified.

Search being made, no will was found. The papers, indeed, were all right, with one important exception: the leases were nowhere to be seen. My uncle searched strenuously. The attorney was at his elbow, and the doctor helped with a suggestion now and then. The old serving man seemed an honest, deaf creature, and really knew nothing.

My Uncle Watson was very much perturbed. He fancied—but this possibly was only fancy—that he had detected for a moment a queer look in the attorney's face, and from that instant it became fixed in his mind that he knew all about the leases. Mr. Watson expounded that evening in the parlour to the doctor, the attorney and the deaf servant.

Ananias and Sapphira figured in the foreground, and the awful nature of fraud and theft, or tampering in any wise with the plain rule of honesty in matters pertaining to estates, etc., were pointedly dwelt upon; and then came a long and strenuous prayer, in which he entreated with fervour and aplomb that the hard heart of the sinner who had abstracted the leases might be softened or broken in such a way as to lead to their restitution; or that, if he continued reserved and contumacious, it might at least be the will of Heaven to bring him to public justice and the documents to light. The fact is, that he was praying all this time at the attorney.

When these religious exercises were over, the visitors retired to their rooms, and my Uncle Watson wrote two or three pressing letters by the fire. When his task was done, it had grown late; the candles were flaring in their sockets, and all in bed, and, I suppose, asleep, but he.

The fire was nearly out, he chilly, and the flame of the candles throbbing strangely in their sockets shed alternate glare and shadow round the old wainscoted room and its quaint furniture. Outside were the wild thunder and piping of the storm, and the rattling of distant windows sounded through the passages, and down the stairs, like angry people astir in the house.

My Uncle Watson belonged to a sect who by no means reject

the supernatural, and whose founder, on the contrary, has sanctioned ghosts in the most emphatic way. He was glad, therefore, to remember, that in prosecuting his search that day, he had seen some six inches of wax candle in the press in the parlour; for he had no fancy to be overtaken by darkness in his present situation.

He had no time to lose; and taking the bunch of keys—of which he was now master—he soon fitted the lock and secured the candle—a treasure in his circumstances; and lighting it, he stuffed it into the socket of one of the expiring candles, and extinguishing the other, he looked round the room in the steady light, reassured. At the same moment an unusually violent gust of the storm blew a handful of gravel against the parlour window, with a sharp rattle that startled him in the midst of the roar and hubbub; and the flame of the candle itself was agitated by the air.

My uncle walked up to bed, guarding his candle with his hand, for the lobby windows were rattling furiously, and he disliked the idea of being left in the dark more than ever.

His bedroom was comfortable, though old-fashioned. He shut and bolted the door. There was a tall looking-glass opposite the foot of his four-poster, on the dressing-table between the windows. He tried to make the curtains meet, but they would not draw.

He turned the face of the mirror away, therefore, so that its back was presented to the bed, pulled the curtains together, and placed a chair against them, to prevent their falling open again. There was a good fire, and a reinforcement of round coal and wood inside the fender. So he piled it up to ensure a cheerful blaze through the night, and placing a little black magohany table, with the legs of a Satyr, beside the bed, and his candle upon it, he got between the sheets, and laid his red night-capped head upon his pillow, and disposed himself to sleep.

The first thing that made him uncomfortable was a sound at the foot of his bed, quite distinct in a momentary lull of the storm. It was only the gentle rustle and rush of the curtains which fell open again; and as his eyes opened, he saw them resuming their perpendicular dependence, and sat up in his bed almost expecting to see something uncanny in the aperture.

There was nothing, however, but the dressing-table and other dark furniture, and the window-curtains faintly undulating in the violence of the storm. He did not care to get up, therefore—the fire being bright and cheery—to replace the curtains by a chair, in the position in which he had left them, anticipating possibly a new recurrence of the relapse which had startled him from his incipient doze.

So he got to sleep in a little while again, but he was disturbed by a sound, as he fancied, at the table on which stood the candle. He could not say what it was, only that he wakened with a start, and lying so in some amaze, he did distinctly hear a sound which startled him a good deal, though there was nothing necessarily supernatural in it.

He described it as resembling what would occur if you fancied a thinnish table-leaf, with a convex warp in it, depressed the reverse way, and suddenly with a spring recovering its natural convexity. It was a loud, sudden thump, which made the heavy candlestick jump, and there was an end, except that my uncle did not get again into a doze for ten minutes at least.

The next time he awoke it was in that odd, serene way that sometimes occurs. We open our eyes, we know not why, quite placidly, and are on the instant wide awake. He had had a nap of some duration this time, for his candle-flame was fluttering and flaring, *in articulo*, in the silver socket. But the fire was still bright and cheery, so he popped the extinguisher on the socket, and almost at the same time there came a tap at his door, and a sort of crescendo 'hush-sh-sh!' Once more my uncle was sitting up, scared and perturbed, in his bed.

He recollected, however, that he had bolted his door; and such inveterate materialists are we in the midst of our spiritualism, that this reassured him, and he breathed a deep sigh, and began to grow tranquil. But after a rest of a minute or two, there came a louder and sharper knock at his door; so that instinctively he called out: 'Who's there?' in a loud, stern key. There was no sort of response, however.

The nervous effect of the start subsided; and after a while he lay down with his back turned towards that side of the bed at which was the door, and his face towards the table on which stood the massive old candlestick, capped with its extinguisher, and in that position he closed his eyes. But sleep would not revisit them. All kinds of queer fancies began to trouble him—some of them I remember.

He felt the point of a finger, he averred, pressed most distinctly on the tip of his great toe, as if a living hand were between his sheets, and making a sort of signal of attention or silence. Then again he felt something as large as a rat make a sudden bounce in the middle of his bolster, just under his head.

Then a voice said: 'Oh!' very gently, close at the back of his head. All these things he felt certain of, and yet investigation led to nothing. He felt odd little cramps stealing now and then about him, and then, on a sudden, the middle finger of his right hand was plucked backwards, with a light playful jerk that frightened him awfully.

Meanwhile the storm kept singing, and howling and ha-ha-hooing hoarsely among the limbs of the old trees and the chimney-pots; and my Uncle Watson, although he prayed and meditated as was his wont when he lay awake, felt his heart throb excitedly, and sometimes thought he was beset with evil spirits, and at others that he was in the early stages of a fever.

He resolutely kept his eyes closed, however, and, like St. Paul's shipwrecked companions, wished for the day. At last another little doze seems to have stolen upon his senses, for he awoke quietly and completely as before—opening his eyes all at once, and seeing everything as if he had not slept for a moment.

The fire was still blazing redly—nothing uncertain in the light— the massive silver candlestick, topped with its tall extinguisher, stood on the centre of the black mahogany table as before; and, looking by what seemed a sort of accident to the apex of this, he beheld something which made him quite misdoubt the evidence of his eyes.

He saw the extinguisher lifted by a tiny hand from beneath, and a small human face, no bigger than a thumb-nail, with nicely proportioned features peep from beneath it. In this Lilliputian countenance was such a ghastly consternation as horrified my uncle unspeakably.

Out came a little foot then and there, and a pair of wee legs, in short silk stockings and buckled shoes, then the rest of the figure; and, with the arms holding about the socket, the little legs stretched and stretched, hanging about the stem of the candlestick till the feet reached the base, and so down the Satyr-like leg of the table, till they reached the floor, extending elastically, and strangely enlarging in all proportions as they approached the ground, where the feet and buckles were those of a well-shaped, full-grown man, and the figure tapering upwards until it dwindled to its original fairy dimensions at the top, like an object seen in some strangely curved mirror.

Standing upon the floor he expanded, my amazed uncle could not tell how, into his proper proportions; and stood pretty nearly in profile at the bedside, a handsome and elegantly shaped young man, in a bygone military costume, with a small laced, three-cocked hat and plume on his head, but looking like a man going to be hanged—in unspeakable despair.

He stepped lightly to the hearth, and turned for a few seconds very dejectedly with his back towards the bed and the mantelpiece, and he saw the hilt of his rapier glittering in the firelight; and then walking across the room, he placed himself at the dressing-table, visible through the divided curtains at the foot of the bed. The fire was still blazing so brightly that my uncle saw him as distinctly as if half a dozen candles were burning.

The looking-glass was an old-fashioned piece of furniture, and had a drawer beneath it. My uncle had searched it carefully for the papers in the day-time; but the silent figure pulled the drawer quite out, pressed a spring at the side, disclosing a false receptacle behind it, and from this he drew a parcel of papers tied together with pink tape.

All this time my uncle was staring at him in a horrified state, neither winking nor breathing, and the apparition had not once given the smallest intimation of consciousness that a living person was in the same room. But now, for the first time, it turned its livid stare full upon my uncle with a hateful smile of significance, lifting up the little parcel of papers between his slender finger and thumb.

Then he made a long, cunning wink at him, and seemed to blow out one of his cheeks in a burlesque grimace, which, but for the horrific circumstances, would have been ludicrous. My uncle could not tell whether this was really an intentional distortion or only one of those horrid ripples and deflections which were constantly disturbing the proportions of the figure, as if it were seen through some unequal and perverting medium.

The figure now approached the bed, seeming to grow exhausted and malignant as it did so. My uncle's terror nearly culminated at this point, for he believed it was drawing near him with an evil purpose. But it was not so; for the soldier, over whom twenty years seemed to have passed in his brief transit to the dressing-table and back again, threw himself into a great high-backed arm-chair of stuffed leather at the far side of the fire, and placed his heels on the fender.

His feet and legs seemed indistinctly to swell, and swathings showed themselves round them, and they grew into something enormous, and the upper figure swayed and shaped itself into corresponding proportions, a great mass of corpulence, with a cadaverous and malignant face, and the furrows of a great old age, and colourless glassy eyes; and with these changes, which came indefinitely but rapidly as those of a sunset cloud, the fine regimentals faded away, and a loose, grey, woollen drapery, somehow, was there in its stead; and all seemed to be stained and rotten, for swarms of worms seemed creeping in and out, while the figure grew paler and paler, till my uncle, who liked his pipe, and employed the simile naturally, said the whole effigy grew to the colour of tobacco ashes, and the clusters of worms into little wriggling knots of sparks such as we see running over the residium of a burnt sheet of paper.

And so with the strong draught caused by the fire, and the current of air from the window, which was rattling in the storm, the feet seemed to be drawn into the fireplace, and the whole figure, light as ashes, floated away with them and disappeared with a whisk up the capacious old chimney.

It seemed to my uncle that the fire suddenly darkened and the air grew icy cold, and there came an awful roar and riot of tempest, which shook the old house from top to base, and sounded like the yelling of a bloodthirsty mob on receiving a new and long-expected victim.

Good Uncle Watson used to say: 'I have been in many situations of fear and danger in the course of my life, but never did I pray with so much agony before or since; for then, as now, it was clear beyond a cavil that I had actually beheld the phantom of an evil spirit.'

Now there are two curious circumstances to be observed on this relation of my uncle's, who was, as I have said, a perfectly veracious man.

First: The wax candle which he took from the press in the parlour and burnt at his bedside on that horrible night was unquestionably, according to the testimony of the old deaf servant, who had been fifty years at Wauling, that identical piece of 'holy candle' which had stood in the fingers of the poor lady's corpse, and concerning which the old Irish crone, long since dead, had delivered the curious curse I have mentioned against the Captain.

Secondly: Behind the drawer under the looking-glass, he did actually discover a second but secret drawer, in which were concealed the identical papers which he had suspected the attorney of having made away with. There were circumstances, too, afterwards disclosed, which convinced my uncle that the old man had deposited them there preparatory to burning them, which he had nearly made up his mind to do.

Now, a very remarkable ingredient in this tale of my Uncle Watson was this, that so far as my father, who had never seen Captain Walshawe in the course of his life, could gather, the phantom had exhibited a horrible and grotesque, but unmistakable resemblance to that defunct scamp in the various stages of his long life.

Wauling was sold in the year 1837, and the old house shortly after pulled down, and a new one built nearer to the river. I often wonder whether it was rumoured to be haunted, and, if so, what stories were current about it. It was a commodious and staunch old house, and withal rather handsome; and its demolition was certainly suspicious.

THE WHITE CAT OF DRUMGUNNIOL

There is a famous story of a white cat, with which we all become acquainted in the nursery. I am going to tell a story of a white cat very different from the amiable and enchanted princess who took that disguise for a season. The white cat of which I speak was a more sinister animal.

The traveller from Limerick towards Dublin, after passing the hills of Killaloe upon the left, as Keeper Mountain rises high in view, finds himself gradually hemmed in, up the right, by a range of lower hills. An undulating plain that dips gradually to a lower level than that of the road interposes, and some scattered hedgerows relieve its somewhat wild and melancholy character.

One of the few human habitations that send up their films of turf-smoke from that lonely plain, is the loosely thatched, earth-built dwelling of a 'strong farmer', as the more prosperous of the tenant-farming classes are termed in Munster. It stands in a clump of trees near the edge of a wandering stream, about half-way between the mountains and the Dublin road, and had been for generations tenanted by people named Donovan.

In a distant place, desirous of studying some Irish records which had fallen into my hands, and inquiring for a teacher capable of instructing me in the Irish language, a Mr. Donovan, dreamy, harmless, and learned, was recommended to me for the purpose.

I found that he had been educated as a Sizar in Trinity College, Dublin. He now supported himself by teaching, and the special direction of my studies, I suppose, flattered his national partialities, for he unbosomed himself of much of his long-reserved thoughts, and recollections about his country and his early days. It was he who told me this story, and I mean to repeat it, as nearly as I can, in his own words.

I have myself seen the old farm-house, with its orchard of huge moss-grown apple trees. I have looked round on the peculiar landscape; the roofless, ivied tower, that two hundred years before had afforded a refuge from raid and rapparee, and which still occupies its old place in the angle of the haggard; the bush-grown 'liss', that scarcely a hundred and fifty steps away records the labours of a bygone race; the dark and towering outline of old Keeper in the background; and the lonely range of furze and heath-clad hills that form a nearer barrier, with many a line of grey rock and clump of dwarf oak or birch. The pervading sense of loneliness made it a scene not unsuited for a wild and unearthly story. And I could quite fancy how, seen in the grey of a wintry morning, shrouded far and wide in snow, or in the melancholy glory of an autumnal sunset, or in the chill splendour of a moonlight night, it might have helped to tone a dreamy mind like honest Dan Donovan's to superstition and a proneness to the illusions of fancy. It is certain, however, that I never anywhere met with a more simple-minded creature, or one on whose good faith I could more entirely rely.

When I was a boy, said he, living at home at Drumgunniol, I used to take my Goldsmith's *Roman History* in my hand and go down to my favourite seat, the flat stone, sheltered by a hawthorn tree beside the little lough, a large and deep pool, such as I have heard called a tarn in England. It lay in the gentle hollow of a field that is overhung towards the north by the old orchard, and being a deserted place was favourable to my studious quietude.

One day reading here, as usual, I wearied at last, and began to look about me, thinking of the heroic scenes I had just been reading of. I was as wide awake as I am at this moment, and I saw a woman appear at the corner of the orchard and walk down the slope. She wore a long, light grey dress, so long that it seemed to sweep the grass behind her, and so singular was her appearance in a part of the world where female attire is so inflexibly fixed by custom, that I could not take my eyes off her. Her course lay diagonally from corner to corner of the field, which was a large one, and she pursued it without swerving.

When she came near I could see that her feet were bare, and that she seemed to be looking steadfastly upon some remote object for guidance. Her route would have crossed me—had the tarn not interposed—about ten or twelve yards below the point at which I was sitting. But instead of arresting her course at the margin of the lough, as I had expected, she went on without seeming conscious of its existence, and I saw her, as plainly as I see you, sir, walk across the surface of the water, and pass, without seeming to see me, at about the distance I had calculated.

I was ready to faint from sheer terror. I was only thirteen years old then, and I remember every particular as if it had happened this hour.

The figure passed through the gap at the far corner of the field, and there I lost sight of it. I had hardly strength to walk home, and was so nervous, and ultimately so ill, that for three weeks I was confined to the house, and could not bear to be alone for a moment. I never entered that field again, such was the horror with which from that moment every object in it was clothed. Even at this distance of time I should not like to pass through it.

This apparition I connected with a mysterious event; and, also, with a singular liability, that has for nearly eight years distinguished, or rather afflicted, our family. It is no fancy. Everybody in that part of the country knows all about it. Everybody connected what I had seen with it.

I will tell it all to you as well as I can.

When I was about fourteen years old—that is about a year after the sight I had seen in the lough field—we were one night expecting my father home from the fair of Killaloe. My mother sat up to welcome him home, and I with her, for I liked nothing better than such a vigil. My brothers and sisters, and the farm servants, except the men who were driving home the cattle from the fair, were asleep in their beds. My mother and I were sitting in the chimney corner chatting together, and watching my father's supper, which was kept hot over the fire. We knew that he would return before the men who were driving home the cattle, for he was riding, and told us that he would only wait to see them fairly on the road, and then push homeward.

At length we heard his voice and the knocking of his loaded whip at the door, and my mother let him in. I don't think I ever saw my father drunk, which is more than most men of my age, from the same part of the country, could say of theirs. But he could drink his glass of whiskey as well as another, and he usually came home from fair or market a little merry and mellow, and with a jolly flush in his cheeks.

Tonight he looked sunken, pale, and sad. He entered with the saddle and bridle in his hand, and he dropped them against the wall, near the door, and put his arms round his wife's neck, and kissed her kindly.

'Welcome home, Meehal,' said she, kissing him heartily.

'God bless you, mavourneen,' he answered.

And hugging her again, he turned to me, who was plucking him by the hand, jealous of his notice. I was little, and light of my age, and he lifted me up in his arms, and kissed me, and my arms being about his neck, he said to my mother:

'Draw the bolt, acuishla.'

She did so, and setting me down very dejectedly, he walked to the fire and sat down on a stool, and stretched his feet towards the glowing turf, leaning with his hands on his knees.

'Rouse up, Mick, darlin',' said my mother, who was growing anxious, 'and tell me how did the cattle sell, and did everything go lucky at the fair, or is there anything wrong with the landlord, or what in the world is it that ails you, Mick, jewel?'

'Nothin', Molly. The cows sould well, thank God, and there's nothin' fell out between me an' the landlord, an' everything's the same way. There's no fault to find anywhere.'

'Well, then, Mickey, since so it is, turn round to your hot supper, and ate it, and tell us is there anything new.'

'I got my supper, Molly, on the way, and I can't ate a bit,' he answered.

'Got your supper on the way, an' you knowin' 'twas waiting for you at home, an' your wife sittin' up an' all!' cried my mother, reproachfully.

'You're takin' a wrong meanin' out of what I say,' said my father. 'There's something happened that leaves me that I can't ate a mouthful, and I'll not be dark with you, Molly, for, maybe, it ain't very long I have to be here, an' I'll tell you what it was. It's what I've seen, the white cat.'

'The Lord between us and harm!' exclaimed my mother, in a moment as pale and as chap-fallen as my father; and then, trying to rally, with a laugh, she said: 'Ha! 'tis only funnin' me you are. Sure a white rabbit was snared a Sunday last, in Grady's wood; an' Teigue seen a big white rat in the haggard yesterday.'

' 'Twas neither rat nor rabbit was in it. Don't ye think but I'd know a rat or a rabbit from a big white cat, with green eyes as big as halfpennies, and its back riz up like a bridge, trottin' on and acorss me, and ready, if I dar' stop, to rub its sides against my shins, and maybe to make a jump and seize my throat, if that it's a cat, at all, an' not something worse?'

As he ended his description in a low tone, looking straight at the fire my father drew his big hand across his forehead once or twice, his face being damp and shining with the moisture of fear, and he sighed, or rather groaned, heavily.

My mother had relapsed into panic, and was praying again in her fear. I, too, was terribly frightened, and on the point of crying, for I knew all about the white cat.

Clapping my father on the shoulder, by way of encouragement, my mother leaned over him, kissing him, and at last began to cry. He was wringing her hands in his, and seemed in great trouble.

'There was nothin' came into the house with me?' he asked, in a very low tone, turning to me.

'There was nothin', father,' I said, 'but the saddle and bridle that was in your hand.'

'Nothin' white kem in at the doore wid me,' he repeated.

'Nothin' at all,' I answered.

'So best,' said my father, and making the sign of the cross, he began mumbling to himself, and I knew he was saying his prayers.

Waiting for a while, to give him time for this exercise, my mother asked him where he first saw it.

'When I was riding up the bohereen'—the Irish term meaning a little road, such as leads up to a farm-house—'I bethought myself that the men was on the road with the cattle, and no one to look to the horse barrin' myself, so I thought I might as well leave him in the crooked field below, an' I tuck him there, he bein' cool, and not a hair turned, for I rode him aisy all the way. It was when I turned, after lettin' him go—the saddle and bridle bein' in my hand—that I saw it, pushin' out o' the long grass at the side o' the path, an' it walked across it, in front of me, an' then back again, before me, the same way, an' sometimes at one side, an' then at the other, lookin' at me wid them shinin' eyes; and I consayted I heard it growlin' as it kep' beside me—as close as ever you see—till I kem up to the doore, here, an' knocked an' called, as ye heered me.'

Now, what was it, in so simple an incident, that agitated my father, my mother, myself, and finally, every member of this rustic household, with a terrible foreboding? It was this that we, one and all, believed that my father had received, in thus encountering the white cat, a warning of his approaching death.

The omen had never failed hitherto. It did not fail now. In a week after my father took the fever that was going, and before a month he was dead.

My honest friend, Dan Donovan, paused here; I could perceive that he was praying, for his lips were busy, and I concluded that it was for the repose of that departed soul.

In a little while he resumed.

It is eighty years now since that omen first attached to my family. Eighty years? Ay, is it. Ninety is nearer the mark. And I have spoken to many old people, in those earlier times, who had a distinct recollection of everything connected with it.

It happened in this way.

My grand-uncle, Connor Donovan, had the old farm of Drumgunniol in his day. He was richer than ever my father was, or my father's father either, for he took a short lease of Balraghan, and made money of it. But money won't soften a hard heart, and I'm afraid my grand-uncle was a cruel man—a profligate man he was, surely, and that is mostly a cruel man at heart. He drank his share, too, and cursed and swore, when he was vexed, more than was good for his soul, I'm afraid.

At that time there was a beautiful girl of the Colemans, up in the mountains, not far from Capper Cullen. I'm told that there are no Colemans there now at all, and that family has passed away. The famine years made great changes.

Ellen Coleman was her name. The Colemans were not rich. But, being such a beauty, she might have made a good match. Worse than she did for herself, poor thing, she could not.

Con Donovan—my grand-uncle, God forgive him!—sometimes in his rambles saw her at fairs or patterns, and he fell in love with her, as who might not?

He used her ill. He promised her marriage, and persuaded her to come away with him; and, after all, he broke his word. It was just the old story. He tired of her, and he wanted to push himself in the world; and he married a girl of the Collopys, that had a great fortune—twenty-four cows, seventy sheep, and a hundred and twenty goats.

He married this Mary Collopy, and grew richer than before; and Ellen Coleman died broken-hearted. But that did not trouble the strong farmer much.

He would have liked to have children, but he had none, and this was the only cross he had to bear, for everything else went much as he wished.

One night he was returning from the fair of Nenagh. A shallow stream at that time crossed the road—they have thrown a bridge over it, I am told, some time since—and its channel was often dry in summer weather. When it was so, as it passes close by the old farm-house of Drumgunniol, without a great deal of winding, it makes a sort of road, which people then used as a short cut to reach the house by. Into this dry channel, as there was plenty of light from the moon, my grand-uncle turned his horse, and when he had reached the two ash trees at the meering of the farm he turned his horse short into the river field, intending to ride through the gap at the other end, under the oak tree, and so he would have been within a few hundred yards of his door.

As he approached the 'gap' he saw, or thought he saw, with a slow motion, gliding along the ground towards the same point, and now and then with a soft bound, a white object, which he described as being no bigger than his hat, but what it was he could not see, as it moved along the hedge and disappeared at the point to which he was himself tending.

When he reached the gap the horse stopped short. He urged and coaxed it in vain. He got down to lead it through, but it recoiled, snorted, and fell into a wild trembling fit. He mounted it again. But its terror continued, and it obstinately resisted his caresses and his whip. It was bright moonlight, and my grand-uncle was chafed by the horse's resistance, and, seeing nothing to account for it, and being so near home, what little patience he possessed forsook him, and, plying his whip and spur in earnest, he broke into oaths and curses.

All on a sudden the horse sprang through, and Con Donovan, as he passed under the broad branch of the oak, saw clearly a woman standing on the bank beside him, her arm extended, with the hand of which, as he flew by, she struck him a blow upon the shoulders. It threw him forward upon the neck of the horse, which, in wild terror, reached the door at a gallop, and stood there quivering and steaming all over.

Less alive than dead, my grand-uncle got in. He told his story, at least, so much as he chose. His wife did not quite know what to think. But that something very bad had happened she could not doubt. He was very faint and ill, and begged that the priest should be sent for forthwith. When they were getting him to his bed they saw distinctly the marks of five fingerprints on the flesh of his shoulder, where the spectral blow had fallen. These singular marks—which they said resembled in tint the hue of a body struck by lightning—remained imprinted on his flesh, and were buried with him.

When he had recovered sufficiently to talk with the people about him—speaking, like a man at his last hour, from burdened heart, and troubled conscience—he repeated his story, but said he did not see, or, at all events, know, the face of the figure that stood in the gap. No one believed him. He told more about it to the priest than to others. He certainly had a secret to tell. He might as well have divulged it frankly, for the neighbours all knew well enough that it was the face of dead Ellen Coleman that he had seen.

From that moment my grand-uncle never raised his head. He was a scared, silent, broken-spirited man. It was early summer then, and at the fall of the leaf in the same year he died.

Of course there was a wake, such as beseemed a strong farmer so rich as he. For some reason the arrangements of this ceremonial were a little different from the usual routine.

The usual practice is to place the body in the great room, or kitchen, as it is called, of the house. In this particular case there was, as I told you, for some reason, an unusual arrangement. The body was placed in a small room that opened upon the greater one. The door of this, during the wake, stood open. There were candles about the bed, and pipes and tobacco on the table, and stools for such guests as chose to enter, the door standing open for their reception.

The body, having been laid out, was left alone, in this smaller room, during the preparations for the wake. After nightfall one of the women, approaching the bed to get a chair which she had left near it, rushed from the room with a scream, and, having recovered her speech at the farther end of the 'kitchen', and surrounded by a gaping audience, she said, at last:

'May I never sin, if his face bain't riz up again the back o' the bed, and he starin' down to the doore, wid eyes as big as pewter plates, that id be shinin' in the moon!'

'Arra, woman! Is it cracked you are?' said one of the farm boys as they are termed, being men of any age you please.

'Ahg, Molly, don't be talkin', woman! 'Tis what ye consa, .ed it, goin' into the dark room, out o' the light. Why didn't ye take a candle in your fingers, ye aumadhaun?' said one of her female companions.

'Candle, or no candle; I seen it,' insisted Molly. An' what's more, I could a'most tak' my oath I seen his arum, too, stretchin' out o' the bed along the flure, three times as long as it

295

should be, to take hould o' me be the fut.'

'Nansinse, ye fool, what id he want o' yer fut?' exclaimed one scornfully.

'Gi' me the candle, some o' yez—in the name o' God,' said old Sal Doolan, that was straight and lean, and a woman that could pray like a priest almost.

'Give her a candle,' agreed all.

But whatever they might say, there wasn't one among them that did not look pale and stern enough as they followed Mrs. Doolan, who was praying as fast as her lips could patter, and leading the van with a tallow candle, held like a taper, in her fingers.

The door was half open, as the panic-stricken girl had left it; and holding the candle on high the better to examine the room, she made a step or so into it.

If my grand-uncle's hand had been stretched along the floor, in the unnatural way described, he had drawn it back again under the sheet that covered him. And tall Mrs. Doolan was in no danger of tripping over his arm as she entered. But she had not gone more than a step or two with her candle aloft, when, with a drowning face, she suddenly stopped short, staring at the bed which was now fully in view.

'Lord, bless us, Mrs. Doolan, ma'am, come back,' said the woman next her, who had fast hold of her dress, or her 'coat', as they call it, and drawing her backward with a frightened pluck, while a general recoil among her followers betokened the alarm which her hesitation had inspired.

'Whisht, will yez?' said the leader, peremptorily, 'I can't hear my own ears wid the noise ye're makin', an' which iv yez let the cat in here, an' whose cat is it?' she asked, peering suspiciously at a white cat that was sitting on the breast of the corpse.

'Put it away, will yez?' she resumed, with horror at the profanation. 'Many a corpse as I sthretched and crossed in the bed, the likes o' that I never seen yet. The man o' the house, wid a brute baste like that mounted on him, like a phooka, Lord forgi' me for namin' the like in this room Dhrive it away, some o' yez! out o' that, this minute, I tell ye.'

Each repeated the order, but no one seemed inclined to execute it. They were crossing themselves, and whispering their conjectures and misgivings as to the nature of the beast, which was no cat of that house, nor one that they had ever seen before. On a sudden, the white cat placed itself on the pillow over the head of the body, and having from that place glared for a time at them over the features of the corpse, it crept softly along the body towards them, growling low and fiercely as it drew near.

Out of the room they bounced, in dreadful confusion, shutting the door fast after them, and not for a good while did the hardiest venture to peep in again.

The white cat was sitting in its old place, on the dead man's breast, but this time it crept quietly down the side of the bed, and disappeared under it, the sheet which was spread like a coverlet, and hung down nearly to the floor, concealing it from view.

Praying, crossing themselves, and not forgetting a sprinkling of holy water, they peeped, and finally searched, poking spades, 'wattles', pitchforks and such implements under the bed. But the cat was not to be found, and they concluded that it had made its escape among their feet as they stood near the threshold. So they secured the door carefully, with hasp and padlock.

But when the door was opened next morning they found the white cat sitting, as if it had never been disturbed, upon the breast of the dead man.

Again occurred very nearly the same scene with a like result, only that some said they saw the cat afterwards lurking under a big box in a corner of the outer room, where my grand-uncle kept his leases and papers, and his prayer-book and beads.

Mrs. Doolan heard it growling at her heels wherever she went; and although she could not see it, she could hear it spring on the back of her chair when she sat down, and growl in her ear, so that she would bounce up with a scream and a prayer, fancying that it was on the point of taking her by the throat.

And the priest's boy, looking round the corner, under the branches of the old orchard, saw a white cat sitting under the little window of the room where my grand-uncle was laid out and looking up at the four small panes of glass as a cat will watch a bird.

The end of it was that the cat was found on the corpse again, when the room was visited, and do what they might, whenever the body was left alone, the cat was found again in the same ill-omened contiguity with the dead man. And this continued, to the scandal and fear of the neighbourhood, until the door was opened finally for the wake.

My grand-uncle being dead, and, with all due solemnities, buried, I have done with him. But not quite yet with the white cat. No banshee ever yet was more inalienably attached to a family than this ominous apparition is to mine. But there is this difference. The banshee seems to be animated with an affectionate sympathy with the bereaved family to whom it is hereditarily attached, whereas this thing has about it a suspicion of malice. It is the messenger simply of death. And its taking the shape of a cat—the coldest, and they say, the most vindictive of brutes—is indicative of the spirit of its visit.

When my grandfather's death was near, although he seemed

quite well at the time, it appeared not exactly, but very nearly in the same way in which I told you it showed itself to my father.

The day before my Uncle Teigue was killed by the bursting of his gun, it appeared to him in the evening, at twilight, by the lough, in the field where I saw the woman who walked across the water, as I told you. My uncle was washing the barrel of his gun in the lough. The grass is short there, and there is no cover near it. He did not know how it approached but the first he saw of it, the white cat was walking close round his feet, in the twilight, with an angry twist of its tail, and a green glare in its eyes, and do what he would, it continued walking round and round him, in larger or smaller circles, till he reached the orchard, and there he lost it.

My poor Aunt Peg—she married one of the O'Brians, near Oolah—came to Drumgunniol to go to the funeral of a cousin who died about a mile away. She died herself, poor woman, only a month after.

Coming from the wake, at two or three o'clock in the morning, as she got over the stile into the farm of Drumgunniol, she saw the white cat at her side, and it kept close beside her, she ready to faint all the time, till she reached the door of the house, where it made a spring up into the white-thorn tree that grows close by, and so it parted from her. And my little brother Jim saw it also, just three weeks before he died. Every member of our family who dies, or takes his death-sickness, at Drumgunniol, is sure to see the white cat, and no one of us who sees it need hope for long life after.

THE FAMILIAR

Out of about two hundred and thirty cases of similar type studied by Dr. Martin Hesselius, I select the following, which I call 'The Familiar'.

To this MS. Dr. Hesselius has, after his wont, attached some sheets of letter-paper, on which are written, in his hand nearly as compact as print, his own remarks upon the case. He says——

'In point of conscience, no more unexceptionable narrator, than the venerable Irish Clergyman who has given me this paper, on Mr. Barton's case, could have been chosen. The statement is, however, medically imperfect. The report of an intelligent physician, who had marked its progress, and attended the patient, from its earlier stages to its close, would have supplied what is wanting to enable me to pronounce with confidence. I should have been acquainted with Mr. Barton's probable hereditary predispositions; I should have known, possibly, by very early indications, something of a remote origin of the disease than can now be ascertained.

'In a rough way, we may reduce all similar cases to three distinct classes. They are founded on the primary distinction between the subjective and the objective. Of those whose senses are alleged to be subject to supernatural impressions—some are simply visionaries, and propagate the illusions of which they complain, from diseased brain or nerves. Others are, unquestionably, infested by, as we term them, spiritual agencies, exterior to themselves. Others, again, owe their sufferings to a mixed condition. The interior sense, it is true, is opened; but it has been and continues open by the action of disease. This form of disease may, in one sense, be compared to the loss of the scarf-skin, and a consequent exposure of surfaces for whose excessive sensitiveness, nature has provided a muffling. The loss of this covering is attended by an habitual impassibility, by influences against which we were intended to be guarded. But in the case of the brain, and the nerves immediately connected with its functions and its sensuous impressions, the cerebral circulation undergoes periodically that vibratory disturbance, which, I believe, I have satisfactorily examined and demonstrated, in my MS. Essay, A. 17. This vibratory disturbance differs, as I there prove, essentially from the congestive disturbance, the phenomena of which are examined in A. 19. It is, when excessive, invariably accompanied by *illusions*.

'Had I seen Mr. Barton, and examined him upon the points, in his case, which need elucidation, I should have without difficulty referred those phenomena to their proper disease. My diagnosis is now, necessarily, conjectural.'

Thus writes Dr. Hesselius; and adds a great deal which is of interest only to a scientific physician.

The Narrative of the Rev. Thomas Herbert, which furnishes all that is known of the case, will be found in the chapters that follow.

I

FOOTSTEPS

I was a young man at the time, and intimately acquainted with some of the actors in this strange tale; the impression which its incidents made on me, therefore, were deep and lasting. I shall now endeavour, with precision, to relate them all, combining, of course, in the narrative, whatever I have learned from various sources, tending, however imperfectly, to illuminate the darkness which involves its progress and termination.

Somewhere about the year 1794, the younger brother of a certain baronet, whom I shall call Sir James Barton, returned to Dublin. He had served in the navy with some distinction, having commanded one of His Majesty's frigates during the greater part of the American war. Captain Barton was apparently some two or three-and-forty years of age. He was an intelligent and agreeable companion when he pleased it, though generally reserved, and occasionally even moody.

In society, however, he deported himself as a man of the world, and a gentleman. He had not contracted any of the noisy brusqueness sometimes acquired at sea; on the contrary, his manners were remarkably easy, quiet, and even polished. He was in person about the middle size, and somewhat strongly formed—his countenance was marked with the lines of thought, and on the whole wore an expression of gravity and melancholy; being, however, as I have said, a man of perfect breeding, as well as of good family, and in affluent circumstances, he had, of course, ready access to the best society of Dublin, without the necessity of any other credentials.

In his personal habits Mr. Barton was unexpensive. He occupied lodgings in one of the *then* fashionable streets in the south side of the town—kept but one horse and one servant—and though a reputed free-thinker, yet lived an orderly and moral life—indulging neither in gaming, drinking, nor any other vicious pursuit—living very much to himself, without forming intimacies, or choosing any companions, and appearing to mix in gay society rather for the sake of its bustle and distraction, than for any opportunities it offered of interchanging thought or feeling with its votaries.

Barton was, therefore, pronounced a saving, prudent, unsocial sort of fellow, who bid fair to maintain his celibacy alike against stratagem and assault, and was likely to live to a good old age, die rich, and leave his money to a hospital.

It was now apparent, however, that the nature of Mr. Barton's plans had been totally misconceived. A young lady, whom I shall call Miss Montague, was at this time introduced into the gay world by her aunt, the Dowager Lady L——. Miss Montague was decidedly pretty and accomplished, and having some natural cleverness, and a great deal of gaiety, became for a while a reigning toast.

Her popularity, however, gained her, for a time, nothing more than that unsubstantial admiration which, however pleasant as an incense to vanity, is by no means necessarily antecedent to matrimony—for, unhappily for the young lady in question, it was an understood thing, that beyond her personal attractions, she had no kind of earthly provision. Such being the state of affairs, it will readily be believed that no little surprise was consequent upon the appearance of Captain Barton as the avowed lover of the penniless Miss Montague.

His suit prospered, as might have been expected, and in a short time it was communicated by old Lady L—— to each of her hundred and fifty particular friends in succession, that Captain Barton had actually tendered proposals of marriage, with her approbation, to her niece, Miss Montague, who had, moreover, accepted the offer of his hand, conditionally upon the consent of her father, who was then upon his homeward voyage from India, and expected in two or three weeks at the furthest.

About this consent there could be no doubt—the delay, therefore, was one merely of form—they were looked upon as absolutely engaged, and Lady L——, with a rigour of old-fashioned decorum with which her niece would, no doubt, gladly have dispensed, withdrew her thenceforward from all further participation in the gaities of the town.

Captain Barton was a constant visitor, as well as a frequent guest at the house, and was permitted all the privileges of intimacy which a betrothed suitor is usually accorded. Such was the relation of parties, when the mysterious circumstances which darken this narrative first begun to unfold themselves.

Lady L—— resided in a handsome mansion at the north side of Dublin, and Captain Barton's lodgings, as we have already said, were situated at the south. The distance intervening was considerable, and it was Captain Barton's habit generally to walk home without an attendant, as often as he passed the even-

His shortest way in such nocturnal walks, lay, for a considerable space, through a line of street which had as yet merely been laid out, and little more than the foundations of the houses constructed.

One night, shortly after his engagement with Miss Montague had commenced, he happened to remain unusually late, in company with her and Lady L——. The conversation had turned upon the evidences of revelation, which he had disputed with the callous scepticism of a confirmed infidel. What were called 'French principles', had in those days found their way a good deal into fashionable society, especially that portion of it which professed allegiance to Whiggism, and neither the old lady nor her charge were so perfectly free from the taint, as to look upon Mr. Barton's views as any serious objection to the proposed union.

The discussion had degenerated into one upon the supernatural and the marvellous, in which he had pursued precisely the same line of argument and ridicule. In all this, it is but truth to state, Captain Barton was guilty of no affectation—the doctrines upon which he insisted, were, in reality, but too truly the basis of his own fixed belief, if so it might be called; and perhaps not the least strange of the many strange circumstances connected with my narrative, was the fact that the subject of the fearful influences I am about to describe, was himself, from the deliberate conviction of years, an utter disbeliever in what are usually termed preternatural agencies.

It was considerably past midnight when Mr. Barton took his leave, and set out upon his solitary walk homeward. He had now reached the lonely road, with its unfinished dwarf walls tracing the foundations of the projected row of houses on either side—the moon was shining mistily, and its imperfect light made the road he trod but additionally dreary—that utter silence which has in it something indefinably exciting, reigned there, and made the sound of his steps, which alone broke it, unnaturally loud and distinct.

He had proceeded thus some way, when he, on a sudden, heard other footfalls, pattering at a measured pace, and, as it seemed, about two-score steps behind him.

The suspicion of being dogged is at all times unpleasant: it is, however, especially so in a spot so lonely: and this suspicion became so strong in the mind of Captain Barton, that he abruptly turned about to confront his pursuer, but, though there was quite sufficient moonlight to disclose any object upon the road he had traversed, no form of any kind was visible there.

The steps he had heard could not have been the reverberation of his own, for he stamped his foot upon the ground, and walked briskly up and down, in the vain attempt to awake an echo; though by no means a fanciful person, therefore, he was at last fain to charge the sounds upon his imagination, and treat them as an illusion. Thus satisfying himself, he resumed his walk, and before he had proceeded a dozen paces, the mysterious footfall was again audible from behind, and this time, as if with the special design of showing that the sounds were not the responses of an echo—the steps sometimes slackened nearly to a halt, and sometimes hurried for six or eight strides to a run, and again abated to a walk.

Captain Barton, as before, turned suddenly round, and with the same result—no object was visible above the deserted level of the road. He walked back over the same ground, determined that, whatever might have been the cause of the sounds which had so disconcerted him, it should not escape his search—the endeavour, however, was unrewarded.

In spite of all his scepticism, he felt something like a superstitious fear stealing fast upon him, and with these unwonted and uncomfortable sensations, he once more turned and pursued his way. There was no repetition of these haunting sounds, until he had reached the point where he had last stopped to retrace his steps—here they were resumed—and with sudden starts of running, which threatened to bring the unseen pursuer up to the alarmed pedestrian.

Captain Barton arrested his course as formerly—the unaccountable nature of the occurrence filled him with vague and disagreeable sensations—and yielding to the excitement that was gaining upon him, he shouted sternly, 'Who goes there?' The sound of one's own voice, thus exerted, in utter solitude, and followed by total silence, has in it something unpleasantly dismaying, and he felt a degree of nervousness which, perhaps, from no cause had he ever known before.

To the very end of this solitary street the steps pursued him —and it required a strong effort of stubborn pride on his part, to resist the impulse that prompted him every moment to run for safety at the top of his speed. It was not until he had reached his lodging, and sat by his own fireside, that he felt sufficiently reassured to rearrange and reconsider in his own mind the occurrences which had so discomposed him. So little a matter, after all, is sufficient to upset the pride of scepticism and vindicate the old simple laws of nature within us.

II

THE WATCHER

Mr. Barton was next morning sitting at a late breakfast, reflecting upon the incidents of the previous night, with more of inquisitiveness than awe, so speedily do gloomy impressions upon the fancy disappear under the cheerful influence of day, when a letter just delivered by the postman was placed upon the table before him.

There was nothing remarkable in the address of this missive, except that it was written in a hand which he did not know—perhaps it was disguised—for the tall narrow characters were sloped backward; and with the self-inflicted suspense which we often see practised in such cases, he puzzled over the inscription for a full minute before he broke the seal. When he did so, he read the following words, written in the same hand:

'Mr. Barton, late captain of the *Dolphin*, is warned of DANGER. He will do wisely to avoid —— Street—[here the locality of his last night's adventure was named]—if he walks there as usual he will meet with something unlucky—let him take warning, once for all, for he has reason to dread
'THE WATCHER.'

Captain Barton read and re-read this strange effusion; in every light and in every direction he turned it over and over; he examined the paper on which it was written, and scrutinised the handwriting once more. Defeated here, he turned to the seal; it was nothing but a patch of wax, upon which the accidental impression of a thumb was imperfectly visible.

There was not the slightest mark, or clue of any kind, to lead him to even a guess as to its possible origin. The writer's object seemed a friendly one, and yet he subscribed himself as one whom he had 'reason to dread'. Altogether the letter, its author, and its real purpose were to him an inexplicable puzzle, and one, moreover, unpleasantly suggestive, in his mind, of other associations connected with his last night's adventure.

In obedience to some feeling—perhaps of pride—Mr. Barton did not communicate, even to his intended bride, the occurrences which I have just detailed. Trifling as they might appear, they had in reality most disagreeably affected his imagination, and he cared not to disclose, even to the young lady in question, what she might possibly look upon as evidences of weakness. The letter might very well be but a hoax, and the mysterious footfall but a delusion or a trick. But although he affected to treat the whole affair as unworthy of a thought, it yet haunted him pertinaciously, tormenting him with perplexing doubts, and depressing him with undefined apprehensions. Certain it is, that for a considerable time afterwards he carefully avoided the street indicated in the letter as the scene of danger.

It was not until about a week after the receipt of the letter which I have transcribed, that anything further occurred to remind Captain Barton of its contents, or to counteract the gradual disappearance from his mind of the disagreeable impressions then received.

He was returning one night, after the interval I have stated, from the theatre, which was then situated in Crow Street, and having there seen Miss Montague and Lady L—— into their carriage, he loitered for some time with two or three acquaintances.

With these, however, he parted close to the college, and pursued his way alone. It was now fully one o'clock, and the streets were quite deserted. During the whole of his walk with the companions from whom he had just parted, he had been at times painfully aware of the sound of steps, as it seemed, dogging them on their way.

Once or twice he had looked back, in the uneasy anticipation that he was again about to experience the same mysterious annoyances which had so disconcerted him a week before, and earnestly hoping that he might *see* some form to account naturally for the sounds. But the street was deserted—no one was visible.

Proceeding now quite alone upon his homeward way, he grew really nervous and uncomfortable, as he became sensible, with increased distinctness, of the well-known and now absolutely dreaded sounds.

By the side of the dead wall which bounded the college park, the sounds followed, recommencing almost simultaneously with his own steps. The same unequal pace—sometimes slow, sometimes for a score yards or so, quickened almost to a run—was audible from behind him. Again and again he turned; quickly and stealthily he glanced over his shoulder—almost at every half-dozen steps; but no one was visible.

The irritation of this intangible and unseen pursuit became gradually all but intolerable; and when at last he reached his home, his nerves were strung to such a pitch of excitement that he could not rest, and did not attempt even to lie down until after the daylight had broken.

He was awakened by a knock at his chamber door, and his servant entering, handed him several letters which had just been received by the penny post. One among them instantly arrested his attention—a single glance at the direction aroused him thoroughly. He at once recognised its character, and read as follows:

'You may as well think, Captain Barton, to escape from your own shadow as from me; do what you may, I will see you as often as I please, and you shall see me, for I do not want to hide myself, as you fancy. Do not let it trouble your rest, Captain Barton; for, with a *good conscience*, what need you fear from the eye of

'THE WATCHER.'

It is scarcely necessary to dwell upon the feelings that accompanied a perusal of this strange communication. Captain Bartin was observed to be unusually absent and out of spirits for several days afterwards! but no one divined the cause.

Whatever he might think as to the phantom steps which followed him, there could be no possible illusion about the letters he had received; and, to say the least, their immediate sequence upon the mysterious sounds which had haunted him, was an odd coincidence.

The whole circumstance was, in his own mind, vaguely and instinctively connected with certain passages in his past life, which, of all others, he hated to remember.

It happened, however, that in addition to his own approaching nuptials, Captain Barton had just then—fortunately, perhaps, for himself—some business of an engrossing kind connected with the adjustment of a large and long-litigated claim upon certain properties.

The hurry and excitement of business had its natural effect in gradually dispelling the gloom which had for a time occasionally oppressed him, and in a little while his spirits had entirely recovered their accustomed tone.

During all this time, however, he was, now and then, dismayed by indistinct and half-heard repetitions of the same annoyance, and that in lonely places, in the daytime as well as after nightfall. These renewals of the strange impressions from which he had suffered so much, were, however, desultory and faint, insomuch that often he really could not, to his own satisfaction, distinguish between them and the mere suggestions of an excited imagination.

One evening he walked down to the House of Commons with a Member, an acquaintance of his and mine. This was one of the few occasions upon which I have been in company with Captain Barton. As we walked down together, I observed that he became absent and silent, and to a degree that seemed to argue the pressure of some urgent and absorbing anxiety.

I afterwards learned that during the whole of our walk, he had heard the well-known footsteps tracking him as we proceeded.

This, however, was the last time he suffered from this phase of the persecution, of which he was already the anxious victim. A new and a very different one was about to be presented.

III

AN ADVERTISEMENT

Of the new series of impressions which were afterwards gradually to work out his destiny, I that evening witnessed the first; and but for its relation to the train of events which followed, the incident would scarcely have been now remembered by me.

As we were walking in at the passage from College Green, a man, of whom I remember only that he was short in stature, looked like a foreigner, and wore a kind of fur travelling-cap, walked very rapidly, and as if under fierce excitement, directly towards us, muttering to himself, fast and vehemently the while.

This odd-looking person walked straight towards Barton, who was foremost of the three, and halted, regarding him for a moment or two with a look of maniacal menace and fury; and then turning about as abruptly, he walked before us at the same agitated pace, and disappeared at a side passage. I do distinctly remember being a good deal shocked at the countenance and bearing of this man, which indeed irresistibly impressed me with an undefined sense of danger, such as I have never felt before or since from the presence of anything human; but these sensations were, on my part, far from amounting to anything so disconcerting as to flurry or excite me—I had seen only a singularly evil countenance, agitated, as it seemed, with the excitement of madness.

I was absolutely astonished, however, at the effect of this apparition upon Captain Barton. I knew him to be a man of proud courage and coolness in real danger—a circumstance which made his conduct upon this occasion the more conspicuously odd. He recoiled a step or two as the stranger advanced, and clutched my arm in silence, with what seemed to be a spasm of agony or terror! and then, as the figure disappeared, shoving me roughly back, he followed it for a few paces, stopped in great disorder, and sat down upon a form. I never beheld a countenance more ghastly and haggard.

'For God's sake, Barton, what is the matter?' said ——, our companion, really alarmed at his appearance. 'You're not hurt, are you?—or unwell? What is it?'

'What did he say?—I did not hear it—what was it?' asked Barton, wholly disregarding the question.

'Nonsense,' said ——, greatly surprised; 'who cares what the fellow said. You are unwell, Barton—decidedly unwell; let me call a coach.'

'Unwell! No—not unwell,' he said, evidently making an effort to recover his self-possession; 'but, to say the truth, I am fatigued—a little over-worked—and perhaps over-anxious. You know I have been in Chancery, and the winding-up of a suit is always a nervous affair. I have felt uncomfortable all this evening; but I am better now. Come, come—shall we go on?'

'No, no. Take my advice, Barton, and go home; you really do need rest; you are looking quite ill. I really do insist on your allowing me to see you home,' replied his friend.

I seconded ——'s advice, the more readily as it was obvious

that Barton was not himself disinclined to be persuaded. He left us, declining our offered escort. I was not sufficiently intimate with —— to discuss the scene we had both just witnessed. I was, however, convinced from his manner in the few commonplace comments and regrets we exchanged, that he was just as little satisfied as I with the extempore plea of illness with which he had accounted for the strange exhibition, and that we were both agreed in suspecting some lurking mystery in the matter.

I called next day at Barton's lodgings, to inquire for him, and learned from the servant that he had not left his room since his return the night before; but that he was not seriously indisposed, and hoped to be out in a few days. That evening he sent for Dr. R——, then in a large and fashionable practice in Dublin, and their interview was, it is said, an odd one.

He entered into a detail of his own symptoms in an abstracted and desultory way, which seemed to argue a strange want of interest in his own cure, and, at all events, made it manifest that there was some topic engaging his mind of more engrossing importance than his present ailment. He complained of occasional palpitations and headache.

Dr. R—— asked him, among other questions, whether there was any irritating circumstance or anxiety then occupying his thoughts. This he denied quickly and almost peevishly; and the physician thereupon declared his opinion that there was nothing amiss except some slight derangement of the digestion, for which he accordingly wrote a prescription, and was about to withdraw, when Mr. Barton, with the air of a man who recollects a topic which had nearly escaped him, recalled him.

'I beg your pardon, doctor, but I really almost forgot; will you permit me to ask you two or three medical questions— rather odd ones, perhaps, but as a wager depends upon their solution, you will, I hope, excuse my unreasonableness?'

The physician readily undertook to satisfy the inquirer.

Barton seemed to have some difficulty about opening the proposed interrogatories, for he was silent for a minute, then walked to his book-case, and returned as he had gone; at last he sat down, and said——

'You'll think them very childish questions, but I can't recover my wager without a decision; so I must put them. I want to know the first about lock-jaw. If a man actually has that complaint, and appears to have died of it—so much so, that a physician of average skill pronounces him actually dead—may he, after all, recover?'

The physician smiled, and shook his head.

'But—but a blunder may be made,' resumed Barton. 'Suppose an ignorant pretender to medical skill; may *he* be so deceived by any stage of the complaint, as to mistake what is only a part of the progress of the disease, for death itself?'

'No one who had ever seen death,' answered he, 'could mistake it in a case of lock-jaw.'

Barton mused for a few minutes. 'I am going to ask you a question, perhaps still more childish; but first, tell me, are the regulations of foreign hospitals, such as that of, let us say, Naples, very lax and bungling. May not all kinds of blunders and slips occur in their entries of names, and so forth?'

Dr. R—— professed his incompetence to answer that query.

'Well, then, doctor, here is the last of my questions. You will, probably, laugh at it; but it must out nevertheless. Is there any disease, in all the range of human maladies, which would have the effect of perceptibly contracting the stature, and the whole frame—causing the man to shrink in all his proportions, and yet to preserve his exact resemblance to himself in every particular—with the one exception, his height and bulk; *any* disease, mark—no matter how rare—how little believed in, generally—which could possibly result in producing such an effect?'

The physician replied with a smile, and a very decided negative.

'Tell me, then,' said Barton, abruptly, 'if a man be in reasonable fear of assault from a lunatic who is at large, can he not procure a warrant for his arrest and detention?'

'Really, that is more a lawyer's question than one in my way,' replied Dr. R——; 'but I believe, on applying to a magistrate, such a course would be directed.'

The physician then took his leave; but, just as he reached the hall door, remembered that he had left his cane upstairs, and returned. His reappearance was awkward, for a piece of paper, which he recognised as his own prescription, was slowly burning upon the fire, and Barton sitting close by with an expression of settled gloom and dismay.

Dr. R—— had too much tact to observe what presented itself; but he had seen quite enough to assure him that the mind, and not the body, of Captain Barton was in reality the seat of suffering.

A few days afterwards, the following advertisement appeared in the Dublin newspapers:

'If Sylvester Yelland, formerly a foremast man on board His Majesty's frigate *Dolphin*, or his nearest of kin, will apply to Mr. Hubert Smith, attorney, at his office, Dame Street, he or they may hear of something greatly to his or their advantage. Admission may be had at any hour up to twelve o'clock at night, should parties desire to avoid observation; and the strictest secrecy, as to all communications intended to be confidential, shall be honourably observed.'

The *Dolphin*, as I have mentioned, was the vessel which Captain Barton had commanded; and this circumstance, connected with the extraordinary exertions made by the circulation of handbills, etc., as well as by repeated advertisements, to secure for this strange notice the utmost possible publicity, suggested to Dr. R—— the idea that Captain Barton's extreme uneasiness was somehow connected with the individual to whom the advertisement was addressed, and he himself the author of it.

This, however, it is needless to add, was no more than a conjecture. No information, whatsoever, as to the real purpose of the advertisement was divulged by the agent, nor yet any hint as to who his employer might be.

IV

HE TALKS WITH A CLERGYMAN

Mr. Barton, although he had latterly begun to earn for himself the character of an hypochondriac, was yet very far from deserving it. Though by no means lively, he had yet, naturally, what are termed 'even spirits', and was not subject to undue depressions.

He soon, therefore, began to return to his former habits; and one of the earliest symptoms of this healthier tone of spirits was his appearing at a grand dinner of the Freemasons, of which worthy fraternity he was himself a brother. Barton, who had been at first gloomy and abstracted, drank much more freely than was his wont—possibly with the purpose of dispelling his own secret anxieties—and under the influence of good wine and pleasant company, became gradually (unlike himself) talkative, and even noisy.

It was under this unwonted excitement that he left his company at about half past ten o'clock; and, as conviviality is a strong incentive to gallantry, it occurred to him to proceed forthwith to Lady L——'s, and pass the remainder of the evening with her and his destined bride.

Accordingly, he was soon at —— Street, and chatting gaily with the ladies. It is not to be supposed that Captain Barton had exceeded the limits which propriety prescribes to good fellowship—he had merely taken enough wine to raise his spirits, without, however, in the least degree unsteadying his mind, or affecting his manners.

With this undue elevation of spirits had supervened an entire oblivion or contempt of those undefined apprehensions which had for so long weighted upon his mind, and to a certain extent estranged him from society; but as the night wore away, and his artificial gaiety began to flag, these painful feelings gradually intruded themselves again, and he grew abstracted and anxious as heretofore.

He took his leave at length, with an unpleasant foreboding of some coming mischief, and with a mind haunted with a thousand mysterious apprehensions, such as, even while he acutely felt their pressure, he, nevertheless, inwardly strove, or affected to contemn.

It was this proud defiance of what he regarded as his own weakness, which prompted him upon the present occasion to that course which brought about the adventure I am now about to relate.

Mr. Barton might have easily called a coach, but he was conscious that his strong inclination to do so proceeded from no cause other than what he desperately persisted in representing to himself to be his own superstitious tremors.

He might also have returned home by a *route* different from that against which he had been warned by his mysterious correspondent; but for the same reason he dismissed this idea also, and with a dogged and half desperate resolution to force matters to a crisis of some kind, if there were any reality in the causes of his former suffering, and if not, satisfactorily to bring their delusiveness to the proof, he determined to follow precisely the course which he had trodden upon the night so painfully memorable in his own mind as that on which his strange persecution commenced. Though, sooth to say, the pilot who for the first time steers his vessel under the muzzles of a hostile battery, never felt his resolution more severely tasked than did Captain Barton, as he breathlessly pursued this solitary path—a path which, spite of every effort of scepticism and reason, he felt to be infested by some (as respected *him*) malignant being.

He pursued his way steadily and rapidly, scarcely breathing from intensity of suspense; he, however, was troubled by no renewal of the dreaded footsteps, and was beginning to feel a return of confidence, as more than three-fourths of the way being accomplished with impunity, he approached the long line of twinkling oil lamps which indicated the frequented streets.

This feeling of self-congratulation was, however, but momentary. The report of a musket at some hundred yards behind him, and the whistle of a bullet close to his head, disagreeably and startlingly dispelled it. His first impulse was to retrace his steps in pursuit of the assassin; but the road on either side was, as we have said, embarrassed by the foundations of a street, beyond which extended waste fields, full of rubbish and neglected lime- and brick-kilns, and all now as utterly silent as though no sound had ever disturbed their dark and unsightly solitude. The futility of, single-handed, attempting, under such circumstances, a search for the murderer, was apparent, especially as no sound, either of retreating steps or any other kind, was audible to direct his pursuit.

With the tumultuous sensations of one whose life has just

been exposed to a murderous attempt, and whose escape has been the narrowest possible, Captain Barton turned again; and without, however, quickening his pace actually to a run, hurriedly pursued his way.

He had turned, as I have said, after a pause of a few seconds, and had just commenced his rapid retreat, when on a sudden he met the well-remembered little man in the fur cap. The encounter was but momentary. The figure was walking at the same exaggerated pace, and with the same strange air of menace as before; and as it passed him, he thought he heard it say, in a furious whisper, 'Still alive—still alive!'

The state of Mr. Barton's spirits began now to work a corresponding alteration in his health and looks, and to such a degree that it was impossible that the change should escape general remark.

For some reasons, known but to himself, he took no steps whatsoever to bring the attempt upon his life, which he had so narrowly escaped, under the notice of the authorities; on the contrary, he kept it jealously to himself; and it was not for many weeks after the occurrence that he mentioned it, and then in strict confidence, to a gentleman, whom the torments of his mind at last compelled him to consult.

Spite of his blue devils, however, poor Barton, having no satisfactory reason to render to the public for any undue remissness in the attentions exacted by the relation existing between him and Miss Montague, was obliged to exert himself, and present to the world a confident and cheerful bearing.

The true source of his sufferings, and every circumstance connected with them, he guarded with a reserve so jealous, that it seemed dictated by at least a suspicion that the origin of his strange persecution was known to himself, and that it was of a nature which, upon his own account, he could not or dared not disclose.

The mind thus turned in upon itself, and constantly occupied with a haunting, anxiety which it dared not reveal or confide to any human breast, became daily more excited, and, of course, more vividly impressible, by a system of attack which operated through the nervous system; and in this state he was destined to sustain, with increasing frequency, the stealthy visitations of that apparition which from the first had seemed to possess so terrible a hold upon his imagination.

It was about this time that Captain Barton called upon the then celebrated preacher, Dr.——, with whom he had a slight acquaintance, and an extraordinary conversation ensued.

The divine was seated in his chambers in college, surrounded with works upon his favourite pursuit, and deep in theology, when Barton was announced.

There was something at once embarrassed and excited in his manner, which, along with his wan and haggard countenance, impressed the student with the unpleasant consciousness that his visitor must have recently suffered terribly indeed, to account for an alteration so striking—almost shocking.

After the usual interchange of polite greeting, and a few commonplace remarks, Captain Barton, who obviously perceived the surprise which his visit had excited, and which Dr. —— was unable wholly to conceal, interrupted a brief pause by remarking——

'This is a strange call, Dr. ——, perhaps scarcely warranted by an acquaintance so slight as mine with you. I should not under ordinary circumstances have ventured to disturb you; but my visit is neither an idle nor impertinent intrusion. I am sure you will not so account it, when I tell you how afflicted I am.'

Dr. —— interrupted him with assurances such as good breeding suggested, and Barton resumed:

'I am come to task your patience by asking your advice. When I say your patience, I might, indeed, say more; I might have said your humanity—your compassion; for I have been and am a great sufferer.'

'My dear sir,' replied the churchman, 'it will, indeed, afford me infinite gratification if I can give you comfort in any distress of mind! but—you know——'

'I know what you would say,' resumed Barton, quickly; 'I am an unbeliever, and, therefore, incapable of deriving help from religion; but don't take that for granted. At least you must not assume that, however unsettled my convictions may be, I do not feel a deep—a very deep—interest in the subject. Circumstances have lately forced it upon my attention, in such a way as to compel me to review the whole question in a more candid and teachable spirit, I believe, than I ever studied it in before.'

'Your difficulties, I take it for granted, refer to the evidences of revelation,' suggested the clergyman.

'Why—no—not altogether; in fact, I am ashamed to say I have not considered even my objections sufficiently to state them connectedly; but—but there is one subject on which I feel a peculiar interest.'

He paused again, and Dr. —— pressed him to proceed.

'The fact is,' said Barton, 'whatever may be my uncertainty as to the authenticity of what we are taught to call revelation, of one fact I am deeply and horribly convinced, that there does exist beyond this a spiritual world—a system whose workings are generally in mercy hidden from us—a system which may be, and which is sometimes, partially and terribly revealed. I am sure—I *know*,' continued Barton, with increasing excitement, 'that there is a God—a dreadful God—and that retribution follows guilt, in ways the most mysterious and stupendous—by agencies the most inexplicable and terrific;—there is a spiritual system—great God, how I have been convinced!—a system malignant, and implacable, and omnipotent, under whose persecutions I am, and have been, suffering the torments of the damned!—yes, sir—yes—the fires and frenzy of hell!'

As Barton spoke, his agitation became so vehement that the Divine was shocked, and even alarmed. The wild and excited rapidity with which he spoke, and, above all, the indefinable horror that stamped his features, afforded a contrast to his ordinary cool and unimpassioned self-possession striking and painful in the last degree.

V

MR. BARTON STATES HIS CASE

'My dear sir,' said Dr.——, after a brief pause, 'I fear you have been very unhappy, indeed; but I venture to predict that the depression under which you labour will be found to originate in purely physical causes, and that with a change of air, and the aid of a few tonics, your spirits will return, and the tone of your mind be once more cheerful and tranquil as heretofore. There was, after all, more truth than we are quite willing to admit in the classic theories which assigned the undue predominance of any one affection of the mind, to the undue action or torpidity of one or other of our bodily organs. Believe me, that a little attention to diet, exercise, and the other essentials of health, under competent direction, will make you as much yourself as you can wish.'

'Dr ——,' said Barton, with something like a shudder, 'I *cannot* delude myself with such a hope. I have no hope to cling to but one, 'and that is, that by some other spiritual agency more potent than that which tortures me, *it* may be combated, and I delivered. If this may not be, I am lost—now and for ever lost.'

'But, Mr. Barton, you must remember,' urged his companion, 'that others have suffered as you have done, and——'

'No, no, no,' interrupted he, with irritability—'no, sir, I am not a credulous—far from a superstitious man. I have been, perhaps, too much the reverse—too sceptical, too slow of belief; but unless I were one whom no amount of evidence could convince unless I were to contemn the repeated, the *perpetual* evidence of my own senses, I am now—now at last constrained to believe—I have no escape from the conviction—the overwhelming certainty—that I am haunted and dogged, go where I may, by—by a DEMON!'

There was a preternatural energy of horror in Barton's face, as, with its damp and death-like lineaments turned towards his companion, he thus delivered himself.

'God help you, my poor friend,' said Dr. ——, much shocked. 'God help you; for, indeed, you *are* a sufferer, however your sufferings may have been caused.'

'Ay, ay, God help me,' echoed Barton, sternly; 'but *will* He help me—will He help me?'

'Pray to Him—pray in an humble and trusting spirit,' said he.

'Pray, pray,' echoed he again; 'I can't pray—I could as easily move a mountain by an effort of my will. I have not belief enough to pray; there is something within me that will not pray. You prescribe impossibilities—literal impossibilities.'

'You will not find it so, if you will but try,' said Dr. ——.

'Try! I *have* tried, and the attempt only fills me with confusion: and, sometimes, terror: I have tried in vain, and more than in vain. The awful, unutterable idea of eternity and infinity oppresses and maddens my brain whenever my mind approaches the contemplation of the Creator: I recoil from the effort scared. I tell you, Dr. ——, if I am to be saved, it must be by other means. The idea of an eternal Creator is to me intolerable—my mind cannot support it.'

'Say, then, my dear sir,' urged he, 'say how you would have me serve you—what you would learn of me—what I can do or say to relieve you.'

'Listen to me first,' replied Captain Barton, with a subdued air, and an effort to suppress his excitement, 'listen to me while I detail the circumstances of the persecution under which my life has become all but intolerable—a persecution which has made me fear *death* and the world beyond the grave as much as I have grown to hate existence.'

Barton then proceeded to relate the circumstances which I have already detailed, and then continued:

'This has now become habitual—an accustomed thing. I do not mean the actual seeing him in the flesh—thank God, *that* at least is not permitted daily. Thank God, from the ineffable horrors of that visitation I have been mercifully allowed intervals of repose, though none of security; but from the consciousness that a malignant spirit is following and watching me wherever I go I have never, for a single instant, a temporary respite. I am pursued with blasphemies, cries of despair, and appalling hatred. I hear those dreadful sounds called after me as I turn the corners of the streets; they come in the night-time, while I sit in my chamber alone; they haunt me everywhere, charging me with hideous crimes, and—great God!—threatening me with coming vengeance and eternal misery. Hush! do you hear *that*?' he cried, with a horrible smile of triumph; 'there—there, will that convince you?'

The clergyman felt a chill of horror steal over him, while, during the wail of a sudden gust of wind, he heard, or fancied he heard, the half-articulate sounds of rage and derision mingling in the sough.

'Well, what do you think of *that*?' at length Barton cried, drawing a long breath through his teeth.

'I heard the wind,' said Dr. ——. 'What should I think of it—what is there remarkable about it?'

'The prince of the powers of the air,' muttered Barton, with a shudder.

'Tut, tut! my dear sir,' said the student, with an effort to reassure himself; for though it was broad daylight, there was nevertheless something disagreeably contagious in the nervous excitement under which his visitor so miserably suffered. 'You must not give way to those wild fancies; you must resist these impulses of the imagination.'

'Ay, ay; "resist the devil and he will flee from thee",' said Barton, in the same tone; 'but *how* resist him? ay, there it is—there is the rub. What—*what* am I to do? what *can* I do?'

'My dear sir, this *is* fancy,' said the man of folios; 'you are your own tormentor.'

'No, no, sir—fancy has no part in it,' answered Barton, somewhat sternly. 'Fancy! was it that made *you*, as well as me, hear, but this moment, those accents of hell? Fancy, indeed! No, no.'

'But you have seen this person frequently,' said the ecclesiastic; 'why have you not accosted or secured him? Is it not a little precipitate, to say no more, to assume, as you have done, the existence of preternatural agency; when, after all, everything may be easily accountable, if only proper means were taken to sift the matter.'

'There are circumstances connected with this—this *appearance*,' said Barton, 'which it is needless to disclose, but which to *me* are proofs of its horrible nature. I know that the being that follows me is not human—I say I *know* this; I could prove it to your own conviction.' He paused for a minute, and then added, 'And as to accosting it, I dare not, I could not; when I see it I am powerless; I stand in the gaze of death, in the triumphant presence of infernal power and malignity. My strength, and faculties, and memory, all forsake me. O God, I fear, sir, you know not what you speak of. Mercy, mercy; heaven have pity on me!'

He leaned his elbow on the table, and passed his hand across his eyes, as if to exclude some image of horror, muttering the last words of the sentence he had just concluded, again and again.

'Dr. ——,' he said, abruptly raising himself, and looking full upon the clergyman with an imploring eye, 'I know you will do for me whatever may be done. You know now fully the circumstances and the nature of my affliction. I tell you I cannot help myself; I cannot hope to escape; I am utterly passive. I conjure you, then, to weigh my case well, and if anything may be done for me by vicarious supplication—by the intercession of the good—or by any aid or influence whatsoever, I implore of you, I adjure you in the name of the Most High, give me the benefit of that influence—deliver me from the body of this death. Strive for me, pity me; I know you will; you cannot refuse this; it is the purpose and object of my visit. Send me away with some hope—however little—some faint hope of ultimate deliverance, and I will nerve myself to endure, from hour to hour, the hideous dream into which my existence has been transformed.'

Dr. —— assured him that all he could do was to pray earnestly for him, and that so much he would not fail to do. They parted with a hurried and melancholy valediction. Barton hastened to the carriage that awaited him at the door, drew down the blinds, and drove away, while Dr. —— returned to his chamber, to ruminate at leisure upon the strange interview which had just interrupted his studies.

VI

SEEN AGAIN

It was not to be expected that Captain Barton's changed and eccentric habits should long escape remark and discussion. Various were the theories suggested to account for it. Some attributed the alteration to the pressure of secret pecuniary embarrassments; others to a repugnance to fulfil an engagement into which he was presumed to have too precipitately entered; and others, again, to the supposed incipiency of mental disease, which latter, indeed, was the most plausible, as well as the most generally received, of the hypotheses circulated in the gossip of the day.

From the very commencement of this change, at first so gradual in its advances, Miss Montague had of course been aware of it. The intimacy involved in their peculiar relation, as well as the near interest which it inspired afforded, in her case, a like opportunity and motive for the successful exercise of that keen and penetrating observation peculiar to her sex.

His visits became, at length, so interrupted, and his manner, while they lasted, so abstracted, strange, and agitated, that Lady L——, after hinting her anxiety and her suspicions more than once, at length distinctly stated her anxiety, and pressed for an explanation.

The explanation was given, and although its nature at first relieved the worst solicitudes of the old lady and her niece, yet the circumstances which attended it, and the really dreadful consequences which it obviously indicated, as regarded the spirits, and indeed the reason of the now wretched man, who made the strange declaration, were enough, upon little reflection, to fill their minds with perturbation and alarm.

General Montague, the young lady's father, at length arrived. He had himself slightly known Barton, some ten or twelve years previously, and being aware of his fortune and connections, was disposed to regard him as an unexceptionable and indeed a most desirable match for his daughter. He laughed at the story of Barton's supernatural visitations, and lost no time in calling upon his intended son-in-law.

'My dear Barton,' he continued, gaily, after a little conversation, 'my sister tells me that you are a victim to blue devils, in quite a new and original shape.'

Barton changed countenance, and sighed profoundly.

'Come, come; I protest this will never do,' continued the General; 'you are more like a man on his way to the gallows than to the altar. These devils have made quite a saint of you.'

Barton made an effort to change the conversation.

'No, no, it won't do,' said his visitor laughing; 'I am resolved to say what I have to say upon this magnificent mock mystery of yours. You must not be angry, but really it is too bad to see you at your time of life, absolutely frightened into good behaviour, like a naughty child by a bugaboo, and as far as I can learn, a very contemptible one. Seriously, I have been a good deal annoyed at what they tell me; but at the same time thoroughly convinced that there is nothing in the matter that may not be cleared up, with a little attention and management, within a week at furthest.'

'Ah, General, you do not know——,' he began.

'Yes, but I do know quite enough to warrant my confidence,' interrupted the soldier, 'don't I know that all your annoyance proceeds from the occasional appearance of a certain little man in a cap and greatcoat, with a red vest and a bad face, who follows you about, and pops upon you at corners of lanes, and throws you into ague fits. Now, my dear fellow, I'll make it my business to *catch* this mischievous little mountebank, and either beat him to a jelly with my own hands, or have him whipped through the town, at the cart's tail, before a month passes.'

'If *you* knew what *I* knew,' said Barton, with gloomy agitation, 'you would speak very differently. Don't imagine that I am so weak as to assume, without proof the most overwhelming, the conclusion to which I have been forced—the proofs are here, locked up here.' As he spoke he tapped upon his breast, and with an anxious sigh continued to walk up and down the room.

'Well, well, Barton,' said his visitor, 'I'll wager a rump and a dozen I collar the ghost, and convince even you before many days are over.'

He was running on in the same strain when he was suddenly arrested, and not a little shocked, by observing Barton, who had approached the window, stagger slowly back, like one who had received a stunning blow; his arm extended towards the street —his face and his very lips white as ashes—while he muttered, 'There—by heaven!—there—there!'

General Montague started mechanically to his feet, and from the window of the drawing-room, saw a figure corresponding, as well as his hurry would permit him to discern, with the description of the person whose appearance so persistently disturbed the repose of his friend.

The figure was just turning from the rails of the area upon which it had been leaning, and, without waiting to see more, the old gentleman snatched his cane and hat, and rushed down the stairs and into the street, in the furious hope of securing the person, and punishing the audacity of the mysterious stranger.

He looked round him, but in vain, for any trace of the person he had himself distinctly seen. He ran breathlessly to the nearest corner, expecting to see from thence the retiring figure, but no such form was visible. Back and forward, from crossing to crossing, he ran, at fault, and it was not until the curious gaze and laughing countenances of the passers-by reminded him of the absurdity of his pursuit, that he checked his hurried pace, lowered his walking cane from the menacing altitude which he had mechanically given it, adjusted his hat, and walked composedly back again inwardly vexed and flurried. He found Barton pale and trembling in every joint; they both remained silent, though under emotions very different. At last Barton whispered, 'You saw it?'

'*It*—him—some one—you mean—to be sure I did,' replied Montague, testily. 'But where is the good or the harm of seeing him? The fellow runs like a lamplighter. I wanted to *catch* him, but he had stolen away before I could reach the hall door. However, it is no great matter; next time, I dare say, I'll do better; and, egad, if I once come within reach of him, I'll introduce his shoulders to the weight of my cane.'

Notwithstanding General Montague's undertakings and exhortations, however, Barton continued to suffer from the self-same unexplained cause; go how, when, or where he would, he was still constantly dogged or confronted by the being who had established over him so horrible an influence.

Nowhere and at no time was he secure against the odious appearance which haunted him with such diabolic perseverance.

His depression, misery, and excitement became more settled and alarming every day, and the mental agonies that ceaselessly preyed upon him, began at last so sensibly to affect his health, that Lady L—— and General Montague succeeded, without, indeed, much difficulty, in persuading him to try a short tour on the Continent, in the hope that an entire change of scene would, at all events, have the effect of breaking through the influences of local association, which the more sceptical of his friends assumed to be by no means inoperative in suggesting and perpetuating what they conceived to be a mere form of nervous illusion.

General Montague indeed was persuaded that the figure which haunted his intended son-in-law was by no means the creation of his imagination, but, on the contrary, a substantial form of flesh and blood, animated by a resolution, perhaps with some murderous object in perspective, to watch and follow the unfortunate gentleman.

Even this hypothesis was not a very pleasant one; yet it was plain that if Barton could ever be convinced that there was nothing preternatural in the phenomenon which he had hitherto regarded in that light, the affair would lose all its terrors in his eyes, and wholly cease to exercise upon his health and spirits the baleful influence which it had hitherto done. He therefore reasoned, that if the annoyance were actually escaped by mere locomotion and change of scene, it obviously could not have originated in any supernatural agency.

VII

FLIGHT

Yielding to their persuasions, Barton left Dublin for England, accompanied by General Montague. They posted rapidly to London, and thence to Dover, whence they took the packet with a fair wind for Calais. The General's confidence in the result of the expedition on Barton's spirits had risen day by day, since their departure from the shores of Ireland; for to the inexpressible relief and delight of the latter, he had not since then, so much as even once fancied a repetition of those impressions which had, when at home, drawn him gradually down to the very depths of despair.

This exemption from what he had begun to regard as the inevitable condition of his existence, and the sense of security which began to pervade his mind, were inexpressibly delightful; and in the exultation of what he considered his deliverance, he indulged in a thousand happy anticipations for a future into which so lately he had hardly dared to look; and, in short, both he and his companion secretly congratulated themselves upon the termination of that persecution which had been to its immediate victim a source of such unspeakable agony.

It was a beautiful day, and a crowd of idlers stood upon the jetty to receive the packet, and enjoy the bustle of the new arrivals. Montague walked a few paces in advance of his friend, and as he made his way through the crowd, a little man touched his arm, and said to him, in a broad provincial *patois*:

'Monsieur is walking too fast; he will lose his sick comrade in the throng, for, by my faith, the poor gentleman seems to be fainting.'

Montague turned quickly, and observed that Barton did indeed look deadly pale. He hastened to his side.

'My dear fellow, are you ill?' he asked anxiously.

The question was unheeded, and twice repeated, ere Barton stammered:

'I saw him—by ——, I saw him!'

'*Him!*—the wretch—who—where now?—where is he?' cried Montague, looking around him.

'I saw him—but he is gone,' repeated Barton, faintly.

'But where—where? For God's sake speak,' urged Montague, vehemently.

'It is but this moment—*here*,' said he.

'But what did he look like—what had he on—what did he wear—quick, quick,' urged his excited companion, ready to dart among the crowd and collar the delinquent on the spot.

'He touched your arm—he spoke to you—he pointed to me. God be merciful to me, there is no escape,' said Barton, in the low, subdued tones of despair.

Montague had already bustled away in all the flurry of mingled hope and rage; but though the singular *personnel* of the stranger who had accosted him was vividly impressed upon his recollection, he failed to discover among the crowd even the slightest resemblance to him.

After a fruitless search, in which he enlisted the services of several of the bystanders, who aided all the more zealously, as they believed he had been robbed, he at length, out of breath and baffled, gave over the attempt.

'Ah, my friend, it won't do,' said Barton, with the faint voice and bewildered, ghastly look of one who had been stunned by some mortal shock; 'there is no use in contending; whatever it is, the dreadful association between me and it is now established —I shall never escape—never!'

'Nonsense, nonsense, my dear Barton; don't talk so,' said Montague, with something at once of irritation and dismay; 'you must not, I say; we'll jockey the scoundrel yet; never mind, I say—never mind.'

It was, however, but labour lost to endeavour henceforward to inspire Barton with one ray of hope; he became desponding.

This intangible, and, as it seemed, utterly inadequate influence was fast destroying his energies of intellect, character, and health. His first object was now to return to Ireland, there, as he believed, and now almost hoped, speedily to die.

To Ireland accordingly he came, and one of the first faces he saw upon the shore, was again that of his implacable and dreaded attendant. Barton seemed at last to have lost not only all enjoyment and every hope in existence, but all independence of will besides. He now submitted himself passively to the management of the friends most nearly interested in his welfare.

With the apathy of entire despair, he implicitly assented to whatever measures they suggested and advised; and as a last resource, it was determined to remove him to a house of Lady L——'s, in the neighbourhood of Clontarf, where, with the advice of his medical attendant, who persisted in his opinion that the whole train of consequences resulted merely from some nervous derangement, it was resolved that he was to confine himself strictly to the house, and make use only of those apartments which commanded a view of an enclosed yard, the gates of which were to be kept jealously locked.

Those precautions would certainly secure him against the casual appearance of any living form, that his excited imagination might possibly confound with the spectre which, as it was contended, his fancy recognised in every figure that bore even a distant or general resemblance to the peculiarities with which his fancy had at first invested it.

A month or six weeks' absolute seclusion under these conditions, it was hoped might, by interrupting the series of these terrible impressions, gradually dispel the predisposing apprehensions, and the associations which had confirmed the supposed disease, and rendered recovery hopeless.

Cheerful society and that of his friends was to be constantly supplied, and on the whole, very sanguine expectations were indulged in, that under the treatment thus detailed, the obstinate hypochrondria of the patient might at length give way.

Accompanied, therefore, by Lady L——, General Montague and his daughter—his own affianced bride—poor Barton—himself never daring to cherish a hope of his ultimate emancipation from the horrors under which his life was literally wasting away—took possession of the apartments, whose situation protected him against the intrusions, from which he shrank with such unutterable terror.

After a little time, a steady persistence in this system began to manifest its results, in a very marked though gradual improvement, alike in the health and spirits of the invalid. Not, indeed that anything at all approaching complete recovery was yet discernible. On the contrary, to those who had not seen him since the commencement of his strange sufferings, such an alteration would have been apparent as might well have shocked them.

The improvement, however, such as it was, was welcomed

with gratitude and delight, especially by the young lady, whom her attachment to him, as well as her now singularly painful position consequent on his protracted illness, rendered an object scarcely one degree less to be commiserated than himself.

A week passed—a fortnight—a month—and yet there had been no recurrence of the hated visitation. The treatment had, so far forth, been followed by complete success. The chain of associations was broken. The constant pressure upon the over-tasked spirits had been removed, and, under these compara-tively favourable circumstances, the sense of social community with the world about him, and something of human interest, if not of enjoyment, began to reanimate him.

It was about this time that Lady L—— who, like most old ladies of the day, was deep in family receipts, and a great pre-tender to medical science, dispatched her own maid to the kitchen garden, with a list of herbs, which were there to be carefully culled, and brought back to her housekeeper for the purpose stated. The handmaiden, however, returned with her task scarce half completed, and a good deal flurried and alarmed. Her mode of accounting for her precipitate retreat and evident agitation was odd, and, to the old lady, startling.

VIII

SOFTENED

It appeared that she had repaired to the kitchen garden, pur-suant to her mistress's directions, and had there begun to make the specified selection among the rank and neglected herbs which crowded one corner of the enclosure, and while engaged in this pleasant labour, she carelessly sang a fragment of an old song, as she said, 'to keep herself company'. She was, however, interrupted by an ill-natured laugh; and, looking up, she saw through the old thorn hedge, which surrounded the garden, a singularly ill-looking little man, whose countenance wore the stamp of menace and malignity, standing close to her, at the other side of the hawthorn screen.

She described herself as utterly unable to move or speak, while he charged her with a message for Captain Barton; the substance of which she distinctly remembered to have been to the effect, that he, Captain Barton, must come abroad as usual, and show himself to his friends, out of doors, or else prepare for a visit in his own chamber.

On concluding this brief message, the stranger had, with a threatening air, got down into the outer ditch, and, seizing the hawthorn stems in his hands, seemed on the point of climbing through the fence—a feat which might have been accomplished without much difficulty.

Without, of course, awaiting this result, the girl—throwing

323

down her treasures of thyme and rosemary—had turned and run, with the swiftness of terror, to the house. Lady L—— commanded her, on pain of instant dismissal, to observe an absolute silence respecting all that passed of the incident which related to Captain Barton; and, at the same time, directed instant search to be made by her men, in the garden and the fields adjacent. This measure, however, was as usual, unsuccessful, and, filled with undefinable misgivings, Lady L—— communicated the incident to her brother. The story, however, until long afterwards, went no farther, and, of course, it was jealously guarded from Barton, who continued to amend though slowly.

Barton now began to walk occasionally in the courtyard which I have mentioned, and which being enclosed by a high wall, commanded no view beyond its own extent. Here he, therefore, considered himself perfectly secure: and, but for a careless violation of orders by one of the grooms, he might have enjoyed, at least for some time longer, his much-prized immunity. Opening upon the public road, this yard was entered by a wooden gate, with a wicket in it, and was further defended by an iron gate upon the outside. Strict orders had been given to keep both carefully locked; but, spite of these, it had happened that one day, as Barton was slowly pacing this narrow enclosure, in his accustomed walk, and reaching the farther extremity, was turning to retrace his steps, he saw the boarded wicket ajar, and the face of his tormentor immovably looking at him through the iron bars. For a few seconds he stood riveted to the earth—breathless and bloodless—in the fascination of that dreaded gaze, and then fell helplessly insensible upon the pavement.

There he was found a few minutes afterwards, and conveyed to his room—the apartment which he was never afterwards to leave alive. Henceforward a marked and unaccountable change was observable in the tone of his mind. Captain Barton was now no longer the excited and despairing man he had been before; a strange alteration had passed upon him—an unearthly tranquillity reigned in his mind—it was the anticipated stillness of the grave.

'Montague, my friend, this struggle is nearly ended now,' he said tranquilly, but with a look of fixed and fearful awe. 'I have, at last, some comfort from that world of spirits, from which my punishment has come. I now know that my sufferings will soon be over.'

Montague pressed him to speak on.

'Yes,' said he, in a softened voice, 'my punishment is nearly ended. From sorrow, perhaps, I shall never, in time or eternity, escape; but my *agony* is almost over. Comfort has been revealed to me, and what remains of my allotted struggle I will bear with submission—even with hope.'

'I am glad to hear you speak so tranquilly, my dear Barton,' said Montague; 'peace and cheer of mind are all you need to make you what you were.'

'No, no—I never can be that,' said he mournfully. 'I am no longer fit for life. I am soon to die. I am to see *him* but once again, and then all is ended.'

'He said so, then?' suggested Montague.

'*He?*—No, no: good tidings could scarcely come through him; and these were good and welcome; and they came so solemnly and sweetly—with unutterable love and melancholy, such as I could not—without saying more than is needful, or fitting, of other long past scenes and persons—fully explain to you.' As Barton said this he shed tears.

'Come, come,' said Montague, mistaking the source of his emotions, 'you must not give way. What is it, after all, but a pack of dreams and nonsense; or, at worst, the practices of a scheming rascal that enjoys his power of playing upon your nerves, and loves to exert it—a sneaking vagabond that owes you a grudge, and pays it off this way, not daring to try a more manly one.'

'A grudge, indeed, he owes me—you say rightly,' said Barton, with a sudden shudder; 'a grudge as you call it. Oh, my God! when the justice of Heaven permits the Evil one to carry out a scheme of vengeance—when its execution is committed to the lost and terrible victim of sin, who owes his own ruin to the man, the very man, whom he is commissioned to pursue—then, indeed, the torments and terrors of hell are anticipated on earth. But heaven has dealt mercifully with me—hope has opened to me at last; and if death could come without the dreadful sight I am doomed to see, I would gladly close my eyes this moment upon the world. But though death is welcome, I shrink with an agony you cannot understand—an actual frenzy of terror—from the last encounter with that—that DEMON, who has drawn me thus to the verge of the chasm, and who is himself to plunge me down. I am to see him again —once more—but under circumstances unutterably more terrific than ever.'

As Barton thus spoke, he trembled so violently that Montague was really alarmed at the extremity of his sudden agitation, and hastened to lead him back to the topic which had before seemed to exert so tranquillising an effect upon his mind.

'It was not a dream,' he said, after a time; 'I was in a different state—I felt differently and strangely; and yet it was all as real, as clear, and vivid, as what I now see and hear—it was a reality.'

'And what *did* you see and hear?' urged his companion.

'When I wakened from the swoon I fell into on seeing *him*,' said Barton, continuing as if he had not heard the question, 'it was slowly, very slowly—I was lying by the margin of a broad lake, with misty hills all round, and a soft, melancholy, rose-coloured light illuminated it all. It was unusually sad and lonely, and yet more beautiful than any earthly scene. My head was leaning on the lap of a girl, and she was singing a song, that told, I know not how—whether by words or harmonies—of all my life—all that is past, and all that is still to come; and with the song the old feelings that I thought had perished within me came back, and tears flowed from my eyes—partly for the song and its mysterious beauty, and partly for the unearthly sweetness of her voice; and yet I knew the voice—oh! how well; and I was spellbound as I listened and looked at the solitary scene, without stirring, almost without breathing—and, alas! alas! without turning my eyes towards the face that I knew was near me, so sweetly powerful was the enchantment that held me. And so, slowly, the song and scene grew fainter, and fainter, to my sense, till all was dark and still again. And then I awoke to this world, as you saw, comforted, for I knew that I was forgiven much.' Barton wept again long and bitterly.

From this time, as we have said, the prevailing tone of his mind was one of profound and tranquil melancholy. This, however, was not without its interruptions. He was thoroughly impressed with the conviction that he was to experience another and a final visitation, transcending in horror all he had before experienced. From this anticipated and unknown agony, he often shrank in such paroxysms of abject terror and distraction, as filled the whole household with dismay and superstitious panic. Even those among them who affected to discredit the theory of preternatural agency, were often in their secret souls visited during the silence of night with qualms and apprehensions, which they would not have readily confessed; and none of them attempted to dissuade Barton from the resolution on which he now systematically acted, of shutting himself up in his own apartment. The window-blinds of this room were kept jealously down; and his own man was seldom out of his presence, day or night, his bed being placed in the same chamber.

This man was an attached and respectable servant; and his duties, in addition to those ordinarily imposed upon valets, but which Barton's independent habits generally dispensed with, were to attend carefully to the simple precautions by means of which his master hoped to exclude the dreaded intrusion of the 'Watcher'. And, in addition to attending to those arrangements, which amounted merely to guarding against the possibility of his master's being, through any unscreened window or open door, exposed to the dreaded influence, the valet was never to suffer him to be alone—total solitude, even for a minute, had become to him now almost as intolerable as the idea of going abroad into the public ways—it was an instinctive anticipation of what was coming.

IX

REQUIESCAT

It is needless to say, that under these circumstances, no steps were taken towards the fulfilment of that engagement into which he had entered. There was quite disparity enough in point of years, and indeed of habits, between the young lady and Captain Barton, to have precluded anything like very vehement or romantic attachment on her part. Though grieved and anxious, therefore, she was very far from being heart-broken.

Miss Montague, however, devoted much of her time to the patient but fruitless attempt to cheer the unhappy invalid. She read for him and conversed with him; but it was apparent that whatever exertions he made, the endeavour to escape from the one everwaking fear that preyed upon him, was utterly and miserably unavailing.

Young ladies are much given to the cultivation of pets; and among those who shared the favour of Miss Montague was a fine old owl, which the gardener, who caught him napping among the ivy of a ruined stable, had dutifully presented to that young lady.

The caprice which regulates such preferences was manifested in the extravagant favour with which this grim and ill-favoured bird was at once distinguished by his mistress; and, trifling as this whimsical circumstance may seem, I am forced to mention it, inasmuch as it is connected, oddly enough, with the concluding scene of the story.

Barton, far from sharing in this liking for the new favourite, regarded it from the first with an antipathy as violent as it was utterly unaccountable. Its very vicinity was unsupportable to him. He seemed to hate and dread it with a vehemence absolutely laughable, and which, to those who have never witnessed the exhibition of antipathies of this kind, would seem all but incredible.

With these few words of preliminary explanation, I shall proceed to state the particulars of the last scene in this strange series of incidents. It was almost two o'clock one winter's night, and Barton was, as usual at that hour, in his bed; the servant we have mentioned occupied a smaller bed in the same room, and a light was burning. The man was on a sudden aroused by his master, who said:

'I can't get it out of my head that that accursed bird has got out somehow, and is lurking in some corner of the room. I have been dreaming about him. Get up, Smith, and look about; search for him. Such hateful dreams!'

The servant rose, and examined the chamber, and while engaged in so doing, he heard the well-known sound, more like a long-drawn gasp than a hiss, with which these birds from their secret haunts affright the quiet of the night.

This ghostly indication of its proximity—for the sound proceeded from the passage upon which Barton's chamber door opened—determined the search of the servant, who, opening the door, proceeded a step or two forward for the purpose of driving the bird away. He had, however, hardly entered the lobby, when the door behind him slowly swung to under the impulse, as it seemed, of some gentle current of air; but as immediately over the door there was a kind of window, intended in the day time to aid in lighting the passage, and through which at present the rays of the candle were issuing, the valet could see quite enough for his purpose.

As he advanced he heard his master—who, lying in a well-curtained bed, had not, as it seemed, perceived his exit from the room—call him by name, and direct him to place the candle on the table by his bed. The servant, who was now some way in the long passage, and not liking to raise his voice for the purpose of replying, lest he should startle the sleeping inmates of the house, began to walk hurriedly and softly back again, when, to his amazement, he heard a voice in the interior of the chamber answering calmly, and actually saw, through the window which overtopped the door, that the light was slowly shifting, as if carried across the room in answer to his master's call. Palsied by a feeling akin to terror, yet not unmingled with curiosity, he stood breathless and listening at the threshold, unable to summon resolution to push open the door and enter. Then came a rustling of the curtains, and a sound like that of one who in a low voice hushes a child to rest, in the midst of which he heard Barton say, in a tone of stifled horror—'Oh, God—oh, my God!' and repeat the same exclamation several times. Then ensued a silence, which again was broken by the same strange soothing sound; and at last there burst forth, in one swelling peal, a yell of agony so appalling and hideous, that, under some impulse of ungovernable horror, the man rushed to the door, and with his whole strength strove to force it open. Whether it was that, in his agitation, he had himself but imperfectly turned the handle, or that the door was really secured upon the inside, he failed to effect an entrance; and as he tugged and pushed, yell after yell rang louder and wilder through the chamber, accompanied all the while by the same hushed sounds. Actually freezing with terror, and scarce knowing what he did, the man turned and ran down the passage, wringing his hands in the extremity of horror and irresolution.

At the stair-head he was encountered by General Montague, scared and eager, and just as they met the fearful sounds had ceased.

'What is it? Who—where is your master?' said Montague, with the incoherence of extreme agitation. 'Has anything—for God's sake is anything wrong?'

'Lord have mercy on us, it's all over,' said the man, staring wildly towards his master's chamber. 'He's dead, sir, I'm sure he's dead.'

Without waiting for inquiry or explanation, Montague, closely followed by the servant, hurried to the chamber door, turned the handle, and pushed it open. As the door yielded to his pressure, the ill-omened bird of which the servant had been in search, uttering its spectral warning, started suddenly from the far side of the bed, and flying through the doorway close over their heads, and extinguishing, in his passage, the candle which Montague carried, crashed through the skylight that overlooked the lobby, and sailed away into the darkness of the outer space.

'There it is, God bless us,' whispered the man after a breathless pause.

'Curse that bird,' muttered the General, startled by the suddenness of the apparition, and unable to conceal his discomposure.

'The candle is moved,' said the man, after another breathless pause, pointing to the candle that still burned in the room; 'see, they put it by the bed.'

'Draw the curtains, fellow, and don't stand gaping there,' whispered Montague, sternly.

The man hesitated.

'Hold this, then,' said Montague, impatiently thrusting the candlestick into the servant's hand, and himself advancing to the bedside, he drew the curtains apart. The light of the candle, which was still burning at the bedside, fell upon a figure huddled together, and half upright, at the head of the bed. It seemed as though it had slunk back as far as the solid panelling would allow, and the hands were still clutched in the bed-clothes.

'Barton, Barton, *Barton!*' cried the General, with a strange mixture of awe and vehemence. He took the candle, and held it so that it shone full upon the face. The features were fixed, stern, and white; the jaw was fallen; and the sightless eyes still open, gazed vacantly forward towards the front of the bed. 'God Almighty! he's dead,' muttered the General, as he looked upon this fearful spectacle. They both continued to gaze upon it in silence for a minute or more. 'And cold, too,' whispered Montague, withdrawing his hand from that of the dead man.

'And see, see—may I never have life, sir,' added the man,

after another pause, with a shudder, 'but there was something else on the bed with him. Look there—look there—see that, sir.'

As the man thus spoke he pointed to a deep indenture as if caused by a heavy pressure, near the foot of the bed.

Montague was silent.

'Come, sir, come away, for God's sake,' whispered the man, drawing close up to him, and holding fast by his arm, while he glanced fearfully round; 'what good can be done here now—come away, for God's sake!'

At this moment they heard the steps of more than one approaching, and Montague, hastily desiring the servant to arrest their progress, endeavouring to loose the rigid grip with which the fingers of the dead man were clutched in the bedclothes, and drew, as well as he was able, the awful figure into a reclining posture; then closing the curtains carefully upon it, he hastened himself to meet those persons that were approaching.

It is needless to follow the personages so slightly connected with this narrative, into the events of their after life; it is enough to say, that no clue to the solution of these mysterious occurrences was ever after discovered; and so long an interval having now passed since the event which I have just described concluded this strange history, it is scarcely to be expected that time can throw any new lights upon its dark and inexplicable outline. Until the secrets of the earth shall be no longer hidden, therefore, these transactions must remain shrouded in their original obscurity.

The only occurrence in Captain Barton's former life to which reference was ever made, as having any possible connection with the sufferings with which his existence closed, and which he himself seemed to regard as working out a retribution for some grievous sin of his past life, was a circumstance which not for several years after his death was brought to light. The nature of this disclosure was painful to his relatives, and discreditable to his memory.

It appeared that some six years before Captain Barton's final return to Dublin, he had formed, in the town of Plymouth, a guilty attachment, the object of which was the daughter of one of the ship's crew under his command. The father had visited the frailty of his unhappy child with extreme harshness, and even brutality, and it was said that she had died heart-broken. Presuming upon Barton's implication of her guilt, this man had conducted himself towards him with marked insolence, and Barton retaliated this, and what he resented with still more exasperated bitterness—his treatment of the unfortunate girl—by a systematic exercise of those terrible and arbitrary severities which the regulations of the navy placed at the command of those who are responsible for its discipline. The man had at length made his escape, while the vessel was in port at Naples, but died as it was said, in an hospital in that town, of the wounds, inflicted in one of his recent and sanguinary punishments.

Whether these circumstances in reality bear, or not, upon the occurrences of Barton's after-life, it is, of course, impossible to say. It seems, however, more than probable that they were at least, in his own mind, closely associated with them. But however the truth may be, as to the origin and motives of this mysterious persecution, there can be no doubt that, with respect to the agencies by which it was accomplished, absolute and impenetrable mystery is like to prevail until the day of doom.

JOSEPH SHERIDAN LE FANU

Joseph Thomas Sheridan Le Fanu was born in
Dublin in 1814. His was a literary family of
Huguenot origins; both his grandmother Alicia
Sheridan Le Fanu and his great-uncle Richard
Brinsley Sheridan were playwrights, and his niece
Rhoda Broughton would go on to become a
successful novelist. Le Fanu's family lived in a
variety of locations around rural Ireland during his
youth – the folk superstitions of which are said to
have left a deep impression on him – and were
financially hard-hit by the agitations of the Tithe
Wars. In 1833, not long after the death of his father,
Le Fanu entered Trinity College, Dublin to study
law. While there, he was elected Auditor of the

College Historical Society, and between 1838 and 1840 published his first series of short stories, which were later collected as *The Purcell Papers.*

Le Fanu was called to the bar in 1839, but he never practiced and soon abandoned law for journalism. During the 1840s, he married, and spent time mounting a protest against the indifference of the government to the Irish Famine. He also produced his first two novels - *The C'ock and Anchor* (1845) and *The Fortunes of Colonel Torlogh O'Brien* (1847); both works of historical fiction – and in 1851 he and his wife Susanna moved to their house on Merrion Square, Dublin, where le Fanu was to remain until his death. In 1858, Le Fanu's wife Susanna died in unclear circumstances, and he became a recluse, setting to work in his most productive and successful years as a writer. Between 1864 and 1872, he produced ten novels, all in the 'sensation fiction' genre popular at the time.

At his peak, le Fanu was the leading ghost-story writer of the nineteenth century, and he is now seen as central to the development of the genre in the Victorian era. His work is credited with turning the Gothic's focus from the external sources of horror to the inward effects of terror, thus helping to create the psychological basis for supernaturalist literature that continues to this day. Arguably le Fanu's most enduring works are *Uncle Silas*, published in 1864, and the vampire novella *Carmilla* (1872), which influenced Bram Stoker in the writing of *Dracula* and has inspired several films. Le Fanu died in his native Dublin in 1873, at the age of 58.

www.ingramcontent.com/pod-product-compliance
Lightning Source LLC
Chambersburg PA
CBHW030402030726
47497CB00002B/452